BOUND IN BLOOD

BROKEN BLOODLINES: BOOK 3

SADIE KINCAID

Copyright © 2025 by Sadie Kincaid

All rights reserved.

No part of this book may be reproduced in any form or by any electronic or mechanical means, including information storage and retrieval systems, without written permission from the author, except for the use of brief quotations in a book review.

The moral right of the author has been asserted

Cover Design: Christian Bentulan/ Covers by Christian

Editing: Baker Street Revisions

Proofreading: Dee's Notes: Editing Services

Formatting: Red House Press Ltd

All characters and events in this publication, other than those clearly in the public domain are fictitious and any resemblance to any real person, living or dead is purely coincidental and not intended by the author.

For all the Montridge faithful who have made it this far, I'm sorry I tore out your hearts, and I hope this little sliver of mine makes up for it.

Thank you for loving Ophelia and her vampires as much as I do,

Love Sadie xx

CONTENT ADVISORY

This book is a dark paranormal romance and contains the following topics which may be sensitive for some readers:

Blood play (well, they are vampires)
    Violence
    Scenes of an explicit sexual nature

THE LOST PROPHECIES OF FIERE

***VI.** Including the elusive final stanza, known as the forgotten verse.*

Until the balance tips to inevitable destruction,
    the sands of fate shall shift unrelenting.
    And those who cannot live in peace,
    shall thrive amongst the anarchy.
    Until Chaos swallows whole the universe once more
    and Gaea, Tartarus, and Eros do mourn.

But there is one who can save the fates of all.
    For the child borne of fire and blood
    shall be our ruin or our redemption.
    Bringing balance to the new world order,
    be it through peace or total annihilation.

Though, take heed—
    the one who first drinks from the untouched vessel,
    pale as alabaster stone,
    for it is they who will determine its poison or its nectar.

*And those who thirst for the crimson rivers of mortal veins
shall face the insurmountable task of their birthright.
They must choose the path of the righteous,
or face the damnation of the eternal.*

*But if the Chosen One can slay the three-headed dragon—
    if the untamable beast does kneel at its new master's feet,
    and the light is tempted back from the darkness,
    then they shall awaken the protector of man.
    And the sun must swallow the shadows
    to bring a balance that reigns through the ages.*

PROLOGUE
NAZEEL DANRAATH

The intense wave of Kameen's fury washes over me before I step foot inside our mountain hideaway. The stone beneath my feet shakes with the ferocity of his rage, and I close my eyes and prepare myself for his wrath. As truly saddened as I am to have defied him so blatantly, it had to be done. And whatever my punishment, it is a price I have always been willing to pay. For too long, our world has existed in chaos and disharmony. Ophelia Hart will bring balance and, with it, peace. Magical creatures of all kinds shall thrive once more.

"Nazeel!"

I bow my head in deference as he approaches.

"What have you done?" His growl is low and dangerous. Accusatory. Designed to bring lesser immortals to their knees. But it has no such effect on me.

"I did what was necessary, Kameen. To unlock the girl's—"

"You did what you wanted," he bellows, his deep voice echoing off the old stone walls of the grand entrance hall. "Why could you not just leave it be?" His jaw tics, his dark eyes imploring me to tell him what he wants to hear. If I begged for his forgiveness, would he show me any mercy? No, for he cannot. His position within the Order does not allow for favoritism.

"The Skotádi grow in power, Kameen. I feel their darkness closing in, and I know that you must too. If they were to intercept the girl before her powers were fully formed ... If they had even a chance to corrupt her ..." I ball my hands into fists at my sides. How can a man so wise fail to see such obvious truths?

"*If* they corrupt her, then it will be because that is the natural order of things, Nazeel. It will be because she was always meant for the dark."

"No." I shake my head, refusing to believe his nonsense. "You know what the prophecy says. There is a chance for her to be swayed to either good or evil."

"And why are you so quick to assume that her bond with the vampires places her on the right side of the line, my little witch?" he scoffs.

My lip curls back, and I have to work to tamp down my frustration, for it will be of no use to me where he is concerned. He does not respond to emotion. Only cold, hard logic. "You know she is an elementai, and therefore, a vampire is her only true mate. Vampires are not inherently evil, as you are well aware. In fact, some of the best men I have ever known have been the most bloodthirsty."

He arches one thick eyebrow. "Men like Giorgios and Alexandros Drakos?"

I roll back my shoulders. "Exactly."

He traces a fingertip over my cheekbone, causing a shiver to run the length of my spine. "Perhaps you are not my caring little witch, after all, Nazeel. You claim to care for this girl, yet you were willing to cause her immeasurable pain in order to further your own ends."

Anger prickles beneath my skin. "To enable her to fulfill her destiny."

His eyes narrow on my face with laser focus. "You know I will have no choice but to punish you for this."

I lower my gaze, saddened that even for me, whom he loves beyond all others, he will not bend. "I know, my lord and commander."

He grips my jaw and squeezes hard. "Do not mock me, Nazeel. It will bring me no pleasure to cause you any pain."

My eyelids flutter, my gaze flickering over his handsome face until I meet his eyes. "I know, Kameen. And I know what you must do. I am ready to meet my fate."

"You could have run from me, little witch. You believe in this girl so much you are willing to face whatever punishment I see fit?"

"I do. But regardless, I would never run from you, my love."

His features soften a little, and he lets out a long sigh full of anguish and frustration. "How did you do it? How did you convince Giorgios Drakos to betray his only brother?"

"Giorgios knows who Ophelia is, and any fool can see Alexandros's love for the girl. Protecting her is the ultimate act of devotion to his brother, even if Alexandros did not see it in such a way."

Kameen tilts his head, still scrutinizing my face. "And the boy? What are his intentions toward the girl?"

I blink, confused. "You heard me talking with Lucian?"

His nose wrinkles. "As with every single time you have met with him these past five hundred years, I can smell him on you."

I take a moment to gather my thoughts. I was not surprised to see Lucian earlier this day. Since the greatly exaggerated rumors of his death, he has taken a distant interest in the Order and in my quest to restore balance to the world. Although he has never spoken of that grave day over five hundred years ago or any of the circumstances which led to it, there is much to learn from him. However, he remains frustratingly silent on anything related to the Skotádi or the elementai downfall.

I am still unclear on his role in the upcoming war, for that is surely what we are headed for, though I am certain he has one—one of the utmost importance. Whether that be for good or bad, I cannot yet tell. "I do not know of his intentions," I admit. "He still refuses to discuss his past. Still so untrusting of me even after what my sisters did for him."

"Is he aware of the girl? Of who she is?"

I nod. "He has been watching her for many years."

His disappointment in me is so acute, and it weighs as heavily as a cloak made of iron. Despite my belief in what I did this night, it still pains me to betray him so. His expression remains stern, unyielding, but his eyes can never deceive me. Can never hide the depth of feeling that exists between us. My mate of over a thousand years, the other half of my being. His fingers tangle in the hair at the nape of my neck, and I am suddenly enveloped in him, in his scent and his arms. I bury my face in his cloak and soak in his comfort. Whilst my actions were necessary to tip the weight of the scale in favor of the light, they still weigh on my heart.

He rests his lips on the top of my head. "You are grounded until I decide what to do with you."

"I know."

A second later, he removes a bronze collar from his pocket and slips it around my neck. It locks into a place with a deliberate click, and he traces a fingertip over the metal band. "It was made in the sacred forge of our ancestors and is imbibed with old earth magic. It will not permit you to leave this mountain."

I nod my understanding and return my cheek to his chest. He wraps his arms around me in response, holding me tightly to him. "It will all work out, Kameen. The prophecy will be fulfilled, and all magical beings shall flourish once more."

He murmurs something I cannot quite catch, but he continues holding me. I close my eyes, content in his arms. Content that Ophelia Hart will claw a path through her pain and that it will make her the woman she was born to be. For one day, she will realize that her importance to this world was too great to risk, even for true love.

CHAPTER ONE

OPHELIA

The pain is excruciating. I can't breathe from the weight of it crushing my chest. But I must fix this. I will not lose them. I will find a way to bring him back.

"Do you really think ..." Malachi's voice cracks.

"No." Xavier shakes his head vehemently. "No fucking way. He can't be. He's Alexandros fucking Drakos."

We're still huddled together on the kitchen floor. A bundle of arms and legs, refusing to untangle.

"C-can you feel him? Even a little?" I frantically search my own mind for any sign of him and find nothing but his absence. Like a deep, gaping chasm of ... nothing.

"I can't," Axl says solemnly, his voice little more than a whisper.

"Me neither," Malachi answers.

Xavier's deep-blue eyes swim with tears. "That doesn't mean he's gone."

I place a hand on his cheek and swipe away the lone tear with the pad of my thumb. One thing I am sure of is that they need me to be strong. There will be time to hurt and to heal, but it's not now. Not when we don't know for sure whether he's truly gone. "We'll find him. We'll get him back."

Malachi shakes his head. "But we don't even know where to start."

"We'll ask Enora for help. She has contacts with the Order, and they must know something. She can at least give us a starting point. But we need to act fast." Their eyes are clouded with so much sadness and fear that my fragile heart struggles to continue beating. "No good can come from us sitting here."

Axl nods, his throat working as he swallows. "Ophelia is right. We can't give up on him."

Xavier licks his bottom lip. "So, we go to Enora, then?"

I nod. Then slowly, we free ourselves from the huddle we've been in for who knows how long and stand.

I HAVE no idea how the four of us managed to put one foot in front of the other enough times to reach Silver Vale just as the sun crested over the horizon. Even less of one as to how we spoke to Cadence when she opened the door, full of her usual wide-eyed excitement although we obviously woke her up. At least for a few seconds. Then her face fell and her anxiety became as apparent as the smell of jasmine from inside the house. But her distress was so weak compared to my own that it barely registered.

Such was the anguish radiating from the four of us, Cadence showed us to Enora without asking a single question. She simply squeezed my hand and held it tight until we reached the professor's study.

"What has happened, child?" Enora asks before all of us make it in the room. Our intense feelings no doubt arrived here

CHAPTER ONE

before we did. Cadence lets go of my hand and, with a final concerned look in my direction, closes the door behind us.

I'm not sure I can tell Enora what happened without crumpling into a heap on the floor. What if saying the words somehow makes it all real? The boys' despair is as sharp as mine. It swirls around us like our own personal tornado of emotional anguish, tearing every shred of happiness and joy from the room and leaving nothing but devastation in its wake.

"Alexandros is ..." Xavier chokes out the words but is unable to finish the sentence.

"Our connection with him was severed," I manage to say, not willing to admit our worst fears quite yet. "We all felt it."

Enora's hand flies to her mouth. Her flushed cheeks pale instantly, and she lets out a soft cry. In the face of her sadness, I feel like I may crumple to the ground. I need her to tell me this will be okay. I need her to tell me there is a chance he's still alive—that, while it is rare, bonds can be severed in other ways. I need it more than I need my next breath.

"That doesn't mean he's dead though, does it?" I plead with her. "It could simply be his connection was severed. Just like ..." I clamp my lips together. Nobody else knows Lucian is still alive. But if he's responsible for what happened to Alexandros, and if he's still out there somewhere, then surely the time for keeping him a secret is long gone.

Not seeming to pick up on my unfinished sentence, she turns her attention to Axl, Malachi, and Xavier. "Did you all feel his ... passing?" She whispers the last word as though it will somehow make it less powerful. Less devastating. It doesn't work.

They glance at me, their expressions etched with guilt and agony, and nod.

"Then it must be true." Enora draws a shaky breath. "A sired vampire experiences the death of—"

"We don't know that!" If we don't say it aloud, then it need never be true. "Don't you dare say that he is!"

Malachi and Xavier take my hands while Axl moves to stand behind me.

"I understand you want that to be true, Ophelia. Believe me, so do I. But if you all felt the bond sever, then it can mean only one thing."

Anger swirls inside my chest, and I have to focus on my light to stop my rage from tearing through the room. Control comes surprisingly easy. "No. There have been instances of bonds being severed so effectively that the other vampire was believed to be dead when they weren't."

Enora's eyes narrow, and she takes a few steps forward. "I am unaware of any such instances."

I harden my gaze as though daring her to challenge me. Daring her to provoke me so I have an excuse to erupt and do something with this is swirling vortex of emotion inside me. "Well, I am."

Are we going to tell her about Lucian? Malachi asks through our bond.

Doesn't seem much point in keeping it a secret now. Alexandros went to find him, and now he's ... Like the rest of us, Axl refuses to voice our greatest fear.

Malachi squeezes my hand in his. *I agree.*

I take a deep breath and focus on my light once more, allowing it to send a wave of calming energy over me, and with another breath, I send the same wave over the boys too. Their anger is still palpable, their grief still heavy and thick in the air, but they are notably less agitated.

What did you do, Cupcake? Xavier asks.

I don't reply because I don't fully understand. I don't recall ever being able to do that before, and I figure it was a rhetorical question anyhow. Besides, I need to tell Enora about Lucian

CHAPTER ONE

before I change my mind. There must have been a reason Alexandros didn't want anyone to know about him, and disclosing his existence feels like a betrayal of trust, no matter how necessary it might be.

"Lucian is alive." I'm surprised at how calm and steady my voice sounds given the gamut of emotions coursing through me.

Her eyes flicker with recognition, but still, she says, "Lucian?"

"Lucian Drakos."

Her brow pinches, and she takes another step closer. "No. You are mistaken, Ophelia. He died a long time ago. Shortly after his mother and sisters. Despite what he did, Alexandros mourned his death."

"I know that, but it's true. Alexandros did indeed believe him dead until recently, but he's alive, Enora. That's where Alexandros is—where he went last night. To find Lucian."

"That is impossible." Her eyes dart between the four of us, wild and accusatory. "Lucian Drakos is dead."

"I'm afraid you're very much mistaken, Enora."

For a wonderful millisecond, I think the deep voice belongs to Alexandros, but Enora's eyes dart to the now-open door. "Giorgios! How did you ...?"

Cadence rushes in, apologizing for not being able to stop him.

"You invited me into this house decades ago, and my invitation was obviously never rescinded." He clears his throat. "I am aware I should have knocked and announced my arrival, but now is not the time for etiquette." His eyes fix on me, and he holds out a hand. "We must leave."

"Where is Alexandros?" I demand as Axl, Xavier, and Malachi draw closer to me like my own protective shield.

"Neither is it the time for explanation. You are in great

danger, Ophelia. We must leave. Now," he barks, but he lacks the commanding tone of his younger brother.

I tip my chin up. "I am not going anywhere with you until you tell me where Alexandros is."

His blue eyes fill with tears. My poor broken heart is about to be decimated again. "You already know the answer." He glances at the boys. "All of you do. You felt it as I did."

"No!" I shake my head. "Take us to him. I can save him. I can use my earth powers. They can heal him, I know it. Alexandros told me that earth is—"

"Ophelia," Giorgios cuts off my babbling. "He is gone."

Axl, Xavier, and Malachi come even closer, their bodies holding mine up as we take comfort from each other.

"How, Giorgios?" Enora asks, a distinct tremor in her voice.

He swallows harshly and shifts from one foot to the other as though uncomfortable in his skin. "Lucian was expecting us. He had an army waiting for us, and he took his father's head before I could ..." He drops his face into his hands.

"So Lucian is alive?" Enora's whispered question is drowned out by Axl's wounded cry.

I let go of Xavier's and Malachi's hands and spin around to face Axl before pulling the three of them closer. Once again, the indescribable agony of his loss tears us open, and we cling to one another, holding onto the memory of him, as well as the only thing we have left—hope.

There is a way to bring him back. I know it, I say through the bond, finding a strength from deep inside me, from the power within my light. I call on it, drawing on its energy to keep me standing on my own two feet and to keep them standing too.

"It is only a matter of time before he comes looking for you, Ophelia," Giorgios says. "He knows who and what you are. We must leave."

CHAPTER ONE

"We can't. We have to stay here," I mumble, my face pressed against Axl's chest.

Giorgios's heavy footsteps signal his approach. "His last words were of you."

Tears burn my eyes, and I refuse to look at him. Refuse to listen to his lies.

"He asked me to protect you."

"We can protect her," Xavier growls.

"You are going to grow weaker with each passing day. How will you protect her then?"

"They won't get weaker. I'll think of something." I'm already mentally searching through all the spells and ancient practices I've learned of these past few months. Surely there must be something that can save them. Even if ... No! It's unthinkable. I shake my head, refusing to believe.

"Regardless." Giorgios's voice becomes a low growl. "I gave him my word that I would protect you, Ophelia. I will not break my final oath to my only brother."

Spinning around to face him, I roll back my shoulders, tip my jaw, and look him square in the eye. "Then you'll have to keep that oath right here, because I'm not leaving Montridge. The books we need are here. Our friends are here."

"Yeah, Ophelia has everything she needs right here," Cadence chimes in like she's been waiting for an opportunity to say something. Her loyalty makes me want to hug her.

"Friends and books will be of no use to you when Lucian arrives, silly little girl," he snaps.

The ground shakes beneath us with the force of my ire, and flames lick at my fingertips, but I douse them quickly, somehow managing to keep my emotions in check.

The boys growl, their anger threatening to spill out too. Giorgios holds up a hand in surrender. "I am sorry," he says, his tone gentler now. "Forgive my curtness, but I have just had to watch the man I love and respect more than any in this world die in my arms." The image he evokes causes my knees to buckle, and the boys hold onto me once more. I briefly wonder whether any of us will ever be capable of standing on our own two feet again. "If I am harsh, it is only because I am so concerned for your wellbeing," Giorgios continues. "You have no understanding of the power Lucian wields."

"Ophelia is way more powerful than him," Xavier argues.

Cadence bounces on her toes, her hands balled at her sides as though she's spoiling for a fight. "And she has plenty of powerful friends here at Montridge."

"This is true," Giorgios concedes. "But whilst you are here, you put everyone at this institution at risk. Both a young witch and a wolf have already died on these grounds, Ophelia. How many more must die before you realize how dangerous it is for you to be here? How many must die at the hands of Lucian Drakos before he finally finds you?"

How many more like Meg and Esme. Like Alexandros. He didn't have to say I am responsible for his brother's death—I know I am. And he's right. I cannot allow anyone else to die because of me. But no matter how sure I am that we must go with him, I don't want to leave Montridge. Not only because this is our home and the place where our friends are, but it's the place where *he* is. Abandoning Montridge feels like abandoning Alexandros.

I hate to admit it, but maybe we are safer away from here, Malachi says. *Somewhere Lucian can't find us.*

Yeah, I know none of us want to admit it, but we're all gonna get weaker, and we have no idea when that will start to happen, Axl adds.

I shove aside the tsunami of emotion that threatens to overwhelm me. I can't think about them getting weaker on top of

CHAPTER ONE

everything else. It will surely crush me until I am nothing but dust and tears.

Giorgios sighs. "Lucian just took the head of the most powerful vampire alive without breaking a sweat. We have no idea what he is truly capable of."

A sharp pain lances through my chest, and I shake my head, trying to dislodge the images of Alexandros's death from my mind.

As if searching for an ally, Giorgios looks to Enora now, and she shakes her head sadly. "I believe Giorgios is right, Ophelia. Lucian is capable of horrors that you cannot comprehend. If he finds you before you are ready to face him ..." A tear breaks free, and she swats it away.

"I am not leaving Montridge!" I yell.

Giorgios comes close enough that I can see the congealed blood on his dark cloak. I squeeze my eyes closed. Without asking, I know it belongs to *him*.

"His final words were spent imploring me to protect you, Ophelia." His voice is gentle. Pleading. "Please allow me to keep my promise to him. Please do not let his death have been in vain."

Keeping my eyes closed, I concentrate on my light, allowing it to ground me. When I reopen them, I'm centered and able to speak without crying. "Where do you suggest we go if we leave Montridge?"

"I have a fortress in the Tibetan mountains. It is impenetrable, and it is the safest place for you." He looks behind me and nods. "All of you."

"Tibet? You want us to go to Tibet?"

"I have medicines," he says. "A library that almost rivals Thucydides. If there is a remedy for the death of one's sire, then we will find it. There is nowhere more equipped for us to stay hidden, educate ourselves, and regroup."

Giorgios is a scholar, sweet girl, Malachi says. *Alexandros told me about him. He understands the ancient texts better than anyone. If there is a cure to be found for us or a way to bring Alexandros back, then he will surely be able to help us discover that information.*

What do you think, Axl? Xavier? I ask through our bond.

I don't trust him, but Alexandros did, Axl replies.

And it got him killed, Xavier adds.

But if Lucian killed him, it's only a matter of time before he comes for our girl, right? Malachi says.

Enora takes a step forward and beckons Cadence to her. She takes my friend's hand in hers and locks eyes with me. "I know you do not wish to leave, Ophelia, and I will miss you so, but ..." She swallows. "Giorgios is right. He is capable of protecting you in ways that I, or even Osiris, cannot."

"This is not the end of your time at Montridge, Ophelia," Giorgios says, forcing a tight smile. "You will see all of your friends again. But Lucian's return and his callous act of betrayal cannot be ignored. There is a war coming, and every magical being must choose a side. We will all face Lucian when the time is right, but until that time, you must be protected. For you are our greatest weapon."

"She's not a weapon," Xavier snaps. "You don't get to use her for any side."

Giorgios tilts his head and regards Xavier with curiosity. "I know my brother well enough to know he has not left his sireds with such little knowledge of the burden they carry being bonded to Ophelia. You must be well aware that there are those who would manipulate her to use her power for their own ends. Therefore, Ophelia must embrace her own power and use it for her true purpose, and only she can decide what that is to be."

This is all too much. The weight of guilt and all the responsibility threaten to crush me under their combined force. Why can't I just be me again? No magical powers and nobody's

CHAPTER ONE

weapon? What if my only purpose were to love Alexandros and the boys? It feels like enough. I would trade these powers for that life in a single heartbeat.

Xavier edges forward, bringing his face close to Giorgios's. "Exactly. She decides! She's not some fucking magical object for you to fight over. If she wants to walk away and leave all this shit behind her, we will do exactly that."

"I think you will find that the time for walking away has passed, young Xavier. If it were an option, I assure you Alexandros would have done it."

Xavier doesn't back down, and I squeeze his hand. "It's okay," I assure him. "I know what he means."

Giorgios offers me a faint smile of appreciation. "So you will come with me? At least until we can determine what our next moves should be?" He holds out his hand. "Please allow me to fulfill my oath to my brother, Ophelia."

I don't take his hand, but I nod. This is the best course of action at the moment. "But how will we get to Tibet? Won't traveling there be dangerous?"

"With my powers of teleportation, along with your magic, and if she will kindly oblige, a spell from Enora, I believe there is a way for us all to get there safely and quickly."

"Of course," Enora says. "I will do whatever I can."

Cadence rushes forward and wraps me in a hug. "I'm gonna miss you so much, Ophelia," she wails, tears running down her cheeks. They're enough to break the dam holding back my own, and I cry freely now too. She was my first real friend, and she represents so many of the positive things that have happened for me in the past few months. More than that, she's a huge part of the person I've become. She taught me to believe in myself and was the first person outside of my mates to really see me for who I am, and that's without her having any desire for my vamp-nip blood. I don't want to do any of this without her.

"We'll be back before you know it," Malachi says, but his voice cracks.

None of us bring up the fact that when we return, it will probably be to confront Lucian. The idea that we are all destined for some epic magical battle is both too terrifying and too absurd to contemplate right now. All we can do is keep taking one breath after another.

Finding out how to save my boys and bring Alexandros back are my priorities. And having a purpose is what is keeping me on my feet. It gives me strength and determination.

As soon as we reach the safety of Giorgios's mountain fortress, I can get to researching and working on a plan. One thing I've come to realize in the past few months is that knowledge is everything. The more I learn about my power, the stronger I become.

CHAPTER
TWO
XAVIER

Never in my life have I been one for sentimentality, but as we stand on the porch of our house, the place that's been our home for decades, I can't believe this is goodbye. Because even though we'll come back, it won't be the same. *He* won't be here. And he is the only thing worth coming back for.

Axl shrugs his bag onto his shoulder. Giorgios told us to pack light and gave us a few minutes to throw some stuff into a backpack while he went over the logistics of the spell with Enora. "Giorgios said he'll speak to Eugene about looking after the Ruby Dragons while we're gone."

I shrug. "Seems kinda pointless if we're all headed for some epic fucking battle with Lucian."

"Yeah, one we're gonna win, so everything has to keep running as it was," he retorts. "We figure out how to bring Alexandros back, then we kill his evil fucking spawn, and then we go back to normal."

I turn and give him my full attention now. "You really fucking believe any of that?"

His dark-brown eyes fill with sadness. "I have to, Xavier,

because if I don't, then I'll ..." He swipes his tongue over his bottom lip. "I can't think about any of that not being true, or I'll fucking stop. And if I stop ... Tell me you believe it too."

Fuck, I wish I believed it. I wish I could stop feeling like my entire world fucking imploded around me. Like I'm not staring into a future filled with nothing but darkness and pain. Maybe then I could fucking breathe. With my hand on the back of his neck, I pull him toward me and rest my lips on his forehead. "Yeah, I believe it." I lie with ease to give him an iota of comfort and wonder when the fuck I became this person.

Right then, the very reason I've become this sentimental asshole—the guy who does what he can to make the people he cares about feel better—comes walking down the stairs, holding onto Malachi's hand. She's changed from her usual uniform of miniskirt and tank top to jeans and a hoodie. Her hair is tied up in a ponytail, her dark roots peeking through.

"Did you get everything you need, Cupcake?"

She bites down on her bottom lip and nods.

Axl clears his throat. "Giorgios is waiting outside. He said we should go to the mouth of the river, near the ancient pagan ruins because magic is stronger there."

"And then what?" Malachi asks.

Ophelia reaches the bottom of the stairs and slips her hand out of Malachi's and into mine. "From what I gather, he'll be able to transport two of us at a time to his fortress in Tibet."

"I don't think I like the idea of splitting up," Axl says, a distinct snarl in his tone.

"Me neither," I agree.

"From what I overheard, there's too great a risk of transporting too many people at once," Ophelia says. "Like our atoms could tear apart or something."

I can't say I love the thought of my cells being strewn about

CHAPTER TWO

the earth like some kind of vampire confetti, but I still don't want us separating.

Malachi slides his arm around Ophelia's waist. "Transportation fucks with your body's molecules as it is. As much as I'd prefer to all go together, best not to fuck with the science too much."

"And I should definitely go last," Ophelia declares.

"Why, so you can make sure one of us doesn't get torn to pieces before you risk it?" I can't resist teasing her despite—or maybe because of—the heavy cloud that's still looming over us all.

"No!" She bumps her arm against mine. "But ..." She chews on her lip, looking uncomfortable all of a sudden.

And now I feel uneasy again too. Her presence allows a little light back into my world, but not enough to banish the darkness. "But what, Cupcake?"

"I don't want to risk Giorgios not coming back for you all. I'm not saying he'd do that, but what if something went wrong and he didn't want to try the group teleportation thing again? He's more likely to risk it to come back for me than for two of you." She whispers the last few words, her cheeks turning pink like she's embarrassed to be more important than us, even though it's an obvious fact of life.

Axl tips his face up to the ceiling and sighs. "Girl has a point."

Yeah, she does. I wouldn't put it past Giorgios to pull a stunt like that either. It would be so much easier for him to only have one of us with Ophelia. Unlike our girl, we're dispensable to him. But it doesn't matter if I trust him. Right now, he looks like our best option for keeping Ophelia from Lucian. "You and Kai go ahead then, and I'll wait with Ophelia."

Malachi glares at me. "Why do you get to wait with Ophelia?"

"Because I said it first, numbnuts."

"Boys." Ophelia shakes her head. "We'll be apart for like a minute. I believe the actual teleportation takes a matter of seconds."

"It's as good an idea as any," Axl says. "None of us want to be apart from each other, but we also don't want to be torn to shreds. So let's just suck it up and make the best of it."

"And once we get to Giorgios's fortress, we start working on bringing Alexandros back." Ophelia's eyes are alight with hope. A hope I cannot bring myself to dash despite being painfully aware that people cannot be brought back. If it were possible, Alexandros would have brought his mom and his wife and kids back. Some clever fuck would have brought the elementai back. But they didn't.

∽

"I will be back for you both before you have time to notice we are gone," Giorgios says.

He clasps Axl's and Malachi's hands in his. "Are you both ready?"

They cast a final look at Ophelia and me before nodding. Before we can say another word, they disappear into nothing. No puff of smoke, no crack in the air. I wasn't sure what I was expecting, but it wasn't nothing. It wasn't three people disappearing without a trace. I stare at the spot on the ground where their feet just were and pray to all the demons in hell that they got there safely.

"What now?" Cadence breaks the eerie silence.

"Giorgios will be back in a moment and then ..." Enora sniffs and wipes her cheeks with the backs of her hands.

Ophelia lets go of my hand and launches herself at the two women. "I'm going to miss you both so much. Can you say

CHAPTER TWO

goodbye to Sienna for me? Tell her I'm sorry I didn't have time to ..." She sniffs.

The three of them embrace. "We will tell her. And I will miss you too, sweet child," Enora says, while Cadence sobs quietly. The professor looks at me over Ophelia's shoulder. "You will take care of her, yes?"

I nod. "With everything I have."

She blinks away another tear and buries her face in Ophelia's neck. In all my years at this university, I've never seen such an overt display of emotion from Professor Green. But then, Ophelia has a habit of bringing out people's sentimental side.

Giorgios's voice cuts through my thoughts. "We must leave."

"You're back already?" Ophelia disentangles herself from the two witches.

"I told you it would take but a few moments. I would have been back sooner had Malachi not asked me half a dozen questions as soon as we arrived."

A smile tugs at the corner of my mouth in spite of all the awful shit that's happened in the past twelve hours. That sounds exactly like the kind of thing Malachi would do, so I guess they arrived safely, and that's something.

"And the boys are okay?" Ophelia asks.

With a nod, he holds out his hand and beckons her to him. "Yes, and they are anxious for your arrival."

Ophelia comes to me first and snakes her slender fingers through mine before she allows Giorgios to take her hand. Only after she has does he take hold of mine too. His palms are smooth and soft, no rough patches like the professor had. A fresh wave of sadness hits me, and I mentally shake it off. Ophelia needs me. I squeeze her fingers in mine.

"Does it hurt?" she whispers to Giorgios.

I look to him, waiting for his answer. Not that I care about me—vampires can feel physical pain, but we experience it much differently than humans. Certainly we have a much higher tolerance.

"I am told it is akin to walking through a little static electricity," Giorgios replies. "Nothing to be afraid of."

"You'll call me, won't you?" Cadence says, tears dripping from her face onto the winter-brown grass.

"Every day," my girl replies.

"And you will warn us if you hear any reports of Lucian?" Enora asks.

"Of course," Giorgios says. "The cell service is very limited; however, we shall remain in regular contact in the coming weeks. But now, the spell please."

Once again, Enora chants the incantation that allows Giorgios to tap into Ophelia's power and enhance his own abilities. There's a strange whooshing in my ears, like I'm being pulled underwater. A second later, my hands are still clasped in Ophelia's and Giorgios's, but we're no longer surrounded by the cool night air of Havenwood. The air in the dimly lit room is warm and heavy with the scent of sandalwood.

"They're here!" Malachi's relieved voice greets us, and before I can blink or ask him why he's surprised, Ophelia and I are wrapped up in his arms as Giorgios tactfully steps aside. Axl comes running into the room not a second later, and the four of us take a moment to enjoy being reunited. We were apart for less than a minute, but it felt like so much more.

"Are you okay, princess?" Axl asks. Her usually flushed cheeks are much paler than normal.

She presses one palm to the side of her face. "I feel a little lightheaded."

"Here, sit down." Axl drags over a chair, and I take the opportunity to survey my surroundings. Six arched windows line two walls of the large dining room, but all that can be seen

CHAPTER TWO

through them right now is pitch-black darkness. A massive chandelier hangs above the long dining table, its bulbs emitting a soft orange glow.

The fireplace, complete with blazing, crackling logs, occupies the far wall, and a worn leather armchair sits beside it, a pile of leatherbound books nestled at its base.

When I look back to Ophelia, she's blinking fast. I drop to a crouch and feel her forehead, noting her clammy skin. "What's wrong, Cupcake?"

Her bright-blue eyes focus on mine. "I feel a little, I don't know ... weak."

I look to Giorgios. "Is that a side effect of the transportation?"

He shrugs, coming closer to her. "Perhaps. Or maybe the thin mountain air is making her feel out of sorts. You will get used to it in a day or two."

"No." She shakes her head. "I feel weak—like my powers. They don't feel the same."

"Oh." Giorgios purses his lips and glances at the fireplace.

My hackles rise and a growl rumbles in my throat, similarly to Malachi and Axl. Something's wrong. Every one of my senses is hyperalert, and I'm about ready to pounce on Giorgios and tear out his heart. "What do you mean, *oh*?"

He shakes his head and sucks air through his teeth, appearing both contrite and annoyingly smug at the same time. "I assure you I simply did not think," he offers.

I advance toward him, hands balled into fists and teeth bared. The fragile hold I've had on my temper since the moment we lost *him* threatens to boil over. "Didn't think about what?"

"Just because I swore an oath to your sire to look out for you does not mean I will not take your head for your insolence, Xavier." Giorgios bares his fangs. "Do not forget who I am."

"Giorgios, please?" Ophelia says, and that's enough to direct his attention from me to her. "Xavier is only protecting me. Tell me why my powers are weakened." There's a tremor in her voice that I hate to hear. We've made a grave mistake in coming here.

"My fortress is built upon the ruins of an old monastery, Ophelia. It has never caused an issue for me before, because, of course—"

"Vampire magic is not affected by hallowed grounds," Malachi finishes for him.

The confusion serves to tamp down my anger at least. "Hallowed grounds?"

"Witch and elementai magic are not as powerful on holy ground. It's something to do with the sacred energy," Malachi explains, and I vaguely recall being told that before. I wish I paid more attention to all this stuff when I had the chance.

"And I'm sure there are few places more imbibed with sacred energy than a former Tibetan monastery." Axl snorts. "Yet you didn't think to warn us of that before we came here?"

"Because he knows there's no way we would have brought Ophelia here if we knew," I snap, wondering what the hell Giorgios's game plan is here. I already know I don't trust him.

Giorgios glares at me, his rage palpable, but it has nothing on mine. "That is not true. I did not consider the ramifications of Ophelia being an elementai. Time was of the essence. I simply wanted her where she is safest, and like it or not, that place is here. I promise you I do not intend any of you any harm."

"You think she's safest in a place where she can't use her powers?" Malachi asks.

Giorgios removes his cloak and places it over the back of a dining chair. "They are severely lessened, not entirely useless." He pulls a chair up next to Ophelia and takes a seat. "I promise you that you can still learn to control your powers, even when they are not at their strongest. In fact, it may be more beneficial to practice when they are weakened."

Is he seriously trying to convince us this is a good thing? The more time I spend in his company, the less I trust him. "And what if she needs to protect herself? How the fuck is she supposed to do that if her powers are weakened?"

He trains his glare on me again. I seem to be adept at pushing all of his buttons—just like I could with his brother. I swallow down the despair brought to life at the thought of Alexandros.

"Should there be any danger to Ophelia within these walls, I would immediately take her somewhere safe before any harm could befall her. A place where she would be free to access all of her powers. Her safety is my utmost concern. No matter what else you refuse to believe, please believe in that."

I crouch in front of Ophelia again and take her hands in mine while Malachi and Axl stand on either side of her. *Let's at least give him a chance*, she implores us through our bond.

I grind my jaw, stopping myself from yelling out all the things I want to say about how wrong this feels, about not believing we should trust the man simply because he's Alexandros's brother. I'm angry and scared and grieving. But for her, I will give him a chance. One chance. *You look tired, Cupcake.*

She stifles a yawn. *I am tired.*

I direct my attention back to Giorgios. "Can you show us where we'll be staying?" We haven't slept in over a day, and it feels like it's been a lifetime. It was certainly in a whole different life, at least. A life with *him* very much a part of it. I should have told him so many things. Even if he wouldn't have wanted to hear them, I should have told him anyway.

"Imari will show you to your quarters" comes Giorgios's reply.

"Imari?" Malachi asks.

XAVIER

Giorgios is saved from responding by the arrival of a woman I assume must be Imari. She walks toward us, smiling, her long black ponytail swishing back and forth like a horse's mane.

"Imari is one of my companions," he explains.

"Are you her sire?" I ask him.

"I am. She will take care of all of your needs when I am not here. Simply call for her, and she will hear you."

I scrutinize her carefully. I'd say she was in her late twenties when she was turned, and it is impossible to tell how old, and therefore how powerful, she is as a vampire.

"And will you fetch Ophelia some tea, Imari?" he adds.

My girl shakes her head. "I don't want tea."

"This is an old Tibetan recipe, Ophelia," Imari says, and for some reason, I'm surprised she has an American accent. "It will help with your altitude sickness and the lightheadedness. I'll sweeten it with some honey. It's delicious."

Ophelia tilts her head and acquiesces with a nod. "Thank you."

Imari smiles again. Everything about her demeanor is warm and friendly, but in contrast, she is tall and angular, with the contours of her muscular arms clearly visible in the tight shirt she wears. She's a fighter, I have no doubt.

I'm suspicious and on edge. I'll feel better when I can get my girl alone.

"I'll show you to your rooms." Imari gestures for us to follow her.

"Um, room. Singular," I snap. That shit is not gonna fly. Not here. Not anywhere.

"Yeah, we don't sleep separately," Malachi adds.

Imari glances at Giorgios, and he must give some sign of agreement because she nods. "Very well. Follow me."

I put Ophelia's backpack over my shoulder with mine, and Malachi scoops our girl into his arms where she nestles herself

CHAPTER TWO

against his chest. Axl slings his arm around my shoulder and flashes me a what-the-fuck-have-we-gotten-ourselves-into look.

I hope we've done the right thing, I tell him.

Alexandros trusted him, he reminds me. *And when have you ever known him to be wrong about anything?*

He was wrong last night about going to find Lucian, and it got him fucking killed. A fresh jolt of pain cuts through my bones, and I grit my teeth and feel every second of it. It's better than having nothing. But I keep my thoughts to myself once more.

Chapter Three
MALACHI

"This room isn't so bad, I guess," I say. It's got a big enough bed for all four of us. One that a quick bounce on the mattress tells me is comfortable. Ophelia strips to her panties and crawls under the covers.

She flops onto her back and yawns. "Does anyone have any idea what time it is?"

I check my watch. "It's three a.m. here, baby. Tibet is thirteen hours ahead of us back home."

Her eyelids flutter closed. "Three a.m.? Maybe that's why I'm so tired." Tears leak from the corners of her eyes, and I hurriedly pull off my clothes and crawl into bed alongside her while Axl and Xavier undress.

As soon as I'm next to her, I pull her into my arms and press her head to my chest. "We didn't sleep last night, baby. Remember?"

"I miss him so much, Kai," she says through a sob.

I kiss the tears from her cheeks and want to do more to comfort her, but I am as broken as she is. She always feels like home to me, but without him here, nowhere feels right. Nowhere feels safe. "I know, baby. So do I."

CHAPTER THREE

She shudders as sobs rack her slender body, and I hold her tighter, wishing I could absorb her pain. Instead, she feels mine as strongly. Just as we both feel Axl's and Xavier's. It's all-encompassing. Overwhelming.

The bed dips behind me as Xavier joins us. He trails his teeth over the back of my neck, and I shiver.

"I feel like I can't breathe," Ophelia whimpers. "It hurts so much. Like an actual physical pain."

Axl slides into bed behind her and nuzzles her shoulder. "We can make it a little better, princess. You want us to try?"

"It feels wrong when he's gone."

I run my hand up and down her spine, and her body arches into mine. My cock stiffens against her. "This is our way of dealing, sweet girl. Bringing each other a little comfort doesn't mean we don't all miss him like hell."

"Alexandros would do the same, and you know he would, Cupcake. There is no greater distraction and no better way of soothing this gaping hole inside us all than being together."

She tips her chin up, wetting her plump lips with her tongue. I dip my head and gently press my lips against hers. *We can stop if it doesn't feel good, baby.*

Xavier shifts into position behind me. *Let me make you feel good while you're feeding on our girl, Kai.*

A groan rolls out of me. The pleasure he gives me might only last a few fleeting moments, but anything has to be better than this living hell.

Axl voices his agreement. *Sounds good to me.*

I slip my tongue into Ophelia's mouth while Axl works her panties down her slender legs. My hand slides over her ribs, down her hip to her thigh, and I lift her leg so her knee is resting on my waist. And I go on kissing her while Xavier sinks his fangs into my neck.

Ophelia moans, and I realize Axl is already edging the crown of his dick at the entrance to her pussy.

Help me out, Kai, and loosen our girl up for me, Axl says softly, lacking his usual commanding growl.

There's nothing I'd rather do. I slip my hand between her thighs and apply light pressure to her clit, teasing her in slow circles until she moves her hips to meet my hand. Her moans turn more needy and desperate, and I increase the pressure.

Xavier presses the head of his thick cock at the seam of my ass, and I grunt into Ophelia's mouth.

How about we take them together, Xavier? Axl asks.

Please! I beg while Ophelia whines her agreement.

Xavier slides the full length of his cock into my ass at the same time Axl takes Ophelia's now-dripping pussy. And fuck, it feels so good. The burning sensation of him filling me with no prep is the exact amount of pain and pleasure I need.

You feel so good, Kai.

You're soaking now, princess.

Our bodies move in a perfect, wordless rhythm as we take whatever solace we can find in each other. Their groans, her whimpers, my own heavy grunts as Xavier fucks me hard—they all meld together in a symphony of our impending release. I pull my lips from Ophelia's and trail them across her jaw and down the pulsing vein in her neck. She smells so sweet and intoxicating, and I can't hold off from sinking my fangs into her for another second. Her rich blood fills my mouth. Xavier's hard cock fills my ass. Axl grabs the back of my neck right before he bites down on Ophelia's shoulder.

And together, all four of us chase a release we all share in, just as we share in our grief and loss.

After, we fall asleep wrapped around each other, taking solace from each other's bodies, temporarily sated from the only comfort we have.

CHAPTER FOUR

XAVIER

My eyes open to warmth and familiarity. Ophelia's soft body is curled against mine, her face nestled into my chest, with Malachi's hard torso at my back and Axl's face on the pillow next to me. The feeling of contentment lasts for all of half a second before my entire world comes crashing down around me and a fresh new agony engulfs me like a forest fire. He's gone. Just like that. All his power and his knowledge and his ... I choke down a sob. Everything he was—it's gone. And soon, we will be too. It all hurts so fucking much I can't breathe.

Ophelia's fingertips skate over my chest before landing on the place directly above my heart, as though she's still checking that I have one. I do, even if it feels broken beyond all repair.

"Xavier." Her warm breath rushes over my skin, reminding me I'm alive, and soon her pain merges with my own, swirling into one raging torrent of grief.

Malachi and Axl must feel it because they stir awake. It takes but a few moments for the anguish to soak through the room like a sponge soaking up water.

I throw back the covers. "I need to get the fuck out of this room and do something. Or at least feel like we're doing something."

Axl and Malachi voice their agreement, but Ophelia remains silent. Her eyes are filled with tears, their tracks carved into her pink cheeks. She closes her eyes.

"Ophelia?" My concern for her fate is so much greater than for my own.

She screws her eyes closed.

Axl traces his fingertips across the palm of her outstretched hand. "Princess?"

"I'm … I'm …" She lets out a frustrated growl and angrily scrubs the tears from her reddened cheeks. "I was trying to use my powers, but they won't work. Not even a little."

"It's the hallowed ground thing," Axl says. "We never would have brought you here if we'd known."

She shakes her head and pushes herself out of bed. "I should have realized. I knew about the holy ground. Kai and I read about it, but I had no idea Giorgios's fortress would be built on an old temple."

I pull her into my arms and rest my lips on top of her head. "None of us did, Cupcake."

"I should have asked."

Axl runs a hand through his hair. "Maybe we all should have asked, but the reality is that we were in shock, and Giorgios was there telling us we had to leave. We did what we thought was best. And now we have to make the best of it."

"Make the best of it how?" Malachi asks.

"For a start, we can go ask Giorgios what the fuck is going on. Why did Lucian …" He shakes his head hard, unable to say the words aloud. "We can start with some answers."

CHAPTER FOUR

AFTER WE GET DRESSED, we make our way downstairs to find Giorgios sitting alone in what appears to be his study. The walls are lined with shelves upon shelves of books, a large wooden antique globe fills one corner, and a vast mahogany desk, piled high with more books, dominates the center of the room.

He looks up from the book he was poring over. "Good morning. Did you sleep well?"

I crack my neck. "I guess."

Ophelia murmurs something, but we're all too distracted to be making small talk.

"We want to do something," Axl snaps, nervous energy radiating from him.

Giorgios closes his book and arches a dark eyebrow. "Such as?"

"Such as finding Lucian—"

"And tearing his fucking head off," I add with a vicious snarl.

With a low hum, Giorgios nods and indicates the small sofa off to the side of the room. "Please take a seat."

The four of us squash onto it with Ophelia perched on Malachi's lap. "I can assure you that searching for Lucian is my top priority, along with keeping you all safe."

"And what can we do to help?" Axl asks.

Giorgios strokes his long fingers through his beard. "At this stage, nothing, I am afraid. Lucian is skilled and powerful. Skilled enough to have eluded his own father for over five hundred years. Skilled enough to have lured the most powerful vampire alive into a trap neither of us saw coming, and then to take his head before Alexandros could do a thing to stop him."

Ophelia's pain rips through all of us, and I gasp at the intensity, glaring at the man in front of us. Did he have to be so callous in the way he talked about his death?

Giorgios sighs. "I am sorry for my bluntness, Ophelia, but

this is the awful truth we must face. Lucian Drakos must be hunted and killed, but in order to do that, we must find him. You four must give me the time and space to do so using whatever means I have. It is safer and less conspicuous if I make my inquiries alone. There are people in the old country who must know of his whereabouts. I will find the man who killed my brother, but none of you are equipped to face him right now."

My anger threatens to boil over. I hate feeling this useless. This completely helpless. "And in the meantime, we do what? Sit around here and wait for him to find Ophelia?"

"This is the safest place in the world for all of you. Lucian will not get past these walls, I assure you. My guards are all my sireds, some of them former Ruby Dragon members. They are highly skilled and trained." I can't help but wonder if he's telling us this to warn us rather than make us feel safe, but I don't challenge him on it and allow him to continue. "And when he finally reveals himself, then we will be ready for him."

"But we don't have the time to sit around and wait to fucking die!" Axl shouts, and Ophelia flinches so hard that he immediately pulls her onto his lap and wraps her in his arms, murmuring his apologies for frightening her.

"Then that is your task, at least until I can find some more information about Lucian's whereabouts. You must find a cure for the deterioration. My library is at your disposal. The books on these shelves are yours to peruse. Please, do all the research you can."

"Why did he kill him?" Ophelia's voice is quiet and calm but loaded with a conviction that fills me with pride.

"Pardon?" Giorgios asks, but we all know he heard her.

"Why did he kill him after all this time? Why now?"

Giorgios swallows hard and glances between Malachi, Xavier, and me. When we don't speak, he finally does. "Surely you know the reason why, Ophelia."

CHAPTER FOUR

"Because of me?" Her voice is a mere whisper.

"Yes, because of you," he says with a solemn nod.

I wind my fingers in her hair, if only to stop myself from going for Giorgios's throat. "No, not because of you, Cupcake," I assure her. "Because he is a twisted fuck, that's why." Malachi offers her similar assurances while Axl kisses a lone tear from her cheek.

I hate every single fucking thing about this. Every single fucking thing.

"Of course he is responsible for his atrocious act." Giorgios sighs. "But there is not a doubt in my mind that he did what he did to get to you. Lucian has been to Montridge. He knows who and what you are, Ophelia."

I sit up straighter and pay closer attention.

Ophelia scrubs her cheeks with the sleeves of her sweater. "He's been to Montridge? When?"

"When the young wolf girl was killed. That was Lucian." Giorgios frowns. "Did Alexandros not tell you this?"

I refuse to believe him. Alexandros would never have kept such important information from us. "If he was actually there, close to Ophelia, Alexandros would have told us."

He scoffs. "Of course, because he has never kept secrets from you before, has he?"

Rage explodes inside me, propelling me up from the sofa and halfway across the room until I have my hands planted flat on the mahogany desk and my teeth bared. "Do not dare to speak ill of him in front of me."

He growls right back, rolling his neck. "I am simply pointing out that he has kept things from you before, Xavier, not that he was at fault for doing so. Now sit down!"

"Xavier, please." Ophelia's sweet voice soothes the feral beast inside of me enough that I return to my seat on the couch beside them.

"How do you know he was there at Montridge?" Malachi asks, keeping a lid on his temper much more effectively than I have, even as I feel his simmering beneath the surface. "The professor told us he thought he might be connected to the attack on the wolf girl, but not that he was there."

"Alexandros told me so. That Lucian was responsible for warping the two vampires' minds and causing the girl's death. But Lucian was there. Watching. Waiting for his moment to strike. I wonder if he was at Montridge the night before last and he followed us, sensing his chance to attack his father whilst he was away from the protection of the university." He purses his lips like he's deep in thought, and I comb my memories of the day the wolf girl was killed, trying to remember what exactly Alexandros told us. But it doesn't matter what he said—anything he did was to protect us. To protect Ophelia.

"What do you think he wants with me?" Ophelia laces her fingers through mine, and when I look up, I see she's done the same with Malachi. With her in Axl's lap, she's touching all of us.

Giorgios looks puzzled, his expression almost amused. "He wants what all magical creatures want from you, Ophelia. Your power."

"But my power is mine. Surely no one else can have it."

He makes his way over to us and cups her chin in his hand. Tilting her head back, he forces her to look at him. Only Malachi using the bond to tell us we can't afford to make a scene when Ophelia is vulnerable stops Axl and me from wrenching Giorgios's arm from its socket. "You have much to learn, Ophelia. Your power is so raw, so new, that it can easily be manipulated."

"But how?" she whispers.

His eyes narrow. "If Alexandros were here, would you not crumble this mountain to dust if he asked you to? If he told you it was necessary?"

CHAPTER FOUR

Her slender throat works as she swallows. She doesn't answer, but she doesn't need to.

"A bond is a powerful thing, Ophelia. It tricks the brain into believing all manner of things that are not true. For instance, leading you to believe that the mere chemical reaction that comes with sharing a vampire's blood is something deep and meaningful."

"It fucking is," I say, snarling, and Giorgios glares in my direction.

Xavier, he's going to tear your fucking head off if you don't stop. Now, for the love of fuck, calm down. Malachi growls the warning in my head.

But my heart is racing and blood is rushing in my ears. *Do you really expect me to sit here and listen to this shit? Let him fill her head with this shit?*

She doesn't believe it, and you know it. Just let him say his piece and we can get out of here.

"Regardless, Xavier, it is what many of our kind hold to be true." Giorgios redirects his attention to Ophelia. "That what you believe to be love or fate is merely vampire evolution at work in its purest form. Both vampire and elementai are slaves to the bond once it is in place, and blood is the drug which feeds the addiction. With Alexandros gone and your bond severed, there is space for a new bond. A new *love* for whom you would burn the world to ash if he asked you nicely enough."

"The fuck she would," Axl snaps, but Giorgios keeps his attention on Ophelia.

Her lip trembles, and she shakes her head. "No. It's not only a vampire blood thing. It's real. I love them. He loved me. They love me."

Yes we fucking do. Who the fuck does he think he is trying to convince her otherwise?

Giorgios's smug, patronizing smile makes me wants to

punch his fangs down his throat. "I am sure that is also true, sweet Ophelia. Which is why you cannot trust anyone but the people in this room. Do you understand me?"

She nods, her lip still quivering.

He straightens his jacket. "Lunch will be served in the dining room at one. Fresh human blood is delivered here every day at noon." Without a backward glance, he strides from the room, and as soon as he's gone, Ophelia looks between the three of us, her eyes wet with tears.

I speak before she has a chance to. "He was fucking wrong, Cupcake. We all love you. We fucking adore you, and Alexandros did too. If you believe anything in your entire life, then please believe that."

She nods, a shaky smile spreading over her lips. "I do believe that."

Axl kisses her forehead. "Good girl," he mumbles.

Malachi squeezes her tighter and taps her on the thigh. "I think we should check out this library. It will give us something to focus on."

I look to Axl. Books have never really been our thing. "Maybe you and I should check this place out a little more? See what we're dealing with?"

He nods his agreement, and we jump up, eager to be doing something productive. I kiss Ophelia and lick the salty residue from her lips. "No more tears today, okay, Cupcake? We're gonna fix everything, all right?" I don't believe it for a second, but it breaks my heart to see her cry.

She nods. "Promise."

Axl and I leave the study and go in search of an exit. "Can you believe that shit?" he growls as soon as we're out of earshot. "Trying to convince her we don't love her. That Alexandros didn't love her. What the fuck!"

"I know, but she doesn't believe it," I assure him.

CHAPTER FOUR

He swallows hard and opens and closes his mouth a few times before he finally says, "Do you?" He speaks quietly, like he's ashamed to say the words.

As he fucking should be. I stop in my tracks and glare at him. "What the fuck, Axl?"

He closes his eyes and blows out a breath. "Do you think this could be some weird ancient vampire mumbo jumbo? Because the way I feel about her, Xavier, it's unnatural. I'm obsessed with her. And I'm more terrified by the thought of leaving her alone than I am of fucking dying. Is that fucking normal?"

I slap the back of his head. "No, it's not fucking normal, dickface. It's love. All-consuming, life-altering, soul-shattering love."

He nods and looks away as his eyes glisten with tears. "I don't want to lose her. I can't even think about losing her without losing my ability to fucking breathe."

Holy fucking shit, this hurts like a motherfucker. "We're not gonna lose her," I say, making a promise I have no idea how to keep.

I throw an arm around his shoulder, and we step outside into a courtyard. I look up to the sky. Not knowing who or what is up there, I make them an oath: Let me keep her and I will do anything you want. Anything. Because Ophelia Hart is ours, and we will not fucking lose her.

CHAPTER
FIVE
AXL

I pace the perimeter of the courtyard, my eyes scanning every nook, every stone, and every turret, looking for a weakness in Giorgios's fortress. The house itself is built into the bedrock of the mountain, using the former monastery structure as its base. It has been fortified and extended since it was first built, but there is one way in and one way out.

A gray stone wall, twenty feet high and three feet deep, runs around the entire perimeter of the half-acre courtyard, which was once the temple gardens. Six turrets loom over the area, vast and imposing. Two on either side of the gate, two on the east wall, and two on the west, each manned by at least six guards armed with swords. There are more guards patrolling the perimeter wall and at the gate. There is nowhere in this entire courtyard where we cannot be seen.

Xavier falls into step beside me. *Any luck finding a way out of this place yet?*

Nope. Giorgios has this place locked down tighter than Shawshank. You?

No. He nudges my arm. *But Andy did get out of Shawshank, remember.*

CHAPTER FIVE

Why does a vampire who claims to spend all his time reading books need this many guards? Is he expecting an invasion?

Xavier raises an eyebrow at me. *I asked one of the guards, an old Ruby Dragon member I recognized, and he said one can never be too careful.*

Yeah, well, there's careful and there's planning for a full-on military invasion. This is the latter. Isn't keeping Lucian out a new development?

Xavier looks around, his deep-blue eyes narrowed. *Apparently so. And I can't help thinking that these guards are designed to keep us in as much as they're supposed to keep anyone out. Something is very off in this place.*

I spoke to one of the guards too, asked about using a cell phone, and he said there's no chance we can get a signal this deep into the mountains. So we're basically cut off from all civilization.

"Everything okay, gentlemen?" The voice comes out of nowhere, and we spin around to find Giorgios standing behind us.

I immediately bring down the shutters in my mind like Alexandros taught us all to do in the presence of powerful vampires. I'm not as good at it as Xavier and Ophelia, but I'll do whatever the hell I can to keep Giorgios out until I know for sure whether we can trust him. "Yup. Just taking a walk and checking the place out."

"These mountains are amazing." Xavier looks up at the one looming over us. "I'd love to climb one."

"The Himalayas are treacherous mountains to climb. Especially this far inland. Very few try to climb the cliff faces here."

"Yeah, well, being a vampire and all, I'm not too worried about falling to my death." He flashes Giorgios a grin that seems friendly, but those of us who know him well know better. "Can I get out there and give it a try?"

"You do not have the appropriate equipment, Xavier, and

vampire or not, climbing mountains in these conditions even with the appropriate gear is dangerous. Do we not have plenty to worry about without having to launch a search and rescue party to find you?" His tone is pleasant enough, but there's an underlying hint of annoyance.

"How about a walk, then?" Xavier rolls his neck. "I really could use a little exercise."

"There is a well-equipped gym in the house and all the space you need here in the courtyard." Giorgios scowls, no longer bothering to mask his irritation. "There is no need for you to leave these grounds. Any of you."

My hackles rise, and I roll back my shoulders, but Xavier speaks before I do. "But what if we want to anyway? You wouldn't stop us, would you? I mean, we're guests here, not prisoners."

Giorgios's blue eyes flash with anger. "Not prisoners, no, but you are here under my protection, and the best way to protect you until we learn of Lucian's whereabouts and his intentions toward Ophelia is for all of you to remain here. I swore an oath to my brother that I do not intend to break, Xavier, no matter how insolently you ask me to."

Back off, Xavier. You're pissing him off, and we need to keep him on our side while we figure shit out.

Xavier nods, conveying his acceptance of the rules. "I understand. I was just asking. I hate being cooped up, is all. But I guess we can handle it for a few weeks while we figure shit out."

Giorgios stares at me, his eyes narrowed in suspicion as though he's waiting for my objection, but I give him no cause to doubt my compliance. I learned to mask my feelings from the best, and no matter how powerful Giorgios is, he's no Alexandros Drakos. He doesn't even come close. "That is good to know. Ophelia's protection is our most important priority."

CHAPTER FIVE

I nod my agreement.

Xavier voices his. "Damn straight."

Giorgios glances at his watch. "To that end, I have a meeting I must get to. A lead on Lucian's whereabouts."

That sparks my curiosity. "Let us come with you."

He shakes his head. "Alas, I must transport there, and without Enora's spell combined with Ophelia's power, I can only do so alone. I will update you upon my return if I learn anything of use."

He offers a nod of farewell and then walks through the gate, the guards standing aside as he passes.

Growling, I watch him go and wish we could walk out of here just as easily. He insists this is for our protection, but Xavier was right before—we're little more than prisoners here. Every fiber of my being urges me to rail against that. To walk out of here with Ophelia, Xavier, and Malachi and never look back. Only my concern for Ophelia's safety stops me, and there's no chance in hell we would leave without her.

Why the fuck did he do that? Xavier asks.

Do what?

Walk outside to transport. Why not do it right here?

Dunno. Something to do with the holy ground thing?

Xavier shakes his head, and we resume our walk around the courtyard. *No, I'm pretty sure that's only for a witch's or an elementai's powers. It has no effect on vampire powers.*

I stare at the gate, unable to see anything through the thick steel grid and the guards standing in front of it. But Xavier is right, why bother leaving to transport?

You guys find anything yet? Malachi asks through the bond.

No. Not yet, I answer. *Either of you?*

No. But Giorgios's library is huge. He was right about it rivaling Thucydides. Ophelia is grabbing books and sorting them into piles like a demon. The quicker we can identify the useful ones, the quicker we can read and find some answers.

I glance back at the gate again. Giorgios has disappeared, and there's little else to do out here while the guards seem to be watching us so intently. *You want us to help out?*

Yeah, before our girl works herself into a frenzy. I've never seen her so determined.

Necessary determination. Her sweet voice fills our heads now too. Kai should have known that nothing gets by her.

It's not a criticism, sweet girl. I just don't want you to strain yourself carrying fifty books while I'm not looking.

Still have my vampire strength. That's not affected at all, she retorts.

Xavier rolls his eyes at me. "We'd better go and see what she's doing, yeah? Kai is right—it will go quicker with all of us." Plus, if Giorgios won't let us do anything else practical, then at least this is a good use of our time.

When we reach Giorgios's library, I drag her into my arms and squeeze her tight, feeling immense guilt for what I said to Xavier earlier. The strength of my feelings for Ophelia scares the fuck out of me sometimes, but that's only further proof of how real they are. I have bitten plenty of people in my long life, and I have never felt the need to see a single one of them ever again. From the moment I tasted her, I have been hers. If I am under some kind of fucking spell, I never want to break it.

"Hi," she says, her eyes sparkling with determination. It's a damn sight better than the despair I've seen in them recently.

"Hey, Cupcake." Xavier gives her a quick kiss on the cheek. "Tell me what we can do."

She gives us both instructions on what kinds of books and topics to look for and points out the various piles she's been sorting them into. The concentration needed for the task at least gives us all something to focus on other than the obvious.

CHAPTER FIVE

While we work, Xavier and I explain what we learned while we were in the courtyard. Malachi and Ophelia share our concern, but none of us has the headspace to examine it in great detail right now. By the end of the afternoon, we have eight distinct piles of ledgers and books waiting to be pored over.

With her hands on her hips, Ophelia blows a strand of hair from her eyes and triumphantly declares, "These are some of the oldest and rarest books in here. Some even rarer than the ones back at Montridge. I'm sure we're going to find the answers we need."

Her enthusiasm and determination are infectious, and they filter through all of us, reinvigorating and purposeful. And for the first time since we lost him, I feel a genuine spark of hope that we're going to fix it. If anyone can find a way, it's our girl. The most powerful creature who ever lived.

CHAPTER
SIX
AXL

I sit on the edge of the bed, holding my head in my hands. It's been over two hundred years since I felt the adverse morning-after consequences of overindulging in alcohol —a major perk of being a vampire is the lack of hangovers—but I remember it clearly. And it's the only comparison I have for the way I'm feeling. Is this how the deterioration starts? Does it really start this early?

In the two weeks since our arrival, our first Christmas and New Year's with our girl came and went without notice, and Ophelia has remained steadfastly dedicated to her ambition of reading every single book in Giorgios's fortress. After we got through the first lot of piles and found nothing, she simply created a new catalog and sorted out more books and more topics and has been unwavering in her certainty that the answers are in there somewhere. And for the first week and a half, we were equally committed. But with every book we read and discarded came more failure, more hopelessness. And while it seemed to spur her on, the rest of us only grew more miserable and dejected. Or perhaps the misery has more to do with how we all started feeling like crap yesterday.

CHAPTER SIX

Giorgios leaves every day, usually returning a few hours later with no news of Lucian's whereabouts and no answers about any-fucking-thing at all. For a powerful ancient vampire, he seems pretty damn useless to me. I almost told him as much yesterday, but Ophelia persuaded me not to. She's grateful to him for helping us scour through books and pointing us in directions we wouldn't have otherwise considered. So I relented after begrudgingly admitting that—other than essentially keeping us prisoner—he's been a gracious host.

Ophelia kneels behind me, running her warm hands over my back and shoulders. Despite my delicate state, pleasure courses through me at the feel of her skin on mine. The animal inside me has no ability to hold back where she's concerned.

"Are you okay?" she asks, her lips against my ear. "Is there something I can do?"

I groan. "Just keep doing that, princess."

Xavier comes in through the bathroom door, dark circles under his eyes and a pallor to his usually olive skin that makes him look waxy. "You still feeling like shit too?"

"Yup."

"Kai too. He went for some fresh air to clear his head. What the fuck, dude? I haven't felt this bad since I was human."

Ophelia's despair washes over me in a thick wave, threatening to pull me under. I take her hand in mine and link our fingers. "We'll be okay. Maybe it's the thin air up here or something."

"Vampires aren't affected by mountain air, Axl," she says.

Xavier falls onto the bed and lies back with his hands behind his head. "Cupcake isn't stupid, dude. She knows what this is."

She rests her chin on my shoulder, and I feel her emotions cut off, as though she's barricading her despair behind a wall of steel so it won't bleed into us. "I didn't realize it would happen so soon."

"We have time," I assure her. But I don't know how long. It could be weeks or months. Maybe even days. The thought of leaving her behind without us makes my heart splinter into a million shards. I can't think about it for more than a second or it will render me immobile.

"We should go ask Giorgios if he has any answers for us," she says, jumping to her feet. "It's been over a week. There must be something, and he knows more about this than any of us."

It takes a lot of grumbling and groaning for Xavier and me to get on our feet and get dressed, but a few minutes later, we're following her out of the room to go find Kai.

∼

WE'VE BEEN SITTING in Giorgios's study for ten minutes already, having disturbed him reading through some scrolls which he informed us are related to the Order. He has also declared them of no help at all and given us permission to read them ourselves.

We asked him about the sickness, about Lucian, and what he's learned in the time we've been here. Surely he must have discovered something useful on one of his daily trips to wherever the hell it is he goes. But thus far, he's revealed nothing more than we already knew. He did make sure to reiterate the fact that he doesn't know of a single recorded case of a vampire ever surviving without their sire, but I guess the bright side is how it could take up to two years. Asshole.

Giorgios runs his fingers through his beard and brings them to a point underneath his chin. He reminds me so much of Alexandros. I blink away the tears burning my eyes before he

CHAPTER SIX

can see them, but the cyclone of grief has already taken up residence where my heart once used to beat.

"Who was the first of you to bite Ophelia?" he asks.

What the fuck has that got to do with how long we have before the deterioration takes us?

He doesn't look at us as he waits for an answer, and my hackles rise. I guess Ophelia feels the same because she asks, "Does that make a difference?"

Giorgios shakes his head, flashing us all an easy smile. "No. I was merely curious." He stares at the four of us like he's waiting for our answer, and we stare back, the room thick with our silence.

Giorgios's smile remains in place, but still, he waits.

Is this weird or what? Xavier asks through our link.

Definitely weird, I reply.

"I was the first," Malachi says aloud.

None of us bat an eyelid at his blatant lie.

Giorgios frowns, his eyes narrowing. "You were?"

Malachi folds his arms across his chest, tipping his chin up. "Yeah. Isn't that right, sweet girl?"

Closing her book, she flashes him a sweet smile and lets him pull her onto his lap. "Yep. My first everything, Kai."

I suppress the growl that the beast inside me is intent on expressing. I know I was her first, and so do they. It doesn't fucking matter what we tell Giorgios. But I don't like the guy. I don't like him asking us questions that are none of his business. He might be protecting us from Lucian, but I can't bring myself to fully trust him. One thing I do know is he should have protected Alexandros, and I will never forgive him for allowing him to die.

"I assume, then, given your questions this morning, you have not yet found anything in your research to indicate a potential cure for your mates' certain fate, Ophelia?" Giorgios asks. Why is he being such an asshole today?

A cloud of sorrow passes over her face for only a second before being replaced with her usual look of steely determination. "No. Not yet, but I will. There must be something, mustn't there?"

He taps his steepled fingers against his lips and hums. Finally, he says, "I believe there must, if only we could be certain of where to find it."

Malachi coughs. "Well, if you could find it real quick, we'd sure appreciate it."

I lean forward in my chair and watch Giorgios intently. "Do you not think it's odd we all started to get sick at exactly the same time?"

"Perhaps." He shrugs. "I have not been in the company of vampire brothers who have lost their sire before, so I cannot say for certain."

"You've never come across groups of vampires who've lost their sire before?" My tone is accusatory, but I don't care. He's over two thousand years old, and I don't buy it.

"Groups, yes. Many groups. But not families such as yourselves. Alexandros raised you like brothers, and I am sure it must have an impact on your …" He pauses like he's searching for the word. "Deterioration."

Fucking asshole.

Malachi shifts in his seat, jostling Ophelia on his lap. "But I thought age and strength were the determining factors?"

"Usually, yes. But given how you have all started to weaken at the same time, then perhaps it is affected by more than that. Perhaps it is the strength of the bond which determines the speed of deterioration. It is not an exact science, so we simply cannot know for sure. But we must learn. I have arranged to meet with an ancient seer in five days' time."

CHAPTER SIX

I sure as fuck hope that's the good news he's presenting it to be. "Why five days? Can't you transport straight to this person?"

He shakes his head. "She refuses to meet with me anywhere but the country of our birth, and it will take her time to clear her schedule and travel to Greece. But I am hopeful she will have some of the answers we seek."

"Please, can we come with you?" Ophelia asks. "I'm sure Enora will give you the spell if you ask her, and we can tap into my power. Elementai magic is similar to witch magic, only channeled differently. I'm sure we can make it work."

"There's no way we'd risk your safety like that, princess." I lock eyes with Giorgios. "But I could go with you." Both Malachi and Xavier immediately add their willingness to participate too.

Giorgios narrows his deep-blue eyes and pauses for a few seconds before shaking his head. "We cannot be absolutely sure it would work without a powerful witch's spell. If the circumstances were so dire that we had to try ..." He shakes his head again. "I am confident you are powerful enough, Ophelia, but Axl is right, we cannot risk you. Any of you." He indicates all of us with a nod. "I know our relationship has been somewhat strained, but please believe me when I tell you that I am doing all I can to protect each of you. I will find a cure for the deterioration, and I am hopeful the seer will point me in the right direction. Besides, she does not welcome strangers." He huffs a small laugh. "It took some convincing to persuade her to meet with me."

My attention is drawn to the other side of the room by a clearing throat. "Sire, you are needed in the courtyard," Imari says.

Is that a look of relief on his face? Maybe he summoned her here with a fake emergency to avoid further pressure to take one of us with him.

We trust him, don't we? Ophelia asks through our bond after he leaves the room.

Let's see what he has to say after his visit to the seer, Malachi says.

I give my agreement.

The guy has been nothing but accommodating since we got here, but ... I don't know. Xavier's brow furrows. *Something just doesn't feel right about the way we all got sick.*

Ophelia shifts on Malachi's lap, her book clasped in her hands. *Wait? Do you think he's somehow making you sick?*

What, like poisoning us? I ask.

Xavier huffs and flops down on the sofa beside Malachi and Ophelia. *I'm saying we shouldn't rule anything out. He could be doing all he can to try to find a cure for us, or he could be giving us poisoned blood. He's always been very generous with his supply. And outside of the people in this room, I truly don't know who or what I trust anymore.*

Malachi wrinkles his nose like he's deep in thought. *You really think he'd do that, though? I mean, why risk it when the sickness will get us all at some point eventually?*

Speed up the process? Xavier shrugs. *Get Ophelia all to himself a little faster?*

Ophelia's sadness is profound, but she masks it quickly. Malachi presses a kiss against her forehead. "You okay, sweet girl?"

She nods. "Yeah, it's just a lot to think about."

"Yeah, it really fucking is." Xavier sighs. "My fucking head hurts."

My mind is racing with questions and suspicions and doubts, and I would give anything to hear Alexandros's calm voice. The way he could cut through the chatter and help me focus was a skill I didn't realize I'd miss so much. *Let's think this through. If we're actually considering the possibility that Giorgios is*

CHAPTER SIX

poisoning us to make us get sicker faster, why? What would be his endgame?

I already told you. Getting us out of the way so he can have Ophelia to himself, Xavier replies. *You heard what he said about Lucian, about why people want our girl. Power. What if that's all Giorgios is after too?*

He may even believe it would be easier to protect her without us around, Malachi suggests, ever the optimist.

That's still a pretty big accusation to make, guys, Ophelia says.

It's a fucking huge accusation, and the ramifications are even bigger. Because if it's true, then we all willingly walked into the lion's den and put our girl in a whole heap of fucking danger. *Yeah, but we're all thinking it, aren't we?*

Ophelia sits up straighter, her eyes wide and shining. *We need to test the theory.*

How, Cupcake?

For the next week, you only feed on me. If you stop getting sick, then we'll know you're being poisoned. And meanwhile, we keep reading and researching and looking for a way out of here.

I shake my head. *While I wholeheartedly agree with the second element of your plan, there's not a chance you're sustaining three hungry vampires all on your own. That's a hell of a lot of blood, princess. You need to keep your own strength up. You're already weakened here because of the whole sacred ground shit.*

My blood still replenishes more quickly than when I was human, or at least when we thought I was human. I'll make sure to eat and drink plenty and look after myself in every other way. Please, Axl? This is the one way we can know for sure.

Logically it makes sense, but I still hate the thought of us being so reliant on her. We should be the ones protecting her. Even if, in a roundabout way, this still achieves that. *I don't know.*

Xavier runs a hand through his hair and sighs. *She has a*

point, Axl. Ophelia isn't sick. If we only drink from her, then we'll know for sure.

If I get too weak, we can stop, she insists, her pleading blue eyes locked on my face.

Finally, I relent, hoping we are in fact being poisoned. The alternative is too terrifying to contemplate.

CHAPTER SEVEN

MALACHI

It's a strange feeling—the deterioration—and nothing at all like I expected it to feel. I expected to grow weaker over time as I wasted away to nothing, but thus far, it seems the worst symptom is extreme fatigue which makes us feel weak and lethargic. Something we are all unaccustomed to. The onset of the deterioration was sudden, and while not unexpected, the timing sucks balls. Ophelia needs us. Alexandros needs us to find a way to bring him back from the netherworld.

Even after feeding exclusively from Ophelia for the past five days, our symptoms show no sign of improving. As she shows no sign of illness, we can only assume it is our worst fear—the deterioration has taken hold a lot more quickly than we hoped it would.

Ophelia and I lie on the sofa together in the den, her head on my chest while I curl a thick strand of her hair between my fingers. I had hopes for at least a couple more years with our girl, but it seems it wasn't meant to be. Axl and Xavier lie on the opposite sofa, and a pervasive sense of defeat hangs heavy in the air. We have searched through every single book in Giorgios's library, and there's nothing about the deterioration in any of them. Nothing helpful in any case.

"You will not find any of the answers you seek lounging in here."

Giorgios is back! A sudden rush of excitement has me opening my eyes. He sits in the armchair beside the roaring fire and clears his throat. It seems like he's about to say something, but he remains silent. Ophelia sits up, swinging her legs over mine and leaning back against the sofa cushions. "Did you meet with the seer? What did she say?" she asks.

I prop myself up on one elbow and watch him with curiosity.

He sucks on his top lip, appearing to wrestle with his conscience.

"Giorgios?" Ophelia pleads. "What did she tell you?"

He nods once. "She told me there is a way." We all sit up now, like he's injected a shot of adrenaline into all of our hearts. "But I am not sure you will like it," he adds, his tone grave and his expression even darker.

"If there's a way, then we'll learn to like it," Xavier says.

Ophelia nods eagerly. "Anything."

His right eye twitches, and he appears nervous, which is something I haven't seen from him before. Nor sensed, but I don't sense much of anything from Giorgios. He's a closed book, adept at masking his emotions. Alexandros once told me that his brother's powers of the mind were not as well-developed as his, but he's certainly adept at guarding himself from others. I only hope he's not as skilled at reading thoughts. We've all kept our guards up around him, but right now, I want to trust him. I want to believe he has the answers we've been searching for.

"Turned vampires cannot be re-sired because you already have, or had, a sire, and your state as a vampire is very much dependent on his bloodline. But ..." His tongue darts out across

CHAPTER SEVEN

his lower lip, and we all lean forward, breaths held in anticipation. "It seems there are a number of factors at play which have created a solution to this unique situation."

"And they are?" I ask, wishing he'd get to the point.

"It is because of Ophelia and her unique abilities that I believe there may be a way to reverse the deterioration."

Reverse the deterioration. So we're not going to die and leave her. Relief, warm and hopeful, flows through all four of us as we stare at Giorgios, the man with the answers we seek. I squeeze Ophelia's hand, and she gives me an optimistic smile.

"Ophelia's bond with Alexandros somehow connected her to you on a deeper level than is usual. As your bond with Ophelia is so unique, and because it remains intact, it is possible to—" He presses his lips together like he's searching for the word. "Transfer the sire bond."

"Transfer it to who?" Axl asks, blinking with confusion. "To Ophelia?"

Giorgios shakes his head. "No. To another vampire. Ophelia would have to …" He clears his throat again, and my hope evaporates. No way is our girl bonding to another vampire. Over my dead fucking body. Which, I realize, is highly likely. "Ophelia would have to bond to another vampire. Specifically to a blood relative of Alexandros to ensure the greatest chance of success."

And the final flicker of hope is snuffed out entirely. There's no way any of us would expect her to bond with Giorgios, and surely he must know that. And there's not a chance in hell we'd accept him as our new sire. We're all still devoted to the one we lost. Ophelia squeezes my hand tighter as a horror-filled gasp falls from her lips.

"And that would be you, I guess?" Xavier growls.

"Not necessarily." Giorgios holds up his hands. "I am not the only member of House Drakos, although I can guarantee I am the only one you should consider for such a role. My father has been advised of my brother's demise, but I have managed to keep Ophelia's identity from him thus far. I am not sure how much longer it will be before I am forced to endure a visit from him."

"Alexandros said he was a danger to me if he found out what I am," Ophelia says, still frowning, but I can practically hear the cogs in her brain working overtime.

"And he is, Ophelia. He would lock you in a cage and breed you until you produced him a whole army of elementai and vampire children. It is what he planned to do when the last few elementai were herded into the apparent safety of his castle. I do not know whether it is fortunate that he did not succeed." He winces and swallows hard. "And let us not forget the other son of House Drakos—Lucian. An even darker fate than my father. Neither of them is a pleasant choice, Ophelia. Neither would be so considerate as to seek your permission first. The safest way for you to ensure neither of them force a bond with you is to bond with another first."

"And again, that leads us all straight back to you." Xavier's voice drips with disdain.

"I will protect you whatever the outcome. But regardless of which path you choose, I am merely presenting you with the options. You need not take any of them if you do not wish to."

Ophelia's skin is pale, and her lip is trembling. Her fear and anxiety spike so alarmingly that I quickly wrap her in my arms and utter soothing words in her ear.

No fucking way, princess, Axl growls in our heads. *You don't have to fucking bond with him.*

No, sweet girl. I smooth back her hair. *Stop trembling. You're safe. This isn't going to happen.*

I don't want to bond with him. She rolls back her shoulders and twists her head from side to side. *But if it's the only way to save you, then I—*

CHAPTER SEVEN

There'll be another way, Xavier assures her. *We don't want another fucking sire, Cupcake.*

He's right, princess, Axl adds.

She ignores our objections and narrows her eyes at Giorgios. "Are you even sure it would work?"

He gives a single nod, his face entirely unreadable now. "After I met with the seer, I did a little research of my own, which also led me to believe it would."

A lone tear runs down her cheek, and she angrily swats it away. "But wouldn't I be ... betraying him?"

"How is saving his sireds—your mates—and protecting your own precious life, the one he so willingly gave his own for, a betrayal of him, Ophelia? He is gone. He cannot save you. And I cannot be sure, but ..."

"But what?" Hope ignites in her heart once more. Hope is a dangerous thing—without it, we are lost, but with it, we are doomed.

"Alexandros asked me to protect you all, and I cannot help but wonder if this is what he meant. What he would have wanted."

The fuck he would have. A rumbling growl rolls deep in my chest, and before I can react, Axl is already on his feet. "I can guarantee with one hundred percent certainty that Alexandros Drakos would not, under any circumstances, have wanted you to bond with Ophelia."

"Not even to protect her?" Giorgios scowls. "To protect you?"

Axl falters, but I don't. "Not even," I bark.

Giorgios stands and brushes imaginary creases from his suit pants. His ire simmers directly beneath the surface. Dangerously close. And I suppose I can't entirely blame him. He presented us with a solution he worked hard to find, and we threw it straight back in his face. "As I said, I am merely presenting you with a choice, it is entirely up to you whether you take it." He walks out of the room.

"You're not fucking bonding with him, princess," Axl snaps, his teeth bared.

"But if it saves you ..." she protests.

"I can't believe you're considering this." Xavier snarls. "Never mind that we don't want him to be our sire."

I glare at them. "She's only considering it to save our fucking lives, you pair of fuck-knuckles." I don't want her to do this either, but she's clearly struggling here.

Sufficiently chastened, my brothers cross the room and kneel in front of us. Axl rests his forehead on her knees. Xavier takes his hands in hers. "I'm sorry, Cupcake, but you don't have to do this. We'll find another way."

She strokes his cheek, and I keep my arms banded tightly around her. "But what if there is no other way? I cannot bear the thought of bonding with Giorgios. Or of replacing Alexandros in any way, even if he will never be replaced in my heart. But I cannot bear the thought of losing all of you even more."

I press my lips against the skin of her neck. "You will never lose us, sweet girl. I will cling to this life for eternity for you. I will make all the bargains I am able to with Death himself before I leave you alone."

Axl presses a kiss on the inside of her wrist. "Me too, princess."

Xavier stands and scoops her up into his arms. "You're never gonna lose us, Cupcake. If there's one way to stop this thing, there must be another. You're stuck with us forever. I promise. Now let's get the fuck out of here and go to bed, huh?"

She offers him the faintest of smiles, and together, we head to our room. The place where we can be together in one mass of beating hearts and tangled limbs. Where we can try to forget we're facing an uncertain future without him in it.

CHAPTER
EIGHT
OPHELIA

"You can do this, Ophelia," Giorgios says in a commanding voice that sounds a little too much like his brother's to not cause me pain. "Your powers are severely weakened, but they remain."

I flick my wrist again, and tiny sparks flicker across the fallen tree branch in front of me, but that's all I'm able to summon. Raindrops fall onto my face, and I blink the moisture from my heavy lashes.

"It is raining, Ophelia. The sky was cloudless not a moment ago, therefore you are not in control of your powers. You must focus!"

Thunder rolls above. A swirling tornado of emotion rages inside me, and I glare at him. How am I supposed to control my powers when I cannot *feel* them? He blinks at me expectantly, seemingly unaware of my inner tirade, which I'm thankful for. I keep my walls up around him at all times, and at least those powers still work.

After his ludicrous suggestion that I bond with him—ludicrous yet still not completely ruled out—I asked if he could at least help me with something practical. And that is learning to control my powers, which he said I could still do even while they're diminished. I expected him to give me some tips I could use with the guys, not instruct me himself. But I suppose he is doing the best he can under the circumstances, as we all are.

Closing my eyes, I focus on the orb of white light in my center and take a brief second to bask in its warmth. It makes me feel deeply connected to Alexandros because he's the one who helped me discover it. He's the one who unlocked all of this, and yet he's not here to help me control it. It feels so impossible without him. A sob wells up in my throat.

"Focus, Ophelia. Stop the storm." Giorgios's calm voice cuts through my turmoil. I reconcentrate on my light and imagine the sun shining in the clear blue sky. The rain stops as quickly as it started, and when I reopen my eyes, the sun is casting Giorgios's shadow in front of me.

"Well done, Ophelia." He places a reassuring hand on my shoulder. "But I sense you are tired, and I must continue my search for Lucian. We will resume your lessons tomorrow."

With a polite farewell, Giorgios leaves me in the courtyard, and Xavier and Malachi, who have been watching from the sidelines, join me.

I slump down against the thick tree trunk. "I hate not being able to use my powers properly. I feel so useless sitting here, waiting for Lucian to show up and take me." I swipe away the tear rolling down my cheek, annoyed with myself for being so emotional. Alexandros would figure out a way around this hallowed ground issue. He'd think of something.

"I know he would, Cupcake, but he's not here," Xavier says, his voice sad as he sits down beside me.

Malachi sits on my other side. "And we won't let Lucian take you, baby."

"I didn't mean to think that aloud. I know you're all doing the best you can. I just miss him so much." The tears flow faster

CHAPTER EIGHT

now, and the weight of guilt and despair and utter helplessness threatens to overwhelm me. This is why I try not to cry—once I start, I can't seem to stop. I've gotten through the last three weeks running on optimism and determination, but now those are in short supply, slowly being replaced with absolute hopelessness.

Malachi wraps a comforting arm around my shoulder, and Xavier rests his hand on my thigh, giving me a reassuring squeeze. "We know, Cupcake, we miss him too. And the truth is, he would know what to do." He plucks a few blades of grass before tossing them aside. "And I feel completely fucking useless in this place. We're trapped here, and I don't know what the fuck to do about it." We're surrounded by snow-topped mountains, clear blue skies, and some of the most stunning views I've ever seen. But a beautiful prison is still a prison.

If only I could figure out how to make these stupid powers work better. Or if they were strong enough that I could do something. Anything.

What if we just walked through the fucking gate and kept going? It's Axl's voice in our heads now, and I smile at the familiar sound. Despite my powers being lessened here, our bond is as strong as ever, if not stronger. Unfortunately, though, the boys aren't strong enough to fight off Giorgios's guards if they tried to stop us from leaving, and without my powers, neither am I.

How are you feeling? I ask him. He was extra tired this morning, so we left him sleeping in bed.

I'm so exhausted. I feel like I've been awake for two centuries. He laughs softly. *But I'm good. I'll take a shower and then come join you all.*

Axl's voice disappears, but I still feel him. His sadness and his fear. His guilt at not being strong enough to fix this mess we've found ourselves in. "Do you think it's strange my powers are lessened, but I can still hear and feel you all as much as I ever have?"

Xavier pops out his bottom lip like he's thinking, but it's Malachi who answers first. "Maybe our bond isn't affected by your powers?"

"Maybe." I rack my brain for an answer I'm sure is there, even if I'm not entirely sure of the question.

Xavier spins to face me, his blue eyes wide. "Or maybe it's because your ability to read our thoughts and connect with us isn't part of your elementai powers."

I'm unable to stop my own exhilaration at the sudden upswing in his mood. "What do you mean?"

"Part of your deal is that you take on our powers, right? Our strength? Our power to speak through thought? That's vampire power, Cupcake. Not elementai."

Xavier's right; none of those powers have been affected at all by being here.

"And you could use Alexandros's powers too, right?" Malachi asks, his face breaking into a smile. "You were able to speak to the dragons, so that probably means you can speak to all the people he's ever shared blood with?"

"Or made a blood oath with," Xavier adds. "So Enora, Osiris, and your friends back at Montridge too."

"I—I guess so, but I've never really tried it." My burgeoning elation is brought to a halt at the memory of his loss. Like ice water being poured onto a flickering flame. I slump back against the tree. At least twenty times a day, I search for Alexandros. Yet I've never found him. "But it probably only worked while he was still here." I choke back a sob.

"But you don't know that for sure." Xavier nudges my arm. "And you won't know unless you try."

"Yeah, sweet girl. What the fuck have we got to lose?"

I take a deep breath, my body trembling with anticipation

CHAPTER EIGHT

and nervous energy. What if this actually works? I could speak to Cadence and Enora. Osiris.

Xavier takes my hand and squeezes. "Try it, Cupcake. Try Cadence back in Havenwood."

"But I tried it already." I swallow down my trepidation. "I tried to connect to Alexandros's mind and couldn't."

Xavier's face falls. He brushes a strand of hair from my face. "Because he's gone, Ophelia."

"But what if there's a chance he's not?" I can't bear to admit there's no hope.

Malachi sniffs, and when I glance at him, he's wiping away a tear. "We're not getting any better, sweet girl. We know now we're not being poisoned, so what other explanation could there be? He's gone."

I drop my head and take a moment to feel his loss before I center myself again.

"You can do it, Cupcake."

I take a deep breath and again focus on my light—the root of all my power, both elementai and vampire—and I search for Cadence. I recall her voice, her sweet laugh. The freckles on her nose. The delicate, almost undetectable southern notes of her accent. Then I call out her name.

Ophelia! Her voice bursts into my head, filling it up with joy and color. *Is that really you, girl?*

It's not only her voice that warms me now, but her feelings too. I'm flooded with happiness and relief. *Yes, it's me.*

"Did you find her, baby?" Malachi asks, hopeful.

I nod, my smile growing wider when I open my eyes and see the happiness in both his and Xavier's eyes.

Where the hell have you been? she asks. *Why didn't you call me?*

There's no cell signal here. I have so much to tell you, Cadence. I can barely hold back a sob. *I hate it here. We're trapped. I can barely use my powers. The boys are sick.*

OPHELIA

Oh, Ophelia. Her concern bleeds into my pores. *Tell me where you are. I'm gonna come get you. Sienna will help me for sure. Enora and Osiris—*

It's pointless. Giorgios won't let us leave. And he has an army of guards. I don't know what they'd do if we tried to, but I wouldn't want to risk your safety.

What? He's actually keeping you prisoner there?

He says it's for our own protection. Maybe it is. I don't know anymore.

"There you all are," Giorgios says. "I assumed you would have come into the house to continue your research." A shiver dances down my spine. Fearful he'll somehow discover that I'm talking to her, I bid Cadence a hasty goodbye and tell her I'll speak to her again later.

"Just enjoying a little more of the morning sunshine," Malachi says.

"Yeah, while we still can," Xavier adds, his tone dripping with snark.

Giorgios hums softly. "Well, we know it will not come to that, Xavier, for if we cannot find an alternative cure, then we will utilize the only one we know, yes?" His eyes rake over me when he says that, and I resist the urge to squirm. The thought of Giorgios biting me and bonding me to him repulses me, but I would do it in a heartbeat to save my boys, a fact he is no doubt aware of. I nod, offering him a fake saccharine smile.

"I have an email from my cousin regarding the Ruby Dragons which requires your attention, gentlemen. I would answer his query myself, but I do not know the intricate workings of your operation at Montridge. If you would follow me?"

"An email?" all three of us say at once. He's told us repeatedly there's no cell service or internet connection here.

"Yes. One of my guards managed to get our old router to work." Smiling, he shrugs. "I have no use for such modern tech-

CHAPTER EIGHT

nologies, but I sensed you were all feeling increasingly cut off from your lives at Montridge. It is a very old dial-up connection, but it will suffice for the occasional email."

All of that is entirely plausible, I guess. And if it's true, it would have been much more useful to know before I realized I could speak to my friends back at Montridge without the need of anything but my mind. Still, I suppose he's making an effort.

"Shall we?" Giorgios says, indicating we should follow him.

Xavier and Malachi stand dutifully, continuing to play the part of grateful house guest to perfection, even if they remain unsure of Giorgios's motives. "You coming, Cupcake?"

I want to play around with my rediscovered ability a little more, so I shake my head. "I'm going to stay out here and enjoy a little more sunshine. I'll catch up with you before lunch."

Have fun reaching out to some of our friends, sweet girl. Malachi flashes me a wink before he and Xavier follow Giorgios back into the house.

I close my eyes and lean back against the tree. I could tap back into Cadence and continue our chat—hearing her voice felt like going home. Or I could talk to Sienna. Or Enora. But none of those things would do much to help our current situation. If only I could talk to Alexandros.

Something tickles my arm, and I open my eyes to find a bright orange butterfly. And it hits me like a thunderbolt. Of course I can talk to Alexandros. Or at least talk to someone who can speak to him on my behalf. Hope flares white hot in my chest, and I can't believe I didn't think of it before now.

The butterfly flutters away, and I whisper my thanks to whatever goddess sent it to me this morning, then take a deep breath and focus on my light. I've never tried this on my own before, but surely it's the same as connecting to any being here in the mortal realm. Which should I try to contact? Elpis is surely less likely to be aggravated at my intrusion, but my connection with Anikêtos felt stronger, so it might be easier for me to connect with him.

I recall what the professor taught me about reaching another's mind. How there will be something which will create a bridge between you—a spark—that, once accessed, will allow you to speak into the other's mind. With Cadence, it was picturing her clearly in my mind's eye and recalling the way she says my name. But with Anikêtos? I've never seen him, not even via the professor's memories, and I have no idea what he looks like. No idea how to breach the veil between this world and his. I screw my eyes closed and think about the last time we spoke. His haughty almost-laugh. The pride in his voice when I addressed him by his full title: Anikêtos, heir of Herôs, seer of truths, and keeper of the cradle of magic.

Ophelia Hart. His gruff voice fills my head and sends a current of warmth shuttling through my body.

Ani? Is that really you? So relieved to have found him, I use his informal name, but he doesn't seem to mind.

Why are you straying so far from your world without Alexandros to guide you, child? There are forces here who would use your mind if you are not strong enough to withstand them.

I suck in a deep breath and steel myself to say the words, stifling the sob which seems to have taken up permanent residence in my throat. *I can't reach him, Ani. I've tried but ... I don't know why because he could breach the veil when he was alive.*

You are making no sense, Ophelia. Do not speak to me in riddles. His annoyance bleeds into his tone.

Alexandros is dead, Ani.

He is not! His reply is swift and said with so much conviction it rattles my bones.

My entire body comes alive, every nerve ending electrified with hope and expectation.

CHAPTER EIGHT

But we felt his loss. A little over three weeks ago now. Our bond was severed. We were told someone took his head.

Anikêtos snorts, and then his voice takes on a sinister edge that makes my toes curl. *Who told you such folly, child? For I assure you, the Dragon Whisperer is not in the netherworld.*

That spark of hope keeps growing, burning brighter and brighter. *Could he be somewhere else? Is there another place people go when they die?*

Not vampires. They either live amongst the mortals or they linger here in the darkness for eternity.

And you're sure he's not there?

He makes a noise between a growl and a snarl, but it effectively communicates his unwillingness to answer the same question again.

Who told you of his death? he asks again.

His brother, Giorgios. He said he saw it happen.

Then he lies to you, child. For Alexandros Drakos remains in the realm of the living.

Why did Giorgios lie? Who is he protecting us from if Lucian didn't kill Alexandros? Where is Alexandros? So many questions are buzzing around my head, and it's hard to keep a lid on them all. I feel like they're about to fly straight out of my ears and go buzzing off to Giorgios to let him know I'm onto him.

I focus on Anikêtos. *Can you speak to him? Have you heard from him?*

Not for some time now. If I were in the mortal realm, I could reach him through our bond, but I am not capable of reaching his mind through the veil. He must choose to contact me.

The tears I've been holding back run freely down my face, but for the first time in three weeks, they are tears of sheer happiness. Alexandros isn't dead. I knew it couldn't be true. If he departed this world, then surely the boys and I would too, our earthly shells unable to sustain the horror of his loss. Our bond was severed, and that is cruel enough, but surely bonds can be restored. Alexandros Drakos is alive. I yearn to tell the boys immediately, but I don't dare while they're with Giorgios in case he should become suspicious. Hell, I want to scream it through these mountains and let the echoes of my joy shake the snow from the peaks.

But I must not get distracted. I force myself to refocus on the connection. *But the boys are sick and getting sicker. If he's not dead, how can that be happening?*

Anikêtos snorts again, and I get the feeling he's growing tired of me.

I'm sorry, Ani. I know our problems are not your concern, but we feel so alone and scared without him. The boys grow weak, and I don't know what to do. Please?

Pay him no mind, Ophelia. It's Elpis's voice I hear now. *He is hungry and you interrupted our mating.*

My face heats from sheer mortification. *Oh, dear god. I'm so sorry.*

It will do him no harm to wait a few more moments. If dragons laugh, I'm sure she just did. *If Alexandros's sireds are weakened, then it is due to something other than the deterioration, for as Anikêtos told you, your fated mate is very much alive. However, there are very few things which can poison a vampire.*

I know. I read everything I could get my hands on about vampire toxins. We've ruled everything out. We know it isn't infected blood, crushed dragon bone, or silver nitrate.

Then there must be something else which you have not yet considered. Something you have not yet read about or is not commonly known, she replies.

Elpis! Anikêtos's voice rumbles so loudly in my head I fear it may shake the mountains around me and alert Giorgios to what I'm doing.

Be safe, Ophelia, she says.

CHAPTER EIGHT

Then they're both gone, and I'm alone in my mind once more. It races at lightning speed, my thoughts no longer buzzy little bees but a plethora of fireworks, igniting and sparking every millisecond. Why did Giorgios lie, and what the hell is his master plan? What's making the boys sick? Where is Alexandros, and why can't I reach him? Is he hurting? Does he call for us the way we call for him?

I jump to my feet and brush the dirt from my jeans. My questions will find answers in time, of that I'm sure. But the most important thing is that he's not dead. The boys aren't going to die, because their sire is still alive. Now we need to find a way out of this place as soon as possible. We're going to find him and bring him home.

And then I'm going to rain down hell on Giorgios and anyone else responsible for taking him from us.

CHAPTER NINE

AXL

After getting Xavier's and Malachi's approval on the wording, I send the email to Eugene Jackson under the watchful eyes of Giorgios. Apart from the few people who know where we are, the rest of the faculty and students at Montridge believe we're all taking a sabbatical, Professor Drakos included. While Alexandros's father, the head of House Drakos, has learned of his youngest son's fate, the news does not appear to have filtered down to the Ruby Dragons yet. And aside from us not being there, it very much appears to be business as usual.

"All done?" Giorgios asks.

I lean back in the chair, hands locked behind my head. "Yeah."

"Good." Under the heat of my furious gaze, he quickly closes the laptop in front of me and unplugs it from the router. It's an old dial-up kind that I haven't seen since the nineties and had no idea still existed—no Wi-Fi here in Tibet—but right now, it's our only link to the outside world.

Xavier winks at me. *Relax, we don't need it.*

CHAPTER NINE

Why the fuck not? The look on his face tells me I'm going to like the answer, and while I'm confused, I know better than to ask why in front of Giorgios. So I simply smile at our host as he bids us farewell and leaves the den with the laptop in his hand.

Xavier stretches and yawns before declaring loudly, "I'm so fucking tired. Let's get the cupcake and go for an afternoon nap."

That was clearly said for Giorgios's benefit. There's something going on that I am unaware of. Before we can go look for our girl, her chirpy voice fills our heads. *I have something really, really important and really, really good to tell you all.*

What is it, princess?

I need to see you to tell you. Like look at your faces and tell you.

What the hell has been going on this morning? I sure as fuck pray her news is as exciting as she's making it sound, because I am fresh out of rays of hope. Xavier and Malachi look as confused as I feel.

Where are you guys?

Xavier shakes his head at me like he has no idea what her news could be. *We're in the den, but we're headed to our room. Want to meet us there?*

Yes!

Despite us growing weaker, our bond with Ophelia seems to have grown stronger here, and she was definitely feeling all kinds of perky.

"What do you think all that's about?" I ask Xavier and Malachi as we make our way upstairs.

"No idea, but it has to be some good news," Malachi answers.

Xavier nods. "Yeah, she was way too happy for it not to be."

Like a toddler must feel on Christmas morning, I'm unable to dampen the flurrying flakes of excitement building up in my

AXL

stomach. I'm trying my hardest not to get too carried away with myself, but ... "She did say it was *really* good."

Malachi bumps his shoulder against mine. "Really, really good."

We feel Ophelia's nervous energy way before she arrives at our room, almost like it's bubbling out of her. She bursts in like a tornado and closes the door behind her.

"What the hell is it, sweet girl?" Malachi asks.

She jumps onto the bed and sits cross-legged between the three of us, her lips pressed tightly together. *Alexandros is alive.* She speaks through our bond, but it doesn't make her squeal of pure joy any less pronounced.

I must have misheard. That news is much too good to be true. I take her hand in mine and stroke a fingertip over her racing pulse point. *What did you say, princess?*

Alexandros. Is. Alive. She says each word slowly, her blue eyes sparkling.

There's no way. I blink at her, too scared to believe it's real in case she's wrong.

Xavier turns her head toward him. *How do you know this, Cupcake?*

The dragons, she announces proudly.

Huh? *The dragons?*

She nods, bouncing up and down on the bed.

Malachi takes her free hand and laces her fingers through his. *Take a breath, sweet girl, and tell us everything.*

She explains to me how she managed to speak with Cadence earlier, and then she tells us all about her conversation with the dragons. By the end of it, the three of us are staring at her with our mouths open, wanting desperately to believe he's still alive but unable to bring ourselves to.

I knew you wouldn't believe me. A tear rolls down her cheek.

CHAPTER NINE

I brush it away before pulling her into my arms. I fucking hate seeing her cry, but this is all way too much to take in. My inner cynic reminds me she could be mistaken. Before we get our hopes up and cruelly dashed again, we need to make sure she's absolutely sure. *First of all, princess, I believe every single thing you just told us.*

What's hard to wrap our heads around is that he's still alive, and not because we don't want to believe. But if we do and he's not ... Xavier's throat works as he swallows. *Then we lose him all over again.*

But I swear to you he is. If he's not in the netherworld, he cannot be dead. That is an irrefutable truth. She looks to Malachi. *Please, Kai, tell them it's true.*

Wincing, Malachi nods. *Every single thing we know about the netherworld says it's true.*

A spark of hope flickers to life inside me. *What if these dragons are lying, princess?*

She gasps and gives me a look that could turn me to stone. *Dragons do not lie!*

Also true, Malachi adds.

That spark turns to an ember.

Xavier holds up his hand, halting the current direction of our conversation. *Okay, so if he's not dead, where is he? Why did we feel him die? And why did Giorgios tell us Lucian killed him?*

Ophelia holds up three fingers. *I don't know. We didn't feel him die; we felt the severing of the bond, like Alexandros felt with Lucian.* She puts a finger down with each answer. *And I don't know. But I do know who might have some answers.*

Giorgios has already lied to our faces, I remind her.

I'm not talking about Giorgios. I'm talking about Lucian. He shares Alexandros's bloodline, now our bloodline. I think I could at least try.

AXL

Is she fucking serious? She wants to willingly connect her mind to that murderous psychopath's? *No fucking way, princess.*

Both Xavier and Malachi echo my sentiment.

But don't you want to know where Alexandros is? And what Giorgios's game plan is?

I shake my head. *Not at the expense of your safety, Ophelia.*

She crosses her arms over her chest. *Like it or not, we're all in more danger here than we realized. If Alexandros is alive, which I know he is, then you're all not going to die. You are not sick with the deterioration, and you are being deliberately poisoned. Giorgios brought us here to weaken us all, knowing my powers wouldn't work properly. He lied about his own brother being murdered.*

She has a fucking point. Xavier sighs with frustration, and I feel it in my own bones. Of course she's right, but that doesn't mean we have to like it.

She untangles herself from my arms and sits up straight, her shoulders rolled back and her eyes darting between us. *So if I reach out to him, you'll stay with me. Like hold my hand?* Her voice sounds small despite her courage.

I take her hand and press her knuckles to my lips. *Alexandros couldn't reach his own son. Their bond was effectively severed, so it's highly unlikely Ophelia will be able to make contact. Regardless, I'll be here for her anyway. Every single step of the way, princess.*

We've got you, sweet girl.

Always, Cupcake.

I pull her back against my chest and rest my lips on top of her hair, inhaling her ginger-scented shampoo, the one that was already in the bathroom here. I much prefer her candy one from home. *And how about we discuss the fact that you can contact the netherworld and talk to fucking dragons?* I'm so fucking proud of her I could burst.

She giggles. *I know. Cool, right?*

CHAPTER NINE

It's better than cool. It's fucking incredible. She is incredible. Astounding. Amazing. There aren't enough adjectives in the English language to describe her. And if anyone can find Lucian Drakos—and even more importantly, his father—then it's our girl.

CHAPTER
TEN
OPHELIA

This is dangerous, Ophelia. What if he discovers where you are? The plea in Malachi's voice makes me falter, but only for a second.

And what if he does, Kai? I ask. *We already know Giorgios lied about Lucian killing Alexandros. We know he's been alive all these years and has never harmed his fath—*

We also know he killed his own mom and his sisters just because they were elementai, Axl reminds me.

Dammit. They have me there. *That was a long time ago. Perhaps he's changed?*

Xavier snorts. *Doubt it.*

Frustrated, I throw my hands in the air. *And perhaps he's still a psychopath who's hellbent on feasting on my soul, but the reality is that we're running out of options and time. You're all getting weaker. We don't know what's making you sick. We don't know where Alexandros is, and we don't know what Giorgios's plan is. One person who might have those answers is Lucian. If he somehow reads my mind and figures out we're here, we'll deal with it, but I'm fresh out of any better ideas. How about you?*

Xavier lies back on the bed, locking his hands behind his

CHAPTER TEN

head. *I say go for it, Cupcake. Your mind is strong enough to hold him, and if it's not...*

We'll be ready for him, Axl says. *Whatever happens.*

I look to Kai, who's staring at me while chewing his bottom lip. *Are you okay with this too?*

He shrugs. *I guess so.*

I was looking for a little more enthusiasm, and the nonchalance stings. Especially coming from him, the one who's most likely to be on my side. Does he think this is easy for me? *Kai, do you really think I'd do this if I didn't think there was no other way? You think I want to have my heart cut out by some psychotic killer who hates my entire species?*

He crosses the room, wraps me in his arms, and rests his chin on top of my head. Despite my annoyance at him, I melt against his hard body. *No, sweet girl. I'm sorry. We've got you. Tell us what you need.*

I roll back my shoulders, so much more confident about trying this with all of their support. *Just some quiet is all.*

Malachi winks at me. *Then we'll be quiet as church mice.*

I sit on the bed, my back against the headboard, and close my eyes. Again, I search for something in Lucian that I can use as a bridge. I've seen his face in Alexandros's memories, so I start with that. Aside from his hazel eyes, his features are so similar to his father's that it throws me off balance. Instead of focusing on my target, I recall Alexandros's voice. His scent. His power. The fire of his blood running through my veins. I do my best to block him out and search for Lucian, but it's impossible. He is everywhere. In every memory. In every thought. Every sound and smell and sight is him.

Ophelia Hart. The voice is deep, sinister. Mocking. Familiar, yet unknown. *I wondered how long it would be before you attempted to contact me. Your feeble grasping in the dark is almost comical.*

Not all that feeble. I found you, didn't I?

His laugh bounces around my head like it's trying to escape—as though aware it doesn't belong there. *Perhaps I simply allowed myself to be found.*

Fear snakes a path up my spine. The solid, reassuring presence of the boys' heartbeats soothes me, but otherwise they remain silent.

You know who I am?

Of course I know who you are, Ophelia Hart. I have known you for longer than those boys you bonded with. Longer than my father.

My stomach rolls. My heart hammers. I have so many questions to ask, but I have no idea how long this connection will last—or how long I want it to last. Instinct tells me the longer it remains open, the greater chance he has of finding me. Finding us. I channel all my emotion into the light in my center until it's a dazzling bright orb.

Giorgios told me you killed your father.

That does not surprise me. You would be wise not to trust my uncle.

So you didn't.

Are you asking me or telling me, little elementai?

Goosebumps break out over my flesh. *I don't think you did.*

As pleasant as our little chat has been, is there a purpose to it? I'm a little busy right now.

Probably tearing out the hearts of some innocent women and children.

Now, that's not a very nice thing to say to someone whose help you're seeking, is it, Ophelia?

Damn, he heard that. I have to break our connection and fast. *Where is Alexandros?*

I don't know.

Are you lying to me?

CHAPTER TEN

If you were as strong as they say you are, then you would know the answer already. But no, I am not lying, Ophelia Hart.

I have no idea if he's telling the truth. Operating purely on instinct, I'd say he is, but I no longer trust my gut. He's unlikely to help me, but I ask another question anyway. *If he's not dead, why are his sireds so sick?*

There are few things that are toxic to our kind.

I know, and I've read all the books I can, but—

Not all answers can be found in a book. Even Giorgios, for all his papers and his books in that vast library of his, can attest to that.

So, where can I find the answer, Lucian? I inject a mocking tone into my voice. I've learned a thing or two about manipulation from the way people have treated me over the years. *If you're so smart, tell me what's making them ill.*

Look around you, Ophelia Hart. There is a reason Giorgios built his fortress in the only mountains where blue poppies grow.

Blue poppies? Is that what he's using to poison them?

No reply comes, and the odd buzzing that seems to come from connecting to the minds of those other than my mates is absent. Did he figure out where we are because I went looking for him? No, of course not. He already knew.

My eyes fly open. "He knows where we are."

Malachi responds first. "What?"

Xavier sits up. "Did he tell you that, Cupcake?"

I shake my head and speak through our bond so as not to risk anyone overhearing. *He spoke of Giorgios's vast library and his fortress in the mountains like he already knew where it was. He's known we were here this whole time.*

Axl frowns. *But he hasn't come looking for you?*

At least not that we're aware of, Xavier says.

Malachi sits beside me on the bed and slips an arm around me. I lean against him. *What else did he say, baby?*

He said not to trust his uncle.

Xavier rolls his eyes. *Yeah, we already got that.*

I tell them his cryptic message about the blue poppies, and although he never actually said they were poisonous, that's definitely what I understood it to mean.

How are they poisonous to us if we don't ingest them? Axl asks.

Do we inhale them somehow? The seeds or ... I dunno. Xavier shrugs, his face a mask of confusion. *But then they'd be poisonous to him too.*

Or Ophelia has been unknowingly ingesting them, Malachi offers. *We have been feeding exclusively on her.* The guilt is immediate and overwhelming, but Malachi soothes me. *And that's not your fault, sweet girl. Is it?*

I know. I just hate how it might be me making you guys sick.

He drops a kiss on the top of my head. *How do we find out more about these blue poppies? I haven't seen anything about them in the books in Giorgios's library. Have you?*

I rack my brain and recall everything I've ever learned about poppies in my entire life, which doesn't take long. But I do recall that vampires developed a tolerance to the opiates derived from red poppies a few millennia ago. *No. But there must be something somewhere, right? Maybe it's in a spell book or a book on herbs rather than a book related to vampire toxins. I'll ask Cadence to help too. There must be something in Thucydides. Enora will give her access to the faculty library.*

Malachi hums his agreement. *Tell her to speak to Professor Chowdry. If anyone knows every single book in that library, it's her. She keeps her own cross-referencing system. Tell Cadence to tell her I asked especially for her help.* He winks at me, and I don't pick at that particular thread right now, having no desire to learn why the theology professor would be more likely to help if his name is mentioned.

I'll ask her now. Having spoken to Cadence earlier today, I find her quickly and easily. It's like the connection between us is

CHAPTER TEN

already open and simply waiting for me to tap into it. I wonder for a second whether I will ever need a cell phone again. At least for calling people—there's no replacing *Candy Crush* or mindless doomscrolling on *TikTok*.

When I'm done explaining what we're looking for and passing on Malachi's message, she gives me her assurance that she's on it and will get back to me as soon as she can. I keep the news of Alexandros from her for now—not because I don't trust her but because there are still too many unknowns, and I don't want to put her in any unnecessary danger.

I tell the boys she's in, and we agree that the sooner we know more about the blue poppy, the better we'll all feel. Collectively, we decide they'll stop feeding from me and fake being sick if they start to feel better so Giorgios doesn't suspect we're onto him.

"You're such a good girl," Malachi whispers, and my cheeks flush with heat.

"You know what those words do to our pretty little cupcake, Kai," Xavier says with a low growl.

"Yeah, I know." Malachi chuckles. "It's been too long since we've had much to celebrate, so I think we should enjoy every little victory we can get."

With a hum of agreement, Xavier sits up and pulls my hair back, giving himself space to trail his lips over my neck. *Alexandros is alive. We're probably not gonna die. Those seem like victories worth celebrating to me.*

And how do you suggest we celebrate without drawing attention from Giorgios? I ask.

Xavier's tongue snakes a path from my collarbone to my ear, making my skin tingle with anticipation. "In here. Quietly."

Malachi pops open the button on my jeans. "Well, maybe not all that quietly."

The bed dips as Axl crawls onto it. "Yeah, I like to hear our girl's pretty little moans."

Malachi's lips are pressed against my skin now too, his warm breath making goosebumps break out over my arms. "Shall I make her moan for you now, Axl?"

Axl simply grunts his response while Malachi unzips my jeans and slides his hand into my panties. "It has been way too long since we've had this kind of fun, sweet girl." He slips a thick finger inside me, making my back arch off the bed.

I bite down on my lip to stifle a groan. Yes, it's been too long. But it didn't seem right to have mind-blowing orgasms while our world was torn apart. We've had sex for comfort and connection, but not for the sheer pleasure of it. But now we have something that's eluded us for the past few weeks.

Hope.

CHAPTER ELEVEN

MALACHI

Fuck me, she feels so good. Hot and wet and tight. I sink my finger deeper inside her, massaging the tender spot that makes her mewl and loving the desperate little noises I wring from her perfect body while Xavier and Malachi remove all of her clothes. Not a second too soon, my sweet girl is lying naked and spread out for all three of us to enjoy.

"You make such pretty noises when you come for us, princess," Axl soothes, snaking his hands up the inside of her thighs and pushing them wider. I take the opportunity to slip a second finger inside her, and she hisses.

Xavier trails his mouth down her neck to her nipples, sucking and biting each one in turn until she squeals. "You might have to keep her quiet, Kai," he tells me with a wicked smirk.

Not needing to be told twice, I seal my lips over hers and swipe my tongue along the seam until she parts them, allowing me entry into her warm mouth. I swallow every sound she makes, and they travel straight to my hard cock, making it throb. Ophelia tastes of apples and cinnamon, and I want to eat her. To bite her flesh and suck her blood, and I hate Giorgios for many things, but depriving us of feeding on our girl is top of my list right now. The pulse of her blood screams in my ears, goading me to taste. She snakes her arms around my neck, fingers threading through my hair as though she hears it too and is trying to remind me that this is enough. And it is. For now.

I twist my fingers inside her, causing a rush of wet heat to slick my fingers. Yeah, this is more than enough. *I have missed this, sweet girl. Feeling you come apart for me. For us.*

So have I.

Axl's mouth joins my hand, his tongue swirling over her soaking flesh, lapping at her juices as they run onto my wrist. *I love how fucking wet you get for us, princess. Your cunt is delicious.*

Every single fucking part of her is delicious, Xavier growls, his mouth not leaving her skin as he goes on suckling one of her hard nipples. *It's taking every ounce of willpower I have not to bite into these like apples.*

Fuck, you've got her soaking here, Kai, Axl tells me appreciatively. *You gonna get her ready for my cock?*

Xavier hums. *For all our cocks.*

Ophelia's back arches off the bed as we work her over, hands and mouths exploring, sucking, tasting, kneading, and taking. Her moans grow louder and more insistent as she pleads for release.

We're gonna take care of you, sweet girl. We always do, don't we? I drive deeper inside her while Axl sucks on her clit and Xavier's tongue flicks over her sensitive nipples. When our girl falls apart for us, it's spectacular—the culmination of weeks of hurting and worry and fear releasing into that one single moment of ecstasy. She's still coming down from her orgasm when Axl sinks his cock inside her, fucking her hard, and she comes apart around him. After he's done, Xavier pulls her onto

CHAPTER ELEVEN

his lap and makes her ride him until they both find the relief they so desperately need.

Only after she's filled with their cum, her skin flushed with heat and her body trembling, do I flip her onto her front and press her into the mattress with the weight of my body.

"Kai." She whispers my name like a prayer.

I push her thighs aside with my knee and nudge the crown of my cock at her swollen entrance. "You want this, baby?"

She nods against the pillow, tears streaming down her cheeks.

I rest my lips against the shell of her ear. "Are you sore?"

"A little."

I slice a cut on the pad of my thumb with the tip of my fang and hold it to her lips. "Just take a little, sweet girl. It will make it feel better."

She hesitates for a few seconds. Ordinarily, we give her blood while we're feeding on her, but that's not possible right now. I run my nose over her cheek. "I'd get my mouth on you and use my saliva, but I'm way too desperate to fuck you."

Laughing, she opens her mouth, allowing me to slip my thumb inside. She suckles gently, and she may as well be sucking on my dick for the way it has my balls tightening.

"Feel better?"

She releases my thumb from her mouth with a satisfied moan. I waste no further time sinking inside her with one smooth, need-filled thrust, driving in all the way to the hilt and pushing her up the bed. She cries out my name, her tight pussy spasming around me, bringing me closer to the edge I'm already teetering on. I'm going to come inside her in a few short thrusts if she keeps squeezing me like that.

"Kai," she whimpers.

"I know, baby. You feel so fucking good. You take us all so

well. Such a good fucking girl." I pull all the way out and slam back inside her.

"Oh, god, Kai," she cries out before sinking her teeth into the pillow, her body shuddering through another orgasm.

Heat coils around the base of my spine, and I pick up my pace, driving home with every thrust until I feel the familiar spasm in my balls and empty my load inside her. I collapse onto my forearms and rest my forehead between her shoulder blades when I'm done, panting for breath, my head spinning with the strength of my orgasm.

I kiss her damp skin. "You are incredible, sweet girl."

She turns her head and murmurs something unintelligible, a contented smile on her face. I roll off her and onto my side and pull her close while Axl and Xavier nestle in on either side of us. I close my eyes, a smile spreading across my face. For the first time in three weeks, I feel like I might be able to keep all the promises I've made to Ophelia about how everything will be okay.

CHAPTER
TWELVE
OPHELIA

I wake with Axl's arms around me, Malachi's head on my shoulder, and Xavier's leg draped over him with his foot resting on my calf. My muscles ache with a reminder of last night and the way the three of them took such good care of me.

I stretch my legs and wiggle my toes, trying to disturb my three sleeping giants as little as possible. Managing to roll onto my back, I smile at Xavier's sleepy mumblings and wonder whether Cadence will be awake yet and if she has any news for me. Less than twelve hours have passed since I asked her to look into the blue poppy, but if I know her, she'll have made it her mission to find out what she could.

Closing my eyes, I search for her and have barely said hi when her voice bursts into my head, as though she's been desperate to speak with me. *Ophelia, girl!*

She clearly has something to tell me, and I can only hope it's good news. *Cadence. Did you find something?*

Hell yeah, I did. And I hope you don't mind, but ... She goes quiet, and I hold my breath. *But she's part of the blood oath, and Professor Chowdry wasn't around, and I needed a little help getting into the library, so I told Enora you contacted me, and then we got to talking, and well, she ...*

She what?

She'd love to speak to you too, if that's all right? She has something super important to talk to you about. Can you do that? Speak to her too? Like a three-way thing?

I don't know. I've never tried, I admit. But I'd love to speak to Enora. She's always been kind to me, and she was really supportive when she found out about my powers. Besides, Alexandros trusts her, and therefore, so do I. *But I'm willing to give it a shot.*

I focus on Enora now. The smell of jasmine at Silver Vale. Her warm eyes and the gentle, soothing lilt of her voice. Her mind opens like the click of a lock, allowing me inside. *Hi*, I say quietly.

Ophelia, my sweet child. Her kind voice makes tears spring to my eyes, reminding me of the day we left Montridge and all we left behind.

Wow! Cadence says. *I can hear you both. This is incredible.*

Tell Ophelia what you learned, Cadence.

Her enthusiasm appropriately tamed, Cadence gives me a summary of everything she learned about the blue poppy, most of which she found in an ancient ledger about herbs and sleeping spells. Apparently, vampires never built up any resistance to the plant due to lack of exposure to it, but it only remains in their bloodstream for forty-eight hours. However—and this is the most depressing part—unlike other opiates, it remains in a human, or in my case, an elementai's bloodstream for ten days. Ten long days without my boys being able to bite me. However, the best news is it causes no long-lasting damage, and as soon as it's out of their systems, Axl, Xavier, and Malachi will be perfectly fine again.

That's all so good to know, Cadence. Thank you so much.

CHAPTER TWELVE

It was nothing, girl. Glad I could help. We feel so helpless while you're basically being held hostage by Giorgios.

Had I known of his intentions, Ophelia, I never would have permitted you all to leave with him, I swear to you, Enora adds.

That's part of the problem though, Enora—we don't know exactly what his intentions are. All we know is that he's lied to us about Alexandros. But why? What the hell is he up to?

That is where I believe I may have some more answers for you, she says in a sad voice.

Axl shifts, and I snuggle closer to him, seeking his comfort even as he continues to sleep, unaware of this conversation.

What do you know?

When was your last period, child?

Embarrassment washes over me, but she wouldn't ask if it weren't relevant, so I answer her. *Last week. Why?*

So you would have ovulated shortly after your arrival to Giorgio's fortress, she mumbles like she's talking to herself. *I suppose even he would have thought it was too soon.*

My mouth goes dry. *Too soon for what?*

You have to understand, Ophelia. You are very special, and not only because you are the only elementai to have been born in half a millennium. There are some who believe you are much more.

Much more what? I demand. *And what the hell does this have to do with my period?*

There is a ritual. One that I am not aware has ever actually been effectively performed before because of its barbarity.

A ritual? My stomach rolls with nausea. Barbarity? That's what she said, right?

It can only be performed when an elementai is ovulating.

Oh god, what fresh hell is this? Is Giorgios intending to knock me up with his vampire spawn? *What ritual, Enora? What does it do? Why is it barbaric?*

If Alexandros is truly alive—

OPHELIA

He is!

Then the only way to permanently sever a fated mate bond is for the elementai to be impregnated by a different vampire.

What the hell? If that were true, then why wouldn't it have been performed before? Why wouldn't more vampires try it? I mean, they're not known for their chivalrous behavior. If such a ritual exists, I can't believe some of the unscrupulous types didn't give this a whirl back when there were plenty of elementai to choose from.

Because it requires more than simply an elementai and a vampire. It requires dark magic and immense power. And you, my sweet child, have more power than any living creature in several millennia.

My heart rate spikes alarmingly, so much so, the boys wake. Xavier sits up, his fangs protracted, and Axl and Malachi cocoon me between them.

"It's okay, I'm not in any danger," I whisper. "I'm just talking with Cadence and Enora. I'll explain everything in a minute."

His concerned eyes remain on me, but Xavier lies down, and the guys stay silent while I continue my conversation. It's probably possible for me to pull them in too, but I have a sickening feeling that the things Enora's telling me will only get worse, and I have no idea how they'll react. For the immediate time being, it's probably best they remain unaware, and then I can explain in my own way without any other distractions.

But the dark magic? My magic is good, right? Elementai are inherently good.

Yes, dear, you are correct. But any magic can be used for dark purposes. Even if it is weakened by the act, magic such as yours would still be powerful enough to cast such a spell.

But who can use dark magic like that? I can't. I won't.

I have reason to believe Giorgios is capable of using dark magic.

CHAPTER TWELVE

That doesn't make sense. *How? Vampires can't cast spells.*

You mentioned something to Cadence about him leaving the grounds when he transported. Has he ever transported from within the fortress grounds as far as you are aware?

He transported into the dining room when we first got here.

I am not talking about entering, but leaving, Ophelia. When he left Axl and Malachi and returned for you, did he teleport from within the grounds or outside of them?

I ask the boys the question.

"He left us right outside the fortress gates," Malachi says, a puzzled look on his face that I'm sure mirrors my own. "But then his guards brought us inside. And when he came back with you and Xavier—"

"He brought us straight into the house," Xavier finishes for him.

I relay this information to Enora.

Then it is as I suspected, I am sure. He can transport into the house, but not out of it. He cannot use the power on sacred ground because it is not his latent vampire power.

I screw my eyes closed. My head is hurting, and I'm unsure if it's due to the prolonged connection with two people or the worry of this new development—or both. *What do you mean, not his latent power? So how can he transport?*

Powers can be stolen. A shiver runs down my spine at the terror that has crept into her voice. *It is not common, but it is possible. I have been plagued by doubt as to how he was able to fool Alexandros, whose mind powers were unparalleled, and I can only come to one conclusion. Giorgios is a lot more powerful than he has led everyone to believe.*

My brain works overtime to process all of this new information. Has he been able to read our minds the whole time we've been here? Can he hear me speaking to my friends right now? Did he hear me speak to Ani and Elpis? Surely not, or he would have made it known. *So in order to mask his vampire powers, he stole another power from someone else?*

I believe that is a likely scenario comes her anxious reply.

And he's been lying to Alexandros and their father for all these years? Since they were children?

Alexandros has told me little about his family, but if my memory is correct, Giorgios's transportation powers emerged when he was already a grown man.

My head pounds, blood throbbing against the pulse points in my temples. I don't know if they're able to feel it, but Cadence jumps in. *Tell her about the ritual.*

Of course, I almost forgot about the ritual.

If Giorgios were to bond with you and impregnate you, Ophelia, then he would be able to use the magic of the sacred creation of life and the dark magic of the ritual to break your bond with Alexandros and the boys forever. If he is powerful enough to incant the spell, your power is enough to make it work.

Her words are like a knife to my heart, and I clutch my chest as pain rips through me like wildfire. The guys all say my name and utter curses. Their hands soothe me, brushing my hair back and gliding over my skin while they utter assurances that everything will be okay. But it will not be okay. If this is Giorgios's plan—

Giorgios with his army of guards—

How will we stop him?

I am sorry, Ophelia. Enora's concerned voice cuts through the turmoil in my head. *What can we do?*

My body trembles with fear and deep-seated grief. Not only for me, but for all of my mates. How can Giorgios be so eager to tear apart what the universe has sought to bring together?

Ophelia? Cadence stops the spiral I'm caught in.

For now, please find out all you can about the ritual. About how

CHAPTER TWELVE

we might stop it. Is there a way to stop me from ovulating, maybe? I'm grasping at straws, but I'm desperate.

We will do all we can. Please keep in contact with us, sweet child. We can find a way to get to you. Osiris and Sienna, and I am certain the Ruby Dragon vampires would help.

I'm not sure there's time, and Giorgios has an army, Enora. An actual vampire army that consists of at least a hundred soldiers, and who knows if there are more. I take a deep breath and force myself to add, *But I will stay in contact and let you know if there's anything else you can do. Thank you, friends.*

Be safe, Ophelia, Cadence says around a sob.

After saying goodbye to both of them, I focus on the boys, who are all staring at me with concern. As much as I would love to tell them there's no need for them to worry, this time I can't.

When I'm finished relaying my conversation with Enora and Cadence, I fall silent and allow them space to react with unsurprising rage and thirst for revenge. It takes some time to calm them, especially as I'm feeling those things myself, but I remind them that Giorgios's mind powers are probably a lot stronger than we thought and we need to shield our thoughts and emotions from him as best we can. Speaking via our bond is the safest option when we are discussing anything we'd rather he didn't hear. During one of our long, brain-melting training sessions, Alexandros explained the mate bond to me. My heart clenches at the memory, but his assurance that the sanctity of such a bond prevents it from being breached by others allows me to be confident the boys and I can continue to safely communicate.

Axl sits beside Malachi and in front of me as I sit cross-legged on Xavier's lap on the bed. *How long do we have, princess?*

Doing some math in my head, I count back to the first day of my last period. Seven days ... *We have about a week until I ovulate, I think. But it could be sooner. I've never tracked this kind of thing, but if I go by the days Alexandros has told me I was ovulating during the last few months, I think it happens pretty much right in the middle of my cycle.*

Fear and anger and sadness pour from all of us. But we can't let this happen. We can't wallow in our despair because we don't have time. *At least the blue poppy news is good. One more day, and it will be out of your system and you'll feel normal again. That's something.*

But we still can't feed from you because we have no idea what you're consuming that contains blue poppy, Cupcake. And while it doesn't harm you, you must eat and keep up your strength. We can live without your blood for months if we truly needed to, but you cannot survive without food and water.

I lean back against him, letting him wrap his huge arms around me. *That will be the least of our worries if we don't stop Giorgios from performing the ritual.*

A fresh wave of white-hot rage rolls over all three of them, and they growl their frustration.

I will fucking kill him before I let him lay a finger on you, sweet girl.

Me too, princess.

He'll be dead before he gets the chance, Cupcake.

I force a smile, grateful for their protection. They mean every word of it, but the reality none of us wants to face is that, even with their full strength, they are no match for a two-thousand-year-old vampire and his army. Not with my powers dulled to almost nothing. If Giorgios plans to force me to ...

I balk, unable to even consider such a heinous outcome. But short of escaping this place, there's not a lot we can do to stop him. *We need to get out of here.*

But how? Xavier says. *Every exit is constantly guarded by at least six guards.*

And they're all sired by Giorgios, which means they can all

CHAPTER TWELVE

communicate with each other. It would take them less than a second to summon the rest of their army, Axl adds.

They're right. We've tested the exits. We even discussed scaling the walls, but there are guards surrounding the entire perimeter.

Malachi runs a hand over his face. *We're fucking screwed.*

No. I shake my head. *I refuse to believe all these powers I have are useless just because we're on the grounds of some ancient monastery. We're smart. We're strong. We'll think of something. We've talked about escaping, but we've never been this determined. It's imperative we consider every angle. There must be a weak spot somewhere. A blind spot we can take advantage of. If only I could get past the gate ...* I gather my resolve. There must be a way. I refuse to believe otherwise.

CHAPTER THIRTEEN

OPHELIA

Giorgios's dark-blue eyes narrow. "Why are you refusing to eat, Ophelia?"

I tip my chin. "I'm not hungry."

"Perhaps I would believe that if your stomach were not growling like a mountain lion."

Annoyed at my body's betrayal, I press my hand to my belly and glare at him. Meanwhile, Axl, Xavier, and Malachi grow tenser with each passing second. "I'm not feeling well. I don't feel like eating."

He blows out a long, slow breath and takes his napkin from his lap before rolling it into a ball and tossing it onto the table. "Another lie," he says, his tone unusually calm. The tension in the room grows so thick I can taste it.

We've got you, Cupcake, Xavier assures me. *Whatever happens, we won't let him touch you.*

I glance at them and then quickly back to Giorgios. In their weakened state, I'm not sure the three of them are a match for the eldest son of House Drakos. But I remain forever grateful for their presence, which alone never fails to bring me strength and comfort.

CHAPTER THIRTEEN

"I don't want to eat." I push my chair back. "May I be excused?"

Giorgios brings his fist crashing down onto the table with such force all the silverware and crockery rattle in their place settings.

Xavier growls. Axl snarls. And Malachi rolls back his shoulders like he's ready for a fight. "Have I not been a good host? Have I not protected you all from Lucian?" His face grows redder with each shouted question. "Have I not treated you all kindly? Yet you sit at *my* table and disrespect me by lying to my face."

My pulse increases rapidly, adrenaline spiking through my system. I'm hyperaware of my mates' heartbeats, all of them racing like mine. This needs to stop. We need to discover exactly what Giorgios's plan is and get the hell out of here so we can find Alexandros. Unable to contain the swirling vortex of emotion any longer, I slam my own fist onto the table. "Would a good host poison their guests?" I yell, my voice echoing off the walls.

If he's surprised by my accusation, he doesn't show it. "Excuse me?" he says instead, his demeanor so at odds with his angry outburst a few seconds earlier.

"You've been poisoning me, us, with blue poppy, Giorgios. Why?"

He runs his tongue over his bottom lip and drags his fingers through his beard. "I am surprised it took you as long as it did to figure it out considering how smart Alexandros told me you all are."

The mention of his name has anger and despair surging up from my stomach, and I feel the same emotions raging a war inside the boys too. So much pain and rage contained in one room. It feels like we're sitting in the core of a volcano that's about ready to explode. If we're revealing secrets today, let's reveal them all. "Why did you lie about him being dead?"

Giorgios's lip twitches at the corner like he's trying to suppress a smirk. Axl launches himself across the table, but Giorgios stops him with minimal effort. With one meaty hand wrapped around Axl's throat, he pushes him back down with ease. "Do not make me do something I will regret, children," he says, sneering. "If you are going to sit at the grown-up table, then please act like one."

I place a hand on Xavier's and Malachi's thighs and squeeze. *Please let me handle this. We need answers, and he's not going to give us any if we're fighting. As much as I'd love to claw his eyes out, we must stay calm.*

They voice their agreement in my head, and I focus all my attention back on Alexandros's traitorous brother. "Why did you lie about Alexandros's death, and why are you poisoning us?" I ask again, amazed at the calm command in my voice.

"I did not poison you, Ophelia, for I would never do such a thing. Blue poppy is harmless to humans. In fact, it releases a mild euphoria in the correct dosage."

"Not harmless to vampires though, is it?" Axl growls.

Giorgios tilts his head and regards Axl with curiosity. "Relatively so. It weakens a vampire somewhat, makes them feel a lot less ..." He purses his lips. "Perky," he finally offers. "It is the opioid, you see. An evolutionary flaw. As the blue poppy only grows here in Tibet and so few of our kind have ever ventured to these mountains, a vampire's DNA has never adapted to tolerate that particular strain of opiate. But it causes no lasting damage. You will all be as you were as soon as the blue poppy has left your system."

The way he speaks so coldly about making my boys so weak and sick is astonishing. "And you think that makes it okay?"

"It makes it necessary, sweet Ophelia." Shaking his head, he

CHAPTER THIRTEEN

releases a heavy sigh. "You all know so little of this world. Of the ancient ways and the things that must be done to ensure the survival of our species. You have so little knowledge about humankind, our only viable food source. As much as we can enjoy these tidbits," he says, indicating the rare cut of lamb on his plate, "they cannot sustain us the way humans do."

Conceited, pompous douchebag. This isn't the first time he's tried to use our apparent lack of knowledge against us to make us feel inferior. But it stops now. "So enlighten us, dearest Giorgios," I say, injecting as much snark into my tone as I can muster. "Why was it necessary to poison my mates?"

He drops his gaze for a few beats, appearing contrite. It's so at odds with all of his usual pomp and arrogance that I simply stare. When he looks up again, his eyes are glistening with tears. "So you would all believe he was dead."

He's not dead.

That means my boys are not going to die. I'm not going to lose them. We didn't lose him.

A current of sheer relief runs through the boys and me, lighting us up from the inside. No matter the evidence we already had to prove he was still alive, Giorgios's confirmation was what we needed to fully believe—not that we'd ever admit it to him.

A tear rolls down my cheek. "But why? Why did you tell us he was dead? Why did you—" A sob steals the rest of the sentence from my mouth, and the comforting arms of Xavier and Malachi slide around my shoulders.

He screws his eyes closed and inhales deeply through his nose. "I hoped it would not come to this. I hoped you would simply stop pushing and accept he was gone. Nazeel Danraath asked for my help, and I could not refuse her. She saved my life a long time ago, and I was in her debt."

"In *her* debt?" I screech at him, the injustice of it all burning a hole in my chest. "What about your brother? What about the man who has done nothing but love you for your whole life?"

He snorts. "You know very little of my brother, Ophelia. Do not sully our history by imbibing it with such human emotions as love."

I'm momentarily too stunned to speak. Too many thoughts are racing around my head for me to pin down any one of them. Thankfully, Malachi speaks in my stead. "Why did Nazeel Danraath want us to think Alexandros was dead?"

"There are far greater powers at work here than any of you can begin to comprehend. Nazeel believes Ophelia is the key to an ancient prophecy, and she believed his death was the only way to unlock her full potential. The only way to determine who you truly are. And she would have had him killed. I—" He jabs his thumb into his chest. "I saved him and hid him away from the clutches of Lucian and the Order."

"So this was about me being the key to some prophecy? Me and these stupid goddamn powers? The ones I can't even use here? You tore us apart to unlock my potential? For a stupid. Fucking. Prophecy?!" Anger fizzes in my veins, and the tips of my fingers crackle with electricity. The ground vibrates, and I see something in Giorgios's eyes that I haven't seen there before. Fear.

But he has nothing to be afraid of while my powers remain suppressed. They're still there, simmering inside me, swirling within the core of white light, but they're smothered, and try as I might, I cannot free them.

"I could not deny Nazeel's request, Ophelia. It would have ensured our certain deaths. I did what I could to protect us all. Alexandros too. *He* understood what had to be done. He undertook the sacrifice willingly."

No. I refuse to believe that. No way would Alexandros willingly cause us this much pain. "What sacrifice? To be parted

CHAPTER THIRTEEN

from us? To have us all believe he was dead? To tear out our souls? To let us think we were all going to die—because that would surely be my fate if all my mates were dead. I would refuse to live in a world without them, and he knows that."

Giorgios remains silent, his shoulders rolled back and his eyes full of tears that don't fall.

In my anger and hurt, I forgot the most important questions, but Axl has enough presence of mind to ask them. "Is he okay? When can we see him?"

"He is alive and he is safe. I cannot tell you where he is for fear Nazeel will discover his whereabouts. She is connected to you, Ophelia. She met with you at Montridge, did she not?"

I blink at him, recalling the enigmatic lady with the emerald eyes and fiery hair, and nod.

His expression softens a little. "She has a connection with you. I am unaware of the power behind that connection, and I cannot risk her finding my brother. You must believe I am doing everything I can to keep him alive. Safe from Lucian and the Order."

I recall my conversation with Lucian a few days ago and how he warned me not to trust his uncle. But of course he would, wouldn't he? "The Order? Lucian? Are they working together? Do they know we're here?" Every new revelation makes less sense and only creates more questions.

"They both know of my fortress, yes, but they do not work together. Despite their misguided efforts, Nazeel and the Order do not wish for the world to fall into darkness. Lucian, on the other hand, would prefer the world to fall into an eternal night. I did not wish to alarm you all with that knowledge. It is why I have such an extensive army. For our mutual protection. Lucian will not get past these gates, I assure you. And neither Nazeel nor the Order mean you any harm. Besides, her powers will be as useless here as Ophelia's are."

"But the Order only observes," Malachi says. "They don't interfere."

Giorgios nods once. "They have never had cause to. Until now. They believe you are the child of the prophecy, Ophelia."

I want to scream down the entire house, but I manage to keep my emotions in check. "What prophecy?" I recall Nazeel speaking to me of being "more" and Enora's caution.

"The Order believes you will be the one to bring balance to the world; however, as you are so young and your powers so new, there are also some who believe you could be swayed just as easily to the dark as to the light."

My head is swaying, I know that much. This is all insane. "But elementai are inherently good."

"If we choose to believe you are truly the child of the prophecy, then you are more than an elementai, Ophelia."

The same words Nazeel spoke to me. I shudder. "Do you believe that?"

"I do not know, and it is of no consequence. There are those who do, and that is what put Alexandros at risk. Nazeel believed your powers must be fully unlocked to prevent you from turning toward the dark."

"Then bring him back here to us, Giorgios. He can stay safe here in this fortress with us. Bring him back to us, or I will use this power and I will scorch this earth to goddamn ash."

He frowns. "Ophelia."

"Please, Giorgios!" I beg, my heart cracking into splinters. I hate this power. I hate being an elementai. I hate that they hurt him because of me.

Before Giorgios can reply, Xavier speaks up. "Nah, I don't buy it."

"You do not buy what, Xavier?" Giorgios asks, his tone simmering with annoyance.

"This bullshit about the Order and what had to be done.

CHAPTER THIRTEEN

You chose to lie to us. You made us sick instead of telling us the truth. You could have told us all of this."

"I had to keep you in the dark to ensure Ophelia's powers would be unlocked, to ensure you would come here with me—"

"Where you could keep us prisoner?" Xavier growls. "Weaken us all and leave us fucking defenseless?"

"I already told you—I did not consider the impact on Ophelia. I built this fortress one thousand years ago, for the very purpose of preventing witches from being able to use their magic against me. How was I to know I would one day harbor an elementai here? You are here for your own protection. At Alexandros's request. He may not have killed his father, but if Lucian finds Ophelia, then he will kill her. Make no mistake about it."

"Then bring Alexandros back to us. Surely he is the best person to protect me from his own son."

Sighing, Giorgios closes his eyes and pinches the bridge of his nose. "Or he is the worst. He and Lucian share an unbreakable bond. It can be masked, but not destroyed. He would take you from this place and then he would lead Lucian straight to you, and who knows what choice he would make when faced with such an impossible decision."

But Lucian already knows where I am. Is he simply biding his time, or is Giorgios lying about him? Is his fortress truly as impenetrable as he claims? I have no idea who to believe about what anymore.

"He would choose Ophelia every single fucking time," Axl says, snarling.

Giorgios's right eye twitches. "You are so sure of your sire's noble heart, yet you know nothing of his true nature." He focuses his attention on me. "You are so confident he has your best interests at heart, Ophelia. So sure his intentions are honorable. What if he is on the wrong side of history? How many times has he told you he is not a good man? What if he is the dark and you, my sweet Ophelia, are destined for the light?"

Rage and injustice, guilt and anguish—all are fighting a war inside me, and all of them are winning. "I know what kind of man he is. He would never do anything to harm me. Never."

Giorgios's nostrils flare. "And I am sure Elena and Alyria and Imogen believed the same to be true when he allowed his son to tear out their hearts. When he was too weak to prevent such a despicable act and too weak to take revenge." He stands, planting his hands on the table. "So tell me, little Ophelia, are you still so sure that he would choose you when faced with such a choice? Because nobody else believes him capable of it, and that is why he has been removed from the equation. He is my brother, and I love him. But he cannot be trusted."

My lip trembles, but my voice is clear. "I trust him."

"Then you are a fool."

We glare at each other, and the moment seems to stretch into eternity before Xavier speaks again. "What about the bond?"

Giorgios scowls at him. "The bond?"

"You offered to bond with Ophelia to save us? But we didn't need saving from the blue poppy, did we? So why the fuck did you offer to bond with our girl?"

Giorgios scoffs like he considers the question beneath him, but he holds Xavier's stare when he answers. "Because, Xavier, I am a benevolent man. I knew Ophelia would not agree to bond with me, which is why I did not push her on the matter. But I also know there is one thing sure to crush a spirit more than anything else, and that is the absence of hope. So I told you there was a cure knowing you would never need to use it. Because I could not bear to let you believe there was no hope. Perhaps I was mistaken." With that, he shoves his chair back so

CHAPTER THIRTEEN

hard it crashes to the floor, then stalks out of the room, leaving us staring after him.

There are so many questions, so much emotion, I feel dizzy with it all. But there's one prevailing thought that rises above the noise. One focus for us all, and it's Axl who voices it. "If he won't tell us where Alexandros is, we need to find him ourselves."

CHAPTER
FOURTEEN
OPHELIA

I clear my mind and focus on Anikêtos.

His snort of derision soon fills my head. *What is it now, annoying human child?*

I can't help but smile at his grumpiness. If he found me that annoying, he simply wouldn't speak to me. *Actually, I'm an elementai*, I remind him.

I think you will find that you are still a human. Perhaps an enhanced version of the species, but human all the same.

I hope I haven't interrupted your mating bond this time.

If you had, I would return to the mortal realm simply to burn you to ash. Now, what is it?

I need your help.

I gathered as much when you invaded my thoughts on this otherwise peaceful day. What do you need my help with?

Do you have any idea where Giorgios or maybe even the Order might be keeping Alexandros? Perhaps Giorgios was lying and the Order truly does have him.

The Order will not be keeping him anywhere. They are prohibited from interfering.

Okay. Giorgios, then. Wherever he is, I can't reach him. Which is

CHAPTER FOURTEEN

strange, right? I can speak to you in the netherworld, but I can't speak to him wherever he is.

There are places within the mortal realm where a bond cannot be felt. Nor a mind be read.

I chew on my lip. *Of course. Like Thucydides Library?*

He simply snorts.

It's a library carved into the bedrock of Montridge Peak.

I have no desire to learn of its existence, Ophelia.

I roll my eyes. Dragons are so grumpy. *I'm just explaining what it is. Do you know of other places like that?*

He doesn't reply for a moment, and I'm worried he's decided to end our conversation prematurely, but then he speaks again. *In order to suppress someone with Alexandros's power for a sustained period of time, it would have to be a place with a vast amount of magical energy.*

That makes sense. But like where?

They are often underground caves or chambers, much like the library you spoke of. Which is why the Order makes their home in the base of a sacred mountain in Greece.

So he could be there?

If I am going to acquiesce to these lessons you are forcing upon me, Ophelia, then I insist you pay attention. His ire is quite apparent, and I am sufficiently chastised.

The Order doesn't interfere. I'm sorry, Anikêtos. I take a second before asking my next question. *Are you aware of any other places with that kind of power?*

There are but a few places imbibed with such powerful magic. The slate mountains of Wales, the silver mines of Peru, the Ethiopian Highlands, the Qilian Mountains of China. All have mountains connected to ancient dragon magic and would therefore be strong enough to hold him.

They all sound so far away. The thought of him alone anywhere without us is hard enough. Are they hurting him to keep him compliant? Is he wondering why we haven't come for him?

If that is all.

No! I wince, but he can't disconnect yet, so I hurry to continue before he can chastise me for my tone. *I have one more thing to ask of you, Ani.* I swallow hard. This one's a doozy, and I have no idea how he'll respond. I guess the worst thing he can do is say no. But if he does, I have no idea what my next plan will be. I am all out of options. I've tried reading Giorgios's mind dozens of times, but it's like he's got a wall of granite up inside there. And if Enora's suspicions about him completing the ritual to permanently sever our bond are correct, we have two more days, three if we're lucky.

And that is?

You once said you may one day return to the mortal realm if there was a strong enough reason.

He doesn't reply, but I can still feel him. Breathing. Waiting.

Would helping to save the life of your oldest friend be considered a good enough reason?

Elpis is my oldest friend. Her life is not in danger.

I roll my eyes but manage to keep the irritation out of my tone. *My time is running out, Ani. I have reason to believe Giorgios is going to permanently sever my bond with Alexandros, and I have a terrible feeling that will mean Alexandros becomes dispensable. I figure I have a week at the most before he can perform the ritual.*

He intends to impregnate you with his child?

You know of this ritual?

My kind have lived forever, Ophelia. There is very little we do not know.

So it's an actual thing, then? Tears well in my eyes. *Not just some ancient story told around a crackling fire and then written in a book? It can be done?*

It is a ritual; however, I am not aware of it ever being successfully

CHAPTER FOURTEEN

performed, and I am not sure if Giorgios is capable of such a powerful spell.

Enora thinks he might be. She's a witch, by the way, a powerful one, and another friend of Alexandros's.

He snorts like he has no need of such trivial information, but I'm reminded of what Enora said to me. Something I didn't have time to question her about given the other information she imparted immediately after. *She said some people think I might be more than an elementai, Ani. What does that even mean? What is more than an elementai? And last night, Giorgios mentioned a prophecy. He said some people think it's about me.*

His growl is low and contemplative.

He knows. Of course he does. Dragons know everything, right?

Ani?

There is a prophecy, Ophelia. One that speaks of a child who will bring balance to chaos.

Now I'm even more confused. *What chaos? I know the world is pretty messed up, but it's the way it's always been, isn't it?*

Not always. My kind left your world when the darkness of man's heart began to cast long shadows over the light. And then, when the elementai were destroyed ... A light went out that will never be replenished.

I shiver, overwhelmed by the chill of defeat. I have not known Anikêtos very long, but this is the most sentimental I've heard him. I shake off the negative feelings and refocus. *What does that have to do with me?*

You already know the answer, Clandarragh.

He's called me that before. The Chosen One. *You think it's me too?* I scoff. *I'm this child who'll bring order to chaos?*

I did not say that.

You literally just called me the Chosen One.

113

You are Alexandros's chosen one, that does not mean I believe you are the savior of man and magicalkind, Ophelia.

That's because—

But there are some who believe you are.

Um, hello. Have they met me?

I am not in the habit of massaging egos, Ophelia Hart. I have given you the answers you seek, now leave me in peace.

Please, Ani, I beg, pushing all ridiculous notions of prophecies out of my head. *We're trapped here. I can barely use my powers. The boys will be back to full strength tomorrow, but there's no way they can take on all of Giorgios's guards.*

What exactly are you suggesting I do, Ophelia? Dragons are prohibited from harming sons of House Drakos unless in self-defense.

I did not know that, and I suspect he's not going to give me a history lesson and explain why right now. So as much as I would love to—all these archaic laws fascinate me—I don't press him on it.

I merely want you to orchestrate a breakout.

He snorts.

You just have to land on the grounds and fly me and the boys away from here, and that's it.

And then I leave you all to freeze to death in the Himalayas? That does not sound like a good enough reason to risk returning to the mortal realm.

As soon as I'm away from these hallowed grounds, I'll be able to use my powers. I'll get myself and the boys to safety. I just need out of here. And fast.

And truly what risk is there to you, Anikêtos? Elpis joins the conversation, and I swear, if I ever get to see her in the flesh, I am going to kiss her beautiful dragon-y skin. *You are a dragon. The mightiest dragon to ever stalk this earth. You can cloak your appearance, and there is no army of vampires who can tame you.*

CHAPTER FOURTEEN

Tame us. Because if you think you are returning to the mortal realm without me, then you are very much mistaken.

I did not say I was returning, he huffs.

His protest notwithstanding, I'm flooded with hope and relief, so much so, I can barely contain my exhilaration. He hasn't said no. And Elpis seems on board.

I know I ask a great deal of you, and I know you owe me nothing. But Alexandros is your friend, is he not? And apparently, I'm some super powerful being. You don't need anything from me now, but should you ever need anything, anything at all, say the word and I'm there.

That is a dangerous promise to make to a dragon, Ophelia. For an oath like that cannot be broken and you have no idea what I would demand of you.

I know you are the keeper of the cradle of magic, Anikêtos, and that means you are a creature of honor. And whatever price you ask of me, I will gladly pay it if you will grant me this one request.

He grumbles for a moment. Finally, he says, *Let me take some time to consider it.*

We don't *have* time. But I know better than to say that. *How will I know when you've made a decision?*

You will know, Chosen One.

Then he's gone.

CHAPTER FIFTEEN

AXL

We sit around the table, making small talk and smiling politely, doing our utmost to maintain the pretense of grateful house guests while every cell in my body screams at me to tear out our host's throat. Even back to full strength, I would likely fail, but I'd still give my life to try. What I won't give, however, is Ophelia's heart. Or her safety. And I made her a promise that I wouldn't do anything stupid and get myself killed. But even without that promise, she needs all of us because we need to find our sire, and I will be fucked if I let his piece-of-shit brother get his hands or his fangs on my girl, and I would tear his body to shreds before I'd let him rape her.

Axl, calm down, baby, she cautions through our bond. *If I can hear your heart beating like that, so can he.*

I know, princess. I just fucking hate him so much.

And now he's glaring at me like he knows exactly what I'm thinking, and part of me doesn't give a single fuck if he does.

"You know we're supposed to have a meteor shower tonight," Malachi says, snatching our host's attention away from me. Giorgios offers him a forced smile that's quickly

CHAPTER FIFTEEN

followed by the ground shaking. The windowpanes rattle in their solid wooden frames.

We all look to Ophelia. "That wasn't me," she insists.

"An earthquake, then?" Malachi asks.

Giorgios frowns. "They are very uncommon here."

None of us have a chance to speak again before Imari rushes into the room, her face etched with concern. "Sir, the guards asked me to inform you that there is someone at the front gate."

The spike in his heart rate is immediate, and my interest is certainly piqued. *Please fuck, let it be someone who can help get us the hell out of this place.*

Imari presses her lips together like she's afraid to speak again.

"Spit it out, Imari. Who is at the gate?"

She bends her head and whispers, but not low enough that I don't hear. "A dragon, sir."

"A dragon?" Xavier barks a laugh.

Ophelia yelps with excitement before she contains herself and clamps a hand over her mouth. My eyes dart between her and Giorgios.

"What on earth ..." Giorgios grumbles and tosses his balled-up napkin onto the table. "Stay here. All of you."

"Not a fucking chance in hell I'm missing out on seeing a dragon," Xavier says, standing up. The rest of us do the same, and Giorgios is too distracted to stop us. Or perhaps, based on his accelerated heart rate and the faint smell of fear emanating from his pores, he's too afraid.

Is this one of your and Alexandros's dragons, princess? I ask her, unaware of any other kind, but still, it's good to check. I wouldn't put it past Lucian or the Order to have a dragon stashed somewhere.

She nods excitedly. *It's Anikêtos. I just said hi to him.*

Dear fuck, I love this girl. I slide my hand into hers, and we follow Giorgios and Imari along the hallway and out into the courtyard. Sure enough, sitting before the gate on his haunches, large enough even with his wings tucked into his sides to obscure our view of the mountain in front of us, is a fucking dragon. All shimmering black scales and silver horns. Smoke unfurling from his nostrils, he trains his huge green eyes on us. With the exception of the pink-haired girl standing next to me, I have never in my life seen anything more magnificent.

"Anikêtos?" Giorgios gasps, his usually olive skin paler than the snow covering the mountaintops.

"He said to tell you he's not here for you, Giorgios," Ophelia says, her shoulders rolled back and her jaw tipped defiantly. I have never been prouder of this girl, and that's saying a lot given how she impresses the hell out of me every single day.

He blinks at her. "You can talk to dragons?"

"Oh, yeah. Did I not mention that? Cool, right?"

He shakes his head. "You cannot take her from here, Anikêtos. I made Alexandros an oath to protect her."

The dragon blinks his bright-green eyes at Ophelia. "He says he'll take care of me now. Of all of us. You're relieved of your duties, Giorgios."

"No!" he bellows. "You cannot. Guards!"

The few dozen guards standing at the perimeter of the courtyard step forward, but their reluctance and fear are palpable.

"Ani says if they take one more step toward us, he'll turn them all to ash." With a single, perfectly aimed plume of flames, the dragon scorches the large tree that towers over the left wall. It crumbles to ash. "Just like that," Ophelia adds.

Giorgios holds up his hand and orders his men to stand down.

"You will not get away with this. You will die out there on your own without my protection," Giorgios spits, practically

CHAPTER FIFTEEN

frothing at the mouth. I mean, who can blame him? How often does a dragon rock up at your door in the middle of dinner and put a huge-ass dent in all of your carefully laid plans to rape your brother's fated mate?

"I think we'll take our chances," Ophelia says with a sweet smile. Then she turns to the guards. "We'll be needing some of your furs. Jackets and hats."

They stare at her, frozen, until Anikêtos sets one of their hats on fire. Once they finish scrambling to give us what we need, Anikêtos, via Ophelia, demands an extra set for his friend. Which makes me smile like a fucking idiot because I know who that friend is.

I keep a wary eye on Giorgios, unsure why he hasn't teleported out of here yet.

He can't, Ophelia reminds me. *He can transport in but not out. The hallowed ground thing.*

I vaguely recall her mentioning something about that now, but it was while I was under the influence of blue poppy and feeling decidedly not my best. *But he's a vampire.*

Yes, but his transportation power isn't vampiric. He simply let everyone believe it was. It was how he was able to mask his mind-control powers so well.

I shrug on the fur jacket and ignore the faint smell of body odor that wraps around me. Ophelia's attention is now back on the dragon. By the look on her face, I can only guess I'm not going to like the outcome of the conversation they're having.

She turns to me with a frown, and trepidation curls its way up my spine. "What's wrong, princess?"

"Ani says that the minute we leave here, Giorgios will leave the grounds and transport straight to Alexandros. And then we won't have a chance of getting to him in time. It's going to take us all night to reach him."

Xavier runs his hand through his hair. "So ...?"

"I don't like this any more than you're going to, but he says it's the only way. A dragon is incapable of harming a son of House Drakos, so the only thing we can do is detain him. And the best way to do that without killing everyone here—"

"I'm not against that," Xavier says.

"I am. There are at least fifty guards, maybe a hundred, and none of them have ever done anything but follow Giorgios's orders. We're not slaughtering them all because of that."

"Fucking pacifists," Xavier mutters, but he silences any comeback from her by wrapping his arm around her neck and kissing her forehead.

I roll my eyes at him, but I can't help but smile. I've missed this side of him.

"So what do we do?" Malachi asks.

"Ani is going to take me to Alexandros. He's sure he knows where he's being held. And you guys will make sure Giorgios doesn't leave."

I suck in a breath. "I mean, I'm all for kicking some ass, princess, but as you pointed out, there's an entire army here."

"Oh, don't worry." She smirks. "You're going to have some help."

We follow her gaze to the sky, and fuck me if there isn't another goddamn dragon circling overhead. Not quite as big as the black one, but still big enough to decimate a city with a flick of its tail, I reckon.

"Guys, meet Elpis. She's Ani's mate. And she's going to be your ride as soon as Ani and I have Alexandros."

The dragon swoops lower and, with a single flap of her wings, causes a mini tornado that has Malachi and me holding onto our newly acquired hats. Then she lands and tucks her wings into her side in the same way as Anikêtos. Her scales are green with flecks of amber, and her golden horns shimmer in the moonlight.

CHAPTER FIFTEEN

I stare at her, enthralled. "She's fucking beautiful."

Ophelia giggles. "Ani says she's his, so don't get any ideas."

I glance back at the imposing black dragon still looming over the courtyard, unaware if he's joking or not despite Ophelia's laugh. He doesn't look like he has a joke in him. He looks mean as fuck.

"I'd feel better if one of us could come with you, sweet girl," Malachi says, and both Xavier and I voice our agreement.

"Ani says he doesn't know what we're going to find when we get to Alexandros. Or what kind of magic might be there to disable or harm a vampire. It's safer if he and I go alone and you travel with Elpis once we have Alexandros."

I'm not sure I can let her go without me. I never want to let her out of my sight ever again. The thought alone is enough to have me feeling like I can't fucking breathe.

Her sparkling blue eyes hold my gaze. "I know this is hard, but I know it's going to work and we'll all be together again before you know it." She slides one arm around Malachi's waist, the other around mine, and we grab Xavier so we're all in a huddle, our faces pressed close together. "Anikêtos will protect me, and ... Well, have you taken a good look at him?"

"Yeah, he's pretty fucking fearsome, Cupcake, but no one will protect you like we can."

"I know that, Xavier. But you have to let me protect you all sometimes too. We can be in touch the entire time. He says this is the best way, and I think he's right."

I press my forehead against hers, inhaling her familiar intoxicating scent. It's only been a few days since we fed from her, and already I'm craving the sweet nectar of her blood. What if something goes wrong? What if we lose her? What if ...?

"It will be okay. I promise," she whispers. "Ani is getting impatient. We need to leave."

She gives each of us an all-too brief kiss, and I reluctantly let her go. She pulls the fur-lined hat onto her head so it rests directly above her dark eyebrows, and that along with the coat that's two sizes too big makes her look downright fucking adorable and way too vulnerable to be out flying on the back of a dragon all alone.

She glares at Giorgios. "Elpis may not be able to harm you, but she asked me to remind you that she can stand on you to trap you here. And if you try to leave these gates, she'll burn this fortress to the ground and everyone besides you in it," she says, her voice full of authority and confidence. I'm so fucking proud of her.

His jaw tics as he glares at her, his hands balled into fists at his sides and his eyes full of impotent rage. Then our girl turns back to us. "Ani and I are going to Peru. He said we should be there by first light if the wind stays behind us."

Malachi groans. "Peru? That's over ten thousand miles away."

"I know." She pulls on a pair of fur-lined gloves, her face lit up with a smile that's imploring us to trust her. "But Ani says he's fast."

I study the intimidating dragon again. "Maybe that's what we're worried about. You traveling at insane speeds on the back of a fucking dragon doesn't inspire confidence, princess."

She glances back at him, and her smile grows wider. "He says it's safer than a horse."

Malachi drops his head into his hands. "Horses aren't all that safe, baby."

But there's no talking her out of this. It's the best plan we have. Besides, the sooner she leaves, the sooner she gets to Alexandros. And the quicker we can get out of this fucking prison.

CHAPTER SIXTEEN

OPHELIA

Had someone told me even six short months ago that magic and witches and vampires were real, I would have told them they'd been reading too many fantasy novels. Had they told me I'd one day be soaring over the Himalayas on the back of a freaking dragon, I would have sat them down and called a doctor. But here I am, sitting on Ani's back, which is surprisingly comfortable, his neck so vast that I have plenty of room.

Despite the rush of the wind, I don't feel cold at all as the heat from Ani's skin is enough to keep me warm even without my stolen furs.

Are you still okay up there, sweet girl? Malachi's check-in is the fifth time I've heard from one of the boys since we took flight about fifteen minutes ago.

Yes. I told you, it's super comfy. I'm in no danger of falling, and it's not even that cold. I bet it's more comfortable than an airplane. Not that I've ever been on one of those. *How are things there? Is Giorgios still foaming at the mouth?*

Yeah. Xavier's reply is followed by a chuckle. *Elpis just flattened his entire east wall with her tail.*

OPHELIA

Imagining the look on his face, I suppress a giggle. *Be safe, and I'll update you when we're close to Peru.*

Be careful, princess. Axl's deep voice floods my thoughts now.

I will. Love you all.

Their responding reiterations of love and devotion resound in my head, and I smile, pressing my cheek against Anikêtos's warm scales. They're alarmingly soft, similar to velvet. I had no idea dragons were so cuddlesome. Immediately, I caution myself to never describe Anikêtos as either soft or anything even remotely akin to cuddly within his earshot.

Thank you so much for coming, Ani. You have no idea how much it means to me that you did. If you could have seen Giorgios's face when Imari told him there was a dragon at his gate … The memory makes me snort a laugh, and I can't suppress it this time. Anikêtos doesn't strike me as the kind of creature who finds much of anything amusing, and I don't want to offend him, but Giorgio's startled expression was a picture.

I weighed the options, and helping you save Alexandros seemed like the most logical course of action.

Did Elpis make you do it? I'm unable to resist teasing him.

He simply snorts. But he doesn't attempt to throw me off, so there's that.

How did you discover Alexandros was in Peru?

It is the logical place. I am aware that the Welsh mountains are too densely populated now. The Qilian Mountains are home to far too many demonkind, the Ethiopian Highlands to too many powerful shamans. That leaves the silver mines of Peru, which is also the most powerful of the ancient sites, for it is the place where dragons once laid their eggs.

So you're sure he's there?

I am certain, little elementai. It is the place Giorgios would choose because it is the place Alexandros would choose. He and his brother are alike in so many ways.

CHAPTER SIXTEEN

My lip instinctively curls into a sneer. *I beg to differ.*

You have known each of them for but a brief time, and I have known them both for millennia, child. Trust I know of what I speak.

I refuse to accept that Alexandros is anything like his brother. *Well, I think they're different in all the ways that matter.*

He falls quiet, and I do too, replaying all of my conversations with Giorgios over and over in my head. Looking for any clues as to what his grand plan is. And then I can't help but recall all of the awful things he said about Alexandros—how, given the choice, he would choose Lucian over me, even if it meant my death. I don't believe it. My eyelids flutter closed, and I sit up quickly, sucking in a cold lungful of air to wake myself up.

You may sleep if you must. We have many hours to travel yet, elementai. I will not let you fall.

I lay my head back down on Anikêtos's warm neck. With my eyes closed, I check in with the boys and remind them to be careful, and then I tell them how much I love them and miss them already.

I won't sleep, but I will rest. Just a little.

CHAPTER
SEVENTEEN
OPHELIA

We are drawing near, Ophelia. Anikêtos's deep growl rouses me from a fitful sleep, a sleep plagued by visions of monsters with sharp teeth and claws and hooded figures and fire and blood.

I sit up and allow the cool rush of air to blow away the last remnants of slumber. The bright light of the rising sun causes me to blink as it bathes the land below in its amber glow.

You see the mountain range ahead? You see the highest peak?

Yes.

It is what we dragons call Marata Fyar Arandagar—Birthplace of Dragons. That is the only place capable of holding the great Alexandros Drakos.

You're sure, Anikêtos?

Yes, for I feel his presence as we grow closer. Do you not?

No. I shake my head, saddened at that realization.

Fear not, little elementai. My powers are stronger here than anywhere in this world. I was born in the shadow of this mountain.

You were? Wow!

A long time ago, when the world did not look like this. I shall land at its foot, and you must go in alone from there.

CHAPTER SEVENTEEN

Alone? Fear curls its way around the base of my spine.

I will not be able to go with you, Ophelia.

Of course he won't. He's almost a quarter of the size of the mountain itself. *I know. I guess I'm just scared of what I'll find in there.*

Fear is an inevitable part of life, elementai.

One I'm not used to. I went through most of my life without feeling anything even close to fear. Perhaps because I never had anything to lose before.

And that is why those with nothing to lose are so dangerous.

I can't help but think he's right. It's love that makes us afraid—afraid of losing what we have. Some might say that makes us weak, but I prefer to believe it gives us our greatest strength. There is no one more powerful than someone fighting for something they love. And no one so destructive as one who loves only themselves.

Anikêtos lands softly, and I climb down from his neck using his enormous front leg as a ladder. Glancing around, I get my bearings. We're at the foot of a mountain, with part of a vast abandoned silver mine running around its perimeter. Between that and the mountain base are shrubs and trees that provide good cover, though not enough to hide a dragon.

I am cloaked. None but whomsoever I choose will be able to see me.

Good. I pull off my gloves and coat and wipe my hands on my jeans before scanning the rock face for an entrance. There's what looks like a vast cave through a clearing in the trees. *Is that the way in?*

Yes.

I take a deep breath and try to calm my nerves.

Focus on your light, Ophelia. I hear Alexandros's voice in my thoughts, and I'm unsure whether it's a memory or because I'm so close to him that I can hear him. I hope it's the latter.

You have no need to be afraid, Ophelia. You have power beyond measure. Anikêtos's voice is oddly soothing in my head.

I know that, but I still don't fully understand how to use it. And it's been kind of switched off for a few weeks. This isn't sacred ground here, is it?

Only for dragons. It does not affect you in the way hallowed ground does.

I swallow and wipe my sweaty palms again.

Hold out your hand, Anikêtos orders.

I have no idea why he asks that of me, but I trust him, so I do it without question, noting my trembling fingers. For the first nineteen years of my life, I never felt even a lick of fear, yet now, when I could seriously do without it, it has me almost paralyzed.

There are very few who are powerful enough to wield Dragonfyre, Ophelia. He blows out a small stream of fire, but not like the fire at Giorgios's fortress. Instead of burning with a red and orange flame, it glows yellow with a green hue. It engulfs my hand, and I let out a startled cry of surprise, but I don't feel any pain, only a gentle warmth. My skin does not blister or burn. *It is a gift I do not bestow lightly. Do not let it touch Alexandros's skin, for it will burn him. And should it engulf him entirely, he will die, for it is lethal to both vampires and demons.*

I hold up my hand, marveling at the flickering golden-green flame and how it simply sits there like it's a part of me. *It's incredible. Thank you.*

You can snuff it out with a flick of your wrist, Anikêtos explains. *But it will always remain a part of you now. You can summon it as you would any other fire.*

Thank you so much, Ani. For everything. I rock forward on my toes, desperate to throw my arms around a part of him and give him a hug, but I'm not sure there's a part of him I can get my arms around. Maybe a talon?

CHAPTER SEVENTEEN

Go, Ophelia. Find him so Elpis can leave with the boys.

Of course, the boys! I make my way toward the entrance of the cave and reach out for Axl, Xavier, and Malachi as I dodge rocks and thick, prickly bushes. All three of them respond immediately.

I'm sorry I didn't check in.

It's okay, sweet girl. We felt you sleeping.

Can't believe I fell asleep on the back of a dragon. I shake my head. *But I'm here, and I'm on my way into the mountain to find him.*

Their pleas to be careful and safe fill my head.

I know. I will, I promise. Anikêtos gave me some Dragonfyre. It's lethal to vampires, so if Lucian is in there ... or anyone else who shouldn't be. Anyway, how are things there?

Giorgios veers between raging and pleading with us, Axl says. *It's kind of fun to watch.*

I reach the mouth of the cave, which leads into the heart of the mountain, and my heart starts to hammer so loud in my ears that I can barely hear my own thoughts now.

Focus on your light, Cupcake. You got this, Xavier says, soothing me. He really would make a great teacher. If we ever get back to Montridge and have any kind of chance at a normal life, that is.

To do that, I have to go into this cave and find Alexandros. And I must hope I am enough to save him.

CHAPTER
EIGHTEEN
OPHELIA

I make my way through the cave, my free hand feeling along the rock face. The Dragonfyre has the added bonus of lighting my way, but the space I'm currently in is narrow, and there's little room for the light to shine.

As I edge deeper into the mountain, the air becomes easier to breathe and the space opens out, the tunnel gradually growing wider and wider until I step into a vast open space, easily as big as the main student library building back at Montridge.

In the center of the space is a cage. Not big by any means. Maybe eight feet by eight feet. It's made of thick, close-set metal bars, which I would bet are made of silver. Inside the cage is a sight that stops my heart.

"I knew you'd come for him." The voice that echoes off the cavernous chamber walls sends a chill through my bones. Alien to me, yet familiar. It sounds different out here in the real world.

His shadow dancing from the light of the Dragonfyre, he approaches, and with each step he draws nearer, my breathing grows shallower and faster while my heart beats frantically in

CHAPTER EIGHTEEN

my ears. I know who this is. Instinctively, I feel his presence, our bloodlines irrevocably intertwined. He lowers the hood of his thick, dark cloak, and I see his face for the first time, at least for the first time through my own eyes rather than Alexandros's memories.

"Lucian." I'm impressed by the lack of tremor in my voice when I speak his name aloud.

His tongue darts out quickly, moistening his full bottom lip. He is so much like his father in appearance, I feel like I'm getting a glimpse into Alexandros's past and seeing him as a younger man. Perhaps that is who this truly is. A past self of his, coming here to warn me. To help me. But he nods, confirming my original suspicion.

"Ophelia Hart," Lucian replies, his tone gentler than I imagined it would be.

I glance around, so many questions about what he's doing here—and what he intends to do now that I'm here—galloping around my head.

My eyes are drawn back to the silver cage. To Alexandros's limp body hanging from chains. "Did you do this to him?"

His lip curls up, showing his fangs. "You think *I* did this?"

"Why are you here? How did you find him? I thought you didn't know where he was."

"I didn't. I have been searching for over three weeks, and I found him here only yesterday. I am no threat to him." He indicates the space behind the cage, and I vaguely make out the shadowy figures of what appear to be four bodies with severed heads by the light of the Dragonfyre in my hand. "In fact, I relieved him of his guards."

The hairs on the back of my neck stand on end. What if there are more here? What if this is a trap? Lucian and Giorgios could be working together. "But you are a threat to me." I hold up my hand, and the green Dragonfyre glows brighter.

Lucian takes a wary step back. "You have no idea do you, *Chosen One*?" There's no mistaking the disdain in his tone, and it causes a fresh wave of anger to engulf me.

I step forward, emboldened by the power I feel running through my veins. As though it ignited at the precise moment I needed it to. "I'm tired of this Chosen One bullshit already. Give me one good reason why I shouldn't burn you to ash right now?"

His lips twitch, but he maintains his composure. So much like his father ... Confused, I shake my head.

"Because then neither you, nor he, shall ever know the truth."

"What truth?" I spit out the words like an accusation, glancing around nervously as I anticipate his next move. Does he have an army of sireds ready to pounce? Will I be bound in a cage too?

His laugh is dark and bitter. "So quick to assume you know me, little girl."

Goosebumps break out over my skin. Alexandros groans in pain, and it slices a welt across my heart. I have to get him out of here. "I know enough." I raise my hand once more.

"I have been here protecting him," Lucian shouts, making me freeze.

I don't know if I believe him. I no longer have any idea who to trust, who is an enemy and who is an ally. "What?"

"As sure as I was that you would find him eventually, I didn't know who or what might come for him in the interim. He has many enemies. And I do not know the full extent of my uncle's plan."

My hackles rise at the mention of his uncle.

"Oh, believe me, I hate Giorgios even more than you do, Ophelia." The amount of rage dripping from his words tells me he means it. But that doesn't mean he's to be trusted in any

CHAPTER EIGHTEEN

way. It doesn't discount what he did to his own mother and sisters.

"If you're here protecting him, why didn't you free him?" I demand, my hand still raised and ready to douse him in Dragonfyre if he so much as breathes in a way I don't like.

He snorts and shakes his head. "I thought you were smart."

And I thought you were a murderous psychopath who cared about nobody by yourself! I rein in that remark and fire off another instead. "I have no time for your games, Lucian."

"If *he*, the most powerful vampire alive, is not strong enough to break those silver chains and bars, what makes you think I am? Even at the height of my powers, I could not have withstood the burning of the silver from these sacred mines."

I swallow the retort I planned—he has a point. I glance at the cage again. It has no door. No apparent entrance. It appears to have been forged with no way in or out. The silver isn't harmful to me, but I can't see a way to get to him through the thick bars.

"Your powers are not affected by silver, Ophelia. They will work just fine down here."

"What do you know of my powers?" I growl accusingly.

He takes a step toward the cage, his head tilted as he stares at his father. "I know Nazeel awakened them fully."

Anger snakes through my veins at the mention of her name. Lucian knew what she had planned? Is she in league with him?

"The only limit to your power exists in here, Ophelia." He taps his temple once, his eyes glowing in the firelight, making him look like a monster. "You possess the inherent power to break this cage and his chains without breaking a sweat."

I swallow nervously. "I wish I shared your confidence."

He snorts and folds his arms across his chest. "Such power is wasted on one who has no idea how to use it."

Of course he would think that. Arrogant, conceited, megalomaniacal douchebag that he is. I glare at him, my muscles clenched tight, ready to strike if he takes one step toward me. "Or perhaps that is exactly who should have it. But I don't see how fire or air or any of the elements can help in this situation."

"You don't?" he asks, incredulous.

The asshole is baiting me. "Just let me think."

"There's no time to think, Ophelia. You are taking your powers far too literally."

Patronizing too, huh? Nice.

He shakes his head like I'm annoying him when clearly it's him annoying me. "What is the most powerful force in the world?"

I blink at him and wonder what he'll think of my answer. I assume he and I have very different views on the matter, but his hazel eyes implore me to reply, so I tell him. "Love."

He opens his mouth and stares at me for a few beats before closing it again, whatever he was about to say dying in silence. His jaw tics while he appears to wrestle with something in his mind. What feels like an eternity passes before he speaks again. "The elements, Ophelia. What is the most powerful element?"

I rack my brain for the answer. Fire? No. "Water," I reply confidently.

He nods, and I feel an unexpected—and definitely unwelcome—flush of pride. What do I care if I got his question right? I don't want or need his approval. "It does not matter which element you choose, for they all could break his chains. What matters is which you believe to be most powerful. Water is a solid choice. It can level entire cities in the blink of an eye. And that's only one of the elements running through your veins. That *power* lives inside you. So find your light, focus, and destroy the fucking cage."

I stare at the cage and swallow nervously, wishing I shared his optimism. "Just like that?"

CHAPTER EIGHTEEN

"Just like that." His breath dusts over my cheek, and I flinch at his closeness. He doesn't back away. "Find. Your. Light," he commands.

That will take effort and concentration, and I don't trust Lucian enough to allow myself to go to that place when he's so near. But Alexandros's pained murmurs remind me that I have little choice. Lucian may simply be luring me in and waiting for his moment to strike, but I take a little comfort in the Dragonfyre still warm in my hand.

I close my eyes and find the dazzling orb of light within my core.

"Focus, Ophelia. You have everything you need already inside you." For reasons I don't fully understand, the sound of Lucian's voice soothes me. Perhaps it's as simple as the fact that he sounds a lot like his father.

I draw in a breath, letting it fill my lungs, before I open my eyes and concentrate my energy on the cage and the chains binding Alexandros's wrists.

"Believe it can happen, and it will be so," Lucian says, quietly confident.

So that's exactly what I do. I will the chains to break and the bars of the cage to shatter. And my veins spark up with lightning while power crackles through my body, and I channel the powerful swell of the ocean. I see it all in my mind's eye—the bars exploding from the pressure of the water, their pieces scattering across the cave, then the links in the chains breaking open and falling from Alexandros's arms.

Lucian ducks, pulling his hood over his head, and it happens in one huge blast, just as I imagined it. The broken chains of silver release Alexandros from their hold, and he collapses to his knees as they clatter to the cold ground.

I surge forward and catch him with one arm before he can fall forward onto his face. "Alexandros." His name is half prayer, half plea. Terror and hope wage a war inside me while I wait to see if he's okay.

His eyelids flicker, and I place a hand on his shoulder to steady him, my palm resting gently on his blistered skin. A violent swell of emotion threatens to swallow me whole, but I choke it down. Now isn't the time. I glance back at Lucian, my senses hyperalert to any change in his demeanor. He watches us intently but makes no attempt to move. Still, I don't trust him, and with a flick of my wrist, I form a protective circle of Dragonfyre on the ground around Alexandros and me. Lucian will burn if he tries to cross it, so it buys me a little time at least. And now that the Dragonfyre around us is burning brightly, I douse the one engulfing my hand and pull Alexandros into my embrace. Gliding both my palms over his charred flesh, I channel my earth line to heal him as best as I can. The thick angry welts striping the length of his back begin to heal beneath my touch, and he shivers in my arms.

As much as I believe that speaking into his mind would break through to him more easily, I know better than to try. It won't work down here, so I say his name again. "Alexandros, it's me."

His eyelids flicker, and his nostrils flare. "Ophelia," he growls.

All too quickly, his fangs protract, and with a feral growl, he goes straight for my throat. Despite his weakened state, it takes all my strength to stop him from feeding on me. The pained look he gives me almost breaks my heart all over again. "You can't. Not yet. My blood flows with blue poppy. If you feed now, while you're still weak ..." My voice catches on a sob. I hate denying him, but it's too much of a risk.

He blinks, and for a few seconds, I wonder how much of what I said he understands. But then his dark eyes spark with recognition and anger, and he nods his understanding.

CHAPTER EIGHTEEN

"We need to leave here." I hoist him to his feet. "It's not safe."

"How did you find me, little one?" My knees almost give way at the sound of his voice after too long without him, and my chest heaves with the effort of holding back my tears.

I blink them away. "I'll explain later. We have to leave."

"Then douse the ..." He clings to me. "Is that Dragonfyre?"

"Yes."

"Ophelia?"

My brain races, and I glance around the cave, squinting to see in the dim light. When I extinguish the ring of Dragonfyre protecting us, will Lucian choose that moment to strike? I can't see him or sense him in here. He is no doubt waiting in the shadows, the place he seems most comfortable.

"Ophelia, what are you hiding from me?"

I suck in a deep breath, eyes darting in every direction while I consider our next move. We have to get out of here, and the only way is the way we came, which means leaving the protective circle. Telling him about Lucian now could be a mistake.

"Ophelia!" he barks, snapping me from my racing thoughts. He draws himself up to his full height, forcing himself to stand on his own two feet.

Trepidation floods my chest. As much as I would rather not have this conversation right now, I can't hide this from him. "I'll tell you, but we have to start moving."

His jaw tics, and after only a few seconds' resistance, he nods his agreement. I gather up the Dragonfyre so it again glows around my right hand and wrap my left arm around his waist, not only for his benefit but because I can't bear to not be touching him.

I suck in a lungful of air, and we begin to edge through the dark cave. "Lucian was here."

He stops in his tracks, as I suspected he would. "What?" His voice is a growl, and his eyes roam over my body, possessive and hungry and full of worry.

"He didn't hurt me." I nudge him to keep moving. "I think he's gone. Can you sense him? Hear his heart beating?"

His eyes narrow, and he shakes his head. "But that does not mean he is not here. I would be unable to sense him down here. Was it he who brought the Dragonfyre? What did he want? Was he here for you? For me? Both of us?"

I quicken my steps, anxious to get out of this damn creepy cave and back to Ani's reassuring presence. "Now who's the one asking all the questions?"

"Ophelia!" It sounds like a threat and a promise all rolled into one delicious word, and goosebumps prickle out all over my body. I can't even put into words how much I've missed him or how much I need him to be okay.

"Both, maybe? He said he'd been watching out for you and that he knew I'd come. He told me he killed your guards. And then he ..." I wince at what I'm about to say, but it's the truth. "He helped me."

"He helped you?" His tone is incredulous, unsurprisingly so.

"Yes. Can we please get out of here, and then I'll tell you everything? We really need to move."

He huffs out a breath but doesn't speak again. He's quiet and contemplative, and I take the opportunity to focus all my energy and attention on navigating our way out of this cave.

"Almost there," I tell him, although he's walking much better than I expected he would be after weeks of starvation and silver chains. With each step closer we get to the entrance, he seems to gain strength.

"The silver dulls my power and saps a vampire's strength," he says by way of explanation, and I'm not sure if he's able to read my mind now that we're close to the entrance or if he simply knows me so well.

CHAPTER EIGHTEEN

"We'll be out of here soon. Into the brush, and then we can get as far away from here as possible."

He turns his head and stares at me. "How, Ophelia? How did you get here?"

Motes of dust dance in the rays of midmorning sun streaming in at the cave entrance. I'm almost breathless with anticipation as I imagine Alexandros's reaction to seeing one of his oldest friends waiting for us. "Wait and see."

His brow furrows, but there's no time for him to ask anything more because we step out of the cave and are immediately greeted by the sight of Anikêtos, grand and majestic even as he sits idly on his haunches.

"Ani?" The way his dark eyes light up when he sets them on his old friend has me ready to burst with happiness despite the circumstances that brought us all here.

Ani snorts, and a thick cloud of smoke plumes from his nostrils. *It is about time, Dragon Whisperer.*

Alexandros cracks his neck, and all the childlike wonder on his face disappears behind his mask of cool certainty. "Well, I was a little tied up."

I suppress a snicker as I douse the Dragonfyre in my hand. Did Alexandros just make a joke? Ani blinks rapidly, and I'm one hundred percent certain it's the dragon equivalent of an eye roll. He jerks his head to the side. *If I had waited for your arrival any longer, your dinner would have woken and ran away.*

Alexandros growls, and I follow his gaze to four men slumped under a tree a few feet away from us. They appear to be asleep. "Who are they?" I ask.

Farmers, I suspect, Ani replies.

Alexandros is scanning the perimeter, his eyes narrowed. "Where are the boys? Are they not here with you?"

"No, but they're safe. They're still at Giorgio's fortress. They had to stay and make sure he didn't transport here before we got to you. But Elpis is with them, and they're going to leave as soon as it's safe."

Alexandros blinks. "Elpis is here too?"

She would not allow me to leave the netherworld without her. Anikêtos snorts, and smoke unfurls from his nostrils.

Alexandros reaches out, and Anikêtos drops his head low, allowing him to rest a hand on his nose. The tenderness between the two of them has tears burning behind my eyes. *Thank you, old friend.*

I told you that whenever you truly needed me, I would be here. This seemed like such an occasion, Dragon Whisperer.

Is it safe for the boys to leave now? I ask, eager for them to get away from Giorgios and be with us. *Safe for them to leave Giorgios behind?*

Alexandros growls at the mention of his brother's name. *It is a pity Elpis cannot burn him to ash.*

You know she cannot. And he is not fool enough to give her any cause to, Anikêtos replies.

It is for the best, Alexandros concedes. *That would deny me the pleasure of looking him in the eye whilst I take his head.*

I have no idea how much Alexandros knows about what his brother has done these past few weeks, and there's no time to discuss it right now. "The boys? Is it safe for them to leave?" I ask again.

Alexandros nods. "Giorgios would not be fool enough to transport here and risk meeting me when I am at full strength, and especially not with Anikêtos at our sides. Tell them to leave immediately with Elpis."

"And head where? We're not staying here, are we?"

He shakes his head. "That would be too dangerous."

"Montridge?" I suggest, wanting nothing more than to go back home.

"Even more so, little one. We have no idea who our enemies

CHAPTER EIGHTEEN

are, but all of them will anticipate a return to Montridge. Anikêtos will direct Elpis to where we are going as soon as I figure out where that will be. Tell them to trust her, and we will give them further information as soon as we have it. In the meantime, I will feed."

I glance at the four unconscious men. "Will they be okay? Are you …?" I stop speaking because the answer is obvious. Alexandros needs to feed, and human blood is the quickest and surest way to nourish him and renew his strength.

He brushes his knuckles over my cheek. "I will feed and leave them sleeping when I am done, little one. They will not come to any lasting harm."

I press my cheek into his touch, craving more contact. "I know. I'll speak to the guys and let them know you're okay and it's safe to leave." I reluctantly step away from him so he can feed.

I easily find all three of the boys. *I have him. He's safe. You can leave now. Ani will tell Elpis where to go.*

Their combined exclamations of joy and relief fill up my head and make me smile. *We're on our way, Cupcake.*

Be there as soon as we can, princess.

How rough is it riding a dragon, sweet girl?

I glance at Anikêtos, who's staring at me with his dazzling emerald eyes. Unblinking.

Terrifying if he weren't such a sweetie deep down. Like deep, deep down. *It's actually very comfortable. I'm not sure I want to travel any other way now.*

After telling them to be careful and that I can't wait to see them, I sit on a rock beside Anikêtos and take a deep breath. It feels like the first one I've consciously taken since we left Tibet. The fresh summer air fills my lungs, and I listen to the sound of the wind rustling the leaves of the trees.

Lucian was here, Ani. Did you see him leave the cave?

OPHELIA

I have not seen anyone but the two of you.

A shiver runs down my spine. All my interactions with Lucian thus far have been surprising. While I can sense the darkness in him, I can't deny that he's done nothing but help me. First with the blue poppy, then with figuring out how to use my power to free his father. Perhaps his motives are less than pure, but until we find out for sure, I can't help but feel grateful to him. *I didn't see him when we left.*

There are many caves and tunnels within the mountain. Many layers which have to be explored before we can see the fullness of the picture before us.

I nod my agreement but can't help thinking Ani is no longer talking about the mountain. Lucian Drakos may have been a monster in the past, but that doesn't necessarily mean he's the villain of my story.

CHAPTER NINETEEN
ALEXANDROS

I lick the last drop of blood from my lips and let the fourth man fall from my arms to lie next to his companions. Such was the strength of my thirst, I could have drunk the four of them dry without a second thought. Whilst I am sated enough and my strength is fully returned, it was only Ophelia's concern for their wellbeing that prevented me from doing so. I almost forgot how powerful an influence an elementai could hold over their vampire mate. Although our bond has been severed, she is still my fated mate, and in such close proximity, I feel every one of her emotions as if they were my own.

The irony of the elementai being slaughtered in an attempt to control the vampire race is so obvious, I wonder how our enemies did not see it. Their loss only made us crueler, stripping away what little humanity we inherently possessed. Ophelia's kindness and compassion radiates from her still—despite what she must have endured the past several weeks at Giorgios's hands. I cannot bring myself to think about that at this moment, although I will discover all she has experienced as soon as we are somewhere safe. For now, I am eternally thankful that I do not detect his scent on her and therefore know he has not taken her in any way.

I make my way back to her and Anikêtos and find her sitting on a jagged rock staring out at the trees. "Are you searching for Lucian?"

She shakes her head. "I think he's still inside the mountain. Ani didn't see him leave, and I don't feel him out here like I did in there."

My heart constricts in my chest. "You felt him before? Inside the mountain?" My tone is sharper than I intended.

She chews on her bottom lip and nods, her eyes wide. "Is that bad?"

I take a seat beside her and lace my fingers through hers. "It is merely surprising to me when I have not been able to detect his presence in over five hundred years. And for you to have felt his presence inside the mountain, where even bonds cannot be felt ..." It is perplexing and concerning that she shares such a connection with my son. A man she has never met before.

"I felt him the way I felt you in there. Not a bond, but like ..." She chews harder on her lip as she searches for the words. "I could feel your presence, and I felt his too. Like your ..." Her fear spikes, and she looks away from me.

"You have nothing to fear when I am with you, Ophelia. And certainly never from being honest with me. I am concerned he has a connection with you, but if you feel anything akin to anger in me, it is never aimed at you, I assure you, agápi mou."

"It's like he's a part of me too. Is it because he shares your blood, maybe? Maybe because I spoke with him while we were at Giorgios's house and—"

"You spoke with him? With Lucian?" How? Why? All manner of scenarios, none of them pleasant, run through my head. How has she been able to achieve something even I could not? It is not surprising to learn that her power is far greater

CHAPTER NINETEEN

than mine, but establishing a connection with him is dangerous and unnatural, as she has never connected with him before. Why is she able to do so now? I give her hand a reassuring squeeze. "Tell me what happened, Ophelia. Did he reach you, or did you find him?"

"I found him. I searched for him, using the way you described being able to connect with people. I tried it, and I just ... found him. He said he cannot find me in the same way."

Just found him? A man who has managed to conceal himself from his own father? I cannot believe he would simply allow that to happen. It seems more likely he orchestrated it himself. "And he spoke with you?"

She nods. "He helped us then too. He warned me about the blue poppy."

Anger simmers beneath my skin, along with guilt for trusting Giorgios and, in doing so, putting them all in so much danger. "Revealing your location to him was incredibly dangerous, Ophelia."

"But I didn't. He already knew where we were, I swear."

So many more questions need to be asked, but Anikêtos is growing restless, and we need to leave this place as soon as possible and find somewhere safe. "Come, let us go." I pull her up, and she obediently follows.

Where are we going, Dragon Whisperer?

Head for Venezuela. I have an idea, but I need to speak to a friend.

Ophelia nods toward a tightly wrapped bundle of fur on the ground. "We brought you a coat and hat to keep you warm." She glances down at my bare feet. "No shoes though. I'm sorry, I didn't think."

I have never been particularly affected by the cold, and although it has been over a millennium since I have had cause or opportunity to sit on Anikêtos's back, I can easily recall his warmth. I press a kiss on her lips. "That was very thoughtful, agápi mou. Thank you."

After slipping on the coat and discarding the hat I have no need of, I help Ophelia climb onto Anikêtos's back. Not that she appears to need my assistance, but it gives me a reason to have my hands on her. Having endured so many torturous days without her, I am loath to let a moment pass without touching her.

As soon as we are seated, I rest my mouth against her ear. "How long has it been since we have last seen each other, agápi mou?"

"Twenty-seven days," she whispers.

I will make Giorgios pay for every single one of them as soon as I am able. "Have you been in contact with anyone from Montridge during that time? How much of Giorgios's betrayal are they aware of?" I wrap my arms around her waist and hold onto her tightly as Anikêtos rises to his full height.

"There was no cell signal at the fortress, but I was able to speak with Enora and Cadence. They know Giorgios betrayed you, and they helped us figure some stuff out."

Anikêtos takes flight, and the wind rushing past us makes it impossible to be heard talking aloud. I must not have heard her correctly, so I switch to speaking through our thoughts. *You spoke to them both without a cell phone?*

Yes.

But how? You do not share a bond with them.

I know, but you do, don't you? The blood oath? I'm pretty sure that's how. Like with Ani and Elpis.

None of this should be possible. Those powers of the mind are usually built over hundreds of years. She breached the veil without my help. Contacted Lucian. Reached out to people I have never even established a mind connection with myself,

CHAPTER NINETEEN

like Cadence. While the young witch did swear me a blood oath, that does not explain Ophelia's ability to connect with her.

That's okay, isn't it? Me speaking with Cadence and Enora? We were stuck and didn't know what else to do. They really helped us.

I pull her closer and rest my lips against her neck. It should come as no surprise that Ophelia can achieve the extraordinary when she is herself extraordinary in every conceivable way. And now that my own abilities have grown so exponentially, I am sure I can communicate with many beings whom I could not before. Now is the perfect time to try. *Of course it is okay, Ophelia. I am merely surprised ... and impressed by the strength of your abilities. I am going to speak to Osiris, and you may listen in.* It would take too much effort to keep her out, and there is nothing I need to say which I would not wish her to hear.

I focus on Osiris, the amber flecks in his eyes and the deep timbre of his voice, and it takes but a moment to establish a connection.

Alexandros! comes his rapid reply, his relief apparent from thousands of miles away. I considered for a moment whether anyone at Montridge could be trusted, especially given Nazeel's involvement in my recent imprisonment and the fact that my own brother was able to mask his intentions from me. But the wolves have nothing to gain from betraying Ophelia and me. His reaction only reassures me further. *I don't know if you can hear me, friend, but I hope you can. I am so fucking glad you're alive.*

I can hear you, old friend.

Are you safe? Are Ophelia and the boys with you?

Yes, I am safe. Ophelia rescued me, and we are both well. The boys will join us shortly. But we are in need of some assistance.

Of course. Anything. What can I do?

I need some time, a few days or maybe more, to try to make sense of Giorgios's actions and determine what his endgame is. Time to figure out what other forces are at work in all of this. To do that, we need someplace safe.

How can I help?

Does your family still have the house in Venezuela? The one on the private stretch of beach? He and I visited there once a long time ago, in much less uncertain times.

Yes. My sister and her kids stayed there for a few weeks before Christmas, but there'll be nobody there until the spring now. It's yours until then if you need it.

Relief washes over me. This will give us time to reconnect and regroup, to formulate a plan. *Thank you, Osiris. I owe you a debt.*

It is my pleasure, old friend. The spare key is underneath the elephant flowerpot. You will find the pantry fairly well-stocked and some clothes in the closets should you need any. Feel free to use whatever you find there—the Brackenwolves have collectively left all manner of things in that house over the decades. It's something of a free-for-all.

Ophelia gives the fur coat she is wearing a sniff and wrinkles her nose. *I could use a change of clothes.* The thing does indeed smell offensive, as does the one she kindly provided for me, but the scent is largely masked by her natural aroma, and that is all I am able to focus on.

Ophelia? Wha—I mean ... How?

It is a long story, one we will bring you up to speed on as soon as we are able. I thank him again and bid him goodbye before directing Anikêtos on where to take us.

With nothing left to do but sit patiently on the back of the dragon, I endeavor to enjoy the remainder of our flight. And I enjoy it immensely with Ophelia's warm body curled into mine. The scent of her hair, her skin, and the reassuring, steady thump of her heart beating has need coursing through me like it is my lifeblood. She shifts on Ani's back, no doubt seeking a

CHAPTER NINETEEN

more comfortable position, but the motion has her perfect backside sliding against my rapidly hardening cock.

The surest sign my strength has fully returned is that I can think of nothing but burying myself inside her tight heat. My eyes rake over the vast expanse of Ani's back, noting the large swaths of dark, weathered skin between his horns. Like the apex of his neck where we currently sit, a space large enough for me to lie Ophelia down and—

Anikêtos's vicious growl reverberates around my head. *Do not even think about it, Dragon Whisperer.*

I cannot help but smile at his ire, so strong it makes his scales shudder from nose to tail. *And how would you know what I am thinking, Anikêtos? Have you mastered the ability of mind reading during your time in the netherworld?*

One does not need to be a mind reader to feel the lust spiking in you. I will throw you both off without a second thought if you so much as try.

Ophelia giggles, shifting her hips and rubbing against my now-aching cock again. *You made Ani mad.*

I would never disrespect you in such a way, old friend. No matter how much I desire to. Tuning him out, I rest my lips against her neck and nip gently, careful not to break the skin. *It is all your fault, little one. Stop squirming, or I will be forced to do something about it and risk our certain death. Anikêtos does not make idle threats.*

Sorry. I was just getting comfortable.

I band my arms tighter around her waist and pull her flush to my chest. *Comfortable now?*

Yes sir.

Sweet demons of hell. *How long until we get to Venezuela?* I ask Anikêtos, frustration and desire making me irritable.

Not soon enough, he huffs. *A few hours at most.*

A few hours of beautiful torture during which I will hold

Ophelia in my arms and think about all of the ways I am going to claim her when we get to where we are headed. Because I am already bordering on feral with need for her. To taste and smell. To kiss, touch, and fuck. If we did not need to get to where we are going as fast as possible, I would have Anikêtos stop so I could fuck her en route. And then I would still do it all over again upon arrival.

The pain of silver searing my flesh was nothing compared to the pain of not being with her. Of knowing she was out there without me. Without my protection.

And my boys. I miss them too, much more than I could have imagined.

The spell used to sever the bond between sire and sired has been used only a handful of times in recorded history and requires such ancient powerful magic that very little is known about it. But one thing that has been written about and is known by a select few is that the spell allows sired vampires to survive without the bond in place. My boys could survive, and indeed thrive, if I were to not put it back.

But would I survive without them? That is a different question altogether—one which I cannot be certain of the answer.

CHAPTER TWENTY

OPHELIA

With his hands wrapped around mine, Alexandros helps me down from Ani's back. Then he rolls his neck until it cracks. "Thank you, Anikêtos. I owe you a great debt." His voice cracks too.

Ani snorts. *It was nothing, old friend.*

You will wait here for Elpis, yes? He resumes communicating via thought.

Of course.

How long before she and the boys arrive?

Ani shakes his scales, and smoke unfurls from his nostrils. *Too long*, he growls, clearly unaccustomed to and displeased with being so far from his mate. *They have picked up a healthy tailwind, and Elpis estimates they will be here in a little over seven hours.*

Alexandros entwines his fingers with mine and tugs me forward so I bump against his chest. "Then let us go inside and wait, little one." He dusts his lips over my forehead and slides his arm around my waist. "I may never let you out of my sight ever again." With a nod of farewell toward the dragon, Alexandros leads me to the house.

OPHELIA

The key Osiris spoke of is exactly where he said it would be, and the air inside the house is warm and welcoming. A faint hint of jasmine reminds me of Silver Vale and brings a smile to my face. A shiver runs down my spine at the sound of the lock clicking into place behind me.

Without touching me, he strips away my coat. I swallow harshly, about to spin around, but his hands on my hips hold me in place. My knees tremble, and I have to lock them to stay upright as the warmth from his naked chest presses into my back. He pulls my hair to one side and runs his nose up the side of my neck, inhaling deeply.

My core is on fire. "Please ..." I rasp.

"Please what, little one?"

"Please. I need—" The rest of my words are swallowed by a sob that bursts from my chest.

Without warning, he presses me up against the closest wall and slips his hand inside my jeans and panties, to the place where I'm already aching for him. His fingers slide easily through my wet center. "Tell me what it is you need, Ophelia." His voice is low and dark, and his hot breath sends a shiver down my spine.

"I need you," I whine, working my hips against his hard cock, desperate for him to take me.

He growls, and the sound vibrates through every cell in my body. "Good, because I cannot wait another second to be inside you, agápi mou."

I barely have time to take a breath before my jeans and panties are torn down the middle, and then I'm spun around and in his arms, my legs wrapped around his hips. He sinks inside me, and I cry out, flooded with euphoria as he pulls out and drives inside me over and over. There is no finesse to his movements. No teasing or tenderness. It is brutal and necessary. Two bodies taking what they need from each other.

CHAPTER TWENTY

I rake my fingers through his hair, tugging harshly as I squeeze my thighs around him, wanting more while knowing he is giving me everything he has. Our breathing grows heavy and labored, hearts pounding frantically in our chests. And still, it isn't enough. I crave him harder. Deeper. Faster.

He rests his forehead against mine, our breaths mingling. "You have no idea how much I have longed for this. In my darkest moments, it was all that kept me sane."

"Then show me, Alexandros."

His vicious growl sends pleasure skittering up my spine. I think I may have just awakened something inside him I've never experienced before, and I am here for it.

CHAPTER
TWENTY-ONE
ALEXANDROS

Show her? She has no idea what she asks. If I show her the depth of my feelings for her right now, I will surely break her in two.

"Show you?" It is the feral beast inside me who snarls those words.

She nods, her cheeks flushed pink and her lip caught between her teeth. I sink to the floor, her legs still wrapped around me as I lay her on the cool marble. I should take more care with her, but I cannot. I cannot get far enough inside her to sate the need burning through me. Although, I will try.

I sink into her and roar out her name as bone-deep satisfaction unfurls in every part of my body. I drive deeper and harder with every thrust. Blood thundering in my veins, head spinning. Being driven mad with frantic, clawing need.

My fingers dig into the supple flesh of her ass and hips as I hold her still, ensuring she takes every millimeter of me over and over again.

It does not take any time at all to have her moaning my name whilst her tight pussy squeezes my cock in a death grip, as though she is as averse to letting me go as I am to being

CHAPTER TWENTY-ONE

released. I fuck her harder than I can ever recall fucking anyone in my long years on this earth. And I go on rutting into her until her walls flutter around me and she screams my name to the heavens. Her climax triggers my own, tearing through my very soul as I fill her tight pussy with my cum.

We pant for breath, and I run my nose up from her collarbone to her jaw. Despite my orgasm, her scent has my mouth watering, and both my fangs and my cock continue to ache. The desire to taste her blood is so intense, and it takes all of my carefully curated years of restraint to resist. My strength has returned, and it would do me minimal harm now to sip from her poisoned veins. But as long as Giorgios's whereabouts and intentions are unknown, he is a danger to her. Not to mention the uncertainty of Lucian's role in all of this. It would be reckless to do anything that would weaken me in any way.

Ophelia whimpers, and tremors vibrate through her beautiful body. And whilst I yearn to taste her blood, I will console myself with tasting my other favorite part of her soon enough. Which reminds me ...

"We should get you some food, little one. I am sure we will find you some sustenance in the pantry."

She shakes her head. "I'm not hungry." Her voice is little more than a whisper.

Her pulse flutters. She seems weakened, and I cannot afford to let my desire for her cloud my decision-making. "When was the last time you ate?"

"I don't know. It's been a while. But right now, I can't even think about eating."

Her heart is racing erratically in her chest, her entire body shaking. "Why are you trembling, little one?" Whilst I can read her mind and feel her emotions, I despise not feeling everything through our bond, and I yearn for it to be back in place.

"I ..." She sucks in a harsh breath, and the tear that runs

down her cheek comes to rest on the plump bow of her lip. She licks it off before I can. "I thought you were ... and now you're here ... and I ..." She squeezes her eyes closed, and I do not need our bond to know the myriad of thoughts and what-ifs running through her head or to feel the pain of my loss still clinging to her bones. The deep sense of relief and elation at finding me alive, at having me here, pressed up against her, is so intense I can taste it. I am real, although she cannot bring herself to fully believe it is true. The same emotions threaten to overwhelm me, but the pervading emotion for me is one of sheer joy—I am here with her, and my boys are safe.

All the anguish of the past four weeks—Giorgios's betrayal, Ophelia's revelations about Lucian—everything pales into insignificance now that she is in my arms. I fasten my pants and scoop her up before carrying her through the open-plan living area to one of the bedrooms at the back of the house, where I set her on the edge of the king-sized bed.

My knees thud against the cool marble floor, and I slide my hands down her thighs, still clad in her torn jeans, until I reach her boots and begin to untie them. "I do not believe I have ever seen you in jeans before, little one."

"They're more convenient, don't you think?"

My lips twitch in a smirk. "I suppose that all depends on what you are doing."

She smiles too, but it disappears quickly and is replaced by a sadness in her eyes that I cannot bear to see. "My skirts didn't feel practical anymore. It felt like we had to be prepared for anything ..." The reminder of where she has spent the last few weeks causes a deep well of rage to open up inside me and threaten to swallow me whole.

She traces her fingertips over my cheek, leaving a trail of heat flickering across my skin. "I missed you so much."

I push thoughts of my brother aside, if only for now,

CHAPTER TWENTY-ONE

because Ophelia deserves every single shred of my attention. "And I you, little one." After placing her foot on my thigh, I continue untying her boots.

"What are you doing down there?" she asks.

With a sharp tug, I remove one boot along with her sock, then make a start on the other. "What, you mean kneeling at your feet?"

She flutters her eyelashes. "Yes."

Once her second shoe and sock have been discarded, I lift her leg and press a kiss to her ankle. "There is no more fitting place in the world for me to be, agápi mou." I run my hands back up her thighs and pull the torn fabric of her jeans and panties down her legs before discarding them. "And nowhere on earth I would rather be." The scent of her grows stronger with each passing second, and my cock aches, urging me to bury myself inside her again until nothing exists but the two of us. I force her thighs apart with my shoulders, and with a hand around her throat, I squeeze gently, pushing her to lie back on the bed.

"I have thought about you every second of every day we have been apart." I run my nose up the inside of her thigh, inhaling deeply and allowing her scent to fill me until it floods my senses and my mouth is watering to taste her. She whines for me, the sound loaded with desperation. But I must savor every moment, every single millisecond of this. "You are soaked, little one."

"Because I need you. Please!"

"And you shall have me." I flick the tip of my tongue along the length of her dripping wet center, and her sweet arousal coating my tongue has the beast inside me snapping its teeth, ravenous to be let loose and devour her whole. "But not before I have you."

She lifts her hips to meet my mouth, her loud, unrestrained

moans echoing around the room. Keeping one hand around her throat, where her racing pulse thrums against my fingers, I use my other hand to press her thigh flat to the bed, holding her wide open for me so I can eat. And I eat like she is the only thing on this earth that can sustain me. Her sweet juices are life-giving nectar, coating my tongue along with my own release as I lick and suck and will myself not to bite.

"Alexandros." My name falls from her lips on a satisfied moan, and the sound only makes me more feral for her. More desperate to make her scream my name in rapture once more. When she comes again for me, it is loud and life-affirming and delicious. I lap up every drop she spills, letting her taste overwhelm me. My head is spinning. Cock aching with a need that I have never experienced in over two thousand years. Ophelia Hart is my addiction. My ruin and my redemption.

I flick my tongue over my lips, savoring her taste. As her legs still tremble and she rides the endorphins of her orgasm, I remove her hoodie and bra, exposing her entire beautiful body to me.

I trail my fingertips over her full breasts, down her ribs, and onto the curve of her hips, enjoying the way her body responds to me. Her nipples pucker as she presses herself into my touch.

"I have told you many times that you are exquisite, agápi mou, but I do not believe I could ever truly convey the beauty of you. You are simply ..." I press a single kiss to her lower abdomen. "Perfect."

She lets out a contented sigh. "You flatter me, sir."

Sir. The word elicits a deep growl, one that rumbles through my bones and makes her shiver. The time for gentle ministrations is over. I need to reclaim her in every way I am able. If I cannot mar her with my teeth, then I will think of other ways to leave my mark on her.

"I have warned you about calling me sir, Ophelia." I push

CHAPTER TWENTY-ONE

her up the bed until her head is resting on the pillow and crawl over her. "It makes me want to do very bad things to you."

Her nipples brush against my chest as she sucks in a deep, rasping breath. Her pupils are blown so wide they obscure the vibrant blue of her irises. I swear a man could fall into those eyes and lose himself forever if he stared into them long enough. "I like it when you do bad things to me, sir."

Damn, I want to bite her. I want to sink my teeth into her flesh and have her delicious blood fill me up. I want to be filled with her essence. Her power. Just her. I want to consume her as she consumes me. She runs her hand down my back, her nails lightly scratching my skin. I throw my head back, a loud, frustrated groan tearing itself from my throat. I cannot wait a second longer.

With a sharp tug on the waistband of my pants, I tear them open and free my cock from the confines of the fabric. It offers but a little reprieve from the constant throbbing ache. But when I sink inside her with one smooth stroke a second later, my body is flooded with overwhelming, mind-altering sensations of both relief and euphoria. I still my movements, remaining deep inside her whilst I let the feelings wash over and through me. Savoring each moment of this connection in a way I was unable to earlier, when I was too driven by my desperation to be inside her. Even now, my muscles vibrate with the strength of the need coursing through me.

"Oh, god." Her nails rake down my back again, harder this time, piercing my still-healing skin, but I am too lost in the ecstasy of our connection to register any pain. She could pour molten silver into the open wound right now and I could not bring myself to care.

I press my forehead against hers, sucking in a deep breath that I hope will calm the racing of my heart. "Ophelia. You. Are. Everything."

With Herculean effort, I pull out, reveling in the needy moan it elicits from her, before I sink back in. Her muscles squeeze around me, rippling around my shaft and milking precum from my crown. And every time I pull out to drive back inside her, her pussy holds me tighter than before. I screw my eyes closed and try to stave off my impending release, but it is no use. My sweet little elementai knows exactly what she is doing to me. She wraps her legs around my waist and stares into my eyes. And when she tells me she loves me, I come undone.

With a roar of her name, I empty my release into her once again, filling her tight channel until my cum drips out of her.

"That was amazing," she pants.

I press a possessive kiss on her lips. "And I am not nearly done with you, little one."

Her eyes widen. "Shouldn't you get some rest, maybe?"

"There will be time for rest when I am in the netherworld."

Her eyes flash with hurt, and I kiss her again. "Which will be a very, very long time away. When the world is nothing but dust. But until then, I may never sleep again, for I want to spend every possible second inside you."

Before she can reply, I flip her over and give her a hard swat on the ass that makes her giggle. The sound is so pure and full of joy.

"I am driven mad by my desire for you, Ophelia Hart." Grabbing her hips, I pull her ass up into the air and drive into her again, the ache in my cock not even slightly lessened by my previous two climaxes. I am not sure I will ever get my fill of her.

Her pleasure-filled screams are muffled by the pillow under her face as I fuck her again. And again. Like this. With her riding me. With her legs over my shoulders. Then, finally, with her

CHAPTER TWENTY-ONE

legs locked tight around my waist whilst I stare deep into her eyes.

She unravels me completely before she puts me back together. Over and over again until we collapse in a heap on the bed, both of us panting for breath and fighting exhaustion. The boys are almost here, and for now, I am sated enough.

For now.

CHAPTER
TWENTY-TWO

AXL

Ophelia was right—riding a dragon is a lot more comfortable than you'd expect it to be. And although we can't communicate telepathically with Elpis, she seems way less grumpy than her mate. Through Ophelia, we've been able to get updates on how far we are from Venezuela.

You're almost here. My girl's excited voice infiltrates my thoughts. She's been quiet for several hours, and I felt the block on her feelings. Whether that was her or the professor, I don't know, but we all know they've spent the time *reconnecting*. It's exactly what I would do if I'd been away from her for weeks. And even if I wasn't addicted to her, it's the vampire way. We are physical creatures.

Can't wait to see you, princess.

We missed you, Cupcake.

We sure did, Malachi adds. *Is Alexandros okay?*

Her sweet snorting laugh echoes around my mind, and it has been too long since I have heard the infectious sound. Sure, there have been occasional giggles over the past few weeks, but that particular sound has been sadly and unsurprisingly absent.

CHAPTER TWENTY-TWO

He's doing really well. He's pissed because he can't bite me though. I think he's currently working on a plan to erase blue poppy from the world.

I bet he is. Imagining his frustrated grumbling makes me smile, but the strangeness of not sharing this conversation with him wipes it away. He's been inside my head for over two hundred years, and I miss him being there more than I thought I would.

Are you all warm and soft and naked, Cupcake? Because that is how I'm hoping to find you when we get there soon.

She laughs again. *I am. And this bed is huge. We'll all fit.*

Xavier growls while Malachi grunts his appreciation for our sleeping arrangements. I can't wait to see them both. After everything we've been through these past few weeks, us all being together again feels too good to be true. The entire way here, I've been convinced something would go wrong, and until I am actually with them both, touching them, I won't believe otherwise.

~

We thank Elpis for the comfortable flight, although the landing was decidedly less so—we all had to hold onto her horns to make sure we didn't roll off down the back of her tail. Something tells me she's a minx of a dragon and she did it on purpose.

I have no idea if she understands our words of gratitude, but she blinks her fiery orange eyes at us before joining Anikêtos. He was resting when we made our descent, his vast form taking up half the beach.

As soon as we step foot inside the house, both their scents surround me, and although I've never been here before, it feels like we've come home.

AXL

Malachi's and Xavier's relief and happiness mingle with my own, and the three of us have goofy grins on our faces as we sneak along the hallway, following the sound of their heartbeats. Like there's a chance in hell we could sneak up on them. But as we reach the bedroom and I place my hand on the door, another emotion hits me—trepidation.

My relationship with Alexandros is deep and profound, but I don't think it could ever be described as warm. My respect for him comes from deep-rooted loyalty and a sense of family. But will he believe me foolish if I'm unable to mask how much I've missed him when I step inside this room? His absence in my life felt like a piece of my soul was missing. And not because I believed I was going to die with him gone, but because I felt less of a reason to live without him here. Alexandros Drakos is about to realize how much I've missed him, how much I love him, and I'm not sure I'm ready for him to know that.

Malachi places his hand on the back of my neck. *He won't reject you.*

I swallow down the anxiety clogging my throat.

Malachi continues. *I know you two don't truly believe it, but he needs us as much as we need him.*

Not sure you're right about that, Kai, Xavier says with a snort, trying—and failing—to hide his own insecurities.

We run out of time to discuss it further because the door opens and he's standing right there in front of us. I wince. Our bond isn't in place, but he can still read minds without a bond. A bond is impenetrable, but he's so powerful, I can't help but wonder if he heard every single thing we said. I bet he's hearing this right now. So shut the fuck up, Axl!

He opens the door wider and beckons us inside. "It is good to see you boys." His voice is calm and steady, his face devoid of emotion. No change there, then.

We file past him and stand at the edge of the room while he

CHAPTER TWENTY-TWO

closes the door, all three of us awkward and unsure. I want to hug the fuck out of him, but he's not a hugger by nature, and there's a distinct possibility he'll kick me in the nuts if I try.

Ophelia kneels in the middle of the bed, clapping her hands and squealing at the sight of us. Thank fuck for our girl. I focus my attention on her, and everything feels better. But before we can join her, Alexandros blocks our path, his imposing presence enough to prevent us from taking a step closer.

I swallow. Xavier's and Malachi's heart rates spike.

Alexandros clears his throat. "I missed you boys." His eyes dart between us. "All of you." And then he does the last thing I expected. *He* hugs *us*. He wraps one arm around my neck, the other around Xavier's, and squashes Malachi between the two of us. His hands rest on Malachi's shoulders. "Thank you for believing in me. For rescuing me. Ophelia told me you stayed behind to make sure Giorgios could not transport. How you refused to let him sire you even when you thought it might save your lives."

Oh, shit. I'm gonna cry.

Xavier sniffs. Has he already caved? "It was nothing."

"No." Alexandros's tone is stern. "It was everything." Then he presses his lips to my ear. "You really think I would kick you in the nuts for hugging me?"

I shrug. "You are kind of hard to read."

He barks out a laugh.

Are you going to bond with us again? I can't stop myself from thinking the question, but he simply gives each of us a kiss on the top of our heads.

"It is late. We are all tired. Ophelia is waiting for you. We all need to rest whilst we can. Anikêtos and Elpis will stand guard."

I glance over his shoulder at the large bed and my girl in it, smile brighter than the sun while she waits for us. He said Ophelia is waiting—does that mean he's not joining us?

"If you think I am spending even a minute away from her or any of you this night, you are very much mistaken." His low growl sends a shiver down my spine.

"Fuck," Xavier murmurs, his desire spiking. I have never held such feelings for our sire; he has always been too much of a father figure for me or Malachi to see him that way. But Xavier's relationship with him has been different from the start, and I know how much it costs him to bury those feelings every single day.

I slide my arm around his waist and give his hip a reassuring squeeze. Then we all pull off our clothes and climb into bed with Ophelia. Given that he's been without her for nearly a month, I'm not surprised when Alexandros takes one of the spaces next to her. Malachi lies on her other side with Xavier and me beside him, all of us ensuring we have a hand on our girl.

She asks at least two dozen questions about our trip here on Elpis. When she tells us that Anikêtos was much warmer and cuddlier than she imagined, Alexandros almost chokes on his laughter.

It has been the longest of days. The longest of months. I never slept well at Giorgios's house. Always on alert. With all of us in one place—and two dragons outside—I feel safe for the first time since before we left Montridge. Sleep threatens to pull me under the weight of its heavy blanket.

"We should rest now." Alexandros's commanding voice has us all eager to obey. I rest my hand on Ophelia's hip, and Kai's goes next to mine, Xavier's on the other side, with the professor's on top of them all. And that is how we fall asleep—all of us touching and finally feeling whole again.

CHAPTER
TWENTY-THREE

ALEXANDROS

A face with dark, sunken eyeholes and black fangs dripping with blood looms over me, rousing me from a fitful sleep. Ophelia! I reach for her in the dark and find her gone. They are all gone. The face gets closer. Lucian? Giorgios? I would take its head, but bone-deep fear paralyzes me.

Warm fingertips skate over the back of my hand, and my eyes fly open. I find the room cloaked in darkness, the sleeping form of Ophelia still curled into my side, Malachi, Axl, and Xavier beside her. It is Xavier's fingers trailing over the back of my hand, and I make no move to stop him. His steady breathing tells me he is still asleep. Having him seek my touch when he is at his most vulnerable makes warmth bloom in my chest.

Their proximity and their steady heartbeats are enough to chase away the remnants of the nightmare that has plagued what little fitful sleep I managed in captivity. I cannot help but wonder what they endured whilst I was locked in my silver cage, unable to reach out to them, to comfort them, to protect them.

The sting of Giorgios's betrayal has only grown sharper

since the day he lured me to Corinth under the pretense of finding my son. And the questions raised by his actions have only grown in number and difficulty since that time too. How was Giorgios able to mask his intentions from me? Whilst it is true that I have always afforded him a measure of privacy for the sole virtue of him being my brother, I still should have been able to detect some deceit in his deeds. What is clear is that his powers must be far greater than I ever knew. He has kept the true extent of his mind's abilities to himself for all these years.

How was he able to lure Nazeel Danraath, a trusted healer of the Order and someone I formerly had no quarrel with, to aid him in his plan? Why did he not simply kill me when I was at his mercy? Instead, he locked me in a cage. Why did he take Ophelia and my boys? And what is his endgame in all of this? He spoke of my downfall being a defining moment in our history. Does he believe himself to be on the right side of that line in the sand?

Ophelia stirs beside me. Her blood hums beneath her skin, and my fangs protract. How much I long to sink them into her tender flesh and sip the sweet ambrosia of her blood. Or perhaps I could wake her by sinking inside her tight, wet heat and allow the warmth of her pussy to drive away the questions plaguing me.

Her pink lips part, and she lets out a little whimper that does nothing to calm the ache building in my shaft. But as satisfying as it would be to take her, she needs to rest. And I need answers to something. Anything.

I close my eyes and rest my lips on the top of her head. In place of the usual candy scent that coats her hair is a spicy ginger aroma, and I despise that even the simplest change in her routine was forced upon her by my brother.

I grant myself entry into her mind instead of her body and comb her memories of the last few weeks. This is not an inva-

CHAPTER TWENTY-THREE

sion of her privacy. She belongs to me, and there is nothing I could discover about her that would ever change that. I steel myself for what I might find. Whilst I am certain he has not bitten or forced himself upon her, I am wary of what other terrors he must have inflicted to have her seek the assistance of Anikêtos, and even more so, what made the dragon agree.

I go back to the day our bond was severed and feel her pain as though it is my own. It squeezes a tear from the corner of my eye, and I move on quickly, unable to endure it for a second time. I find Giorgios telling them of my death at the hands of Lucian, Giorgios persuading them to go to his fortress, imprisoning them, poisoning her with blue poppy to make my boys sick. I feel their despair. Their anguish. Their desperation. Their loyalty to me. Their love.

Each new memory adds yet more fuel to the boiling inferno of rage inside me. But there is nothing that can prepare me for what comes next: her sheer terror at discovering the archaic ritual for severing the bond between fated mates. Is that what Giorgios planned? From her memories, she never confronted him to deny or confirm it, but she believed that was his intention, which is enough to have white-hot, blinding rage searing itself into every cell of my body, an anger so visceral it etches itself onto my soul. That he would take her from me. Force himself upon her. Fill her with his treacherous seed. My hand curls into a fist in her hair. She whimpers, causing me to loosen my grip. I grind my teeth together so ferociously, it is a small wonder they do not turn to dust in my mouth.

Such is my anger and sense of betrayal, I am of a mind to go outside and jump on Anikêtos's back right now so we can track down my treacherous snake of a brother. So I can tear out his throat and feed him his own tongue before ripping off his head.

But ... I cannot leave them when they have only just found me again. My heart and soul would not survive. I cannot summon the sheer strength of will it would take to tear myself from them. Not now.

Alexandros? My son? Is that truly you? I close my eyes and curse my own stupidity. Using so much concentration to access Ophelia's mind undoubtedly lowered my defenses enough that my father was able to feel my presence. Although our bond was also severed during the ritual Giorgios and Nazeel performed, without my walls in place, his mind has found mine. Which must mean he was searching for me.

Yes, it is me.

But I felt your passing. Giorgios told me—

Anger again flares hot in my chest once. *It appears the rumors of my death have been greatly exaggerated, Father.*

Son. He says only the one word, but it conveys a whole depth of emotion I have not felt from him in centuries. If I did not know better, I would say he is relieved by the discovery that I am alive. And perhaps he is. I have always fulfilled my family duties to House Drakos without complaint. *Why did Giorgios lie to me?* Anger bleeds into his tone now. *He told me Lucian was alive. That he had taken your head. Why, Alexandros? Did you and he willingly deceive me? Is this what you have been hiding from me?*

Giorgios deceived us both.

But why? How was our bond severed? The magic that would require such a feat is ... Who possesses such a power?

My ire at him is never far from the surface. *Is that all you are concerned about? Who might have more power than the great Vasilis Drakos?*

Watch your tone, he barks.

I draw a deep breath and close my eyes, forcing myself to channel my usual calm. *I am tired, and I do not have the answers you are searching for. I would very much like to know them myself.*

Is Lucian truly alive?

There is no sense in denying the truth any longer. *Yes.*

CHAPTER TWENTY-THREE

Then we must root him out and make him pay for his crimes, Alexandros.

I intend to find him and uncover his secrets, but I have no intention of teaming up with my father to do so. Whether he is in league with Giorgios is unknown at this time, but I would put nothing past him. It is possible my brother has told him of Ophelia's existence and this is their joint ploy to take her. To breed her and spawn a whole army of elementai and vampires. *Perhaps you should focus on finding your own son who betrayed his only brother and leave me to deal with mine.*

I will deal with him in good time.

As will I. I keep that to myself and close my mind off to him. It is too dangerous to allow him inside for longer than a few moments. His powers are as great as mine.

One day soon, I will face Giorgios, but not today. Or even tomorrow. Not whilst they are warm and soft and as in need of me as I am of them. For now, I will stay cocooned in the warmth of my true family. The only one I need.

CHAPTER
TWENTY-FOUR
XAVIER

"Ophelia isn't here." I glance up from the sketchpad I found earlier in the writing desk. "She and Malachi are talking with Elpis and Ani, and then they're going to do some training. Axl went to pick up some food."

The bedroom door closes with a soft click. "I know." His voice, low and deep, sends a current of something unexpected skittering along my spine.

I scrub a hand through my hair. Annoyance, or perhaps frustration, prickles beneath my skin. "Do you need something, Alexandros?"

His eyes narrow to sharp pinpoints that I swear pierce through to the deepest recesses of my soul. "Our bond was severed, Xavier."

I shrug, feigning disinterest when I am all too aware of that fact. "Yeah, I know. So?"

He licks his bottom lip. "So I am here to rectify that problem."

A thick knot of nervous anxiety lodges in my throat, and I swallow it down. When we learned that we don't need his bond

CHAPTER TWENTY-FOUR

to survive, I wasn't sure if he'd want to put it back in place. But I hoped he would. "You're reestablishing our bond?"

He nods.

I don't ask why. Can't imagine he'd tell me anyway. "Here? Now?"

He glances around the room. "Do you have somewhere else in mind?"

"No." I glance at the sketch of Giorgios's mountain fortress I've been working on and rub the back of my neck, finding it clammy with perspiration. My pulse is racing double time. A fact he's no doubt aware of. "I just assumed ..."

"That I would seek out Axl or Malachi first?"

Or that you wouldn't seek us out at all. I don't dare voice that thought. "Yeah."

His only response is a harsh laugh I can't decipher. He walks toward me, and each step he takes sends another jolt up my spine. "You recall how this works, yes?"

I wipe my hands on my jeans and try to tamp down my excitement. It's embarrassing, the effect he has on me after all these years. "We share blood."

He nods, his dark eyes boring into my face.

I shift awkwardly on the chair, and the wood creaks under the uneven spread of my weight. "So you'll cut your tongue while you're feeding on me? Like you did the first time, and like we do with Ophelia?"

He rocks his head from side to side until his neck cracks. "Or you could bite me if you would prefer."

I grip the sides of the chair to prevent myself from falling off it. If I prefer? Fuck yeah, I prefer. Unconsciously, I lick my lips. I refuse to voice my desire to bite him.

He arches an eyebrow. "I can still read your mind, pup. Even without our bond."

Shit, I forgot to block him out of my thoughts, so unused to the need to do it around him. I clear my throat. "You've never allowed me to bite you before."

"Do you want to bite me, Xavier?"

I push my chair back and stand, coming face-to-face with him. His warm breath dusts over my forehead. "You know I do."

He tips his head to the side, exposing the skin at the base of his throat. His blood pulses in the thick vein there, making my fangs ache with hunger and desire. "So do it."

I sink my fingernails into my palms, searing deep grooves into my flesh, fearful of what I'll do if I put my hands on him—and what he'll subsequently do to me as a result. His masculine scent saturates my senses, and I lick my lips. A growl rolls in my chest.

I inch closer, and he doesn't move away, not even when I bring my face close to his neck and inhale, my nose skimming over his skin. His blood calls to me, and my mouth waters to taste him. He threads his fingers through my hair. "You should definitely make this count, pup."

His tone seems to carry a threat, but I don't care. I'm already drooling with the mere anticipation of tasting him. My fangs graze his skin, and he hisses out a breath, tipping his head back farther like he's daring me to take a bite. And how I fucking want to. I've thought about this very moment frequently for over two hundred years but never dared to imagine it would become a reality. Because Alexandros Drakos does not let his sireds bite him. He sure as fuck doesn't let his least favorite one do it.

But here we are. I close my eyes, focusing on my senses of smell and taste and allowing him to overwhelm me. My fangs throb with their own pulse. And when I sink them into his delicious flesh, there's the most satisfying pop of my teeth puncturing his skin before his rich, coppery blood floods my mouth, coating my tongue, my gums, my teeth. I suck greedily, and his

CHAPTER TWENTY-FOUR

power flows through my veins, viral and potent and life-affirming. His short fingernails dig into my scalp, and he groans. He fucking groans—a sound full of pleasure and desire—like he's enjoying this as much as I am. Even though that's impossible because this is fucking *everything*.

Unable to keep my hands to myself a second longer, I palm the back of his neck, pressing his flesh into my hungry mouth. I suck harder, feeling feral. Unrestrained. Powerful and powerless at the same time.

Then his solid hands are on my chest, and he shoves me. I stagger back, his blood dripping from my mouth. I take a few more steps backward, licking him from my lips, before my back hits the wall. The look on his face is nothing short of murderous, and my heart beats double time in my chest as he glares at me. "My turn, pup," he says in a low, menacing growl.

Tension crackles in the air between us, and if I didn't know better, I'd say there was nothing dangerous about his intentions at all. But ... the look on his face can't be what I think it is. I desperately wish our bond was present so I could read him a little easier, but he needs to be the one to cement it back in place. He unbuttons his shirt, revealing his toned torso inch by delicious fucking inch and sending endorphins hurtling through me. "You were so convinced I treat you differently from the other boys, Xavier?"

I swallow, my muscles rigid as the power in his blood races furiously through my veins. Afraid to move in case he stops doing whatever it is he seems to intent on doing. He doesn't give me a chance to answer, not that my mouth is capable of forming a word right now. "And on some level, I suppose you would be right."

I knew it!

His eyes shimmer with something I don't recognize. Or perhaps I recognize it all too well, but I'm too afraid to admit it.

Afraid I'm wrong because it might break me if I've misread what this is. "Because you *are* different."

He tugs his shirt off and lets it drop to the floor as he takes another step toward me. The air is hypercharged, thick with pulsing energy and sexual tension. The fuck I'm wrong about this. Even if he denies it afterward, I know he wants me as much as I want him. He's fucking stalking me, and I'm his willing prey, ready to offer up my throat and whatever else he asks for as soon as he says the word.

I lick my lips and stifle a groan as his taste floods my mouth again. It helps me find my voice at last. "Different how?"

He runs the tip of his tongue across his fangs. "Many vampires feed from and fuck the ones they sire, but I ..." He shakes his head. "I suppose I wanted to try to recreate the family I once had." His hands drop to his belt, and my eyes follow, watching intently while he unbuckles it. He opens his pants, and my dick almost explodes in my boxers.

My mouth waters to taste him again, my synapses misfiring with each move he makes. This has to be a dream, right? Alexandros's pants slide down his muscular thighs, and he steps out of them and stands in front of me, his body barely an inch from my own. Motherfuck. He's as hard as I am.

He slides his hand to the back of my neck and grips it possessively. "But I see now how foolish an endeavor that was. You are not my son." He drags his nose along my throat, and I'm filled with nothing but hot, aching need. "But you are most assuredly *mine*. You will always be mine."

He presses our chests together, and blistering heat sears my skin. His eyes are almost black as he bares his fangs and drops his mouth to my throat, and I wait in breathless anticipation as the moment seems to go on forever. A moment I have waited over two centuries for.

His hot breath dances tauntingly over my skin. "Two

hundred and three years, and I can still recall the taste of your blood, Xavier. So tantalizingly delicious."

He yanks my head back, exposing the full length of my neck, before his fangs pierce my skin. My entire body is overwhelmed with white-hot euphoria, and my already-stiff cock aches painfully. He sucks greedily, hand still firmly gripping the nape of my neck. My knees buckle, but his hold stops me from falling. Pleasure and pain and intoxicating ecstasy rage inside me. And I recall with excruciating agony the first and only other time he bit me so very long ago. The memory of how much he wanted me stings even as it ignites a fire deep in my core. His desire for me matched mine for him, and I now realize that this cruel bastard made me forget afterward.

I place my hands on his chest and push him away, but there's no intent in my actions, and he doesn't move an inch.

Stop fighting me, he commands through our bond, sinking his fangs deeper into my neck and sucking so hard my eyes roll back in my head.

Tears leak from my eyes. *You're back.*

I never left you, Xavier.

But you made me forget. Why?

Because it was easier for me.

I tangle my fingers in his hair and groan, succumbing to the ecstasy that washes over me, threatening to pull me under. I have so many more questions, but I can't think about anything except his mouth on me. And then his free hand dips inside my boxers, and I lose all sense of rational thought. He cups my balls and squeezes hard enough that electric heat sears the base of my spine.

"Oh, fuck!" I groan.

His hand slides to the base of my shaft, and he glides it up and down, working me slowly and firmly while he feeds on me until I'm fucking whimpering with desperation. But I don't give a single fuck. I would drop to my knees and beg him for a taste of what he's offering right now. Our bond is already firmly back in place, so I know for certain this is no longer about that. It's about me and him. It's him choosing me. A sob ricochets through my chest. He stops feeding and looks into my eyes. Then he presses his forehead against mine. "I chose you the moment I saw you, Xavier. And I will *always* choose you."

He swipes the pad of his thumb over the head of my cock, smearing me with my own precum, and my entire body trembles. "So unusually quiet this morning, pup." He licks my blood from his lips and flashes me a wicked grin.

I open my mouth, but when he grinds his hard length against me, I bite down on my lip so hard I draw blood. "I want to taste you."

"You just did," he taunts.

"I mean—"

"I know what you mean." He takes a step back and pulls down his boxers to reveal his thick length, the slit weeping with precum. I'm pretty sure I'm drooling. "So what are you waiting for?"

I sink to my knees with his hand still on the back of my neck. Gliding my palms up his powerful thighs, I flick my tongue over his crown, causing a moan to pour out of him, and it's one of the most erotic sounds I've ever heard in my life. His thick fingers thread through my hair, and he holds me still while he drives his cock into my open, waiting mouth. Saliva collects on my tongue and drips down my chin and onto my chest. When I glance up at him, he's watching me with a look of such pure devotion on his face that only makes me want to please him more. In this moment, nothing matters but the two of us.

"That is my good boy. Open your throat nice and wide for me."

CHAPTER TWENTY-FOUR

Sweet motherfucker. I have no idea how to do that, but I allow him to sink deeper, straight past my gag reflex and deep into my throat until I'm choking on his length and tears are rolling down my cheeks. But I grab onto the backs of his thighs and pull him closer, wanting more of him. Wanting everything he can give me. And he gives me all of it. The grunts and groans I wring from his perfect body have my own cock aching with the need for release.

Before I can bring him to climax, he pulls my head back and stares down at me, his chest heaving. He rubs his thumb across my chin, wiping away the saliva still dripping from my lips. "Such a mess you have made, Xavier."

I flash him a smirk. "I haven't finished yet."

He arches one eyebrow. "Neither have I."

I swallow the nervous anticipation lodged in my throat.

"Stand up and turn around." His voice is deeper than usual. Feral. Animalistic. Goosebumps break out across my entire body.

I do as he asks and face the wall. Before I can take a breath, he's taken off my jeans and boxers, and his hard chest is pressed against my back, sandwiching me between his hot body and the cool wall. He runs his nose up the back of my neck, inhaling deeply. His cock twitches against my ass. "I have waited so very long for this."

His growl has me desperate and panting. "So have I."

He kisses the spot right under my ear. It's soft and gentle and so at odds with the way he just fucked my throat. So at odds with the man he is. "I know you have, pup." His hand slides to the front of my throat, and he tips my head back. "I am desperate to fuck you."

I hiss out a breath. "Then do it."

He laughs, and his breath on my hot skin makes me shiver. "It is a good thing you made such a sloppy mess of my cock."

"I don't care. I don't need lube."

His dark laugh rings in my ear. "You would take me any way you could get me, would you not?"

"Yeah," I grit out. Desperate to feel him inside me, I grind myself on him, and he growls. It's full of warning and a promise of what's to come, and it does nothing to sate this burning need inside me. Instead, it only stokes my desire further. "Please?"

"So sweet to hear you beg, Xavier. But it is beneath you." He tips my head back farther and licks a path from the base of my neck to my jawline before he bites me again.

Relief and euphoria hurtle through me again. My nails scrape down the walls, taking off chunks of paint as I moan and writhe against him. He kicks at my ankles, spreading my legs wider apart before he presses the crown of his cock at my ass. I inhale a deep breath, preparing for the burning pleasure of him finally taking me. And when he sinks his thick cock inside me, my eyes roll so far back in my head that white spots flicker in my vision. He sucks on my neck and fucks me against the wall, relentless and ruthless, and it is everything I've ever wanted from him.

I press my forehead to the cool plaster as I gasp for breath, reveling in the dominance of his body over mine. Willingly accepting every inch of him, every single part of him while he sucks my neck and fucks my ass like he might never stop. I wouldn't care if he drank me dry. It would be worth it for this moment. For this part of him.

When my head is spinning violently and my whole body is shuddering with my impending climax, he slows his thrusts, and his greedy feasting of my blood becomes a gentle suckling, which makes a whole different kind of ecstasy flow through me. I drop my head back against his shoulder, and he bands both his arms around me, locking me in his embrace. Yeah, I could die right here and it would be worth it.

CHAPTER TWENTY-FOUR

But sweet Ophelia would miss you so, he says in my head, his voice tinged with a laugh.

I didn't mean to say that.

You have been saying a lot of things, pup.

Would you miss me? I ask without meaning to. It makes me sound weak and needy, and I fucking hate that.

He stops feeding and laughs out loud this time, his breath ruffling my hair. "Yes, I would miss you, Xavier. So I will not fuck you into the afterlife today." He presses his mouth against my skin again, and I feel him smile. "How about I just fuck you until you moan my name?"

I sag against him. "I'll scream your name if you want me to."

He coasts his hand down my abs and holds my cock in a tight grip. "Whatever you prefer is fine. But I want my name on your lips when you come for me."

"Fuck!"

He drives into me. "That is not my name, pup."

"Well, I'm not coming yet," I say, unable to resist pushing him a little.

He jacks me off and fucks me to the same deliciously torturous pace, keeping me on the precipice of ecstasy for so long that the need to come feels like a thousand shards of silver piercing my skin. And when I feel him teetering on the edge alongside me, he sinks his fangs into my skin once more, and we both fall over the cliff together.

"Alexandros!" It comes out somewhere between a roar and moan.

Good boy is the last thing I hear before everything goes black.

CHAPTER
TWENTY-FIVE
ALEXANDROS

Xavier slumps against me, his eyelids fluttering, and I pick him up and carry him to the bed. My eyes roam his perfectly toned body. I was a fool waiting so long for this. More so for making him think he was the problem when my desire for him made me keep him at arm's length, albeit unconsciously. That my coldness toward him contributed to the way he has underestimated himself all these years does not escape me.

The removal of our bond once again allowed me to truly see him for who he is—the same strikingly beautiful, addictively charismatic young man I first encountered so many years ago. The one who burned with shame because of his father's cruelty to him. I took great pleasure in breaking every bone in that old man's body before drinking him dry. But my desire for his son, which I kept buried for so long, came rushing back to me as soon as I saw him again yesterday.

"Sir?" Xavier's voice cracks as he blinks up at me, questioning whether what happened was real or imagined. He is a paradox. Powerful and vulnerable. Confident yet so unsure of

CHAPTER TWENTY-FIVE

himself. I saw all of that and more in him over two hundred years ago, and it still captivates me now.

I sit on the bed beside him and run the pad of my thumb across his full lips. "Yes, I just fucked you, pup."

His throat works as he swallows, his blue eyes narrowed in uncertainty. I have not been the sire he deserves. Nor the man. "It was ..." He licks his lips and does not finish the sentence.

I crawl over him and press him down with the weight of my body. A groan pours out of him. Running my nose along the thick column of his throat, I inhale deeply, and his unique scent floods my senses. "It was what?"

He sucks in a ragged breath, his fingers skating up my spine until they find my hair. But his movements are cautious and unsure, and I suppose that is to be expected given our history. "Incredible." He closes his eyes, as if embarrassed by his admission.

"I agree, Xavier."

His eyes snap open, and the spark of hope that flares bright in his chest lights me up too. "You do?"

"Did I not fuck you as well as you have ever been fucked in your life?"

The corners of his lips twitch. "Yeah."

I grind myself against him, my cock already stiffening at the sensation of his skin against mine. "And you think I did not enjoy it as much as you did? I am almost hard again, and that is all for you."

His eyes shine with unshed tears. "Why did you shut me out? You made me feel like I was nothing."

A growl of frustration rumbles in my chest, but it is aimed at my own shortcomings, not at him. I rest my forehead against his and speak through our bond. *It was easier for me to ignore this side of myself with you, Xavier. And for that, I am sorry.*

"You could have ... Just once, you could have—"

I cut him off by sealing my lips over his. My tongue slides into his mouth with no resistance, and I devour him. Sinking deeper, I take everything he has and give him all he desires. Everything he deserves. Pouring into him all the things I should have told him but never had the courage to. His hands are no longer cautious as they rake through my hair and down my back, fingers kneading my muscles. Loud, guttural moans bubble up into his throat, and I swallow them whole.

Sir, he says through our bond. *Please don't do this if you're not ...* His chest heaves with a strangled sob, and it is enough to force me to tear my mouth from his.

I do not need to ask him what he was going to say, nor do I need to read his mind. It is written clearly on his face—the fear that I am going to use him and toss him aside. Or even worse, make him forget. I brush his cheek with my knuckles. "I told you, Xavier, that you are mine. Always. I will not ever take this from you. From us. I give you my word."

His hand fists in my hair, and he pulls me back to him, but before I resume our kiss, I dust my lips along his jawline, teasing him until he moans my name.

"You are so beautifully delicious," I murmur, my lips trailing his collarbone as my fangs ache with the need to taste him again. His carotid artery pulses beneath his skin, his blood flowing so tantalizingly close to my mouth. Using my knees, I spread his thighs apart. After settling between them, I notch the head of my cock at his ass. I want to sink inside him again so badly my body aches.

He grunts. "Do it."

I let out a dark laugh. "You want me inside you again, pup?"

He bucks his hips, and his hard length digs into my abdomen. "Yeah. Please!"

Teasing him is delicious torture, for I know the sweet relief

CHAPTER TWENTY-FIVE

that awaits me as soon as I decide to take it. "I have told you not to beg, Xavier. It does not become you."

"So stop teasing me and fuck me already," he says, groaning.

I relent and grant him his wish, and my fangs pierce the tender flesh of his throat at the same time I drive inside him.

"Fuck!" He grits out the word, his arms banded around my back as he bears down on me. His warmth envelopes me as I feed and fuck and take what I have been denying myself for far too long.

Please don't stop. His pained plea rings out inside my head.

I have no intention of stopping, pup. Not until you are a trembling mess and unable to walk.

I feel him smile, his hand sliding up my back until he is gripping my hair. *Are you sure about that, old man?*

His impudence would draw my ire in any other circumstance, but here, with my cock and my fangs buried inside him, it simply fuels the flames of my desire for him. I do slow my thrusts a little, and he whines.

I would make you regret that. Except I am sure the only thing that could make you feel such a way would be for me to stop, and we have already established that is not going to happen.

"Then I guess you'd better prove it."

I rip my teeth from his neck and lick the residue of his coppery blood from my lips. "I intend to."

∽

A SOFT TAPPING comes from the other side of the door, and I already know it is Ophelia before I call out for her to enter. "You do not have to knock."

She gives me a shy smile. "I just wanted to make sure you were both ..." She presses her lips together. "Uh ... done."

ALEXANDROS

I sometimes forget the strange notions humans have about sex. She is perfectly aware and accepting of the boys being together, but is this different for her? As possessive as I am when it comes to her, that does not extend to my boys, and I assumed the same would be true for her. But perhaps I should have spoken with her beforehand. "How much did you feel?"

Her cheeks flush the brightest shade of pink. "All of it."

Xavier opens one eye. "You should have joined us, Cupcake."

She bites on her lip and makes her way to the bed. "I didn't want to interrupt. Bonding is special. Intimate, right?"

I grab her wrist and pull her to lie between us. She squeals, snuggling between our bodies. "Yes it is, little one." I run my nose over her hair. "And I am desperate to bond with you again."

"I'm desperate too. Six more days, right? And then you can bite me all over?"

Sweet demons of the netherworld. She lives to test my willpower. "Six very long and torturous days."

"I can't wait to taste you again, Cupcake," Xavier says with a groan. "No blood is as sweet as yours."

She rests her chin on her hands and flutters her eyelashes. "That's sure good to know."

I catch his eye over the top of her head. "There are other parts of your little cupcake that are almost as sweet as her blood, Xavier."

He smirks. "You know, I believe you're right, Professor."

She squeaks. "I haven't showered yet today."

Xavier tips his face to the ceiling, his plump lower lip caught between his teeth, and groans. "Fuck me, Cupcake. That means you're full of Alexandros's cum too. Is that supposed to make me want to eat you less?"

CHAPTER TWENTY-FIVE

She presses her lips together and covers her eyes. "Axl's too," she whispers.

Xavier gasps, faking shock. "You are a naughty cupcake." He smacks her ass, and she squeals with delight.

I have an idea, I tell Xavier.

His eyes flash wickedly. *I'm in.*

I run my thumb over Ophelia's soft lips. "I have not kissed you nearly enough since we were reunited, Ophelia."

"I agree," she murmurs, staring at me with love and lust shining in her eyes.

I hum whilst using the bond to tell Xavier to lie between my thighs so I can maneuver her into the right place. Before she can make another sound, I quickly remove her T-shirt and panties, and then I dust my mouth over hers. "So I think I am going to kiss these beautiful lips." I lift her to straddle the both of us, with her knees on either side of my waist and her pussy directly over Xavier's mouth. "While Xavier kisses these ones." I swipe a finger through her slick heat.

The skin on her neck is bright pink now too. Her heart beats faster in her chest, and the scent of her arousal has my cock digging into the ridge of muscle between Xavier's shoulder blades.

"Sit down, Cupcake," Xavier orders.

She lowers herself enough that he can swipe his tongue over her flesh. Her eyes roll back as, to my amusement, he growls his frustration. "Sit, Ophelia. Do not squat. Do not hover. I am a vampire. I cannot suffocate—and even if I could, it would be a price worth paying. So sit your sweet fucking cunt all the way down on my face right now."

She looks at me, her expression caught between hesitation and wanton desire. "I can think of few more pleasant ways to pass the time than having my face buried in your sweet pussy, agápi mou. Do as he says."

She gives a jerky nod and drops her full weight. His resulting groan is so dramatic that I am unable to suppress my laugh.

As his tongue flicks out and he begins to work her over, I take her mouth with mine, swallowing her moans and whimpers as he brings her to the edge of ecstasy. Being the benevolent and helpful sire I am, I assist him as much as I am able. I palm her beautiful breasts and tease her hard nipples whilst exploring the recesses of her mouth and savoring the taste of her that I have so deeply missed. Xavier is right—she does taste like cupcakes. Sweet and tempting and too delicious to resist. So we do not hold back, both of us devouring her, taking all we can.

CHAPTER
TWENTY-SIX
MALACHI

Standing in front of the open fridge, I'm impressed at the vast array of groceries Axl managed to source for us earlier today. The shelves are practically groaning under the weight of thick-cut steaks, racks of fresh lamb, gallons of milk and juice, and a couple dozen eggs. There are enough fresh fruits and vegetables to keep our girl's energy up for days, not to mention an array of sweet treats and pastries stacked on the counter. From the smirk on his face when I asked him how he managed to get all this stuff with no money, I figure he bit the store clerk and left them in a bite-induced state of euphoria as he took what he wanted.

We have no idea how long we'll need to stay, but at least we can keep Ophelia well-nourished while we're here. Tonight, I am going to cook up a feast. After all the toe-curlingly awkward and unpleasant dinners we've been subjected to over the past few weeks, we deserve to sit down and enjoy a meal together. I still don't know much about what the professor has been through, but I'm sure he will appreciate a nice slice of normal.

"Do we have coffee, Malachi?" Alexandros asks, and I spin

around to see him sitting at the kitchen table. With him bare-chested in the bright light streaming in through the window, I get my first good look at his body. His shoulder and the tops of his arms are lined with thick red welts. How much must they have hurt for the marks to still be seared on his skin now?

"They do not hurt. Ophelia has healed them well." He peers over his shoulder at his back. "I suspect most of them will not even scar."

"I forgot you can still read my mind, even without our bond. Well, I didn't forget, so much as … You never used to read our minds very often before."

He rests his chin on his clasped hands. "And I did not just now. Your eyes were drawn to the marks on my body, and your sadness and guilt were too acute for me to miss."

Of course he read my emotions and not my thoughts. And I know he would hate my pity, although that's not what I'm feeling. Still, I change the subject. "You want coffee? I'm sure I saw some in the pantry."

He hums softly, that sound he makes when he's deep in thought, but not in a bad way. Humming means good thinking. "Actually, it can wait. There is something much more important to take care of."

My curiosity is piqued. More important than coffee? "And what's that?"

"Come here." His tone is low and commanding, and if not for the fact that he appears more serene than I recall ever seeing him, I would be convinced I'm in some kind of trouble.

I obey him without question, and he spins on his stool so when I reach him, I'm standing in front of him. "Closer," he orders.

I step between his spread thighs, and the sides of my bare knees brush against the linen pants he's wearing. He must have

CHAPTER TWENTY-SIX

rustled them up from one of the closets. My heart is hammering against my ribcage, and adrenaline courses through my veins. He's going to put our bond back in place, and I'm excited and nervous in a way I'm not used to. So much so, my entire body is trembling in anticipation.

"A kitchen is not the ideal place for this. Would you like to go somewhere more private?"

I shake my head, eager to get this done with so we can get back to the way we were before. I'm not entirely myself when he's not a part of me. Our bond was—no, *is* a huge part of who I am. Without it, I am somehow less whole. "Here is good."

His lips curve into a smile. "You are always so sure of me, Malachi." He traces a fingertip over the pulse in my neck. "The most sensitive soul I have ever turned."

My instinctive growl surprises me, but it makes his smile grow wider. "That is not the insult you believe it to be. My daughter Alyria was sweet and sensitive too. She loved horses. Would rather spend time with them than most people she knew. I saw her in you the day I found you."

Sadness and shame form a thick knot in my throat. I had my service revolver and one bullet with me, and I rode out of town on Mabel, my beloved mare, intending to go to the woods where there would be nobody to stop me from taking my own life. Plagued by memories of my fallen comrades being blown to pieces, of the pleas in their dying eyes as they clung to me, I couldn't stand to live a day longer. Until Mabel stepped in a hole and broke her leg.

Her pained whinnies as she lay on the ground tore a hole in my heart, and I couldn't bear to leave her to suffer. So I offered her all I had left to give—my single bullet. When he found me, I was weeping over her still-warm corpse.

"That is nothing to feel ashamed of, Malachi." His voice is

gentle and soothing, and I close my eyes, letting it wash over me. "Horses are loyal creatures. They have served man, vampire, witch, and demon for as long as anyone can recall. Perhaps she gave her life so that I might find you."

That thought brings me comfort. "So you could save me?"

He skims my throat with his fangs, and a shiver runs down my spine. "Or perhaps so that you could save me."

Before I can ask him what he means, his teeth pierce my skin and I'm hit by a blinding, breath-stealing wave of pure ecstasy. My knees buckle, but he holds me up, enveloped in his tight embrace. I wrap my arms around his shoulders and cling to him. I'm lost to the whole moment, aware that I'm whimpering like a puppy but unable to care. And right as the euphoria hits its peak, then comes the lightning. Raw and powerful, it races through my bloodstream, lighting me up from the inside. And I feel invincible. A wolf instead of a puppy now, I tip my head back and roar his name.

Yes, Malachi. Take back what is yours. His voice resounds within my head, and I sag in his arms, relief and the last flickering embers of ecstasy fizzling through me.

When he's done feeding, he gently suckles the wound on my neck until it's fully healed.

I missed you so much, I tell him.

He cradles me in his arms, the same way he did he when he found me over a century ago. *I missed you too. More than you will ever know.*

After I open my eyes, I find the strength to stand on my own two feet again. "What did you mean before, about me saving you?"

His eyes narrow, and he brushes the backs of his knuckles over my cheek. "I always loved Xavier and Axl in my own way, Malachi. But it was not until I found and turned you, a boy who sacrificed the only thing he had to end the suffering of his

CHAPTER TWENTY-SIX

beloved horse, that I was able to recall that such pure selflessness exists in this world. You allowed that part of my heart to beat again, Malachi. Even if it did not beat with the strength it should, it was you who reminded me it was still there. You are one of the most incredible souls I have ever known, and I thank all the stars in the universe and all the demons in the netherworld that I found you."

Fuck, I'm gonna cry. In fact, I already am. He brushes away the tear that drips down my cheek.

"Shit!" Xavier's voice is a welcome reprieve from the intensity of the moment. "I'm sorry, I didn't mean to interrupt. I was—"

"It is okay, Xavier. Malachi and I have recemented our bond."

Xavier flashes me a smile that makes his blue eyes sparkle. "Yeah?"

I mirror his grin and step out of the professor's embrace. "Yeah. Get over here."

He saunters over, flicking his dark hair out of his eyes, and wraps me in a bear hug. He smells of sex and Ophelia. And Alexandros. A slightly surprising, if not entirely unexpected, development. The sexual tension between those two had to give at some point.

Xavier slides his hand into my boxers and squeezes my ass hard as he trails his lips over my neck. Goosebumps skitter along my forearms, and I groan. He's such a fucking tease.

Alexandros pushes back his stool. "Do either of you know where Axl is?"

I shake my head. "Haven't seen him since he dropped the groceries off a little while ago."

Hey, bro, where are you? Xavier asks. *Alexandros is looking for you.*

Out is his clipped reply.

MALACHI

My gaze locks with Xavier's, and I groan inwardly. Can we not all play nicely for a single day? Half a day even?

Xavier rolls his eyes. *Out where, numbnuts?*

Just out. If he wants me bad enough, he can come find me.

I narrow my eyes at Xavier. *Don't repeat that.*

"You do know I can hear the two of you, yes?" Alexandros claps us both on the back. "And even if I cannot hear Axl, I can guess his reply. I will find him. Go and take care of Ophelia."

Well, that's an order he doesn't have to give me twice. I've been desperate to take care of her since we got here last night. It's been far too long since I've tasted her. Fucked her. Felt her soft lips around my—

"Enjoy yourselves, boys, but remain alert at all times." Alexandros's warning stops my train of thought. "Anikêtos and Elpis will need to replenish their energy stores at some point today and will not always be here to guard the house. And whilst my mind is sharp enough to detect intruders before they arrive, Giorgios has fooled me before."

Yes sir, we reply in unison.

As soon as he's gone, Xavier pushes me back against the counter and trails his hands down my abs. "Being bonded to the professor again makes you look so fucking hot, Kai."

"I was already hot," I remind him.

He chuckles wickedly. "Yeah, you were. But I really fucking want you."

I arch an eyebrow at him. I want him too, but I enjoy pushing his buttons a little. "Have you not had your fill already today?"

He shakes his head, a wicked grin spreading across his face. "Not nearly enough. I'm hornier than a fucking mountain goat."

"And exactly how horny are mountain goats?"

"No idea." He shrugs. "Not as horny as me."

Laughing, I grab the back of his neck and pull his face to

CHAPTER TWENTY-SIX

mine so I can capture his lips in a bruising kiss. There's something about Alexandros's bite that has me all fired up too, and I can think of no better way to sate this thirst than with Xavier and Ophelia. An image of him fucking me while I'm inside her pops into my brain. It is so fucking good to be back.

CHAPTER TWENTY-SEVEN
AXL

I flex my toes in the velvety sand as the heat of the late afternoon sun warms my back. Elpis circles overhead, and I watch her, mesmerized. I'm still awestruck over the fact that such majestic creatures exist and that the majority of people on this earth can't see them. Certainly none of the people in the towns below can; otherwise, I'm certain we would have hordes of curious villagers descending upon the house.

"I never figured you as someone who would enjoy the beach, Axl." His voice startles me, and I spin around. It's been over an hour since Xavier told me he was looking for me. I think I've walked the entire length of beach and back in that time.

"I like the sound of the ocean."

He hums softly before he sits down. "How did all those vampire legends get our relationship with sunshine so wrong? I can barely get a tan, let alone burst into flames."

His attempt at humor is very unlike him, and it makes me uneasy. Still, when he pats the space beside him, I take a seat in the sand next to him without hesitation.

"You are aware I have resecured the bond with Xavier and Malachi, yes?"

CHAPTER TWENTY-SEVEN

I nod, avoiding his scrutinous gaze.

"And you have been eluding me since."

I stare out across the ocean, the sheer vastness of it making me feel incredibly small and insignificant. "Have I?"

"I will not dignify that with an answer, for you already know it. Do you not wish to bond again?"

I turn and face him now but find no clue in his expression as to what's on his mind. I wish I could read him more easily, but he's consistently closed off to us. I always thought I was special somehow, being the first vampire he turned in over a millennium. Perhaps I was wrong. "Do I get a choice?"

His right eyelid twitches. "I am afraid you do not."

His response is unexpected, hitting me like a punch to the gut and knocking the breath from my lungs. I wish I could hide my reaction from him, but bond or not, there's nothing I can keep from him. "I don't?"

"You seem surprised by my response, Axl. Did you think I would not want to bond with you again? That I would allow you the freedom to leave our family unit?"

"I would never leave," I insist. How can he even suggest such a thing? The mere thought of it flays me.

He tilts his head. "Well, of course you would never leave Ophelia."

Is that what he thinks? "I would never leave any of you." I ball my hands into fists and grind them into the sand. Anger simmers beneath my skin, and I have no idea why this conversation is eliciting such strong emotion. Better yet, why didn't I simply tell him the truth—that of course I want to bond again? Fear that he wouldn't want to has been tearing me apart since we got here last night. So what the hell is stopping me from being honest with him?

"If you would never leave, why do you want a choice?"

Tears burn my eyes, and I blink them away. "I don't."

"Then tell me why you asked for one."

I clench my jaw tight and turn back to the ocean. Each wave deposits a white foam residue on the shore, leaving behind the parts of itself it no longer wants.

But Alexandros keeps on. He knows I won't be able to avoid answering for much longer. It's a particular skill he has. I've seen him use it in the classroom too. A gentle interrogation that always gets to the root of the truth, even if the person being interrogated didn't realize what that truth was before he dug it out. "Why did you not simply ask me what you wanted to know instead?"

I grind my teeth. "And what is it you think I want to know, Alexandros?"

He holds up a handful of sand and allows it to run through his spread fingers. The silence seems to stretch between us for an eternity before he answers me. Perhaps he's hoping I will find the answer myself, but even if I know it, I'm not sure I can put it into words. "You wish to know why I did not come to you first. And if by not doing so, it means I favor you less now than I did before."

I growl, angry that he's so easily able to verbalize what I'm feeling when I can't.

He sighs, following my gaze out toward the horizon. "I still recall the first day I saw you. Sitting on a bench in the park, staring at the water, much like you are now. So handsome and confident in your finery. Catching the eye of every pretty maid who walked by and so sure of his prowess that no one would dare believe him anything less than a man with the world at his feet. Yet those who cared to look directly below the surface, as I did, would have seen a boy. One filled with sadness and self-doubt and a deep gnawing yearning to be *good enough*."

Some of that self-doubt creeps in right now; it churns in my gut and ignites a chain reaction of negative emotion that swells

CHAPTER TWENTY-SEVEN

inside me. I do my best not to let the memories of my past life take hold and drag me into their abyss.

"I suspected it was to do with your father, but I was not entirely sure. And then I met him, and ... Well, I do not need to remind you of the kind of man Alastair Thorne II was."

That abyss opens up into a soul-sucking chasm at the mention of his name. My old self calls to me, reminding me of my true nature. And I wonder whether we can ever truly escape the lives we were born into. The people we were born as—the ones that are inherent in our DNA.

Alexandros places his hand on the back of my neck and squeezes possessively, and it anchors me back to the present. "I chose you because you reminded me of my daughter Imogen. She was a beautiful, spirited soul, much like you. Your heart had been hardened by a cruel world by the time you and I met, but your humanity has always been what draws me to you. Your passion and your resilience." He turns my head and presses our foreheads together. "You have always been good enough, Axl Thorne. Much too good for your father. But more than good enough for everyone else. For your brothers. Xavier, Malachi, and Frederik. For Ophelia. For me."

"I have?" Tears run down my cheeks, and I cannot recall the last time I cried openly in front of him.

"Yes, you have and you are. I cannot choose between the three of you, and I never will. You are all a part of me in different ways, and without each of you, I am decidedly less. So no, you do not have a choice, Axl Thorne. You already belong to me, and I will never let you go."

I suck in a shaky breath. The memory of being turned creeps up on me unexpectedly, reminding me of the agony I endured to become what I am.

"It was changing that hurt. The bond will not," he says

softly. "Without the agony of the turning to endure, you will no doubt enjoy it."

He straddles me and pulls me into his arms, and the heat from his skin burns against my flesh. He rubs his nose over my throat, and I close my eyes, listening to the gentle sound of the waves caressing the sand. I feel nothing but euphoria when he sinks his fangs into my throat. My blood hurtles to the spot where his mouth greedily suckles, and pleasure ignites in every cell of my body. I tip my head back, my mouth open on a moan when he presses his wrist to my lips, and I act only on instinct, sinking my teeth in and letting his thick, metallic blood coat my teeth and tongue. And then I feel so much more than the pleasure of bonding.

I feel power. His power. He may be less without us, but that is surely true of us without him. I forgot the feeling of invincibility that comes along with his blood. My strength is derived from him. It was not only the blue poppy that made us weaker.

There is my boy. His deep voice washes over me, and I seem to melt bonelessly into the sand, so relieved to have our bond back in place.

It's so good to have you back.

He hums while he goes on feeding. *It is good to be back. I have missed you.*

I've missed you too. It was quiet without you in my head.

He stops feeding and laughs. "Even with Xavier, Malachi, and Ophelia inside there? Surely there is never a quiet moment in any of our heads."

"It's different with you. Like you're always there even if you're not talking."

He presses a chaste kiss on my forehead. "I will do everything in my power to never leave you again."

He jumps up and brushes the sand from his pants before holding his hand out to me. I take it and allow him to pull me

CHAPTER TWENTY-SEVEN

up. I can't help but feel there's something different between us now. Good different.

"So there's only Ophelia left for you to bond with again?"

He tilts his face to the sky and groans. "I am sorely tempted to bite her right now. Blue poppy be damned." He starts to walk back to the house, and I fall into step beside him.

"So why don't you? We're back to full strength now. Elpis and Anikêtos are here. It may weaken you a little, but surely Ophelia's blood is worth the risk."

"Believe me, I have thought the same thing many times in the past twenty hours. But we do not know how long Ani and Elpis will stay. And we do not know what tomorrow brings, Axl. There is nothing worth risking her safety for. Each of us must be at full strength. To purposely weaken myself, no matter how enjoyable it would be, would be dangerous and foolhardy."

"I guess you have a point."

"You are aware what passed between Xavier and me earlier?"

I felt it through him, even though I suspect he tried to block us out. Despite how strong his mind is now, Xavier couldn't mask the strength of his emotion. Which I suppose is unsurprising given how he's craved that kind of connection with our sire for so long. "Yeah, I know. He's ... He's wanted that for a long time."

Alexandros sucks on his top lip and hums. "I am aware."

"Is that why you and he ... Because he wanted to?" I already know the answer. As a rule, Alexandros doesn't do things he doesn't want to do.

"I have wanted it too, Axl. I turned you each for different reasons, even if I were not prepared to admit it until now. You and Malachi have always been like sons to me. Yet with Xavier, from the moment I met him, I experienced a strong desire for him. But you wanted a brother, and I wanted a family, and I thought I could treat you both the same. I was foolish. I caused him a great deal of pain by not admitting the truth a long time ago."

"I always told him he was crazy for thinking you treated him differently, but I guess deep down I knew you did." The realization settles over me, making me feel guilty for all the times I brushed off Xavier's concerns and dismissed his feelings as jealousy.

Alexandros rests a comforting hand on my shoulder. "I am the only person who should feel any guilt over my actions, Axl. And I have a lifetime to make it up to him, do I not?"

"Yeah. Although I wouldn't tell him that, or he'll hold you to it, you know?" It feels good to laugh after the tumultuous month we've all had.

He raises his eyebrows. "I am aware of that also."

We keep walking in silence for a few moments before he speaks again. "And how do you feel about the change in my relationship with Xavier?"

I look out at the ocean while I consider my answer, feeling considerably more significant now than I did a few moments ago. "It changes nothing for me. It makes Xavier happy, and it's not like ... I've just never seen you that way though, you know?"

"I understand that."

Despite this ease between us now, there is still a niggling doubt in the back of my mind. "I do not know the answers where Lucian is concerned, Axl," he says, reading my thoughts.

"Giorgios told us he killed you. Why would he make us think that? It's not like we didn't already mistrust Lucian after what you told us he did. Although, he did help us out with the blue poppy. Ophelia was able to speak to him while we were in Tibet. So why the hell would he help us? None of it makes much sense at all."

CHAPTER TWENTY-SEVEN

"He also helped Ophelia in the cave," Alexandros says, frowning. "He was there when she arrived."

"He was? I knew we shouldn't have let her go alone." The idea of what might have happened to her is too much to consider after everything we've already been through. "She's never going anywhere alone ever again."

"While I agree with that sentiment, he caused her no harm. Nor did he cause any to me. We cannot be sure of his intentions at all. But it appears Giorgios has told you many lies. As for his or Lucian's motives, I am afraid I do not have the answers right now. But perhaps some can be found. I think it is time for us to discuss everything that has happened and try to make sense of this insanity."

"Malachi said he'd make dinner. I think Ophelia would like it if we all joined her. I got plenty of meat."

His smile is brief but genuine, and it reminds me how much we almost lost. How much we could still lose. We walk the rest of the way back to the house in silence, both of us deep in our own thoughts.

I understand so little of his old life. His old world, filled with dragons and oaths and prophecies. But whatever happens next, I'm all in.

CHAPTER
TWENTY-EIGHT
ALEXANDROS

Ophelia's smile is so bright I swear it could light up the entire night sky. Happiness radiates from her and from all my boys too as we sit around the dining table about to devour the feast Malachi prepared. Such an ordinary scene, and one so at odds with the turmoil that surrounds us. While we eat, we keep the conversation light and pleasant. Xavier's joy that the TV here has a sports channel, the surprising array of American foods at the grocery store, how the middle-aged store clerk watched Axl steal three bags full of groceries, staring at him like a lovestruck teenager thanks to the pleasurable bite he gave him. Whom out of Elpis and Anikêtos would be more likely to throw you off mid-flight and actually let you hit the ground if you had sex on their back.

But despite the pleasant food and atmosphere and the feelings of contentment that have settled over us all, there is only so long that we can indulge in this fantasy that our lives are in any way normal. Only so long we can avoid the very obvious topics of Giorgios, Lucian, and Ophelia's fate.

"What happened to you? That day?" I am surprised it is

CHAPTER TWENTY-EIGHT

Ophelia who broaches the subject first. "What did Giorgios do to you to sever our bond like that?"

I set down my fork, having little desire to sample the mashed potatoes Malachi made, as delicious as he and Ophelia seem to find them. I fight back the despair conjured by reliving that day. "Giorgios lured me to a cave, a place where my powers would no longer work, and thus I had no way to detect any danger."

She leans forward and rests her chin on her hands. "Like the cave in Peru?"

I shake my head. "No, this was done with powerful magic. A coven of witches cast a spell that prevented my powers from working. They chained me with silver and then an even more powerful witch cast an ancient spell which severed our bond." I grind my jaw.

"Giorgios told us it was Nazeel. He said she saved his life and because he owed her a debt, she forced him to betray you."

"Nazeel Danraath." My hands ball into fists, and I bare my fangs.

Ophelia gasps. "So it's true?"

My memories are clouded, cloaked in the pain of the silver and their betrayal, and I am not sure I fully trust them where Nazeel and Giorgios are concerned. I cannot be sure what is truth and what is falsehood. "It is true she once saved his life, and yes, she was certainly there. What else did he say of it?"

Ophelia's brow furrows like she is recalling the details, and Axl answers in the interim. "He said she wanted you dead. That the Order wanted you dead, but that he saved you."

"Saved me by chaining me with silver and leaving me to rot in a cage?" I lash out, unable to contain all of my rage. But it serves no purpose here, and I manage to rein in my temper once more.

Axl nods. "That's what he told us."

Malachi blinks at me, his mouth hanging open for a few seconds before he finds his voice. "Did she want you dead though? Or did the Order? Because they're not supposed to interfere, right?"

"They are not. But Nazeel has been involved in Ophelia's fate since the day she was born, and whilst I once believed her intentions were honorable, now I am not so sure."

"Not sure?" Xavier scoffs. "She severed our bond with you at best, tried to kill you at worst. Plus made us all think we were going to die, broke Ophelia's heart wide fucking open … And you're not sure her intentions are honorable? I'd say they are most definitely fucking not."

Do not think the recent change in our relationship allows you liberties regarding the tone you take with me, pup.

His throat works as he swallows, the thick vein pulsing with his blood, and he sits back in his chair, his chin dropping a little, but I do not miss the spike in his heart rate that has nothing to do with my chastisement. *Yes sir.*

I brush aside thoughts of disciplining him for his insolence. As pleasant as it is to imagine how hard I will fuck him whilst feeding from the vein at the nape of his neck, I could do without the distraction for the moment.

I clear my throat and refocus on the after-dinner conversation. "Nazeel left immediately after the ritual. It was Giorgios who transported me to my prison in Peru." I recall how I fought and struggled against him. But still chained in silver and weakened by the ritual, I was no match for him. Coward. "I recall now how he also told me that he was sparing my life and that the Order wanted me dead, but given the many lies he has told and the Order's history, I doubt either of those things were true. There were guards stationed outside my cage, but they refused to speak, and I believe I was in and out of consciousness for

CHAPTER TWENTY-EIGHT

many days before Ophelia freed me. Certainly I did not witness Lucian dispense with the guards."

"Lucian got rid of the guards?" Axl asks, surprised.

I look to Ophelia, for this is her part of the story, and she nods. "That's what he told me, and there were four headless vampire corpses in the cave. At least I assume they were vampires. So if he didn't kill them, who did?"

Malachi's green eyes narrow on her face. "Did he say why he was there? Why he killed the guards?"

She glances at me, and a tear runs down her cheek. "He said he was protecting you."

There is a place on a vampire's throat, directly below the Adam's apple, where if one receives a blow, it causes considerable pain and an inability to breathe for at least a few seconds. I have endured such an assault only twice in my long life, by vampires who were much stronger than I at the time, and it both hurt and affected my breathing less than Ophelia's words did.

He was protecting me?

In order to breathe again, I push all thoughts of him from my head and focus on her sadness instead, for it is much easier to deal with.

Another tear runs down her face. "I hate that you were there all alone. In the dark with no idea of ... of anything." She wipes her eyes.

I beckon her to me, and she pushes back her chair and walks around the table. As soon as she is close enough, I pull her onto my lap and wrap my arms around her. Whilst my time there was spent in more agony than I have experienced in my incredibly long life, I will never let her know that, for it would only cause her more pain. "Do not feel sad for me, little one. What I endured was nothing compared to your heartache. I knew I would see you all again."

She rests her head on my shoulder, and her hot tears fall onto my bare skin.

Axl is staring at me, his brow furrowed with concentration. "So you never saw Lucian that day when our bond was severed? Even though Giorgios told us it was him that killed you?"

I shake my head. "I have not seen Lucian in over five hundred years." I cup Ophelia's chin in my hand and tilt her head up. "You are the only one of us in this room to have seen him recently, are you not, agápi mou?"

She chews on her lip and nods.

"Did he say anything else in the cave, baby?" Malachi asks.

Ophelia explains what happened in Peru and how Lucian helped her focus on her powers. As I expected, this is met with a confusing mix of incredulity, disdain, and gratitude.

"But what I don't get is why didn't Giorgios just kill you." Xavier shakes his head. "Why keep you alive? If his goal was to sever your mate bond with Ophelia and—" He stops speaking and winces. "Hang on, you don't know about that yet, huh?"

I brush Ophelia's hair behind her ear and kiss her forehead. I have not yet had a chance to tell her that I read her mind whilst she slept, and I am not entirely sure how she will react. "I know almost everything that happened in Giorgios's fortress. The pertinent points at least. How he poisoned you all, the lies he tried to make you believe about me, his deceitful offer to bite Ophelia to ensure you would not die. And the ritual too." The rage I feel whenever I am forced to think about that particular plan is indescribable, burning through the muscles and sinew of my body until they feel like they will ignite. I roll my neck and grind my teeth.

Ophelia places a hand on my cheek, and it does more to calm me than my own efforts. "How do you know all of that?" she asks.

I stare into her bright-blue eyes and feel overcome with a

CHAPTER TWENTY-EIGHT

desire to simply take her and the boys and run far away from all of this. "I needed to know what happened to you all. What Giorgios did. And I did not wish for you to have to comb your memories to pick out and regurgitate every piece of information you felt might be useful. It was quicker and easier this way."

She blinks. "You read my mind? My memories?"

Regret and guilt cloud my thoughts now, mingling with the anger and making me feel like there is a dead weight on my chest. "I did, agápi mou."

Her lip trembles and tears run freely down her face. "I'm sorry. I didn't ... It was only ..."

"Ophelia." I stop her nervous babbling and wipe the tears from her cheeks. I am confused and more than a little fearful at what it is she thinks *she* needs to be sorry for. Was there something I did not see? Something I missed? Something she hid from me? "What on earth are you sorry for, little one?"

"I only thought about him biting me to save them. I did speak to the guys about it too because he told us it was the only way to save them. We agreed that none of us wanted to be bonded to him, and I never would have if—" She sucks in a breath and chokes back a sob at the same time, and the torrent of words finally stops pouring from her mouth.

I hold her tighter and, cupping her face with one hand, swipe the pad of my thumb over her lips, brushing away the tears that have collected there. "I did see that memory of you all discussing Giorgios's proposal, but the only thing it proved was your deep loyalty to me." I glance up at the boys, who are watching us intently. "All of you. And I am honored to have that from each and every one of you. So please, agápi mou, do not torture yourself a second longer for considering something that would have saved you all. Can I be selfish enough to ask you to forgive me for reading your mind without your knowledge?"

She gazes at me with eyes full of love and strokes her hand

over my cheek. "What is there to forgive? There's nothing in my head I wouldn't share with you, and you already know that. And I know you'd never read my mind unless you felt you had to."

I dust my lips over hers. She is far too gracious of my darkness, but I am thankful for her light. "No matter what happens, nothing in this universe would ever sever our mate bond, Ophelia. You have been mine and I yours since time began, and we will remain so until the end of days."

She sniffs, a soft smile playing on her lips.

"So, what do we do now? Find Lucian? Go after Giorgios?" Axl asks, reminding me there is still much to discuss. "Hide out here or go back to Montridge?"

"I believe finding Lucian can give us some of the answers we seek. He appears to know something of Giorgios's plans given that he was able to find me in Peru. I do not believe it is safe to return to Montridge yet, neither for us nor any of our allies there."

Xavier nods, running a hand through his thick dark hair. "I agree. It's the first place Giorgios will think to look."

I suck in a deep breath and pinch the bridge of my nose to try to stave off the throbbing ache directly between my eyes. "And as for Giorgios, whilst I would never have breached his trust by reading his mind, I believed he was as guileless as he seemed, but he was able to deceive me. That is of grave concern. I should have been able to pick up on some clue to his betrayal, yet I did not. Perhaps I was blinded by my loyalty to him, or perhaps his powers of the mind are much stronger than I ever knew."

Ophelia shifts on my lap. "Enora thinks his powers of transportation might be stolen."

I recall that from Ophelia's memories. "That makes sense, at least in that it would have allowed him to mask his innate

CHAPTER TWENTY-EIGHT

vampire powers by making us believe his was transporting. But it does not make sense that he would be able to steal another's powers. That requires powerful dark magic." I screw my eyes closed and wish I could find at least some of the answers that elude me.

"Not much about anything makes sense right now," Malachi reminds us all.

"Nothing except this," Ophelia says with a smile as she looks around the room. "This makes perfect sense."

Axl smiles at her. "If only we could hide out here forever and nobody would find us. I think I'd be pretty happy with this life."

If only it were possible. She nestles her head against my chest and sighs. "Me too. And if Ani and Elpis wanted to stay, that would be even cooler."

"Pet dragons." Xavier snorts.

I arch an eyebrow at him. "I would not let either of them hear you even joke about that, Xavier."

He laughs quietly to himself.

Malachi pushes back his chair. "Seeing as we probably can't hide out here forever, I say we enjoy it while it lasts." He holds his hand out to Ophelia. "Fancy a moonlight walk on the beach, sweet girl?"

She nods excitedly, gives me a brief kiss, and then scrambles off my lap. I cannot help myself from swatting her ass when she stands. She is irresistible. I want to take her to bed, but it is selfish of me to keep her to myself. Besides, I have something, or some*one*, else to take care of first.

Axl jumps up and tosses his napkin onto the table. "If that walk is likely to end in me fucking one or both of you, then I'm in too."

Xavier is quick to express his desire to join them, but before he can walk out of the kitchen, I am on my feet and blocking his path. "Not you. Not yet. I believe we have some new ground rules to discuss."

Axl tuts and shakes his head. "Naughty pup."

Xavier flips him the bird and mouths, *Fuck you.* Then the three of them leave, and Xavier and I are alone in the kitchen.

Cupping his jaw with one hand, I press him against the wall. Desire ripples down my spine. "Do you think because there has been a change in our relationship that I would somehow overlook your insolence, Xavier?"

He swipes his tongue over his full bottom lip and stares at me, his eyes sparking with defiance. "No."

"So what was that earlier?"

"I always talk to you like that, Professor."

That is most definitely true. He has always been adept at pushing me to my limits, never quite doing enough to incur any serious punishment. But that was before the idea of punishing him was so appealing to me. I bring my face closer to his until his heated breath dusts over my lips. His pupils blow wide, his pulse spikes, and he is already hard. But then, so am I.

I swipe my thumb over his full lips. "You will watch your tone when you address me, pup."

His eyes bore into mine. "Yes. Sir."

I am certain he said that to goad me into doing exactly what it is I am about to do, but I am too blinded by desire to care. I sink my fangs into his throat, and his rich blood fills my mouth.

"Fuck," he whimpers, wrapping his arms around my neck and digging his fingers into my scalp.

Will you remember who you are speaking to in the future? I sink my fangs deeper, offering him a little pain to go along with his pleasure.

He grinds himself against me and moans.

I slip my hand inside his jeans and grip the base of his rigid length with a hard squeeze. *I did not hear you.*

CHAPTER TWENTY-EIGHT

"Yes!" he cries out. "Yes, I'll remember."

I stop feeding and trail my teeth along his jawline to his mouth, smiling against his lips as I slide my hand free from his jeans. "Let us go and join the others on their moonlit stroll." His surprise is acute, his sudden despair almost enough to make me reconsider, but then that would be no lesson at all. "Surely you did not think I was going to fuck you as a reward for your insolence, Xavier?"

He glowers at me, eyes blazing with fire and defiance. My hand still gripping his jaw, I pull him to me and kiss him. My tongue is granted easy access to his willing mouth. *If you are a good boy, I may fuck you later.*

His muscles tense, but his mouth softens, and there is no fight in him at all. But I am certain the brat in him aches to tell me go to hell.

CHAPTER
TWENTY-NINE
ALEXANDROS

The shade is cool underneath the vast shadow cast by Anikêtos. It has been three days since he and Ophelia rescued me from Giorgios's prison, and I have already grown accustomed to his presence. After a millennium without him in my life, I cannot deny the joy I feel each day he and Elpis choose to remain in the mortal realm.

He stands to his full height, looming over me, and shakes his scales from nose to tail, thus creating a mini sandstorm. I brush the golden grains from my hair. *Where is Elpis?*

He glances out across the ocean. *Taking her midafternoon flight. She is taking her fill of the energy from the mortal realm whilst she can.*

I am grateful for your presence here, my friend.

I know.

I recall with startling clarity the day we met, near a beach much like this one. I was barely fourteen years old when I came face-to-face with the most fearsome creature ever to have roamed the skies. I had met dragons before him, but none so terrifying—or so opinionated as he.

CHAPTER TWENTY-NINE

You never used to be so prone to bouts of nostalgia, Dragon Whisperer.

I never had much cause to be when we were last acquainted.

He tilts his head, his huge green eyes unblinking. *Ask whatever question it is that you are wrestling with, Alexandros. Uncertainty and indecision do not become you.*

They are not traits I value or usually possess, but I am aware that what I am about to ask would keep him from his kind for much longer than he anticipated. *Whilst I am grateful for all you have done, Anikêtos, I must ask for more. Would you and Elpis consider remaining here in the mortal realm for a short while longer? Until I am more certain of Giorgios's intent.*

He blinks at me before looking to the sky. *I must speak with Elpis.* Without another word to me, he takes flight and disappears into the clouds.

I make my way through the thick grasses bordering the garden back toward the house. Her presence sets my teeth on edge, and I spin around to face her, my fangs bared and my blood boiling.

"I am only here to help, Alexandros."

Fury burns hot in my chest, and it is only my many years of practiced restraint that prevent me from tearing out Nazeel Danraath's throat. As powerful as she is, such is the strength of my rage that she would not have a hope of stopping me. A fact she is well aware of.

"Why would I trust a word that comes from your mouth, Nazeel? You betrayed me."

"I did not betray you. I did not learn of your fate until days after it happened."

"Days!" I spit out the word like an accusation. "I was in that place for nearly four weeks. If you knew what he had done, why did you do nothing to fix it? Why did you not tell them I was alive?"

"I could not. I have been grounded. Unable to leave the mountain fortress of our home. I have taken a great risk in coming here today."

Is that supposed to make me pity her? Supposed to undo the pain and torment she caused? Perhaps if her actions had only affected me, it would, but I will never forgive her for breaking their hearts. Especially Ophelia's.

She takes a cautious step closer. "That I had no idea of Giorgios's true motives pains me greatly. Yet, his ability to deceive was so great, he fooled even you, Alexandros Drakos, whose power is unparalleled when it comes to matters of the mind."

"Do you think reminding me of my own failings will be of any benefit to you?"

She shakes her head. "I am simply pointing out the facts. He fooled us all, hiding his true intentions and the full strength of his own power of the mind. How do you suppose he managed such a feat?"

I grind my teeth. "I do not know."

She says nothing for a long moment.

"You also think that his powers of teleportation are not innate?" I ask, mirroring the question she is already asking herself.

"You read my mind?" She blinks at me but does not appear overly surprised.

I did not read her mind as such—more like she is an open book. Which is puzzling given the amount of power she possesses. "I can hear every thought in your head."

She laughs, a musical sound so at odds with the situation that it only fuels my anger. Nothing about this is amusing. A second later, her hypnotizing green eyes are back on me. "If you can hear my thoughts so easily, then you must know I did not betray you, Alexandros. I was of the understanding that you and Ophelia would be reunited within a matter of hours. I

CHAPTER TWENTY-NINE

simply wished to fully awaken the child's powers through the quickest and surest route."

That she was willing to put Ophelia through such torment simply to expedite the awakening of her powers comes as no surprise to me, but it still stokes the flames of my rage. "She is *not* a child."

My snarl catches her off guard, and she flinches before quickly regaining her composure. "No, you are quite right. She is not. You and I both know what she truly is, yes?"

"Do not, Nazeel." Her thoughts are growing increasingly fervent, and I want to ignore them and divert this conversation away from where it is surely headed.

"If you knew the full prophecy, Alexandros. So very few know of the forgotten verse, for it is never spoken of. But the Skotádi know, and that is why they want her. Because she is about to fulfill her destiny. All of the pieces are finally in place."

"She is not the Chosen One." I shake my head. "The world cannot have her!" I roar.

She chants the words in her head so that I am forced to hear.

But if the Chosen One can slay the three-headed dragon—
if the untamable beast does kneel at its new master's feet,
and the light is tempted back from the darkness,
then they shall awaken the protector of man.
And the sun must swallow the shadows
to bring a balance that reigns through the ages.

"They are the ramblings of a madwoman, Nazeel. They mean nothing."

"No, Alexandros, they mean *everything*." There is something in her voice—conviction, perhaps—that makes the hairs on the back of my neck stand on end. Her thoughts race at such speed that it is hard to focus on any one of them, but the dominant emotion is fear—and hope.

I place my hands on her upper arms, hoping to find some calm in her eyes that will help me make sense of the chaos unfolding in her brain.

"I must go, Alexandros," she pleads. "Kameen will—"

"I do not care, Nazeel." I growl my frustration.

"Yes you do." Tears fill her eyes. "You have always cared far too much, and that is why it had to be you. You are the one who will rise by her side."

Me? I almost bark out a laugh at the absurdity of such a notion. Nazeel must be delirious. First Ophelia, and now me? "Stop speaking in riddles."

"I am not!" she insists. "You, of all people, know the innate power of a name, Alexandros."

"Let her go." The deep, snarling voice comes from behind me, and I need not turn around to know who it belongs to.

I growl a warning. "Stay out of this, Kameen."

He moves around me to stand beside her. "I am not your enemy, Alexandros Drakos, but if you harm a hair on her head, I will remove yours from your body."

I roll back my shoulders. "You can try, Kameen, but you will be unsuccessful."

His eyes narrow, but the corner of his lip seems to twitch as he looks me up and down. "You would dare challenge me?"

"I do not *dare* to do anything. As powerful as you are, Kameen Nassari, I am older, wiser, and stronger. And even your disobedient witch will confirm the truth of that."

"Boys, there is no need for such hostility," Nazeel says softly, her hand placed on her mate's forearm.

The ground shakes underneath our feet, and the heat from Anikêtos's breath washes over us all before his vast shadow blocks out the sun. He nudges my shoulder with the tip of his nose, the most significant gesture of affection a dragon would show any creature not of their own kind.

CHAPTER TWENTY-NINE

Both Kameen and Nazeel bow their heads slightly, showing deference to the powerful being now in their presence. "Anikêtos," Kameen says, his tone carrying the appropriate amount of gravitas.

Anikêtos snorts softly in response. Both Kameen and Nazeel are well-versed in dragon communication, although they have not had cause to engage in such for far too long. *Do I need to scorch anyone to ash, Dragon Whisperer?*

"Not quite yet, Anikêtos," I reply aloud. Not that either of the beings standing in front of me needs the reminder of my ability to communicate with dragons, but it cannot hurt.

Kameen rolls his neck, his gaze traveling back to me. "Nazeel is done interfering in matters that do not concern her." Nazeel flashes him a warning glare, but he does not give her any opportunity to argue with him. "We are leaving."

Leaving? Just like that? It is far past the point of Nazeel being done interfering. She already interfered, and she put my family in danger. "There is a great battle surely coming, and you must choose a side. Is it with me or with my brother?"

"It has always been with you, Alexandros, even if we did not know it," Nazeel answers before he can.

Kameen bares his teeth, anger radiating from him, his glare darting between his mate and me. "We do not choose sides. We do not interfere."

"Perhaps you no longer have a choice, Kameen."

His jaw tics, but he does not refute my assertion. Instead, he glances at Nazeel—a paradox of a woman if ever I have known one. Despite everything, I am sure of her inherent desire to bring peace and balance, even if her attempts at doing so have been severely misguided. Still, I do not trust her, particularly where Ophelia is concerned.

"We are leaving," Kameen snaps.

Nazeel places her hand on his cheek and lightly traces the

lines of his scars with her fingertips. "Kameen, please. Just one more moment?"

I witness the precise moment the rigid, unfeeling commander of the Order acquiesces. His shoulders drop a fraction, and he tilts his head to the side, pressing his cheek into her palm. I am not sure I would have detected such a change in him only six months ago, before I met Ophelia. But I understand Kameen more now than I ever have. How difficult his love for Nazeel must make his position in the Order.

Seizing the opportunity, Nazeel steps forward and clasps my hand in hers. Anikêtos inches closer, a protective presence at my back. "You understand the true power of a name, Alexandros. Yes?" Her green eyes glisten with such hope that it is difficult to look away from her intense gaze.

So many underestimate the importance of a name, yet it shapes so much of who we are and what we become. Still, I have no idea how that relates to the situation at hand, so I remain quiet and allow Nazeel to fill the silence. "The forgotten verse, Alexandros. It was never forgotten, simply omitted."

Even as I struggle to comprehend what she is alluding to, there is something in her words that feels so oddly familiar and true, it makes goosebumps prickle over my flesh. "Speak plainly, Nazeel, or do not speak at all."

"Most people operate under the mistaken belief that our parents or the people who are present at our birth choose our names. And whilst that is true for most, you and I know that some of us are born with a name already etched into our soul."

The memory of Lucian's birth comes rushing back, threatening to overwhelm me. I remember the sweat, the screaming, the relief when he was born on a ragged wail that matched his mother's. Most importantly, I remember how the name Elena and I chose for him became irrelevant the moment he took his first breath. Lucian Drakos was the person he was meant to be from the second he was born.

"Nazeel." Kameen's gruff voice cuts through the tension. "We are leaving."

"It was all predestined, Alexandros." With that, she and Kameen disappear, leaving me to stare at the spot on the ground where they stood only a moment ago.

Prophecies. Anikêtos snorts.

Do you know of the Lost Prophecies of Fiere? Of the forgotten verse?

I do, he says, preening his scales. *Although I have never paid them much heed. Dragonkind has no need for the ramblings of other creatures.*

Of that I have no doubt.

But it perturbs you, Dragon Whisperer? Why?

Nazeel is of the belief that Ophelia is the Chosen One.

And you think she is not?

I do not answer him. I cannot bring myself to lie or to confirm the truth I already know.

Recount the forgotten verse to me, I have forgotten its detail, he commands.

I do as he asks, and he is quiet for a few moments. *And Nazeel's riddle about names makes you think ...*

He stops, and I finish the thought for him. *That Lucian is the light that must be turned from the dark.*

Thick smoke unfurls from his nostrils. *That is not the only name Nazeel refers to though, is it?*

My head is crammed with too many questions and memories, some real and some imagined, and I am filled with a sense of dread and déjà vu. I pinch the bridge of my nose, aware of Anikêtos's analyzing gaze as he awaits my response. *What are you talking about, Ani?* I snap at him, unable to keep a lid on my frustration. I should take Ophelia and my boys and disappear where nobody will ever find us. Prophecies and Skotádi and the Order be damned.

Your name, Alexandros.

A current of lightning-laced fear shoots down my spine. *No. I am named after my great-grandfather. My mother chose my name before I was even conceived.*

Regardless, you are aware of its meaning, are you not?

Synapses fire in my brain, and I am transported to my childhood. I recall soft fingers brushing my cheeks, her dark hair falling over her shoulder, and her deep-blue eyes so full of love—my mother, one of the most powerful elementai who ever lived—and how frequently she would tell me the meaning of my name.

Alexandros—defender of men.

The protector of man. Anikêtos's voice rings in my head now.

"I am not ..." I clench my teeth and ball my hands into fists. "I am not a part of some ancient archaic prophecy."

Then why do you rail against it so, Dragon Whisperer?

"I thought you did not believe in such nonsense?"

Another thick plume of smoke drifts from his nostrils. *I have never claimed to not believe; merely to not care.*

There is a flash of pink in my peripheral vision, and I turn to see Ophelia headed straight for us. Despite the grave nature of the situation we all face, she bears, as she often does, the sweetest of smiles. It both pleases and saddens me to see it.

Say nothing of this to her, Anikêtos, I warn him.

You do not believe she deserves to know?

I do not believe it would do any good to burden her with such knowledge. Who in their right mind would want to learn that the fate of an entire world rests upon their shoulders?

He blows out a breath that singes the hairs on my forearms even from thirty feet above me. *She shall not learn of it from me.*

As soon as she is within touching distance, I pull her to my

CHAPTER TWENTY-NINE

side and wrap a protective arm around her waist. "What are you boys talking about?" she asks, glancing between the two of us.

I run my nose over her hair, and she smells so good it takes all of my restraint to stop myself from biting her. "I was simply thanking Anikêtos for his and Elpis's help."

She smiles up at him. "I am forever in your debt."

He dips his head. *I am well aware, Ophelia, as you swore me an oath.*

I glare at her. "You swore a dragon an oath to be in his debt?"

She blinks, confusion all over her face. "Yes. I had to so he would come back and help us."

I speak to her through our bond so he cannot hear. *Ophelia, you do not make such a promise to a dragon. They do not see the world in the same way as you and I.*

But it's Anikêtos. We trust him, don't we?

With my life, agápi mou. But he would ask for yours in an instant to save another dragon. You never make such a promise to a dragon if you are not prepared to wager your soul.

She hardens her gaze, her jaw tipped defiantly. "If that ends up being the cost of getting you back and saving the boys, it was a price worth paying a hundred times over."

Anikêtos snorts. *You are a true warrior, Ophelia Hart, and you, my old friend, underestimate her.*

She folds her arms across her chest and flashes me a triumphant grin. She does not have to say or even think the words *I told you so*. They are clear in every other way.

I press my lips to her ear. "One of these days, little one, I am going to spank all of your sass right out of you."

She flutters her eyelashes. "I hope so, sir. But right now, lunch is ready, and I would love it if we could all sit down to eat together."

The only thing I want to eat is her. The beast inside me growls, desperate to feed. That only makes her laugh, and she rubs her stomach. "You can eat as soon as I have. I'm starving."

We bid Anikêtos goodbye, and I slip my hand into hers, unable to stop staring at her as we walk back toward the house, her skin shimmering in the light of the midday sun.

Anikêtos is wrong—I do not underestimate her. I am all too aware of the things she is capable of. Not her power, for we still lack knowledge of the full extent of her might, but her strength and her courage. Those traits which she had in spades long before her powers were awakened. She is noble and selfless. That is how I know of the sacrifices she would make to save those she loves. And my greatest fear is that she will one day be faced with such a choice, and there will be nothing I can do to prevent her from making it.

CHAPTER
THIRTY
OPHELIA

After I'm finished with training for the day, I sit cross-legged on the ground, absentmindedly plucking blades of grass as I stare up at the mountain of dragon that is Anikêtos. It's been four days since we arrived here, and he and Elpis have remained with us. I don't know how long they intend to stay, and I don't want to ask and tempt fate. I love having them here.

Why are you staring at me, child?

Because you're a dragon! An actual fire-breathing, cool-as-hell dragon who's thousands of years old, and I have six billion questions I want to ask you. I don't say that though. Instead, I ask, "Why can't dragons harm a son of House Drakos?"

It is an oath my father swore long ago to Alexandros's great-grandfather, the first of House Drakos.

"And it lasts forever?"

Until we are no longer beholden to it, and only the head of House Drakos can release us from such an oath.

His shiny black scales shimmer in the sun. He is almost too wondrous to believe. He and Elpis, who is half his size but equally mesmerizing. "Can you tell me everything you know about the blue poppy?"

He snorts and does that thing that looks suspiciously like an eye roll, even though I'm certain he would claim such human reactions are beneath him. Then he tucks his head under his wing in his best effort to ignore me. But I'm not budging.

Ani!

Go ask Alexandros, he says.

I did, and he told me everything he knows, but ... I lick my lips before I go on. *He isn't Anikêtos, son of Herôs, seer of truths, and keeper of the cradle of magic, is he?*

He snorts again and lifts his head, blinking his fiery green eyes at me. *What is it you want to know, curious and annoying child?*

"I know it takes ten days to leave my system, but is there a way to ... you know, hurry the process along?"

He makes a noise like a growl. *Ophelia, you are the most powerful creature to have been born in centuries.* With that cryptic and less than helpful answer, he huffs once more and returns his head to its previous position underneath his wing.

I stare at him, hoping he will elaborate but knowing he won't. He's even more stubborn than Alexandros. Instead, I look to Elpis for some help, but she simply shakes her head and snuggles against him.

I place my hands beside me and press my palms into the plush grass, flattening it down until it tickles my skin. Taking a deep breath, I close my eyes. Alexandros said the earth is the most powerful element—with healing properties, right? So if blue poppy is a toxin, then surely it can be removed, or cleansed, like a bacteria.

A thrill of excitement runs down my spine. I have no idea if this will work or if I'll be able to tell whether it has. But it's worth a shot. Anything that allows Alexandros to reinstate our

CHAPTER THIRTY

bond is worth trying, and I could kick myself for not considering it sooner.

I press my fingertips into the cool soil. Dirt surges up to collect underneath my fingernails, and I breathe, focusing on the orb of light inside me, dazzling like the sun, as well as the movement of the earth beneath my hands. The soil, warm and ticklish, fizzes under my fingertips. And then I feel it—an ancient, powerful energy flowing through my body, making every hair stand on end. It's scary and overwhelming, yet intoxicating and addictive at the same time. I feel invincible, like I could make the mountain in the distance crumble to the ground if I simply stared at it long enough. But I focus on the blue poppy, isolating the remnants of the drug that cling to my red blood cells, and then I channel those remnants through my fingertips and release them all back into the earth.

As soon as I feel the last of it leave my system, I pull my fingers from the dirt and let out a triumphant shout. I did it. And more surprisingly, I instinctively knew how to. Like with the silver cage in the mountain cave, I only had to think about what I wanted to make it happen.

I wipe the dirt from my hands and jump up, eager to get back to the house as quickly as possible. Alexandros is leaning against the open doorway, watching me. I should have realized that one of them would have me in sight.

"What were you doing, little one?" he calls.

I press my lips together, unable to contain my glee as I run across the lawn and throw myself at him. He catches me with ease, and I wrap my legs around his waist. "I just got all of the blue poppy out of my system."

The sound that comes from this man's throat makes me melt. I'm pretty sure one day I will actually do that, and I'll wind up as little more than a puddle on the ground. "Ophelia, do not toy with me."

"I'm not. I did it," I say, heat curling in my core. "I used earth magic."

He carries me inside the house, running his nose along the skin of my neck, and I tip my head back for him, willing him to bite me. I need him to bite me.

"Ophelia." My name is a pained, frustrated groan on his lips.

"What? Is something wrong?"

"You are ovulating."

Dammit all to hell. Of course I am. I knew it was expected, but now? Can Mother Nature not have given me only one more day? "Nooo," I whine.

"One day, I will love nothing more than to see you carry my child, agápi mou. But for now, we cannot take such a risk." I'm way too young to have kids. I've never even thought of having my own before, so why does the thought of having his tiny vampire or elementai babies sound so appealing to me? He presses his forehead to mine while he carries me through to the bedroom. "However, I am still going to feed from you. I am as desperate as you are to have our bond back in place, and the mere scent of your blood has my mouth watering and my fangs aching."

I grind myself against his hard length, still annoyed by this turn of events. As soon as he bites me, I'll want him inside me too. And I've been starved of him for weeks. "It's so unfair."

He laughs softly, his warm breath dancing over my skin. "I am sure I can still make it entirely pleasurable for us both, little one."

I know he can, but it won't be the same.

"Do you recall the first time we bonded?" His voice is low and husky, and it only stokes my need for him further.

"Yes." It was intense and incredible and so very, very hot. "I set your office on fire."

CHAPTER THIRTY

"You turned my books to ash." He kisses me until we get to the bed, and then he tosses me onto it. I bounce in the middle. "And you burned yourself into my soul, Ophelia Hart."

Wow. He is so intense. Sexy, brooding, and intense, and he makes my ovaries melt too, which is not conducive to getting pregnant, I imagine. He kneels between my legs and pulls the sundress off over my head, another item of clothing I borrowed from one of Osiris's relatives.

Alexandros growls as he hooks the finger into the waistband of my panties. "What is this tiny white scrap of cotton, Ophelia? Are you purposely trying to drive me insane?"

"What?" I glance down at them on the floor. They are tiny, and they barely covered my ass, but they were the only new pack of panties available. While I'm grateful to Osiris's family for loaning me some clothes, given the choice between new and previously worn panties, I'm gonna choose new every time. I will reimburse whoever I need to for them as soon as I'm able. "I had limited options. It was those or nothing."

He arches a dark eyebrow and runs the tip of his pointer finger through my aching center. "Nothing would have been a very good choice. You should consider that option in the future." His gaze roams my body and comes to a stop between my thighs. My skin burns under the heat of his scrutiny.

"Yes sir."

He slips a thick finger inside me, and my back arches off the bed as pleasure rockets through me. He moves in and out, massaging the sensitive spot inside me, and my thighs tremble. "You are always so ready for me, Ophelia."

I moan, grabbing for him, but he remains frustratingly out of reach. "Alexandros, please."

"Do you need more, little one?"

I pant out a breath. "Yes."

He adds a second finger, stretching me wide and causing burning hot pleasure to spike in my core.

"Such a responsive little thing for me, agápi mou." He leans over me, holding himself up on one muscular forearm. "I am going to enjoy feeding on you whilst you come on my fingers."

His teeth scrape over my skin, and my pulse flutters violently, like my blood is screaming for him to claim me. Why is he drawing this out? It's torturous. And there's no way he doesn't feel this same clawing need.

"But it is an exquisite torture, agápi mou. Is it not?" He sinks his fingers deeper, swiping them over a sensitive spot deep inside, and my entire body trembles. "You fall apart so beautifully for me."

His tongue flicks over my pulse, and he grinds the heel of his palm against my hypersensitive clit. "Alexandros." His name pours out of my mouth on a keening moan.

"I know, little one," he murmurs while he works his fingers in and out, hitting the same sweet spots over and over until every cell in my body is frantic for release. Frantic for him.

I cling to him, rocking my hips and arching my neck, trying to force my flesh into his fangs. But he's right. This is exquisite torture. I teeter on the edge of heaven, knowing redemption is only a breath away. Tears squeeze from the corners of my eyes. My nails sink into his skin. I beg and moan as I ride his hand.

And when I'm sure I can't possibly take any more, his sharp fangs pierce my neck. And I fall, spiraling into a euphoric haze of pleasure. Down and down I tumble before he pulls me back again, sucking harder on my neck and driving his fingers faster and harder until I'm cresting another wave and crying out his name.

Ophelia. He groans my name, and the word resonates in my mind as our bond is anchored back in place. I can feel his blood thundering in my veins along with my own now, just as it

CHAPTER THIRTY

should be. The euphoria builds within him as his need for release grows, and I work my hand inside the waistband of his pants and push aside his boxers until I'm able to wrap my fingers around his shaft. It pulses in my hand, hot and smooth.

Fuck. He growls the word inside my head.

You like that? I ask, tipping my head back farther so he can have better access to my neck.

He takes the opportunity to sink his fangs deeper. *You know I do, little one.*

I slide my hand up and down his length, collecting precum with my thumb and spreading it over his crown. *How about that?*

He grunts and ruts into my hand while he works his fingers inside me deeper and harder. Once again, I fall into oblivion, only this time, he comes right along with me. I wrap my legs and my arms around him, clinging to him as we both pant for breath and tremble with the aftermath of our climaxes. He keeps his face buried against my neck, the wound from his bite already healed.

"I love you, Ophelia," he whispers.

"I love you too," I murmur as I melt into the mattress. Intense feelings of warmth and contentment have ingrained themselves into my very bones. I am once again bonded to all four of my mates, exactly as I should be. And no matter what the future has in store for us, I know that together we can face anything this crazy universe throws our way.

CHAPTER
THIRTY-ONE
AXL

"You feel that?" Xavier shivers, his eyes flaming with heat and desire.

Yes, I fucking felt it. Every single nerve ending in my body felt it. Despite having already taken our fill of blood this afternoon, my fangs protract. I have never been more ravenous for a taste of anyone since I was first turned over two centuries ago.

Malachi grins. "Alexandros re-bonded with Ophelia."

Xavier cracks his neck. "That means the blue poppy must be gone."

"And that means we all get to feed?" I barely recognize the vicious growl that comes out of my mouth, but it comes from a place of deep yearning. Of a need so profound, I am sure I'll die if I don't taste her soon. Like on the day I first bit her, the beast inside me can no longer be contained.

We increase our speed, each of us as desperate as the other to get back to the house. To her. It takes but a few moments, and the house is quiet except for the sound of their beating hearts. My skin sizzles with anticipation, fangs throbbing with

CHAPTER THIRTY-ONE

a delicious kind of ache, and I know my hunger will be sated very soon.

The bedroom door is open, and she lies on the bed with him, her pink hair fanned out over the pillow while he lazily runs his fingers down her abdomen. I want her so fucking bad it hurts.

"Hi," she whispers, not needing to lift her head and see us to know we're here.

"Hey, Cupcake," Xavier says, already tugging off his clothes.

Malachi does the same. "Is the blue poppy out of your system?"

"Yeah." Her voice is a soft breath I can feel on my skin even from here.

My cock presses painfully against the seam of my zipper. "How?"

It's Alexandros who replies. "Our clever elementai figured out a way to remove the toxins herself using healing energy."

"You're so smart, sweet girl." Naked, Malachi crawls onto the bed, trailing his mouth from her ankles all the way to the tops of her thighs as he goes. "I cannot fucking wait to taste you."

She giggles. "Me too."

Xavier follows him, and Alexandros rolls out of the way, allowing them both to get beside her, his eyes dark as he watches them with her. And I watch too, strangely transfixed by the sight of them together. Their need for her blood feels as keen as my own. Yet despite my feral instinct to bite, to drink from her and slake this thirst, I remain where I am. Watching. Waiting. Prolonging this agony because I know it will make the reward all the sweeter.

"I really fucking need you, Cupcake," Xavier growls. "All of you."

He and Malachi pull her into a kneeling position and situate themselves in front of her and behind her. I stalk around the edge of the bed to obtain a better view. From here, I see them all in profile. Her soft, supple body sandwiched between their hard ones. Her juicy tits pressed up against Xavier's chest. Their stiff cocks digging into her ass and stomach.

Malachi collects her hair and wraps it around his fist, exposing the full length of her neck. "We're gonna fuck while we feed, sweet girl."

She shivers between them. My cock throbs, and I palm it over my jeans, desperate for some relief, and take a seat beside the window. Xavier and Malachi communicate without words or thoughts as they take her together. Their fangs sink into her flesh on either side of her neck while Malachi drives into her wet pussy. Then he pulls out and allows Xavier to do the same. They work together like that, each of them fucking her with a steady rhythm, not letting her tight pussy remain empty for more than a second. She cries out, and overwhelming pleasure permeates the room. Her power intoxicating, her taste addictive and delicious. But it's the sounds the three of them make that nearly tip me over the edge as I slide my hand into my jeans and stroke my cock. Her cries. Their groans. Her wet pussy taking them both so well. A beautiful symphony of their union.

Alexandros watches them too, as transfixed by the three of them as I am. They are a beautiful sight as they come together, one single entity sharing an intense moment of euphoria and release. And by the time they're done with her, I'm already on my feet, tearing off my clothes and growling like a starving animal that's about to make its first kill in weeks. Such is the strength of my desire for her, I feel a spike of anxiety that I'll hurt her as soon as I get my hands on her. Until I remember I can't. Our bond won't allow it, and I thank fuck for that because I have no idea how I'm going to hold back my desperation to take everything from her.

CHAPTER THIRTY-ONE

Malachi gently lays her trembling body down on the bed next to Alexandros, then shuffles out of my way with Xavier close behind. I crawl between her thighs, spreading them wider with my knees. Her chest heaves with every breath. The pulse in her throat flutters violently, silently begging for my fangs. Instead, I trail kisses up her thighs and skim her sweet pussy on my way to her stomach.

"Axl," she moans, bucking her hips and threading her fingers through my hair, her desire still coursing through her despite the orgasm she just had. Not to mention the ones Alexandros no doubt gave her before we arrived.

"I know, princess. I'm fucking desperate to taste you and to fuck you while I do it. Would you like that?" She sinks her perfect teeth into her juicy lower lip and nods. "Did the professor fuck you too?"

She shakes her head, and I look to him, confused.

He arches an eyebrow. "Ophelia is ovulating."

I turn my attention back to her and continue my mouth's exploration of her tender flesh while I speak to them all through our bond. *If only there was a way to fuck Ophelia that wouldn't risk her getting pregnant, huh?*

Xavier snorts a laugh, probably because that's exactly the kind of thing he'd say. I've never been one to provoke the professor unnecessarily, but I am too far gone with need. The thought of taking him with her, of doing something similar to what Xavier and Malachi just did, is much too tempting to resist.

Ophelia's eyes blow wide open, and her racing heart speeds up even farther, but she wants this as much as I do. Alexandros is a little more hesitant. He rolls onto his side and brushes his knuckles across her cheek. "Is that something you would like, Ophelia?"

She nods. "You know it is."

"And you think you could take us both together? At the same time?" His voice is low and smooth, and even if she did have any doubts, I'm sure he just killed them. Flat-out. Dead.

She traps her lip between her teeth and nods.

"Words, Ophelia," he commands.

"Yes sir."

We all feel the effect that word has on him coming from her lips, and I suppress a grin because Ophelia has sealed her fate. "Very well. What do we have for lubrication?"

I swipe a finger through our girl's soaking center and arch an eyebrow at him. "Cum?"

He grunts. "As tempting as that is, I was hoping for something a little more substantial."

I press my lips to Ophelia's ear. "Oh, princess, you are about to get fucked in the ass so hard."

Her breath hitches in her throat, and her titanium-hard nipples graze my chest.

"There's some actual lube in one of the other bathrooms," Malachi says. I imagine he's looking forward to watching the show as much I'm anticipating starring in it. Alexandros gives him a nod, and Malachi disappears from the room.

That figures; I'd expect no less from a house owned by wolves.

This will probably be easiest if Ophelia is riding you, Axl, Alexandros says inside my head. *I am blocking her out, but I am not sure how long I will be able to continue to do so.*

Taking that as my cue to act quickly, I roll onto my back and pull Ophelia to straddle me. "Come up here, princess. Slide yourself onto me."

She does as she's told, resting her palms flat on my abs to steady herself as she slowly impales herself on my rock-hard cock. Her silky-smooth heat envelops me, sending endorphins shuttling through my body at the speed of light. She feels so fucking good, and the ache in my fangs becomes even more painful as they throb with the desire to sink inside her too.

Malachi quickly returns with the lube, and Alexandros kneels behind Ophelia. She shivers when he runs a soothing hand down her back. "I will not hurt you, little one," he says softly. "You might feel the desperate urge to fuck you into a coma within me, but I will not."

She sucks in a breath. "I know."

Hold her still for me, he orders, and I grab her hips, remaining fully seated inside her. Her inner walls ripple around my shaft, milking precum from my weeping slit. I'm gonna nut in her as soon as I taste her blood, but I don't fucking care.

I feel him edge a finger inside, and it causes tremors of pleasure to vibrate through her entire body and into me.

"Oh, sir!" she cries.

"Ophelia." He growls her name in warning, but my girl is on the edge too, and she's not gonna make this easy on him or me. She knows what she does to us. Her power over each of us has nothing to do with her being an elementai and everything to do with the fact that we are addicted and obsessed with her to the point of insanity. We would all do anything in our power to make and keep her happy, and she knows it. We may appear to be in control here, but in truth, she holds the reins. And that's never not true.

"I can take much more." She purrs the words, and his dark eyes blaze with fire.

Please, sir, fuck her so I can bite her, because I'm gonna last about forty-five more seconds here.

I'm unable to tune her out the way he can, and she flutters her eyelashes at me before her eyes roll back in her head with one smooth thrust to the hilt from Alexandros that makes her go nuclear.

"Is this what you wanted, Ophelia?" He pulls out and drives

inside her again as her teeth chatter. Then he looks over her shoulder at me and nods. "You may feed whenever you are ready, Axl."

With a hand on the back of her neck, I pull her body to lie over mine and push her hair out of the way. She smells so incredible. I don't wait a second longer to sink my fangs into her throat, and her delicious, soul-cleansing blood fills my mouth. It has only been a week, but it feels like I've been starved of her forever.

Fuck, princess, you taste even better than I remember. I slide my hands down her ribs and resettle them on her hips, holding her steady as we both drive inside her.

She mewls and whimpers and writhes, but Alexandros lays his body over hers, and between us, we pin her in place. He gathers her hair in one fist and bites into the other side of her neck. Together, we feed on her and fuck her, and I have never felt closer to him than I do at this moment. Ophelia's orgasm tears through her, but we don't give her any reprieve, and soon she's hurtling toward another one.

Alexandros slides his hands between our perspiration-slicked bodies and slowly circles her clit. Her pleasure becomes so intense it borders on pain, but we keep her on the precipice of ecstasy, and I feel everything. Her desire and her euphoria. His. Mine. Xavier's and Malachi's. All of it builds to a crescendo, rising higher and higher until it feels like the air is sucked from the room and the ground shakes beneath us. And when it seems like we're too high, too far gone to come back, we fall over the edge and free-fall into blissful oblivion.

CHAPTER
THIRTY-TWO

ALEXANDROS

Ophelia hands me a wet cloth and flashes me her sweet smile. "Can you wipe down the table, and I'll load the dishwasher?"

I draw a breath through my nose and let it out with a growl. "There are many other things I would rather be doing with and to you right now, little one." Renewing our bond last night has only increased my desire for her and her blood.

She rolls her eyes and giggles. "We agreed to do clean-up duty while the guys went to the store. You cannot possibly need any more sex today after last night and this morning. I won't be able to walk by tonight."

I slide my arms around her waist. "I think you are forgetting that your powers of healing ensure you have no such problems with walking, or any other more pleasant activities, no matter how many times you indulge in them, Ophelia."

She tips her head back, a laugh bubbling from her lips before it cuts off abruptly and her eyes widen in horror. Her fingernails dig into the muscles of my forearm.

I sense no danger nearby, but she is clearly feeling something. "Ophelia? What is it?"

"He's here," she whispers.

"Who is here?"

"Hello, Father." The voice answers my question and cuts through me with surgical precision. An ice-cold shadow passes over my soul, and a dozen different emotions run through my body all at once as the moment seems to stretch out into eternity. I push every single one down where they cannot escape and cloud my judgment.

Spinning around, I push Ophelia behind me and face him. The dam breaks. Everything hits me at once. Rage, betrayal, and despair. Loss, guilt, regret. Relief. They barrel into me with the force of a steam train and steal the breath from my lungs. His face ... No trace of the sunken black holes infested with maggots where his eyes should be, no mouth full of black rotting teeth—the image I always conjure in my mind's eye when I think of him. He is just as he was when he left home as a young man. Almost a mirror image of me.

He cocks an eyebrow. "Surprised to see me?" His voice drips with disdain.

From somewhere deep within, I find the strength to swallow down every feeling he provokes in me, the bad and the good. "Lucian. What do you want?"

"We meet once again, Ophelia." He glances behind me, where Ophelia peers over my shoulder, and I let out a vicious snarl in warning.

Of all the emotions raging against the walls I have built around them, anger is the one that seeps out and simmers directly beneath my skin now. "If you so much as think about touching her—"

He rolls his eyes. "If I had any intention of causing harm to Ophelia, then I would have done it when we came face-to-face within the mountain cave." He tilts his head to the side, his hazel eyes narrowed as he scrutinizes us both. He looks so

CHAPTER THIRTY-TWO

much like his mother and sisters, and all of our faces seem to peer back at me at once, making it impossible for me to look at him. "Or any of the many other times I've met her during the past nineteen years."

Ophelia's breath catches in her throat.

Both jealousy and confusion slam into me. I keep her pinned behind me and demand, "What other times?"

He glances toward the chair Xavier used when we joined Ophelia for lunch only a short time ago. "May I?"

I growl. "After everything you have done? Everything!" I roar, unable to contain the voracity of my fury for a second longer. "And you ask to sit at my fucking table?"

He wrinkles his nose. "The Brackenwolf family table, if I'm not mistaken. So may I?"

We should hear him out. He might have answers. Ophelia's sweet voice seeps into my thoughts and soothes a little of the rage inside me.

"If your little elementai is telling you to listen to what I have to say, I think you should probably heed her. You might despise me, Father ..." He says the word like it is an insult. And perhaps from his lips, it is. But there was a time when he was my greatest joy in life. My firstborn son. He sucks on his teeth, his eyes boring into mine. "But the feeling is mutual. Besides, I think we both have a few things we need to get off our chests, do we not?"

Get off our chests? That is the understatement of the millennium. I have plenty I need to say to him. So many questions to ask. They race around my head at lightning speed. But I would much rather have this conversation without putting Ophelia in danger by having her spend any further time in his presence.

My curious elementai breaks the ice for us. "When have we met before? Other than the cave, I mean. I don't remember you." She takes a cautious step out from behind me, but I keep my arm around her.

Lucian takes the seat he was not offered and runs a hand over his stubbled jaw. "It is far too long and complicated of a story to explain right now."

"You have been to Montridge." My words sound like an accusation, which I suppose they are.

"Yes, I have been to Montridge. Once since Ophelia began attending there."

"On the day the wolf girl was murdered?"

He nods.

"I saw you, but I hoped I was mistaken. In the young vampires' minds. You controlled them somehow. You forced them to kill that girl."

He scowls. "Of course *you* would think that."

I bang my fist on the table. "I saw you, Lucian."

"And you of all people know how easily a memory can be manipulated. Yes, I was there, but I"—he jabs a finger into his chest—"did not force them to do anything. The Skotádi have access to dark magic that can turn even angels into demons. They can do anything they want to ..." He hisses out a breath, his eyes wild.

"You would know. You were their leader, were you not?"

"I was never their leader," he scoffs. "Another lie dear old Uncle Giorgios told you."

I bristle at the mention of my brother's name. "Giorgios told Ophelia and my sireds you killed me."

Lucian growls, his teeth bared in warning. "It wouldn't be the first time my uncle has blamed me for a crime I didn't commit."

All I can see when I look at him is the boy he was—the man he was before the Skotádi turned him to the darkness. And then I recall the sight of him in our family home, holding his sisters

CHAPTER THIRTY-TWO

in his arms and their still-beating hearts in his hands as he sobbed for them. He was the only person in the room. The only person his mother would have allowed to enter the house aside from Giorgios and me, and Giorgios was with me the entire time. Still, there is a part of me that wants to believe he is incapable of such cruelty, just as I did that day. So I ask him again. "Tell me you did not do it. Tell me it was not you, Lucian. Please."

His hazel eyes, so cold and unfeeling before now, fill with tears. "I wish I could. I wish I did not see their faces every single time I close my eyes. That I did not feel their hearts beating in my hands after I tore them from their chests or smell the blood that soaked through my clothes. I wish I could clean their blood from beneath my fingernails." He holds up his hands. "But over five hundred years later and I still cannot!" He drops his head.

Anger and bitter sadness fill the room, and I am no longer sure which feelings are his and which are mine. I do not know how he severed our bond, but it is as though seeing him has put it back in place.

"No." I shake my head. "They were your sisters. And your own mother. You adored them, Lucian. I know you did." Tears stream down my face, and I am unable and unwilling to stop them.

They were everything to me, but that does not mean I am not a monster.

It takes me a few seconds to realize that he did not say those words aloud.

He looks up at me, his expression full of terrified fury now, and he shrieks like a wounded animal. "Get out! Get out of my head!" As he scrambles backward, the chair hits the ground, and he stumbles over it. "How are you doing that? I blocked you. You're not supposed to be in there!" He grabs fistfuls of his hair and pulls. "Get out of my fucking head!" he screams.

ALEXANDROS

Get out. Get out. Get out. He chants the words silently over and over again, preventing me from hearing anything else.

He is in clear distress, his thoughts and actions deranged, and it tugs at something paternal that is buried deep inside me. I cannot resist the urge to soothe him. "I am sorry, Lucian. I did not mean to."

But he carries on like he cannot hear me.

"Lucian." Ophelia says his name, and he whips his head around to look at her, his chest heaving and eyes wild. "It's okay. Sit down, please, and we can talk some more."

"No." He shakes his head vigorously as he backs away toward the door. "I have to get out of here." Before he goes, he points a finger in my direction. "You—stay out of my fucking head. I don't want you there. You have no right. If you couldn't be there when I needed you ... When I really fucking needed you ..." Tears are squeezed from the corners of his eyes. "You have no fucking right."

Frozen to the spot, I can do nothing but watch him leave. I expected to feel anger and betrayal, but the overwhelming feelings that remain now that he is gone are sadness and confusion.

"How did I fail him so badly, Ophelia?"

She does not reply. Instead, she climbs onto my lap and wraps her arms around me. I bury my head against her neck.

And I cry. Not a few tears, but a torrent of them. Every single one that I have held onto for the past five hundred years. I was a terrible father to him. I let them all down so badly. And for the rest of my life, no matter what I do, I will never be able to change that.

CHAPTER THIRTY-THREE

XAVIER

My eyes are always drawn to my little cupcake any time we're in the same room, but now, as she sits on Malachi's lap and lights the wood stacked in the hearth with a flick of her wrist, making flames lick and dance along the thick logs, she is truly mesmerizing.

"I can't believe he was here." Axl's deep growl snaps me from my daze and drags my attention from Ophelia to him—and to the conversation we've all avoided having since we got back here half an hour ago.

The atmosphere in the house was decidedly gloomy when we returned from hunting. All of us were in such high spirits today after feeding on Ophelia together last night that it was easy to forget the middle of the shitstorm we're currently in. Lucian Drakos paying a visit to the house was a stark reminder of that.

The professor was clearly distressed, and the sight of him undone in Ophelia's arms when we got back was enough to turn my blood to ice. I didn't have it in me to make any kind of snarky comment on the prodigal son's return. Even Axl, who seems to hate Lucian more than Malachi and I do—probably because he's the true firstborn—sat down and kept his mouth shut.

Until now.

Malachi looks to where the professor has been sitting for the past twenty minutes, staring out the window in silence. "Is it still safe here?"

Alexandros sucks on his top lip, his focus remaining on the ocean view. "I believe it is. Lucian has made no attempt to harm us. Nor has Giorgios discovered where we are. I do not believe the two of them are colluding."

I guess that's something worth being thankful for. "So why was he here?"

Alexandros shakes his head and finally directs his gaze toward me, and I wince at the pain still lingering in his dark eyes. "I do not know. I ..." He grinds his jaw until the thick vein in his neck bulges.

"We didn't get the chance to ask," Ophelia says.

Malachi tucks her hair behind her ear. "So he wasn't here very long, then?"

She screws up her nose. "Yes, but ..."

"I asked him what he wanted, but he did not answer." Alexandros fills the silence she leaves. "And then we got embroiled in old hurts and the past, and he became angry and left."

Did I hear him right? I bark out a laugh. "*He* got angry? What the fuck does he have to be angry about?"

I'm almost sorry I asked that question when a shadow of intense anguish passes over his face again. "I unintentionally accessed his thoughts."

Axl scrubs a hand over his jaw, visibly bristling. "Why unintentionally? Isn't accessing his thoughts the best way to find out what the hell he's playing at?"

CHAPTER THIRTY-THREE

"Unintentional because I did not know I was capable of accessing his thoughts given that he has hidden himself from me for so long. I have not been able to before today."

"And you didn't get any worthwhile information from him when you were inside his head?" Malachi's soothing voice eases the tension and douses the simmering anger.

Alexandros shakes his head. "Nothing."

His pain is so intense I can taste it, but I don't know how to comfort him. Our relationship is in a state of flux right now, and I'm still navigating these waters, so I focus on the practical instead. "How do we stop him from coming back here?"

His brow furrows, and after a few seconds, he sighs. "We do not."

"We don't, or we can't?" Axl asks, his tone dripping with frustration.

Alexandros stands. "He is no threat to any of you, Axl." Without another word, he walks out of the den, and I feel like shit that we can't do anything to make this easier for him. He has always been there for us, and I hate to see him so fucking broken and not be able to do anything to make him feel better.

Your concern is enough, Xavier. I simply need a little time with my thoughts, he says through the bond. *Take care of Ophelia. She was shaken by his visit as much as I.*

It brings me some comfort to know he at least knows I want to help. I go to sit next to Ophelia, and Axl sits beside me, making me wonder if he received a similar instruction.

I lace my fingers through hers. "How are you doing, Cupcake?"

She smiles, and her blue eyes sparkle. "I'm okay."

Malachi nuzzles her neck. "What was it like seeing him again?"

"I mean, he scared the hell out of me—out of both of us at first, but then ..." She chews on her juicy bottom lip, her nose wrinkled in concentration, and it makes her look even more edible than usual. "I don't know. He seems so full of pain, you know. Especially when he spoke about his mom and sisters. He didn't deny that he killed them, but he was really cut up about it. Maybe he's had five hundred years to regret what he did, and he wishes he could change it? He's not scary, though, you know? But he was scared. When Alexandros read his thoughts, he seemed terrified. And angry. So angry. He accused him of not being there when he needed him …" She sighs. "The whole encounter was just really sad for both of them."

I don't want to think about Alexandros being hurt any longer, and I'm curious about something else about Lucian, which nobody has asked yet. "Does he look like him?"

She nods. "A lot. Same eyes. Same jawline." She chews on her lip again. "Same broody exterior. He looks exactly like I imagine Alexandros would have looked when he was younger."

I arch an eyebrow, wanting to do anything to lighten the mood. "So he's hot, then?"

She rolls her eyes at me. "Stop that."

Axl grunts. "I don't like that he was here, and I don't like that he could just rock back up here at any given moment."

"Me neither," Malachi agrees.

I don't either, but I trust Ophelia's judgment. Alexandros's too, but his is clouded by the fact that Lucian is his son, and as coldhearted as he tries to make the world think he is, we know he feels all too deeply. His loyalty to the people he loves is unparalleled. It's hard to believe that only a week ago, I wouldn't have considered myself part of that elite group of people.

"Fuck," Axl mutters, still stuck in his bad mood.

I grab the remote and switch on the TV before wrapping my arm around his shoulder. "I think there's a game on." Uncharacteristically, he leans into me and rests his head on my shoulder,

CHAPTER THIRTY-THREE

and I flick through the channels while Ophelia stretches her legs over ours.

I find the basketball game, and we watch it in silence, all of us touching one another in some way. As long as the five of us are together, we can face whatever comes next.

CHAPTER
THIRTY-FOUR
ALEXANDROS

Ophelia's fingertips skate over my ribs, and she stares down at me, her chin resting on her hand as she holds herself up on her elbow. "I know he said he hates you, Alexandros, but it isn't true."

"Are you reading my mind, little one?" She came in here shortly after I did to check on me. The weight of all their concern emanated from the next room, and it is both touching and mildly claustrophobic.

"No. I don't have to. I can feel your sadness and guilt eating away at you." She presses a kiss to my chest. "And I would feel that even without our bond."

I roll onto my side and stare at her, brushing my knuckles over her cheek. Her heart is so pure, she cannot comprehend a son hating his father. "How can you be so sure of what he feels, agápi mou?"

"Because he was there in the cave, Alexandros. Watching over you. He said you had many enemies and that he knew I'd come, but he was protecting you until I got there. Why would he do that if he hated you?"

I cup her face in my hand. "I know you see the best in every-

CHAPTER THIRTY-FOUR

one, Ophelia, and it is one of the many things I love about you. But it is more probable he was lying to mask his true intentions."

"But why? Why say that at all? What was his intention if he left as soon as I freed you from the cage? He had a chance to attack when my guard was down and you were weak, and he didn't take it." Her cheeks darken with the strength of her indignation.

"Might I remind you that you were carrying Dragonfyre at the time, agápi mou. He would have been burned alive had he even tried."

"So why bother waiting around to help me free you? He saw I had the Dragonfyre. Why not let me flail around trying to figure it out for myself? And why help us in Giorgios's fortress?" She goes on, her skin growing more flushed with each second. "This may all be new to me, Alexandros, but I am not an idiot." Anger creeps into her tone now.

Where the hell has this come from? My eyes narrow on her face, and my palm twitches, eager to address her defiance. "I have never once given any indication that I think you anything but intelligent, Ophelia. Do not use my justified concern to make such ludicrous accusations."

"Then why do you not trust my judgment the way I trust yours? You are always telling me that an elementai's power is rooted in emotion, so why is it you think I can't detect emotions in others? Lucian may be confused and angry and a whole host of other things, but he does not hate you."

Her pout is adorable and frustrating. Hauling her over my knee and spanking her for her insolence does not seem even mildly appropriate when we are faced with such imminent danger. But one day ... I groan as my cock stiffens.

"Really? Right now?" She shakes her head, still annoyed with me but already softening.

"Always when you are near me, little one. Especially when I provoke such passion in you. Do not pretend that me wanting to fuck you when you are so full of fire surprises you."

Her lips twitch, but she manages to keep a smile from spreading across her face. "Lucian?" she says, bringing us back to the conversation she initiated.

I let out a sigh of frustration. "I believe it is complicated, and whilst I am convinced he was not lying when he told me he despises me—"

"He does not—"

I press a finger to her lips. "That does not mean he does not feel all manner of other emotions where I am concerned, little one."

Her expression softens. "So you're willing to accept that some part of him still loves you?"

I am not sure I am prepared to make quite that bold an admission, no matter how much she craves it. And no matter how much I wish it were true.

"Just like you still love him, even after everything he did."

Her words slice their way into my heart, burrowing into its deepest recesses where I keep my firstborn buried. "How do you do that to me, agápi mou?"

Her eyelashes flutter. "Do what?"

"Make me feel things I have spent the last five centuries conditioning myself not to feel?"

She shrugs. "Just another one of my superpowers, I guess."

I press my lips to hers and roll on top of her, wanting to forget about everything that was dredged up by seeing Lucian again, if only for a short time. Axl, Xavier, and Malachi shout at the basketball game in the next room, and I once again find myself longing for an ordinary life—at least as ordinary of one as four vampires in love with one elementai can have. The realization that we can never have such a thing, except in tiny snatched moments like this, only makes the despair inside me grow stronger.

I love you. Ophelia's voice in my head anchors me back to her and this moment.

And I you, agápi mou. I deepen our kiss and focus only on her and the feel of her supple body underneath mine. Her taste. Her scent. Her velvety smooth skin. How she yields to me so easily, at least with her body, at the slightest pressure. Ophelia gives me everything I need whilst I give her everything I am.

CHAPTER
THIRTY-FIVE

ALEXANDROS

Lucian. My firstborn. A coldhearted murderer. The reason I have torn myself apart for the past five hundred years. But still my son. The apple of his mother's eye. The boy who was born with his name already ingrained into his soul. As soon as we discovered she was carrying a boy, Elena and I wished for him to be named Ares—a strong name for a son of House Drakos. But the moment he was born, we both knew Ares was not his name. It was Lucian.

I can still recall that day with astounding clarity even over seven hundred years later.

I thought I told you to stay out of my head! His wrath fills my consciousness, and I fight his efforts to shut me out. I am not entirely sure why I can reach him now after so many centuries, but I suspect it has something to do with how Ophelia's powers have magnified my own.

I know what you asked of me, but I will take only a few moments of your time, Lucian. Please?

I owe you nothing. Get out of my fucking head! Every word is infused with his pain.

Despite what you think of me, and despite what I believed myself

CHAPTER THIRTY-FIVE

before I saw you again yesterday, I have no desire to cause you any harm.

He is silent.

Allow me a few moments, and then I will leave you in peace. I swear.

What do you want from me? he asks.

Although I planned what to say, now that I am speaking with him, I find myself uncertain of where to start. So I start with her. *How do you know Ophelia, and how long have you known who she is?*

His derisive snort echoes in my head. *Of course you would ask about the elementai.*

It seemed safer than asking why you murdered your innocent mother and sisters.

It is a calculated risk to push him when he is already so angry with me, but it works. It also causes him a fresh burst of pain, and for that, I feel shame and guilt. An apology would only anger him further, so I swallow the words perched on my tongue. In the limited contact I have had with him, I sense that being in pain is the state he is most comfortable in. And I have no time to unpack how much that saddens me. *That, dearest Father, is much too complicated for only a few moments of your time, which is all I am apparently worth.*

He is twisting my words, but I do not take the bait. *Then you can have all of my time that you desire, Lucian. Despite our differences, I do not believe you mean her any harm, and if there is any way for me to know more of her past, then it would surely help to protect her.*

I have no desire to protect the Chosen One.

The Chosen One? Those words are like a dagger to my heart. That he has referred to her by that title is too much to discuss right now. But whatever it is he knows or suspects, I do not believe he has no desire to protect her. *Then why have you protected her for all these years? If you have known her true identity as you claim, why not give her over to the Skotádi?*

I do not work for the Skotádi! he roars.

I close my eyes and breathe. *You said it was complicated, so please uncomplicate it for me. And then I will leave you in peace.*

He is quiet for a moment before his voice fills my head again. *Nineteen years ago, before she was born, the Skotádi learned of a child, a descendant of Azezal himself who was able to summon fire from her mother's womb. Jadon Nassari tried to keep such power a secret, but the magic was detected by warlocks of the Skotádi. They sent a squadron of their finest vampire soldiers to kill the parents and take the child. But once again, the child summoned fire from her mother's womb and burned the vampires who came for her to ash.*

I was aware of this, but why did the Skotádi want Ophelia?

Because they believe she is the Chosen One.

It seems I cannot escape those words and this damn prophecy. *And do you?*

I believed enough to be willing to kill the child myself before I would allow the Skotádi to take her and manipulate her power for evil. To be the first to drink from the untouched vessel. I am too enraged by his admission to explore the words taken straight from the prophecy.

You would have killed a defenseless infant—

To prevent the darkest creatures in the world from getting their hands on the Chosen One? I believe you already know me capable of more heinous crimes than that, Father. Again, the word is more insult than title. He is right; I am acutely aware of the darkness inside him.

But you did not have to because members of the Order saved her?

Nazeel Danraath and Ophelia's uncle, Kameen, yes.

Another burst of rage hurtles through me at the mention of Nazeel's name. *So when did you meet Ophelia?*

CHAPTER THIRTY-FIVE

I have met her many times in her life, but as she got older, I remained at a distance and observed, careful to never let her see me.

To what end were you watching her?

To ensure she was not manipulated by the dark, he snaps, growing impatient. Restless to move on from wherever he currently is. And I have an image of him, always restless, always moving.

I have two more questions, and then I will bother you no further.

He growls.

Did you have anything to do with the attacks on Ophelia whilst she was at Montridge?

I believe you should look closer to home for the answer to that question.

Giorgios?

Is that your second question? he scoffs.

I have two million more questions, but there is one burning to be asked. *Why can Ophelia sense you? It is as though you share a bond when I know you do not.*

Ah. He laughs darkly. *That is because I tasted her blood. A hell of a long time before you did, Father.*

No. That is impossible. I would have known if he had fed from her, would I not? Because then he would have had to bond with her too. He would have been drawn to her the way the boys and I were. Unless she was only a child. The raging maelstrom of emotion in my chest grows wilder and less able to be contained. *When? How? Did you wipe her memory?*

I answered your questions. All trace of amusement is gone. *Now get the fuck out of my head.*

I clench my jaw so hard my teeth ache. Why is it that answers only lead to more questions where Ophelia Hart is concerned? But I will keep my promise and leave him in peace —for now, at least. *I am going. But Lucian ...*

He does not reply, and I wonder whether what am I about to

say will hurt or help, but I cannot live a moment longer without saying it. *I felt your loss as deeply as I did theirs. You are my son. And it does not matter that you removed our bond—you will never not be my son.*

Still, he says nothing, but I am content knowing he heard me. For now, that is all I can hope for where he is concerned.

CHAPTER
THIRTY-SIX
OPHELIA

"You smell so good, princess." Axl trails his lips down my neck as he pins my wrists on either side of my head.

I giggle, squirming against his grip, trapped between him and the floor. "You're supposed to be teaching me to fight."

My protest was feeble at best, and his hand snakes under the hem of my sundress. "So fight me, princess."

"Ophelia." Alexandros's deep voice makes Axl and me bolt upright. Am I in trouble?

He sounds mad, I say to Axl, who mumbles his agreement as we both quickly jump to our feet.

Alexandros arches an eyebrow. "I can hear you."

I press my lips together and watch him stride purposefully through the room before he takes a seat, and we do the same. "Where are Xavier and Malachi?"

"Hunting," Axl replies.

Alexandros hums, sucking on his top lip. "I suppose we will tell them later."

I scooch off Axl's lap and sink onto the sofa cushion beside him. "Tell them what?"

His dark eyes narrow on my face. "Have you ever met Lucian before you saw him in the cave that day?"

I shake my head. "No."

He frowns. "Think carefully, Ophelia. This is important."

"I don't need to think. I have never met him. I mean, I think I'd remember if I did. He's kind of ..." I chew on my lip.

"If you say he's hot, I will spank your ass, princess." Axl's growl contains only a hint of playfulness.

I roll my eyes. "I was going to say he's intense."

"Can we focus, children?" Alexandros barks, and Axl and I turn our attention back to him. I sink farther into the sofa. What have I done to make him think I'm hiding something about Lucian?

He pinches the spot between his brows and sighs. "I am sorry. But I spoke with Lucian a moment ago, and he told me you and he have met many times before."

"I really don't remember if we did. Maybe I was too young to remember?" I offer. But why would Lucian lie about that, and why does Alexandros seem so mad at me because of it?

"He also said he tasted your blood."

The room falls awkwardly silent, and both Axl and Alexandros stare at me. "He has never tasted my blood, I swear!"

Axl snarls. "Fucker."

Alexandros runs a hand over his beard. "It is possible he made you forget afterward, but I am sure I would have detected his scent if he had ever bitten you before, no matter how long ago it was."

"And wouldn't he have had to bond with Ophelia? Or he would've gotten sick like I did, right?" Axl asks.

"Not if he tasted Ophelia's blood before her first menstrual cycle. Elementai cannot be bonded with until they come of age. An evolutionary tactic to prevent babies and children from being bonded for life."

CHAPTER THIRTY-SIX

Ugh! I was twelve when I got my first period. Hardly of age. But I have more pressing matters to deal with. I feel confused and angry and like I'm being accused of something I didn't do. "I have no idea what the hell he did to me or whether he used his vampire Jedi mind tricks on me afterward, but I am telling you that as far as I am aware, the first time I met him was in that cave in Peru!" I seethe, my breathing growing heavier.

Alexandros walks around the coffee table and sits beside me. After taking my hand in his, he dusts his lips over my knuckles. "I am not accusing you of anything, little one. Nor am I angry with you. But it is an alarming development."

"Can't believe he fucking tasted you," Axl grumbles.

I shove him in the arm. "Hey, jerkwad. It wasn't like I asked him to."

He winces like he's only just realized what a dick he's being. "I know, princess." He looks over my head to Alexandros. "Did he say anything else?"

"He was frustratingly vague." Alexandros focuses his attention on me. "But he did tell me it was the Skotádi who killed your parents. They wanted to indoctrinate you into their cause, but you killed them all before they could."

"They're like the evil version of the Order, right?" I ask.

Alexandros tilts his head back and forth. "That would be an overly simplistic yet accurate way of describing them, yes."

Axl rests his hand on my thigh and squeezes. "Wasn't Lucian the head of the Skotádi?"

Alexandros leans back against the sofa and rests his arm on the cushion behind me. "He claims he never was and that on the day of Ophelia's birth, he was trying to stop the Skotádi from taking her."

"Do you think he's telling the truth?"

He blows out a breath, looking incredibly tired all of a sudden. I slip my hand into his and lean into him. He drops a tender kiss on the top of my head, and a little of the tension seeps out of him. "I did not detect any deceit in his answers, but then I have learned not to trust my instincts when it comes to my family."

"Fucker," Axl says again, his hand still firm on my thigh.

"I suspect he has more answers about Giorgios and his intentions, but for now, it is best not to push him. Whatever the truth, it is clear he has been aware of you for some time."

"How, though? Did he say anything else about the day I was born? Or how the Skotádi knew I was an elementai?"

His muscles tense, although it's so subtle I probably wouldn't have noticed if I weren't so in tune with him. "What is it?"

He sighs and runs a hand through his thick hair. "It was not that they thought you to be an elementai that drew them to you, Ophelia."

Sitting up, I search his face for a clue as to why he's become so evasive. "Then what was it?"

"You have to understand that this has no basis in fact. It was written thousands of years ago and is nothing more than the vague notions of a madwoman."

Panic settles in the center of my chest. "What notions? What madwoman? What are you talking about?"

"There is a prophecy." He clears his throat and shakes his head.

My conversations from last week with Enora and Giorgios come back to me, along with what Nazeel Danraath said about how I was something more than an elementai. "About the Chosen One?"

He frowns. "You know about this?"

I explain how Lucian called me that when I met him for the first time and about Enora and Giorgios and Nazeel. With each new piece of information, he grows more tense.

CHAPTER THIRTY-SIX

Axl's mouth hangs open. "So, there actually is a prophecy? About Ophelia? That wasn't Giorgios making up bullshit to justify what he did?"

Alexandros lets out a weary sigh. "There is a prophecy."

"What the fuck does it say?" Axl demands.

"I do not accurately recall the full text, but essentially, it speaks of a child borne of fire and blood who will be the world's ruin or redemption."

"And they think that child is me?" I whisper the words because the thought of being some kind of savior is insane. Insane!

He nods. "Yes."

My stomach rolls, and I fight the urge to be sick. This is too much to process. I long for the time when deciding whether to have beef or chicken burritos for lunch was my biggest dilemma of the day.

Axl lets out a low whistle. "Wow. No pressure, princess."

Alexandros wraps me in his arms and rests his lips on my hair. "You are not anyone's Chosen One but ours, little one."

I bury my face against his shirt and inhale his familiar scent while he runs his hands over my hair, and it works to soothe me a little. I had no idea Enora and Nazeel were referring to such absurd notions when they spoke of me being chosen, of being something more than an elementai. Alexandros's and Axl's concern emanate from them, and it only makes me feel worse. A few short months ago, I didn't even know magic existed. And now I'm hiding out in a werewolf's house with my four vampire mates, trying to learn how to use my powers, speaking to people in other countries with the power of my mind, and being watched over by two dragons. So, if the last six months have taught me anything, it is that anything is possible.

And that is completely terrifying.

CHAPTER
THIRTY-SEVEN
ALEXANDROS

"Alexandros." A familiar voice rouses me from my sleep, and I blink at the apparition of Enora Green standing at the foot of the bed. For that is what she is—an apparition. I have seen enough of them to know.

Enora surely possesses such magic, but I have never known her to use it to contact me before, and that knowledge is enough to have dread settling in my stomach. "Osiris told me of your whereabouts, but only because it was a matter of grave urgency."

Ophelia has been in regular contact with Cadence and Enora whilst we have been here, and although I am still wary of most of witchkind, I am certain I can trust them. The boys and Ophelia remain sleeping, and I slip out of bed and keep my voice low, careful not wake them. "What brings you here to me, filis mou?"

She glances around her, her physical form still back at Silver Vale. "I must be quick in case Giorgios detects this spell." My dread turns to white-hot anger in the blink of an eye. "He is here, Alexandros. He told everyone you are a traitor to House Drakos and has taken control of the Ruby Dragons."

CHAPTER THIRTY-SEVEN

"And President Ollenshaw and Eugene simply allowed it?"

"You know they are both unaware of his gross misdeeds. He is being very persuasive. Charming and convincing in that soothing way he has about him. But he has an army of Skotádi with him, Alexandros. They camp just beyond the woods at the base of Montridge peak. Osiris and some of his pack discovered them last night while hunting."

"How many?"

"Hundreds. Perhaps one thousand."

Giorgios's powers of deception are much greater than I realized. How long has he been planning this, and more concerningly, how did I not know any of it? "A Skotádi army? Of what? Vampires? Demons?"

"Yes. Osiris detected warlocks too."

"Witches?" I growl.

"Warlocks, Alexandros," she bites back. I have always considered them to be the same species, for they are simply witches who use dark magic, but witches who abhor dark magic vehemently disagree with my stance. "I am sure Giorgios suspects Osiris and I know the truth. He has requested entry to Silver Vale twice since his arrival not twelve hours ago. I have refused, but I am not sure how much longer I can put him off. I am worried for my girls' safety, filis mou."

I close my eyes and take a few seconds to process what this means for everyone at Montridge. How long before Giorgios unleashes his Skotádi army? How long before he tortures anyone he suspects may be helping us and discovers where we are? Any concern I have for our allies and the thousands of innocent people at Montridge pales in comparison to my fear for Ophelia.

"I am worried for Ophelia's safety too," Enora says. "For all of you."

Before I can reply, a warm hand on my forearm forces my

eyes open. "Enora?" Ophelia exclaims. "Is that you?" Her delight is quickly drowned out by anxiety. "Why are you here? What's wrong? Is it Cadence?"

"Everyone is well for now, sweet child. But Giorgios is here at Montridge."

Ophelia gasps. "Then we have to go back. He's looking for me, right?" She turns and faces me, her eyes clouded with fear. "They'll all be in danger, Alexandros. We have to go back."

"I must go," Enora says before I can tell Ophelia what a terrible idea her returning to Montridge is. "But know this, Alexandros—he is somehow in possession of dark magic. Some of the darkest I have ever felt. I sensed it as soon as he set foot outside Silver Vale, and he knows I did. But still, he did not care to mask it."

"Go, Enora. I will update you with our intentions as soon as we have discussed my return."

Enora offers a tight smile before her form disappears.

"*Your* return?" Ophelia asks, her voice low.

I am too tired for this argument, but there is no avoiding it. In fact, I have been anticipating it for days now. There have been many times when I considered simply running. Taking her and the boys and hiding, but every lesson I have learned in my long life tells me that plan is futile. "It is far too unsafe for you to return to Montridge and face him, little one. I will confront him alone."

Her skin flushes pink and her hands ball into tiny fists. "The hell you will. We only just got you back."

My frustration and anger boil over. Most of it is for my deceitful brother, but he is not here right now, thus Ophelia bears the brunt of it. "That is what will happen. I will find you a safe place to hide, and you will stay there with Elpis and the boys whilst Anikêtos takes me back to Montridge so I can deal with Giorgios."

CHAPTER THIRTY-SEVEN

"The fuck we will." Xavier joins the conversation, and a second later, he is standing beside us.

Before I can blink, Axl is with us too. "We go everywhere together, or we don't go at all."

He is swiftly followed by Malachi. "Yeah. Because with all due respect, sir, fuck that."

Baring my teeth, I pace away from them, enraged. This is like nothing else they have faced before. They have no idea what we are up against. I spin back around. "Giorgios is not alone. He has an army of vampires, demons, and warlocks with him. They are Skotádi, and they are far greater in number and infinitely more powerful than the army you encountered at his fortress."

Xavier shrugs. "We have two dragons."

"You do not understand. Giorgios is in possession of dark magic." Dragons are powerful, but they are not immune to dark magic. "It is too great a risk for Ophelia to be anywhere near him."

Axl shakes his head. "And what if it's another trap? You go there, then he transports himself to wherever we are?"

"He will not discover your location because you will be leaving here. Only I will know your new location, and I would die before I gave any of you up."

Malachi sighs. "But we're stronger together, Alexandros. You know this. Look what happened last time he split us up. Are you going to risk that again?"

I roar, allowing my anger to spill out in an uncharacteristic display of emotion. Panting, I put my hands atop my head. My voice is thick. "I will not let my fear of losing her, of losing all of you, be the reason he gets his hands on Ophelia."

Axl and Malachi blink, and Ophelia opens and closes her mouth, no doubt trying to think of a counterargument but finding none.

ALEXANDROS

It is Xavier who speaks. "Let me get this straight—Giorgios has an army and some kind of dark magic abracadabra bullshit going on, and he's gunning for you and he wants our girl. So your options are to go face him alone and leave us swinging in the wind." He holds up his hands like he can feel the rage inside me building to a crescendo and knows I am not going to like what he is about to say. "Then he either kills you or he locks you in a cage again, and he comes for us anyway. Or ..." He stares at me, and despite the lightness of his tone, he deep-blue eyes are pleading. "You go there with two dragons, three powerful and ragey-as-fuck vampires who want to tear off Giorgios's head just as much as you do." He takes a breath and jerks his head toward Ophelia. "And the most powerful being who ever lived —the woman who busted you out of a silver cage by simply thinking about it."

She does have power beyond anything any of us can imagine. The child borne of fire and blood who will save us all. That is what I am most afraid of. I do not want her to save us. Those kinds of heroes do not get to live happily ever after once they have fulfilled their destiny. They save the world by making the ultimate sacrifice, and I cannot bear the idea of Ophelia being a martyr.

Ophelia places a hand on my cheek, her bright-blue eyes brimming with tears but her jaw tipped, defiant and strong. "I know you're trying to protect me, but don't you understand that I would rather die by your side than spend an eternity without you?"

I rest my forehead against hers, and for the first time, I do understand her. My instinct is to protect her, but she is more than capable of making her own choices. And if one of those choices is me, then I am not strong enough to deny her.

CHAPTER
THIRTY-EIGHT

OPHELIA

Malachi licks the residual pancake syrup from my lips before giving me a kiss. "You missed some, baby."

The sweet aftertaste of my delicious breakfast still clings to my tastebuds. "They were amazing, as always. Thank you."

"I had to make sure my girl was fully nourished before our trip back to Montridge, now, didn't I?" He grabs my ass with one hand and skims his fangs down my throat. "Especially as you were gracious enough to be breakfast to all of us this morning."

Warm pleasure coils deep in my core, and I shrug out of his grip before things get more heated. "Speaking of our trip, I'm going to go find something more suitable to wear." I flick the hem of the pink sundress for effect.

Xavier flashes me a smirk. "I was always partial to the miniskirt-and-tank-top look on you, Cupcake."

Malachi winks. "Me too."

I look to Axl. "Any special requests from you?"

He slides his arms around my waist and ducks his head to press a kiss at the base of my throat. "Anything that shows off these beautiful curves is fine by me. But yeah, I was also a fan of the miniskirt combo."

As I head to the bedroom, I consider my options. I haven't worn my old "uniform" since we left Montridge. Was that really only a month ago? It feels like it's been a lifetime. So much has changed, especially me.

Returning to Montridge has me giddy, but the reason we are returning has me on edge. How are we supposed to act remotely normal when the apocalypse is supposedly on the horizon? I can't forget what Enora told me about the whole prophecy thing. And I know Alexandros is trying to protect me from the weight of that burden, but what if it is true? What if this is all connected and I am at the center of it all?

A thick knot of trepidation sits in the pit of my stomach, and I lay a hand on my abdomen. I remind myself who I am. What I am. I am an elementai. The last of my kind. Descendant of the great Azezal himself.

Always trust your light. Nazeel's words come back to me, and I close my eyes and immediately find the dazzling orb seated within me. Flickering and sparkling like a miniature supernova. It increases in intensity as my powers grow stronger. And, with a deep breath, I find my inner peace. The calm within the raging storm that has become my life.

I roll back my shoulders and go to the closet to examine the contents. Osiris said we could take what we wanted, and what I want is sitting right there on a hanger in front of me. As if it has been waiting for my arrival. I run my fingertips across the soft black leather and smile. It's definitely time for a new uniform.

~

ALL THE GUYS are in the den by the time I'm dressed. Xavier and Axl have their heads bent over a map. Malachi is reading a book,

CHAPTER THIRTY-EIGHT

and Alexandros is staring out the window, his hands stuffed in the pockets of his dress pants, the white shirt he borrowed pulled taut across his muscular back. He looks every inch the respectable professor again.

He spins around when I walk into the room, and the guys look up from what they were doing.

"Holy fucking shit, Cupcake!" Xavier exclaims while Malachi wolf whistles and Axl groans loudly, biting on his lip and tipping his face to the ceiling. The three of them crowd me and run their hands over my leather-clad skin. Grunts and groans and declarations of approval wash over me.

I look down at my new outfit: black leather pants, a tank top, and a black leather jacket. Skintight but supple and surprisingly comfortable and practical. "So you like the new look?" I ask, unable to stop myself from blushing. "It's not too ... cliché?"

"Like it? Cupcake, I love it. You look hot as fuck." His hand slides down to my ass and gives it a squeeze.

Axl kisses my forehead. "Like an avenging fucking angel. A sexy-as-hell avenging angel."

Malachi twirls me around and then wraps me in a hug. "You look incredible, baby."

I glance over Malachi's shoulder at Alexandros, who has remained silent and stoic, which isn't unusual, but I hoped for a little more of a reaction from him.

I catch his eye. "Do you approve?"

He strides across the room and reaches us in less than a second. With one hand, he grabs the back of my neck and drags me toward him, tilting my head back with his grip. "No, Ophelia, I do not approve." His voice is low and dangerous, and it sends a shiver down my spine. "In fact, I disapprove so much that I have half a mind to march you back into that room where I will relieve you of every scrap of these clothes." He presses a kiss on my lips. "After which, I will fuck your mouth before I dress you in more appropriate attire."

As hot as that sounds, is he serious? I'd be hurt, except I sense a wicked playfulness in his tone. "And what exactly would you deem appropriate, sir?"

He runs his nose across my jawline, inhaling deeply. "Something that does not make me instantly hard every time I look at you." His lips twitch with the faintest hint of a smirk before he swats me hard on the ass. "But alas, we do not have time for such frivolity. We must leave before Anikêtos gets any more annoyed and burns down a small village."

He stalks out of the room, and I glance between the three guys, trying to suppress my grin. "So you think he likes it, then?"

Xavier slips his arm around my waist. "Cupcake, he is going to fuck the brat out of you for wearing this as soon as he can. Yeah, he likes it."

I like it too, and not only because the boys love it and it seems to do something in particular to Alexandros.

I like it because it feels very much like the new me. Ophelia Hart, the girl who is about to ride home on the back of the most powerful dragon that ever lived.

CHAPTER THIRTY-NINE

ALEXANDROS

"So, we're on Elpis, yeah?" Malachi asks as he eyes the spectacular green dragon preening herself in front of us. I nod.

"Seems unfair you get the bigger, faster dragon *and* Ophelia," Xavier grumbles. He stumbles back when Elpis scorches the patch of grass at his feet.

I clap him on the shoulder. "She says to tell you that you are welcome to walk if you would find it more tolerable." I suppress a smirk at the contrite look on his usually cocky-to-the-point-of-annoying face.

He holds up his hands as he gazes up at her. "I meant no disrespect. You're an epic fucking dragon, and you're way prettier than the other guy." Then he places one hand over his heart. "I am actually only pissed I don't get to ride with my girl and that they'll get there before us." Elpis blows a plume of smoke at him, making him sputter.

"She and Ani will fly together, Xavier. I want to ensure we all stay together and arrive at the same time."

He coughs, waving his hand in front of his face. "Good to know."

I turn to face the house as the others lock up, and I sense him before I see him. He appears on the stone path between the house and where Xavier and I stand waiting for Ophelia, Axl, and Malachi.

"Giorgios." I spit his name from my mouth like the poison it is.

Two warlocks shrouded in dark hooded cloaks appear immediately at his side, and the force field they conjure around my brother glows with a faint orange hue.

I run toward him, rage fueling every step I take.

Ophelia calls my name in warning, but I pay her no mind, too mired in my determination to tear my brother's head from his body. But when I reach him, I am met with an immovable wall. Enraged, I slam my fists against it. The warlock to Giorgios's right simply taps the barrier with his finger, and I am thrown back with the force of energy he releases.

Ophelia surges forward with Axl and Malachi on her heels. She conjures a ball of Dragonfyre and throws it in their direction, but it simply bounces off. The grass instantly ignites where it lands, and she douses the flame. I race over to her and pull her to my side. Fear for her safety is the only thing preventing me from running at him again.

"I will kill you, Giorgios." I snarl. "Your magic will not hold for long."

He flashes me a sympathetic look. Arrogant, deceitful fuck. I will kill him, and then I shall travel to the netherworld and kill him again. Xavier is by our side now, bouncing on the balls of his feet.

As Elpis stalks toward us, she flattens the white picket fence surrounding the house.

Giorgios looks up at her. "Delightful to see you again, Elpis."

She aims a plume of fire in his direction, but like Ophelia's Dragonfyre, it bounces off.

CHAPTER THIRTY-NINE

Giorgios's lip curls in a sneer, and I am picturing the moment I tear his entire face to shreds until no features remain. "Should you not be asking me why I am here, brother? How I found you?"

"You found me because magic such as what we have here"—I glance up at the shadow passing overhead to find Anikêtos looming over the house—"cannot be masked forever. I believed we may have a week, but it appears I have underestimated your abilities."

He tilts his head to one side, eyeing me like one would eye an exhibit in a zoo. As though he has never seen me before. "You have always underestimated me, brother, and that will be your downfall."

"No." I shake my head, my teeth gnashing together whilst I keep a firm grip on Ophelia. "I have always trusted you, brother, and that may be my weakness, but it will not be my downfall."

Ophelia closes her eyes, and a gust of wind ruffles the leaves on the trees. She is channeling her powers. The force field shimmers but remains intact.

"You may be powerful, little girl, but these warlocks have been practicing magic for centuries. It will take more than your pathetic little attempts to break their spell." For his mockery alone, I want to tear out his heart and feed it to him whilst it is still beating.

My incredible elementai pays him no heed, but she opens her eyes and remains focused on the orange orb in front of us.

Giorgios inspects his nails like he has somewhere more important to be, and my rage boils hot in my veins. But the longer we can keep him here, the higher chance Ophelia has of breaking down his force field. And then I will have my revenge.

"You did not answer my other question, brother."

I scowl at him and his two cloaked mercenaries, whose faces remain hidden. "The question of why you are here? That is obvious. You are here for Ophelia." I flex my hand on her hip, keeping her close.

Giorgios smirks, and for the first time, the mask slips and I glimpse the evil lurking beneath the veneer of respectability he has cultivated so well these past two thousand years.

"Once again, brother. You underestimate me."

The warm air turns frigid, and darkness falls over the garden as though it is suddenly night.

"No!" Malachi's anguished cry pierces the air. A cold finger of fear slithers down my spine, but it is what I see when I turn my attention from Giorgios that freezes the blood in my veins to ice. The shadowy figure looms over Malachi, and his abject terror hits me straight in the chest. Anxiety and despair and so much anguish grip my throat, making it impossible to breathe. If I were not feeling such things, I would swear the apparition was a lie. A trick. A hallucination.

Ophelia shrieks, and Axl and Xavier call out to their brother, but it is all too late. Their movements appear to happen in slow motion as they run to him, but they have barely taken a single step when the twisted shadows curl around him and absorb Malachi into the darkness. Just like that, the light returns.

But he is gone.

My sweet, sensitive boy.

"Wh-where is he?" Xavier gapes at the spot where his brother just stood.

Ophelia trembles, leaning against me for support as she whispers his name.

"What the fuck was that?" Axl shouts. "Where is he? Professor?"

I am too focused on Giorgios to answer. I can only utter one word. "How?"

"I told you, brother." He winks. "You underestimate me."

I am going to gouge that eye out as soon as I have the

CHAPTER THIRTY-NINE

chance. He and his warlocks disappear, and I am left with a gaping hole in my chest and soul-crushing anguish—not only mine, but theirs too. Xavier drops to his knees and sobs, and Ophelia buries her head against my chest as Axl stares blankly at the void where Malachi was. We are all overcome with shock and the lingering despair left behind by creatures such as the one that took Malachi.

Alexandros. It is Anikêtos's growling voice that overcomes me now.

"Was it? Was that truly a wraith, Ani?" I cannot even form the entirety of his name.

Yes.

"But how?"

His sadness is almost as overwhelming as Ophelia's and the boys'. *It must have slipped through when Elpis and I left the netherworld.*

"What does that mean?" Ophelia fists her hand in my shirt. "Why did they take him? Is he still alive?" Her pleas carve out chunks of my heart.

I suck in a deep breath and swallow down the desolation threatening to drown me. The lingering effects of the wraith's presence continue to cloud my thoughts, but Ophelia and my boys need me, and that is what I must focus on. I clear the sob from my throat. "He was absorbed by the wraith, but that does not mean he is dead. Giorgios clearly needs him for something." Although I have absolutely no idea why he could need my youngest sired.

"S-so he's okay? We can get him back?" She blinks at me, tears running down her face.

I did not say he was okay. I have never known anyone to be swallowed up by a wraith and live to tell the tale. But I cannot consider the possibility that he is gone, and more importantly, neither can they.

My eyes dart between Ophelia, Axl, and Xavier. "We will find Giorgios, and we will get Malachi back." I do not add that even if we achieve such a feat, the man who returns may never again be the man who left.

I am sure Ophelia hears my thoughts anyway, because she clings to me even more tightly and heavy sobs rack her body. But after only a moment, she rolls back her shoulders and stares up at me, her eyes full of fire. "If Giorgios has Malachi, then let's go get him back."

I kiss her forehead. Despite my fear for her safety, I can think of nothing we need to do more.

CHAPTER FORTY

XAVIER

"We need to leave now. It is likely Giorgios will return to Montridge, and although he has taken Malachi, we must assume Ophelia is still his primary target, so we will all travel together on Anikêtos," Alexandros says.

I'm still on my knees, my heart shattering into pieces while I stare at the spot on the ground where he stood until he was swallowed up by that ... that thing. "What the fuck was that thing?" The words come from me, but they can't be mine because I'm pretty sure I've lost the ability to function.

That thing took Kai. It swallowed him up like he was made of air.

Alexandros pulls me to my feet and places a hand on the back of my neck. "It was a wraith."

"A wraith?" Axl asks. He and Ophelia are standing beside us now too, looking like they're holding each other up. "Like a ghost?"

Ophelia's lip wobbles. "Or a demon?"

"More than a ghost and different from a demon. They are immortal, soulless creatures that are able to drain the life of others and steal their souls with merely a touch. They are one of the few creatures able to kill a dragon."

I look overhead to where Anikêtos is still looming over the house. "Where the fuck did it come from? I heard of wraiths back when I was human, but I've never seen one before. And I've never heard you mention them."

"When a warlock casts a dark spell and it backfires, they are doomed for eternity, thus becoming wraiths. However, I have not seen one in over a thousand years. They were once great in number and wreaked havoc on the world of man during the Dark Ages. But their reign came to an end when a powerful white witch banished them to the netherworld, where Lucifer holds them captive. She gave her life to cast the spell, and her sacrifice has kept them there since, at least as far as I am aware."

I scrub the tears from my eyes with the back of my hand. "So why is one here now, and how do we kill it?"

Alexandros glances up at Anikêtos. "I believe they may have taken the opportunity to slip through the veil when Anikêtos and Elpis returned."

Ophelia's eyes widen. "They? You think there's more than one?"

Alexandros frowns. "We cannot discount that possibility. And as for what kills them, it can only be done with a sacred or holy relic."

I need something to hold on to, and this feels like it. A way to kill the shadowy fuck. "Like a crucifix?"

He shakes his head. "Much more than that. It must be the most sacred of artefacts."

Axl throws his hands in the air. "And what the hell kind of thing would that be? Because I don't see any spare ark of the covenants lying around."

CHAPTER FORTY

"It does not have to be a Christian symbol; it can be from any religion, but the relic must be believed in by the user."

Axl drops his head and sighs. "So that means we're out—we believe in fuck all. Ophelia, what about you?"

She shakes her head. "Not religion. But I do believe in something ..."

I run the pad of my thumb over her jawline and tip her chin up so she's staring into my eyes. "And what's that, Cupcake?"

She narrows her eyes with determination. "Us."

Alexandros wraps his arms around all three of us and pulls us into an embrace. All four of our heads press together. "We do not have to kill the wraith. It will be enough to send it back to the netherworld. And I believe I know a witch powerful enough to cast such a spell."

I suspect he's talking about Enora, but I don't ask for clarification. As long as we get Malachi back, I don't care how we get rid of the damn wraith.

We'll get him back. Ophelia's voice is full of conviction as it suffuses our collective thoughts. *If I'm supposed to be some magical Chosen One with all these powers, then we'll get him back.*

～

As Alexandros promised we would be, we're all seated on Anikêtos's back for our return trip to Montridge. We cling to each other out of fear that another one of us may fall prey to the wraith.

Ophelia, being a quick study, has figured out the force field spell and has surrounded us with one. Hers, unsurprisingly, has a pink hue rather than an orange one, and it also handily serves to keep us safe from the elements. Still, it doesn't block sound, and Anikêtos's speed coupled with the wind makes it impossible to hear one another speak aloud, so we stick to our bond.

XAVIER

Did Giorgios show any special interest in Malachi whilst you were at his fortress? Alexandros asks.

No, I say. *He didn't really take much interest in any of us other than Ophelia.*

Axl adds his agreement.

We'll get him back, Ophelia says again. The phrase seems to have become her new mantra. I wish I had her conviction. All I can think about is Kai in pain. Or even worse, not in pain because as long as he's hurting, he's alive. I've tried reaching him at least a dozen times since we left Venezuela, but I can't find him. And I know if Ophelia or Alexandros had, they would have let us know he's alive.

Immortal soulless fuck or not, if the wraith has killed Kai, I will drag him back to the netherworld myself.

CHAPTER
FORTY-ONE
OPHELIA

Anikêtos lands on the football field, one of the few places he can do so entirely undetected. While he remains cloaked from the view of others, his vast size makes it difficult for him to be anywhere where there are people.

Elpis circles overhead.

The campus is eerily quiet for a Friday evening.

"Where will you wait for us, old friend?" Alexandros asks.

Elpis and I will take shelter on the other side of the mountain, far from Giorgios's army but where we can keep a close eye on them.

Alexandros thanks him, and Anikêtos spreads his huge wings and joins Elpis. The rush of wind almost blows me over, and Xavier wraps his arms around my waist. "Got you, Cupcake."

"Be careful to mask your thoughts and emotions as much as possible at all times," Alexandros warns. "Do not search for Malachi yet, for it may open you up to Giorgios's detection. He will be anticipating our arrival, and I would prefer for him to remain unaware of our presence for as long as possible."

Although it hurts not to search for Malachi and to close my

mind off so he can't find us if he's looking, I know he's right. So I do as he asks, bringing down all the walls I've learned to build.

Axl looks around. It has not taken him long to resume his role as Ruby Dragon Commander. Strategic and alert. "Where are we headed? We can't go to either Ruby Dragon house, so where's our base?"

Xavier frowns. "But that's where he'll have Kai, right? Shouldn't we go straight there and get him?"

"My brother took him for a reason, and whatever that reason is, it buys us a little time. We cannot go there immediately when we do not know what we are walking into." Alexandros cups Xavier's face in his hands and presses their foreheads together. "I want him back just as much as you do. I assure you."

Xavier mumbles his understanding.

"We will head for Silver Vale as it is protected from unwelcome vampires. I will inform Enora of our imminent arrival and have Osiris join us there."

My heart gives a tiny flutter of hope. I'll get to see Cadence and hopefully Sienna. Enora too. All of us together will figure out how to get Malachi back.

He must still be alive. I would know if he weren't. We would have all felt the same heart-wrenching agony as when our bond with Alexandros was severed. That is what I'm clinging to, along with Axl's and Xavier's hands, as we race toward Silver Vale.

～

Cadence is waiting for us on the steps of Silver Vale when we arrive. Hurriedly, she ushers us inside, and as soon as the door is closed, she throws her arms around me, wrapping me in the biggest, warmest hug she's ever given me.

CHAPTER FORTY-ONE

"I'm so sorry about Malachi. And Giorgios and everything." She squeezes me tighter. "But I'm so glad you're back."

"Me too, girl." Sienna hugs me from behind, sandwiching me between their warmth and comfort.

Being enveloped in their compassion has tears dripping down my face. "Thank you so much for being here for me."

Cadence presses her cheek against mine. "We've always got your back, Ophelia."

Sienna presses her cheek on my other side. "Ride or die, bitches."

This right here is true magic. True friendship.

"It is good to see you all," Enora says as she strides in our direction. "I only wish it were under much happier circumstances." She gestures toward her study. "Osiris is here too. But I have sent all my other girls home for the weekend to be with their families. It felt like it was for the best."

Alexandros scans the hallway, as though looking for a potential threat. After everything that's happened, it's no surprise he's suspicious of everything and everyone.

"Don't you want to go home to be with your families too?" I ask Cadence and Sienna.

Cadence shakes her head. "No way. I told you we got your back, and we do. Always."

"My family is here anyway," Sienna says, shrugging.

My heart is bursting with love and gratitude for both of them, but I can't help feeling guilty. "It could be dangerous. I would hate for anything to happen to you because of me."

"Ophelia Hart," Alexandros's growl sends a shiver down my spine. "How many times must I tell you that nothing that has happened and nothing that will happen is your fault?"

I can feel my lip lower lip tremble. Logically, I know it's true, but still ...

Enora offers me a kind smile. "He speaks the truth, Ophelia.

And while your compassion is endearing, the guilt will hold you back. We are all capable of making our own choices, sweet child. Now, let us go. I have made tea."

Xavier rolls his eyes. *Oh yeah, because tea is exactly what we need, right?* He winks at me before he follows Enora and Alexandros down the hallway.

Osiris is indeed pouring tea when we reach Enora's study, and he offers us all a cup. All of my mates refuse, but I accept. I find holding the hot mug in my hands oddly comforting. Once the pleasantries are dispensed with, Osiris brings us all up to date. Alexandros, Axl, and Xavier stand near the entrance of the room, arms folded and bodies rigid as they listen to Osiris explain all they have learned since Giorgios's arrival.

He apparently remains the self-imposed head of the Ruby Dragon society; however, many of the vampires have already left at his invitation. "From what I can tell, they refused to denounce you and swear allegiance to him."

Alexandros merely nods. "Go on."

"Jerome is still useless. He has not challenged Giorgios in any way thus far."

I listen intently, with Cadence and Sienna standing either side of me. Giorgios seems to have spent his entire time on campus waging a smear campaign against Alexandros, trying to draw as many as possible to his cause. It's a testament to how respected he is here that so few flocked to his brother's side. But where is Giorgios keeping Malachi, and what the hell does he want with him? A shiver runs down my spine when I recall the wraith's presence and how he filled our heads with darkness and despair.

"And the heads of all the other houses?" Alexandros's voice snaps me from my depressing thoughts, reminding me we need to act, not dwell on what's already been done. That is how we get Kai back.

CHAPTER FORTY-ONE

"The heads of the Crescent houses have been advised that you are not a traitor. They are on your side, even if they do not understand the coming war."

The sip of tea I just took goes down wrong, and I cough violently. When I can speak again, I rasp, "War?"

Alexandros narrows his eyes at Osiris, who winces and clears his throat before continuing. "Merely a figure of speech. But you can count on the Crescent societies, although at my instruction, most of our packs have been sent home. Only a few critical seniors remain. Those I believe would do well in battle should the need arrive."

Alexandros turns to Enora. "And the Vales?"

"They are aware something is afoot, but they do not wish to be a part of Giorgios's coup. However, they have no desire to challenge him either, so they have left. And all members have been advised to return home until told it is safe to return."

As much as I try not to let it, guilt returns to consume me. Safe to return? When will that even be? How long will Giorgios continue his ridiculous scheme? What the hell does he want with Montridge? With Malachi?

With me?

Axl comes to stand behind me and puts his arms around my waist. I lean back against him. "And what about the Dragon houses?" he asks.

"Nicholas Ashe was keen to side with Giorgios from the moment he arrived. All of his vampires have stayed behind."

Alexandros clenches his jaw. "That figures. I should have taken his head five hundred years ago after what he took from me."

My innate curiosity demands I ask for more information about what he took, but now isn't the time to learn about the past. Not unless it helps the present situation, and if it did, I'm sure Alexandros would elaborate.

OPHELIA

Xavier's lip curls up, baring his fangs. "Onyx has always hated us."

Axl rests his chin on top of my head, his warm breath ruffling my hair. "But what about Opal and Lapis?"

"They have always sworn allegiance to House Drakos," Osiris answers, looking at Alexandros. "And without word from you or your father, they have refused to accept Giorgios as the new Ruby head. However, they are not fully aware of the situation. I did not wish to involve myself in vampire affairs as I am unsure who we can trust, but I believe they will be our allies."

"I understand your reluctance, and I concur. But they must be appraised of the situation as soon as possible." Alexandros directs his attention to Axl. "When we are done here, you must make contact and tell them Giorgios has betrayed his house by bringing dark magic and the Skotádi onto campus. Let them send their members home if they must."

Xavier scowls. "But we need some of them to stay behind and fucking fight, Professor. Giorgios has a whole goddamn army."

"They must make that choice for themselves, Xavier. An unwilling soldier is little use to us. They can leave or they can fight for the future of their kind. It is up to them."

Axl voices his compliance while Alexandros refocuses on Osiris. "And Jerome Ollenshaw must advise all other students to return home." He glances at his watch. "It is not too late for them to leave, and as it is a weekend, it is likely to cause less chaos. Have him tell them the school is infested with cockroaches or some other such nonsense that will scare the humans."

Before Osiris can reply, someone hammers on the front door. My heart leaps into my throat, and Alexandros snarls.

"You think that's Giorgios?" Cadence asks, her eyes wide.

Alexandros cracks his neck. "No. It is my father."

CHAPTER
FORTY-TWO

ALEXANDROS

Alexandros. His familiar voice rings through my head. My jaw clenched tight, I fight the urge to roar my frustration. Do we not already have enough to deal with?

Alexandros! he calls again.

Aware of all the eyes in the room currently upon me, I answer him. *What do you want?*

His bellow shakes the foundation of the house. *I wish to speak with you. I demand answers.*

Does Giorgios know you are here?

Do you mean the new head of Ruby Dragon? He scoffs. *No, he does not.*

His powers are much greater than you know, Father. I would not be so sure of that.

I know when my own son is aware of my presence. I hid it from you until just now, did I not? Now let me in this damn house before I summon your brother here and ask him for the answers I seek.

I look at the anxious faces around the room. "He wishes to enter, or he will alert Giorgios to our presence."

Osiris rolls back his shoulders. "Then grant him entry. I am sure he is no threat to the strength in this room."

I glance at Ophelia, safely wrapped in Axl's arms with her friends on either side of her. It is not his strength I am concerned about. It is him finding out what she is. However, as much as I worry about my father's intentions toward Ophelia should he discover her to be an elementai, he is not our concern at the moment. "Will you allow him entry, Enora?"

"If you believe he can be trusted," she replies.

That is a complicated issue, but only one thing truly matters. "I believe he would take our side over Giorgios's. So that makes him our ally. For now." My father is many things. Cruel. Unyielding. Ruthless. But he is not insane. He also understands a fated mate bond, and no matter how much he might covet Ophelia, after what I learned the last time I saw him, I have a small amount of hope he would never take that from me.

Enora goes to admit him entrance, and I beckon Ophelia to me. "Come here, agápi mou."

She glances back at Axl, and he lets her go so she can stand with me—the safest place for her when my father is in the vicinity.

"Is it safe for Ophelia to have him here?" Xavier asks.

I suck in a deep breath as his overwhelming presence grows closer. If I believed he was a risk to her safety, I would not have risked allowing him to enter. However, one can never be sure of anything where my father is concerned. What I am sure of is that I would take his head before I let him touch her. "She will not come to any harm."

She shivers, and I slide my arms around her waist and press my lips to her ear. "He will never hurt you when I am near, little one."

She straightens her spine. "I'm ready for him if he tries. A

CHAPTER FORTY-TWO

force field if he gets too close, and Dragonfyre if he really pisses me off."

My lips twitch, and I am filled with pride. "That is my girl."

"Alexandros, what in the name of the netherworld is going on?" he asks as soon as he steps foot in the room. He does not bother with any pleasantries, but I introduce everyone by name anyway. I leave Ophelia until last.

His tilts his head to the side as he scrutinizes her, and a deep, possessive growl rumbles in his chest. It is instinctive, I know, but it does not make me any less enraged. "Do not touch her," I snarl in warning.

He takes a step closer and inhales deeply. "What is she? She is not human. Not witch."

Ophelia tips her chin. "I'm an elementai."

His eyes narrow to slits. "No."

"She is." I sense Axl's and Xavier's anger growing stronger the closer my father gets to her. "And she is my fated mate as well as that of my sireds."

His throat works as he swallows down the many things he no doubt wants to say. "What is occurring? Why did your brother have me believe you were dead? Why is he claiming to be the head of Ruby Dragon when I"—he jabs his thumb into his chest—"have not approved such a position?"

I look at him, really look at him for the first time in as long as I can remember. The silver flecks in his hair, the faint lines around his eyes. He is almost three thousand years old. How weary would I be of this world if I had lived as long and lost my fated mate half a millennium ago? He has always been cruel. Pushed Giorgios and me past our limits. Pitted us against each other. But perhaps it was because he saw something no one else did in my brother's heart. I will never know the full truth, but right now I make the choice to trust my father, something I have not done since I was a boy.

My father's face grows darker with each new piece of information I reveal. And by the time I have given him a summary of Giorgios's betrayal, Malachi's abduction, and Ophelia's unique powers, he is a breath away from foaming at the mouth.

"I knew your brother was not to be trusted, Alexandros." He holds up his fist and shakes it. "All along, I have known his loyalty to House Drakos, to our family line, was questionable."

"You can spare me the lecture for when I have the time to hear it. Right now, I need to focus on getting Malachi back, and that means getting into the Ruby Dragon house whilst simultaneously preventing Giorgios from discovering our arrival for as long as possible."

My father nods his agreement. "As soon as he realizes you are here, he will likely deploy the army he has on standby. Who do we have other than the people in this room?"

"I'm counting on some vampires from Lapis and Opal," Axl answers. "A few wolves. Our own vampires will likely fight for us once they see you and Alexandros are here."

"If they do not, they will lose their heads," Vasilis growls. "Is that all?"

"No." I have not yet told him of our greatest weapon. "We have two dragons on our side."

If I did not know better, I would say he gazes upon me with pride. "You have brought dragons back to the mortal realm? Tell me Anikêtos is one of them."

"Anikêtos and Elpis, yes. Yet it was not I who ensured their return, but Ophelia."

He blinks at her. "You truly are a wondrous creature."

Axl clears his throat. "We need to move if we're going to have any hope of rallying some support before we try to take Ruby Dragon back and get Kai."

Osiris nods his agreement. "I'll go to Jerome and then speak

CHAPTER FORTY-TWO

with the other heads of houses if Axl can deal with Lapis and Opal."

"And Onyx?" my father asks.

I shake my head. "Onyx has sided with Giorgios already, though I have no idea what lies he has told them or what promises he has made."

He snorts with disdain. "I am sure Vincent will have something to say about his nephew's defiance. He has been a thorn in our sides for far too long."

Vincent Beretti is the head of House Chóma, and he and my father are not exactly allies, but they do have a long-standing mutual respect. "You can ask Vincent to pull Nicholas into line, and perhaps he will, but I still would not trust him."

"And you would have good reason not to after he was already discovered to be an ally of the Skotádi once. But you must recall how he saved his head." I do recall. He swore he would serve Vincent for eternity. "If he breaks that oath, there is only one fate which will await him."

Osiris shakes his head. "I don't trust Ashe either. However, our biggest hurdle will be getting Jerome to agree to send all the human students home. He will want to avoid any kind of confrontation with the board or with parents, but if anyone gets caught in the crossfire, we will have a scandal to cover up."

My father puffs out his chest. "Then I will deal with Jerome Ollenshaw. It should only take a small reminder that he is president of this institution at the grace of House Drakos."

I offer Osiris a nod of appreciation, grateful my father has something to focus on. That will give me some much-needed space to think and plan.

CHAPTER
FORTY-THREE
MALACHI

Despair. Desolation. Black and shadowy and all-consuming, it creeps into every cell of my body, solidifying inside until I am no longer made of flesh and bone, but of only darkness and anguish. There is nothing worth living for. Not even her.

I screw my eyes closed and try to curl myself into a ball, but I realize I'm hog-tied with my ankles and wrists bound together. Even being here, in the cellar in our basement where we brought Ophelia all those months ago, is not enough to bolster any strength of feeling other than abject misery.

I know the creature that took me. I've read enough of wraiths to know this darkness swallowing me whole is its doing. It should have taken my soul but for some reason has not. But I didn't know they existed until today, and I have no idea why I've never come across one before. Surely a being with such powerful dark magic would not have to hide itself.

"Happy to be home, Malachi?" Giorgios asks, his tone mocking.

I don't care where I am. I want to be nowhere, to sink into the ground and disappear. That is the only fate that seems

CHAPTER FORTY-THREE

appealing. But there is something still in me, perhaps it's her blood running through my veins, that flickers with the tiniest spark of something.

It takes me a moment to recognize it as hope, the true enemy of a wraith. But it gives me some fighting spirit. "What do you want with me?" I growl.

Giorgios runs a pointed fingernail over my jaw, and I snap at him, rage and hatred bubbling up from my core. It's only now I realize I am bound with chains of silver. They burn the flesh from my bones, but that pain is nothing compared to the crushing despair.

"You are very important to my plan, Malachi." He cups my jaw almost tenderly. "Of the utmost importance."

I wrench my head from his grip. "What plan?"

He smiles, and his beady eyes light up with glee. "All will be revealed. But you shall be reunited with your precious Ophelia, if only for a short time."

His cruel laugh echoes off the bare brick walls. The air turns ice cold, and the wraith drifts through the room. Giorgios stops laughing and dips his head in deference.

The wraith's screams fill my ears, so sharp and piercing I am sure they burst my eardrums, and Giorgios talks to him like he understands what those screams mean. Yet I cannot hear his words for the incessant cries of anguish ringing in my head. Unable to cover my ears, I simply close my eyes and wait for Death to take me.

CHAPTER
FORTY-FOUR
ALEXANDROS

Cadence accompanied Axl to visit the heads of the Dragon houses, and Sienna went with her father to alert the heads of the Crescent Houses, thus leaving Ophelia, Xavier, Enora, and me alone to discuss how and when we will take back our house and rescue Malachi.

"Why did he take your sired when he could have easily taken Ophelia?" Enora asks.

Does she think me so incompetent that I would have allowed the wraith to take her? The most precious thing in the entire universe? "Because he would not have taken her so easily despite what you think, Enora."

Her eyes narrow, but she does not argue the point with me further. "Why Malachi, though? If Giorgios has been planning something all this time, then every move he makes is a strategic one. Why Malachi?" She directs the last question to Ophelia and Xavier.

Xavier shrugs and runs a hand through his hair.

"Enora is right," I say. "There must be a reason he was taken. Giorgios said as much. Was there anything at all that he said or did to reveal why Malachi may be his target?"

CHAPTER FORTY-FOUR

They stare at me blankly for a few seconds. "Giorgios seemed strangely interested in who bit me first," Ophelia murmurs as if she is talking to herself. "The way he asked when we weren't talking about anything to do with that—it was weird."

"But that has no bearing here because Axl was the first to bite you."

Her eyes grow wide, and panic bubbles up inside her. "Yes, I know, but Malachi said it was him. I don't even know why now, but Giorgios seemed weirdly curious about it."

Enora presses her lips together and flashes me a knowing look. She is thinking about the damn prophecy. I suppress my frustration. "So Giorgios took Malachi because he believes he was the first to taste your blood."

Xavier blinks at me. "And the wraith was actually supposed to take Axl?"

"If we are assuming that is the case, then this could be a good thing. It buys us a little more time."

Xavier shakes his head. "But what the fuck has he taken him for? What the hell has biting Ophelia first got to do with anything?"

Enora speaks before I can stop her. "The one who first drinks from the untouched vessel determines its poison or its nectar."

Ophelia and Xavier stare at her, their faces masks of confusion.

"Stop, Enora," I growl.

She scowls at me, her slender hands balled into fists. "You can deny it no longer, Alexandros! Ophelia is the child of the prophecy."

I advance on her, my muscles rigid with anger. "I will not make decisions based on archaic nonsense."

She straightens her spine and tilts her jaw, her gray eyes

sparking with defiance. "Then make them based on facts. Ophelia was born in fire and blood. She has mastery over four elements, making her one of the most powerful beings who ever lived."

"Stop!" I roar.

She presses her lips into a thin line and glares at me. We are wasting precious time. Ophelia's hand curls into mine, and warmth snakes along my forearm, easing the tension in my muscles. "Alexandros." Her voice is soft and soothing. "I have been told of this prophecy so many times now. Can you at least tell me what it is?"

I turn to her. She is so innocent. So pure. How can I put this on her? She will hear the words, and she will know, as I do, that she is the one it speaks of.

"I will speak it if you cannot," Enora says.

I glance at Xavier, whose eyes are pleading with me too. Every instinct I have tells me to take her and run, but instead, I give Enora a nod.

Her lilting voice fills the room.

"Until the balance tips to inevitable destruction,
the sands of fate shall shift unrelenting.
And those who cannot live in peace,
shall thrive amongst the anarchy.
Until Chaos swallows whole the universe once more
and Gaea, Tartarus, and Eros do mourn.
"But there is one who can save the fates of all.
For the child borne of fire and blood
shall be our ruin or our redemption.
Bringing balance to the new world order,
be it through peace or total annihilation.
"Though, take heed—
the one who first drinks from the untouched vessel,
pale as alabaster stone,

CHAPTER FORTY-FOUR

for it is they who will determine its poison or its nectar.
"And those who thirst for the crimson rivers of mortal veins
shall face the insurmountable task of their birthright.
They must choose the path of the righteous,
or face the damnation of the eternal."

She clears her throat. "There is another verse, but it has been lost or forgotten. Though I am sure there are some who know it well."

I close my eyes and recount the verse Nazeel told me, the one I have been unable to forget since.

"But if the Chosen One can slay the three-headed dragon—
if the untamable beast does kneel at its new master's feet,
and the light is tempted back from the darkness,
then they shall awaken the protector of man.
And the sun must swallow the shadows
to bring a balance that reigns through the ages."

When I reopen my eyes, all three of them are staring at me. Enora's eyes are brimming with tears. "I thought it was the five points of the pentagram that held meaning, and perhaps it does, but it is the three-headed dragon which holds the key."

Xavier rubs his temples. "What the fuck? What three-headed dragon? We have one of them to deal with now too?"

Enora clears her throat to speak, but it is Ophelia who answers. "You're the three-headed dragon, Xavier."

He gapes at her. "Say what now?"

"You, Axl, and Malachi. The three untamable Ruby Dragon commanders." Then she looks up at me. "And you're the protector of man?"

Despite all the evidence to the contrary, I still refuse to accept it as my truth. I am no savior, and I will not let her become one either. Because there is only one fate for those who are born to save the world. "I am the protector of you. Nobody else."

She squeezes my hand and turns back to Enora. "So, whoever first drank from the untouched vessel, which I guess refers to me, gets to determine whether I'm good or bad—is that right?"

Enora nods. "That is the general interpretation, sweet child."

Ophelia presses her lips together, her face screwed up in concentration. "So Giorgios has taken Malachi because he thinks he can somehow use him to persuade me to use my magic for evil?"

I rack my brain for an answer that will not come. "That makes no sense. Elementai are inherently pure and good."

Enora clicks her tongue against the roof of her mouth. "This is true. However, we know Giorgios is in possession not only of powerful dark magic, but that he also has a wraith on his side. A wraith can turn anyone toward the darkness if they have the opportunity to be in proximity for long enough."

I shake my head and pace the length of the room. "A wraith's touch is designed to steal your soul by driving you into a spiral of despair. It would render Ophelia powerless, not powerful, and it would not steal her power."

"What if he's planning some kind of spell or something?" Ophelia asks. "A ritual like the fated mate one he was going to use?"

Enora claps her hands together. "That is it, sweet child. If you had become Giorgios's fated mate, he could have easily used his influence to take your power."

She turns to me, blinking. "So you could do that if you wanted to? You could take my power?"

I pull her into my arms. "In theory, but I would never, little one."

She rubs her cheek against me, fisting her hands in my shirt. "I know, and I love you for that."

CHAPTER FORTY-FOUR

"So, what?" Xavier snaps. "He uses Kai for some ritual to make Ophelia evil? Is that it?"

Breathing through my nose, I shove aside the images of me tearing out my brother's heart before I tear off his head and focus. "Do you know of such a ritual, Enora?"

"Not specifically, as there has never been a Chosen One before. But there are many dark rituals which can be used to steal powers or control the actions of another. It is possible that a ritual for this scenario could be successful if there is enough power."

I run a hand over my face as the true horror of Giorgios's plan becomes clearer. "Ophelia has enough power to ensure the success of any such endeavor."

Enora places a hand on my shoulder. "At least it will not work, for Malachi was not the first to drink from Ophelia."

My heart sinks through my chest and cold dread floods me. "Neither was Axl."

Enora blinks at me. "Then who?"

I vividly recall our conversation from a few nights ago. How he taunted me with his claims. "It was Lucian."

CHAPTER
FORTY-FIVE
XAVIER

We stand around the dining table: Alexandros, Ophelia, Axl, Osiris, Enora, Cadence, Sienna, and Alexandros's father, Vasilis. I've constructed a crude diorama of Montridge University using various kitchen items, and we stare at it.

"Who do we actually have on our side?" Sienna asks.

Vasilis answers, his arms folded over his chest, "The Onyx Dragon vampires have been ordered to fall into line by Vincent, but I cannot imagine they will be our most reliable allies."

"No." Alexandros shakes his head. "If anyone sees Nicholas Ashe, you have my permission to remove his head."

I smirk because that is exactly what I'd like to do. He and his Onyx vampires have had it coming for years. Smarmy fucks.

Alexandros directs his attention to Axl. "Did you speak with Eugene?"

Eugene Jackson—another man I don't particularly like, but he is Alexandros's cousin and a faculty member of Ruby Dragon.

Axl nods. "I got word to him, and he says fourteen Ruby

CHAPTER FORTY-FIVE

members stayed behind. He's aware Giorgios has someone held captive in the basement of our house, but he has no idea who. But that must be our boy, right?"

The thought of Malachi being held prisoner by that evil fuck makes it difficult to focus on anything but my desire to get him back, but I rein it all in and reply, "Of course it is."

"If he is using Malachi as bait to ensnare Ophelia, then that is most likely," Vasilis agrees, his dark brows furrowed.

"And our vampires?" Alexandros asks.

"Eugene is confident they remain loyal to House Drakos, and as soon as we give him the signal, he will have them ready to fight."

Alexandros draws in a breath and blows it out again, slowly.

"I know you have never truly trusted your cousin," Vasilis says, placing a hand on Alexandros's shoulder. "But he is a loyal member of House Drakos. He will not disobey either of us."

Alexandros screws his eyes closed. "I do not sense any deceit in him, but I am unsure whether I can trust my instincts any longer."

"Your brother fooled us both. Do not let his betrayal make you doubt your gifts; they outweigh his by legions."

Alexandros nods and looks back to Axl. "And what of Lapis and Opal?"

"They're fully on board," Axl answers. "Both Professors Benedictine and Morrone, as well as their thirty members between them."

Osiris studies the makeshift model. "We have a dozen of our toughest wolves at your disposal, and James Black is willing to lead them."

"James Black?" Alexandros says, undoubtedly as surprised as I am to hear that the recently appointed head of the Callisto Crescents has volunteered for such a role.

Osiris nods. "I know he can be argumentative at times, but he is a good man from a good family. We can count on him."

"He is strong and will be an asset in battle," Sienna says with a firm nod, and her father shoots her a glare. There's definitely something more going on there, but now isn't the time to wonder about family drama.

Alexandros paces around the table, his eyes narrowed.

"It seems we are vastly outnumbered," Vasilis says, a distinct gleam in his eye. "But I do enjoy a challenge." He winks at me, and I can't help but grin back. I think I'm really gonna like him.

Alexandros rubs a hand through his beard as he goes on scrutinizing the model. "We are, but we have something Giorgios does not. Ophelia and two dragons."

As I knew she would, Ophelia blushes.

Alexandros beckons me forward. "What would you suggest our strategy be, Xavier?"

Well, fuck. Is he really asking me to weigh in when so much is at stake? I glance at Axl. We filled him and the others in on the whole Chosen One–prophecy deal as soon as they got back, and it spooked the hell out of him as much as me. But he simply gives me a reassuring nod.

I roll back my shoulders and clear my throat. "Axl and I head straight for Malachi and get him out of there. If we can trust Eugene, then you let him know when we're there so he can get us inside. But as soon as we step foot in the house, Giorgios will know we're here, and he's gonna deploy his army."

I slide the condiment bottles across the table from the end of the makeshift woods to the edge of campus. Then I move around the table and pick up the salt and pepper. Strategy has always been a strength of mine, but until now, I've only ever used it for the Trials. Being given this much responsibility is new, and it's a little fucking terrifying.

CHAPTER FORTY-FIVE

You are doing well. Go on, Alexandros urges me.

"So I think we set up a perimeter here." I point to the quad. "Then we have the mountain at our backs, and we can set up a solid defense against attacks from the woods as well as maintain an exit over the mountain that no one else has because we have fucking dragons." I'm specifically referring to getting Ophelia out quickly should we need to, but nobody in this room needs me to voice that. We all know her safety is our most important objective. And I know her well enough to know she would oppose such preferential treatment.

When there are no complaints, I go on, placing the salt and pepper in front of my cereal box model of Zeus Hall. "With Anikêtos and Elpis at the rear, burning anything that gets to the edge of the quad to a crisp, we can have Ophelia, Enora, and Cadence directly in front, using whatever magic they have at their disposal and holding the line. And then everyone else will fan out across the quad, picking off any stragglers who get near."

Vasilis stares at me, his eyes even darker than Alexandros's, and for a moment I wonder if I just fucked that whole thing up. But he gives me a small nod, and I feel a rush of pride. The feeling is magnified a hundred-fold when I feel Alexandros's approval shining through our bond.

"Does anyone know where Giorgios is?" Alexandros asks.

Vasilis taps on the carton of eggs that represents our house. "If he is using your sired as bait as we suspect, then surely he will be at your house too. Therefore, you and I will accompany Axl and Xavier."

Alexandros glances at Ophelia and shakes his head. "It is too much of a risk. Perhaps that is his intent. To leave Ophelia vulnerable without our protection."

"But I'll have Anikêtos and Elpis, plus Cadence and Enora."

She waves her hands in the air. "Not to mention all this magic, right?"

He shakes his head. "It is too dangerous. We do not know Giorgios's plan for you yet, agápi mou."

Ever since the discussion of the prophecy, he's definitely been spooked. It's hard to describe, but he isn't his usual calm, assured self. I want to talk to him about what he's feeling, but now is not the time. Whatever the reason, him being freaked out has me spooked too. He's the rock here. If he crumbles, then what the fuck do the rest of us do?

So, what's the real plan here, Professor? Axl asks.

We protect Ophelia at all costs. Whatever Giorgios's plan is, I fear it is bigger than we suspected. She is the key.

So why don't we just run? I ask the question I know we are all thinking. *Get Kai back, grab the dragons, and go live on some tropical island somewhere?*

Alexandros looks to Ophelia, and she gives him a sad smile before she answers me. *Because none of us would ever be safe, and hiding is no way to live.*

I know she's right, but still.

"I agree," Vasilis says, reminding us all that we're still part of a wider conversation involving the rest of the room. "We must lure Giorgios out of the house and confront him on our own terms. He does not get to determine the rules of engagement."

Alexandros looks to me, then Axl. "Are you two ready for this?"

I crack my neck. "Fuck yes, let's go get him."

Alexandros walks around the table, beckoning Axl and me to him. He places a hand on the backs of our necks and pulls us close. "Get Malachi and come straight back to us at Zeus Hall. Once you are all safe, I will decide what to do with Giorgios."

"You got it," Axl says.

CHAPTER FORTY-FIVE

"I love you both," he says, and it's not in our heads. He says it aloud so the whole room can hear him.

"Love you too," Axl mumbles, but I declare it loudly.

He gives us one final squeeze and then a firm nod. "Now go get our boy back."

CHAPTER
FORTY-SIX
ALEXANDROS

94 MINUTES BEFORE THE LIGHT GOES OUT

With Ophelia's hand in mine, we head for the quad alongside Osiris, Enora, Cadence, Sienna, and my father. Under an exceptionally bright moon, we stick to the shadows in case Giorgios has spies around campus. Our allies have been informed of our plan and will meet us there, and I have told Anikêtos and Elpis of our strategy. They have agreed to remain cloaked until the time is right.

I have tried to locate both my treacherous brother and Malachi by accessing their thoughts but have been unable to. Giorgios is likely using some kind of dark magic to block them both.

We emerge from the trees, and Zeus Hall looms into view. All too quickly comes the sound of charging feet, numerous pairs of boots stomping and shaking the ground.

My father is far out in front, and he speaks to me privately. *Giorgios must have learned of our arrival.*

Foolishly, I hoped Axl and Xavier could have rescued

CHAPTER FORTY-SIX

Malachi without alerting my brother. But of course he is there awaiting their arrival. What if he ambushes them? Have I sent my boys to their deaths?

Ophelia squeezes my hand. "They are strong and smart, and you taught them well."

I press a kiss on her forehead and take a moment to breathe in her scent before we face the chaos that is about to ensue. Then I grind my teeth at the sound of Nicholas Ashe's voice.

"The great Vasilis Drakos—what did we do to deserve you gracing us with your presence?"

Ashe is surrounded by a dozen Onyx members as well as half a dozen warlocks. The dark-gray circles surrounding their eyes, caused by decades of practicing the darkest of magic, always give them away.

"I believe you know why we are here, Nicholas," my father replies. "Vincent gave you the order himself, did he not?"

Ashe and his minions start to circle my father like hyenas who have found themselves fortunate enough to corner a lion. I grasp Ophelia's hand in mine. Despite their number, they are no match for Vasilis Drakos.

If anything should happen to me, I have already decreed you my heir and future head of House Drakos, my father says directly into my mind. *And I will decree it again with my last breath if I have to. All the heads of the families have been informed.*

You are not going to die at the hands of a weasel like Nicholas Ashe, Father. I will assist you if necessary.

There will be no need. He will not defy Vincent by attacking us.

I frown, not as convinced of Nicholas's allegiance to his house as my father is.

Do not underestimate him, Father. We need you in this fight.

Proving me right almost before I have finished forming the thought, Ashe and his minions swarm my father. But I move faster than they can, with Ophelia and Osiris on my heels. I throw two of the Onyx soldiers, and their heads crack open against the brick exterior wall of Zeus Hall, spattering the tan brick with vibrant red.

Ophelia reaches my side, standing like she is ready to fight. *Stay by my side and handle the warlocks with Enora and Cadence, agápi mou. They will try to block us with magic, but you are stronger.*

She voices her agreement, and soon the air is filled with static electricity as she blocks all of their spells, one after the other. As I tear out the throat of an Onyx vampire, I realize I have never been more proud of her. Sienna proves herself a strong young wolf as she fights alongside her father. An Onyx vampire pulls her back by her hair and is about to sink his teeth into her neck when she drops to her haunches and throws him over her head before crushing his windpipe with her boot.

Ophelia and the witches go on battling the warlocks, countering their spells as Osiris, Sienna, and I lay waste to the vampires. But where are Ashe and my father?

I scan the quad, and then I see them. My father is on his knees with another half dozen vampires surrounding him. Nicholas Ashe holds a sword above his head.

"No!" I roar.

"You can have me killed, Giorgios, but I have already named your brother as my heir," our father bellows.

I sprint across the quad, but I am not faster than Ashe's blade. I am unable to stop it from slicing off my father's head.

Ashe turns and smirks at me, brandishing the blood-stained weapon. "How about I take yours next?"

I growl, my fangs protracted and every sinew in my body alive with anger. My father and I have had our differences, but he did not deserve to die like that—on his knees at the hands of a man with no honor.

Ashe does not have time to raise his sword again. I pin him

CHAPTER FORTY-SIX

to the ground and tear out his throat with my teeth, shrugging off his minions when they jump onto my back. He chokes on his own blood, coughing and sputtering.

"Are you expecting this will heal soon?" I taunt as I tear out another chunk. "I should have taken your head when I had the chance." I wish I had, but I had taken so many souls by that point and was too weary to take another, so I agreed to let him live.

But I swear no such truce today.

The vampires surrounding me are suddenly set ablaze. Their flesh melts from their bones, and I recognize it as the work of my elementai. "I guess I will take it now." I shove my fingers into the open wound of his throat and shred his neck apart until his head is no longer attached to his body. He stares up at me with blank, lifeless eyes.

Ophelia crouches beside me and lays her head on my shoulder. "I'm sorry," she whispers, and I take a deep breath and allow myself a moment to absorb her love and strength.

If I have learned anything from the many battles I have fought in during my long life, it is that my father will not be the only loss we suffer today.

CHAPTER
FORTY-SEVEN
MALACHI

89 MINUTES BEFORE THE LIGHT GOES OUT

Giorgios cocks his head to the side and narrows his eyes. "Did you hear that?"

I shake my head. I heard nothing.

"I think they have finally come for you."

Please let it be true. I'm not sure how much longer I can stand this.

The wraith's answering screech is ear-piercing and blood-curdling. During the last however many hours or days I've been here, watching the wraith float in and out of here while Giorgios remains frustratingly nearby at all times, I've learned that is how the creature communicates. The despair is still overwhelming, but it lessens when the wraith isn't here, and I have somehow nurtured the tiny flicker of hope in my chest into a small flame. That's the only thing keeping me from trying to tear off my own head.

"I have deployed them now," Giorgios says and follows it up with a cruel laugh.

Deployed who? What the fuck is going on?

CHAPTER FORTY-SEVEN

"Welcome home," he says as he opens the steel door to the basement. "I expected you sooner. Poor Malachi here has suffered so in your absence."

"Where is Kai, you evil piece of shit?" Xavier's voice echoes through the room, and it makes the flame inside me burn a little brighter.

"Where is Ophelia?" Giorgios sneers.

"You seriously think we'd let her anywhere near you, you twisted fuck?" Axl says.

"She is the only one who can break Malachi's chains, so if she is not with you, then your endeavor will be a purposeless one, dear boys."

"The wraith is in here too," I yell. "Don't let him get close to you."

The wraith screeches again, and I assume it's at me, but Giorgios spins around to face it, his hands balled into fists. "I know that, but I want her to see it."

Huh? What is it he wants Ophelia to see?

Another wraith shriek pierces the air, and Axl and Xavier use Giorgios's distracted state to charge into the room and head straight for me. They pull on my chains, wincing at first at the burn of the silver before yanking harder.

"What the fuck?" Xavier grumbles.

"I told you, they cannot be broken other than by Ophelia herself. They are the same chains I used to restrain your sire. Forged from the sacred silver from the mines of Peru and fortified with dark magic, and even he, as powerful as he is, could not break them. If the great Alexandros Drakos could not break those chains, children, what makes you think you can?"

Xavier stands tall and glares at him while Axl goes on trying to find a way to free me, but it's pointless. Everything is pointless.

"So call Ophelia and have her come rescue her beloved Malachi," Giorgios croons.

"No!" I shout. "I'd rather fucking die than let you get anywhere near her."

More wraith screeching. Giorgios smiles at me, cruel and mocking. "And die you shall, boy, but I would really like her to see it."

Xavier lunges for him, but Giorgios swipes his arm through the air, and Xavier is thrown back against the concrete wall.

"What the fuck are you?" Axl growls.

"Oh, you pathetic little boys. I am the true power of House Drakos. Vampire and warlock combined."

"How?" I bark.

"That, dear boy, is far beyond your wildest comprehension." He raises his hand and twists his fingers. Chains of silver wrap around Axl's and Xavier's wrists. They struggle against the bonds as I did, but then the darkness, the pervasive anguish and misery, grows heaver and thicker as the wraith circles them.

They stop struggling and drop to their knees on the concrete floor.

"Let them fucking go," I command. It's a fruitless request, but I have no other power here.

Giorgios snaps his teeth at me. "Call for Ophelia and I will let them go."

"I couldn't call for her even if I wanted to because you suppressed my powers," I remind him.

He crouches and looks me up and down. "If I remove the block on your mind and allow you to call for her, will you?"

"No, Kai," Xavier groans.

"I will let them go; I give you my word," he says, his sour breath making me gag.

CHAPTER FORTY-SEVEN

"He won't," Axl growls. "You know he won't."

If I could hear her voice only one more time, I would be able to accept my death. "I'll call her."

His eyes narrow like he doesn't know if he can trust me, but a second later, my mind clears, and I call for her.

Kai! Her sweet voice makes tears burn behind my eyes.

Hey, baby.

Are you okay? Where are you?

I'm okay, sweet girl. Now that I've heard your voice.

Are you with Axl and Xavier? Are you coming back here?

We'll be back soon, I promise. I lie to her with ease. *But whatever happens, you have to stay away from Giorgios. He wants you to see something, and I don't know what, but—*

"Is she coming?" Giorgios demands.

"Let me fucking speak to her."

We think it's something to do with my blood, Kai. There's this prophecy about whoever drinks from me first can decide whether I'm good or evil.

You will always be good, baby. No matter what.

Kai! She sounds exasperated. *You told him you bit me first, remember?*

Yeah. I look up at Giorgios. *Is that what this is about?*

But it wasn't you who tasted me first, or even Axl. She drifts off, and Giorgios's angry voice is demanding to know what I'm saying to her.

I love you, sweet girl.

I love you too, Kai.

My mind goes dark, and I realize he's put the block back in place. "Is she coming?" he demands.

I shuffle up onto my knees so I can look him in the eye when I crush his twisted plan to dust. "No, she's not, you evil fuck! And she never will."

He roars, grabbing my jaw and pushing me back down to the floor as the wraith caterwauls with more fervor than before.

Looks like I just signed my own death warrant. But at least I got to tell her I love her one final time.

CHAPTER
FORTY-EIGHT

OPHELIA

84 MINUTES BEFORE THE LIGHT GOES OUT

Something is wrong. Very wrong. Malachi sounded so ... Well, he was almost serene. And that is definitely not right.

I turn to Alexandros. "I think the boys are in trouble. And I can't reach any of them now, can you?"

He concentrates for a second and then shakes his head. "But they are alive, for we would have felt them die. We will go to them as soon as we are able to clear a path."

"Behind you!" I yell as four vampires charge at him. He pivots and grabs one by the throat, then tears off his head while I force the other three back with a wave of fire. Our moment of reprieve is over, and we both return to the battle.

Enora is beside me as I channel all my training and weave threads of magic together to stave off the incoming hordes. A warlock manages to get by my magic, and after she dispenses of him, I panic. "Why am I becoming less powerful?"

"Magic is like anything. It uses energy." She casts another

spell. "Not only from the elements, but from you. Are you tired?"

I'm exhausted. "Can't I just channel more?"

She weaves a spell that throws back two hooded figures who were headed for Sienna. "You are powerful, but magic is about stamina and endurance too. You cannot run on endlessly without stopping to recharge."

I drag in a deep breath. "Am I going to get weaker until I can't use any magic?"

"No, child. You will always have some magic to channel. But conserve your energy when you can. Fire uses a lot."

"Got it. Ease off on the fire."

She smiles and returns her focus to the battlefield that was once Gaea's Green. And my mind goes back to Malachi and the prophecy.

There is only one person I can think of who might be able to help us, and he isn't here. Is he close by?

Lucian?

He replies quickly. *Ophelia Hart.*

Your uncle is a megalomaniac, you know, and he's trying to take over the world.

And what does that have to do with me?

You already know what it has to do with you. I duck as a warlock throws a spell at me, and Enora finishes him off before I can retaliate. *You know what the prophecy says, and you know what it means.*

I still do not see what this has to do with me, he says, his tone bland, but I refuse to believe he's the monster he believes himself to be.

We really need you.

Goodbye, Ophelia Hart.

I swallow down the disappointment that lurches up in my

CHAPTER FORTY-EIGHT

chest. I was so sure he would help us. But I won't give up. I will figure out a way to get to Malachi and the boys before we lose them too.

CHAPTER
FORTY-NINE
MALACHI

75 MINUTES BEFORE THE LIGHT GOES OUT

The potency of Giorgios's rage vibrates through the cellar, bouncing off the concrete walls.

The wraith shrieks even louder than before, and I screw my eyes closed as though that will somehow make it less painful.

"I know. I will do it now!" Giorgios bellows, and then he's hauling me up by the back of my neck and dragging me to the center of the room.

"Here?"

The wraith screams in response.

I glance down at the stone circle I'm kneeling on. It's a part of the earth line that runs underneath the university and connects to the ruins at the mouth of Havenwood River. The pagan settlers who lived on this land before the university was here believed it to be magical, and Alexandros once told me it magnifies the demon magic he uses to protect our house. But I can honestly say I have never given it much thought. Until now, that is, when I find myself kneeling on it while Giorgios holds

CHAPTER FORTY-NINE

some evil fucking sword over my head. The whole thing, pommel to point, looks as if it's made of shadows that drift in and out of sight.

"Get the fuck off him," Xavier yells, struggling to his feet and hobbling over to me. But after only a few steps, Giorgios floors him with a swipe of his arm and mutters some kind of incantation in a strange language. Xavier doesn't move, and I almost throw up onto Giorgios's feet.

I glance at Axl, who has his jaw clenched, his lips pressed together in a thin line.

"Now back to the matter at hand." Giorgios raises the blade once more.

"No!" Axl shouts. "It wasn't him. He didn't bite Ophelia first. It was me."

I close my eyes, readying myself for the blow anyway, but it doesn't come.

Giorgios scowls at him. "You are lying."

"I'm not!" Axl spits.

"He is," I snarl.

Giorgios's narrowed eyes rake over my face. "There is an easy way to tell. All we need is a drop of your blood."

He slices a welt into my forearm that burns like a million razor blades, but the pain lifts the fog I've been living under since the wraith took me. My mind is sharper, and I feel like myself again. Holy shit, the block is gone.

My blood drips onto the stone circle. We all hold our breath.

The wraith squalls.

With a roar, Giorgios pushes me away and grabs Axl by his hair. "Then I shall take your head instead."

"Actually, you should probably take mine." The voice sends chills down my spine.

Lucian's lips curl over his teeth in some strange hybrid between a sneer and a smile. It's altogether terrifying, but for now, at least, it appears he's on our side. "The first to drink Ophelia's blood. No, that would be me, Uncle, and I'm not so easy to kill. You've tried before, or have you forgotten?"

Axl and I shuffle over to Xavier and nudge him, but he remains unconscious.

Giorgios spits at Lucian's feet. "You always were a spineless waste of oxygen, nephew. Couldn't even fulfill a simple task without some *encouragement.*"

Whatever that's in reference to, it ignites Lucian's fury. "A simple task," he roars, his hands balled into fists. "They were my sisters. My mother!" Spittle flies from his mouth, and he lunges for his uncle, but the dark magic now surrounding Giorgios seems to keep Lucian at a safe distance.

I call out for my sire now that I'm able to reach him again.

Malachi? His voice is filled with relief. *Are you all okay?*

We're okay. But Lucian is here, and I really think you need to hear this. Can you tap into my mind and hear what's going on through me?

I can try.

"And all you had to do was tear out their hearts and take your father's head when he was kneeling at their feet, crying for the woman who was never his!" Giorgios rages. "Yet you could not even do that. You are weak and pathetic."

Lucian charges again and is again stopped by the wall of dark magic. "I am what you made me!"

"No." Giorgios shakes his head. "I created a true warrior. A beast. A vampire so powerful, nothing would stop him. And you destroyed him, all because you decided to grow a conscience."

Lucian drops to his knees and puts his head into his hands. His entire body seems to sag, his shoulders shaking. A wail is ripped from his throat. "No!" The word is made entirely of pain. It echoes off the walls and seeps into my bones as despair radiates from his center. "You asked me to kill my own mother." A

CHAPTER FORTY-NINE

sob makes him convulse. "My little sisters." His words are muffled by his cries.

I watch him break apart in front of my eyes, wishing I could do something to ease his pain, because it is impossible not to feel it and know his tortured soul.

"It was what needed to be done. Without him, our father would have fallen, and I would have become head of House Drakos. Can you imagine? The head of Skotádi and the head of the most powerful vampire house that ever lived? We would have been kings, Lucian. The Skotádi would have thrived. But you let him live! And we were forced to shrink back into the darkness for centuries."

I can barely believe the scene unfolding before me. I glance at Axl, who looks as stunned as I feel. If I weren't here to witness this for myself, I wouldn't believe it to be true. I only hope Alexandros can hear what's happening for himself.

Something shifts. The air crackles with static electricity. "You could have killed him yourself, but you were too weak." Lucian looks up, his cheeks streaked with tears. His voice is deathly quiet. "You have always been too weak, and that's why you needed me to do what you could not. He has always been a better man than you, and I'm sorry it took me so long to realize it."

Giorgios towers over Lucian's kneeling form. "I may have forced your hand, Lucian, but you will always be the one who tore out their hearts. They took their last breaths believing one of the people they trusted most betrayed them."

"No." Lucian drops his head once more, tears dripping from his face onto the dusty concrete floor. "I would never betray them."

Giorgios raises his hand. I struggle against my bonds, but they refuse to break.

I sense Axl doing the same beside me.

It's only when Giorgios is bringing his hand down that I see the weapon forming before my eyes this time. It appears in his hand as though he has conjured it, a long broadsword with a double-edged blade, like the ones I read of knights using when I was a boy. Except this isn't made of steel, but entirely of shadows. He brings it down in a swift blow, straight toward the back of Lucian's neck.

"No!" I roar.

But the blade does not deliver the killing blow it was aiming for. It only slices through a few inches before it's stopped by something.

No, someone. A blur that passes by so fast, it takes me a moment to recognize him.

Both Axl and I call out his name like a prayer. "Alexandros!"

CHAPTER
FIFTY
OPHELIA

59 MINUTES BEFORE THE LIGHT GOES OUT

Ophelia, do not leave Anikêtos's side! Alexandros warns, and I assure him I won't.

I have no intention of straying far from the huge black dragon, especially now that Alexandros is no longer at my side. Without Alexandros and the boys, I feel safer with Ani and Elpis than with anyone else. The warlocks have created force fields that deflect Dragonfyre, but I'm able to channel enough power to hold back any of the vampires and warlocks who draw too near while taking down the force fields one by one.

Cadence stands to my left and Enora on my right, chanting spells that counteract the warlocks' dark magic. The vampires and wolves who remained, including Sienna and Osiris, have fanned out in front and are picking off Giorgios's army and holding the line. The system is working, and although we've lost two vampires and a wolf—a fact which I cannot give too much consideration to right now because the pain would be debilitating—we're winning. Giorgios's army is no match for two powerful witches, an elementai, and her dragons.

OPHELIA

But my sense of triumph is short-lived. Birds explode into the night sky as a lone moose rockets out of the woods, followed by a herd of deer. What appears at first to be a solid wall of darkness emerges next, but as it clears the gap between Apollo Hall and Erato Hall, I am able to make out individual figures. Every hair on my body stands on end at the sight of thousands upon thousands of shadows approaching us in one massive wave.

"What the hell are they, Enora?" Cadence asks.

"I am not sure," she replies, her face a mask of fear.

I direct a shard of energy toward one, testing its defenses, and it splinters into a thousand fragments of darkness. "I don't know what they are, but we can take them out easily." I flash Cadence a grin. "They have no defenses."

I would not be so sure of that, Anikêtos warns.

I turn back to the horde and watch in horror as the fragments are pulled back together, as though by a magnetic force, and retake the original shape of ... What is their shape? Man? Vampire? Warlock?

What are they, Ani?

They are the undead, child. There is a crack in the veil.

"The undead," I repeat aloud for Cadence's and Enora's benefit. An army of the undead isn't the wildest thing I've seen lately—I mean, I'm communicating telepathically with a dragon—so that's probably why the first thing I ask isn't *what the actual hell*, but instead, "How do we stop them?"

"They will not be so easily stopped, Ophelia," Enora says gravely. "You cannot kill what is already dead."

Ani and Elpis torch the advancing line of dark figures with Dragonfyre, but it simply burns them to an ash that quickly reforms. This is bad. Really, *really* bad.

"But there must be a way to stop them? Have you dealt with them before?"

CHAPTER FIFTY

Enora pulls her hair from its topknot, and her silver locks swirl around her, sizzling and crackling with energy. "Not in any great numbers, sweet child." She begins chanting a spell that has silver sparks of lightning whirling around us and seems to slow the advancing shadows.

I blast energy at them and watch them explode into particles one after one before becoming whole again. Cadence chants a spell that strengthens Enora's, but the shadows move through it like they are passing through a wall of treacle, then pick up speed.

Ani and Elpis continue raining Dragonfyre, but the effort is in vain. At least we are able to keep the shadows from our allies on the quad, who go on fighting the living. "What the hell are we going to do? Keep destroying them and hope they have a distinct number of lives that we'll eventually burn through?"

Enora weaves her arms in a circle above her head. "The only way to stop them is to close the crack in the veil. And the only way to do that is to return the wraith to the netherworld."

"How?"

She glances at me, her usual youthful complexion now old and haggard, and I recall how Alexandros once told me she channels magic to mask her true age. "We must recast the spell of the great white witch, Selena."

"Can you do that? Can *we* do that?"

She turns back to the advancing army. "I believe it is possible, but we will need a little help."

"Help?"

"I have called for Nazeel Danraath and her sisters. I hope they reach us before it is too late." The mass of dark figures grows closer and closer.

I sure hope so too.

CHAPTER
FIFTY-ONE
ALEXANDROS

59 MINUTES BEFORE THE LIGHT GOES OUT

My fingers wrap around my brother's wrist, and I squeeze hard, stopping the blade from slicing any deeper into my son's neck. Giorgios gapes up at me, his face a mask of shock and fear. He should fear me, for nothing in this universe will save him from my rage.

I squeeze harder, crushing the bones in his wrist until he drops the blade, and the writhing shadows spread out and fade before disappearing completely. Malachi and Axl are bound by their hands and feet, kneeling on the floor. Xavier lies bound and unconscious. But they are all breathing. They are all alive.

"You are too late, brother," Giorgios sneers.

The wraith's bloodcurdling shrieks fill the room, then it disappears in a torrent of darkness. My brother does not seem at all perturbed by the wraith's sudden departure. It is almost as though he expected it. A cold shiver runs the length of my spine.

Ophelia, do not leave Anikêtos's side! She quickly voices her compliance.

CHAPTER FIFTY-ONE

Anikêtos, if I have ever asked anything of you before, know that it meant nothing compared to this. Do not let the wraith near her.

I am faster than any wraith, Dragon Whisperer. I will not let him near her, I assure you.

Satisfied he will keep his word and that she is safe in his care, I direct all my attention and anger back at Giorgios. "Not too late to tear your head from your shoulders, dear brother."

He moves backward, his dark-blue eyes fixed on mine. "You can try, little brother, but I think we both know who is the more powerful between us now, do we not? Despite what our father would have you believe."

"Our father is dead, Giorgios. His head was removed by one of your allies. He used his last breath to appoint me as the official head of House Drakos. And the first thing I did was remove the oath placed on dragonkind."

He snorts. "So you will have one of your dragons kill me?"

I can read every thought in his mind. He is trying to figure out why he cannot transport out. "I do not need the aid of a dragon to kill you, Giorgios. And you will find you cannot transport from within either of the Ruby Dragon houses. Had you ever shown any interest in our family enterprise, you may have known that."

His eyes narrow, and he looks past me to the door at my back. I shake my head. "That is not the way you will be leaving this room, big brother."

He surges forward, trying to catch me by surprise, but I am ready for him. The blade he had in his possession when I entered the room is in his hand again, and he swings it toward my neck, but I have always been faster. I dodge him with ease. Dropping to my haunches, I punch him in the kneecap, splintering the bone and causing him to drop to the ground. He swings the blade again, and I dodge backward. It whispers past me, but even without feeling the sting of its blade, I feel the malevolence embedded within it.

When did my only brother align himself with such dark forces, and how did we not know?

"Why, Giorgios?" I ask, standing over him.

"For the same thing we all strive for, Alexandros. Power!" He rises to his feet, wincing as the bones in his knee fuse back together.

I shake my head. "I do not believe you. If it was merely power you wanted, then you would have killed me rather than imprisoning me." I lunge for him, and he surges at me too, trying to defend himself, but I overpower him easily and tear a chunk of flesh from his throat. He holds his hand to the wound and snarls.

"So what was it, brother? You already had power. You are the firstborn son of Vasilis Drakos, heir to the family throne had you not betrayed your own kind."

"No!" he bellows like he has been pained by something greater than the wound I inflicted. "I was never the heir, was I, Alexandros?" He spits my name from his mouth like it leaves a bitter taste. "I was always the second. The spare!"

"If you were ever second in his eyes, it is because you made yourself so."

His lips curl back over his teeth, fangs glinting in the overhead light. "I had no choice. Once he had a son who could talk with dragons, what chance was there for me?" He lunges for me, his sharp fingernails scratching my lip, and I throw him backward.

His back slams against the concrete wall, and I step closer. "You are a whiny, self-serving piece of shit. And yes, Giorgios, I have always been superior to you. And I have spent my entire life trying to make you feel better about that fact. But now you

CHAPTER FIFTY-ONE

are about to learn just how superior I am." I lift him by his collar and slam him into the wall again.

He spits blood from his mouth. "Were you trying to make me feel better when you stole the only woman I ever loved from me? Elena was mine, and you took her."

I should have known. Of course it was always about her. Within the maelstrom of thoughts and memories swirling around his head, she is there at the center of it all. Peaceful and serene, a calm within the eye of the storm. Just as she was in life. "Why did you have him kill her, brother?" I ask, my rage giving birth to a deep well of sorrow. "Why did you force him to kill his own mother and our innocent children? Why not simply kill me and take her for yourself?"

He screws his eyes closed and presses his lips together as though that may stop me from finding the answers I seek. But if he will not tell me, then I will discover them for myself. I comb his memories, shoving aside all the ones he pushes to the forefront of his mind as I delve into the heart of his darkness. His bitterness and jealousy. His cowardice. He knew he was never strong enough to kill me, so he did not even try, at least not in physical deed. Killing me was not enough. He had to make me suffer—to make me feel as he did. To watch me lose everything I ever loved. My beloved first-born son. My kind, beautiful, innocent daughters. My wife. He had her killed simply because she was mine and he could not have her.

"Revenge!" I shake him like he is a puppet on a string before slamming him back against the wall. That he has caused so much pain and suffering for something so petty and human as revenge only makes this all so much more tragic. "This was about your petty, mindless revenge."

He snivels, pathetic and weak. "You never understood. Never loved her like I—"

"You never loved her, Giorgios!" I scream the accusation so

loud I am sure I can be heard in the netherworld, but then I drop my voice and hold him close, for I want him and him alone to hear every word of what I say. "For if you had, you would not have been able to cause her even a moment's pain."

"I loved her," he whimpers. "And she was mine."

I shake my head. "She was never yours."

And now I am assaulted by his thoughts of Ophelia, of his desire to bond with and impregnate her. To defile her. Not because her loves her. But because he hates me. The ugliness of his intent toward my sweet Ophelia makes me recoil, but not long enough for me to forget why I am here or to give him any room to escape.

"You are despicable." I wrap my hand around his throat. He struggles, clawing at my arm, but his strength is no match for mine. It never has been. I have always been the better of us, and it has truly taken me until now to see it. "Is that why you kept me alive? So you could take Ophelia from me? Impregnate her with your spawn and ensure I would live to see it?"

"It is no less than you deserve," he says, snarling.

"Know this, brother. I would have loved her still. You could have bonded to her and sowed your evil seed in her, and still, she would have loved me."

He laughs, and the sound is completely unhinged and so shocking, it makes me inch back, though I keep a firm grip on his throat. "And the irony of it all, dearest brother, is that you have brought about your own downfall."

He is stalling for time, and I have no more patience for his games.

"The downfall of us all." He cackles, his eyes alight with glee.

"Okay, I will relent. Tell me of this downfall I have supposedly brought upon myself." I hoist him higher but loosen my grip enough to allow him to speak freely.

CHAPTER FIFTY-ONE

"That would be far too easy, Alexandros. But if you had let me simply take the girl, then all of this could have been avoided. The dragons were a surprise I was not expecting. Yet they have sown the seeds of destruction even I did not anticipate. I shall be reborn, brother. And your precious little Ophelia will be swallowed by the dark."

Indescribable rage hurtles through my veins. I wrap my other hand around his throat, and in my peripheral vision, I see he has again conjured the sword. But it does not matter. It is too late. My fingers are already digging into the meat of his flesh, crushing his windpipe and tearing through sinew and arteries.

His hand falls to his side, but whilst he still has life in his eyes, I deliver him the cruelest blow of all. "Elena and I were not fated mates, Giorgios, but we did love each other deeply. And she confided in me as soon as we were married." I press my mouth to his ear to ensure he hears every word. "She only ever felt pity for you."

Summoning every ounce of rage in my body, I tear his head from his shoulders. It dangles from my fingers by strands of fascia, and his body drops to the floor.

I drop his head and stare down at the remains of the man who was once my brother.

CHAPTER
FIFTY-TWO
OPHELIA

40 MINUTES BEFORE THE LIGHT GOES OUT

I watch in awe as they stride purposefully toward us, three witches with flaming-red hair glinting in the moonlight, all dressed in emerald-green cloaks. They look like the cavalry from a really badass superhero movie.

"Nazeel," Enora cries, and her face, still aged and weathered, brightens with relief.

"We are here, dearest friend," Nazeel says, stepping in front of the other two. "We felt the tear in the veil. Tell us what must be done."

"A wraith has opened it. He imbibes Giorgios Drakos with powers, and we must return him to the netherworld before the veil falls completely."

One of Nazeel's sisters blanches, but it is the other who speaks. "The spell of the white witch?"

Enora nods.

"Nazeel, it is too dangerous," the sister says. "You must summon Lucifer himself to return a wraith to the netherworld."

CHAPTER FIFTY-TWO

Lucifer? As in the devil? This suddenly feels like a terrible idea.

"It is what must be done, Ameena," Nazeel says. "We cannot allow the veil to fall."

My head is spinning. The world is about to literally descend into hell. Alexandros and the boys aren't here. I'm scared and freaked out, and I don't know what the hell I'm supposed to do.

A warm hand slips into mine. "We got this, girl," Cadence says.

I roll back my shoulders and steel my spine. "Can I help with the spell?"

Nazeel shakes her head. "It is a spell that can only be performed by a descendant of the white witch. One that can channel earth magic. Enora and I have such lineage and power, and we will do all that is necessary."

Ameena nods toward the battlefield. "Zendaya and I will help hold back the hordes. Are you good with incantations, child?" she directs the question to Cadence, who nods her agreement.

"So am I," I insist.

Anikêtos stops me short. *You will stay here, Ophelia.*

"You are too valuable to risk, Ophelia," Nazeel says.

I open my mouth to protest, but Nazeel grabs my hand and squeezes tightly. "Ophelia, your humility and your compassion for others is noble, but not when it will risk your life. Look around you. You see all of these people fighting?"

I do as she asks, noting the fallen and those still valiantly battling, and force myself not to feel the crushing pain of those we've lost.

"They do not fight for you, Ophelia, but for everything you represent. The future of *all* our species. They fight for the light. And if you recklessly endanger yourself because you believe you are not worthy of their sacrifice, then they do all of this in vain."

What Nazeel says is true, and humbling, but I'm stopped from having to reply by Ameena. "Do you know the spell?" she asks her sister.

Nazeel nods. "Both Enora and I do."

"I'll keep fending off the hordes from here, then, alongside Ani and Elpis," I say.

Ameena and Zendaya glance up for the first time, then immediately bow their heads in respect of the dragons looming over us. Without any further words, they make their way to the middle of the quad, where Zendaya immediately beheads a warlock. Cadence gives me a quick look that says *be careful* before she darts off too.

Nazeel takes off her robe and lays it on the ground, then pulls a gold pentagram from around her neck and places it on the cloak. "Let us get to work."

She and Enora kneel beside each other, and I go back to directing my energy toward slowing the advancing line of shadows.

Enora's voice melds with Nazeel's over ancient words I don't understand, and the air fills with their energy.

They chant.

The shadows roar a battle cry. My heart pounds, but I keep channeling my magic into destroying them over and over again.

Thunder rolls and lightning splits the sky in two.

Nazeel and Enora cling to each other.

The shadows scream now.

It's working. The spell is working.

Hope floods my chest.

Anikêtos torches the entire line with Dragonfyre, and they scatter to fragments.

A piercing shriek permeates the night.

The shadows reform.

No! What's happening? The spell was working.

CHAPTER FIFTY-TWO

Darkness falls over the quad like a hand reaching out to cover the moon. The air is filled with the bitter taste of despair and hatred.

Another shriek, loud and terrifying.

And then another scream, but this time it's from Enora. Her face twists with terror as her hair is pulled from her scalp by an invisible force, her skin being peeled from her skull like someone has doused her in acid. Nazeel continues to clasp her friend's hand and goes on chanting the ancient words.

It grows darker, and the sense of anguish is crushing, bearing down on us like the weight of the mountain behind us.

The wraith is here.

Enora takes her last breath and falls.

Nazeel goes on chanting, but there are tears running down her face, and the pentagram has melted into liquid gold.

The ground rumbles. A crashing sound comes from somewhere, followed by the most pained cry I have ever heard another creature make in my life. An unholy, unnatural sound. A roar and a scream and a wail all bound up in a cacophony of pain. It is Anikêtos.

Nazeel stops chanting and slumps to the ground.

The battle on the quad rages on, the horde advancing without Ani's and Elpis's fire to hold them back.

I spin around, and the sight that meets me drops me to my knees. I thought dragons were indestructible, but Elpis lies on her side, her huge frame having crushed the whole west wing of Zeus Hall.

"Ani, what happened to her?"

The wraith. I have never encountered one so powerful.

Alexandros's words come back to me—a wraith is the only creature that can kill a dragon.

My heart gallops erratically. The dark shadows grow closer,

as do the remaining vampires and warlocks from Giorgios's army. "Will she be okay? What can I do?"

You must heal her, Ophelia.

I start to move in her direction, but Nazeel's hand grips my ankle. "If you heal a dragon, Ophelia, it will deplete your own healing energy too much. We cannot take such a risk."

"I c-can't let her die."

Nazeel stares at me, her eyes brimming with tears. "You must."

I shake my head. "No way."

You swore me an oath, Ophelia Hart. Ani's booming voice vibrates through my bones. *I am calling in my debt.*

Nazeel makes another attempt to convince me. "Alexandros would tell you to let her die, child."

"And Alexandros knows I would tell him to go to hell." I look up at Ani. *Hold them back while I heal her.*

I stand beside Elpis's head, and I can just reach the tip of her nose. *I've got you, Elpis. I won't let you die.*

It will deplete your power, child. Her voice is weak inside my head.

Yeah, but it won't kill me, right? And whatever doesn't kill you ... I expect her to finish the adage for me, and when she doesn't, it occurs to me that dragons who've lived in another realm for over a thousand years probably aren't up to date on the latest human sayings.

With my arms outstretched as far as possible, I rest both my palms flat on her snout and close my eyes, blocking out the noise around us, confident Anikêtos will protect us both while I heal her. Channeling my earth line, I pull energy from as deep as I can burrow—from the mountain behind us, the trees in the surrounding forest, and the core of the earth itself. Every drop of healing energy I can muster, I feed into the magnificent creature before me. And I keep going until my fingers are numb and

CHAPTER FIFTY-TWO

my knees are buckling and there is nothing left for me to give. I have no idea how much time has passed when I stagger back and fall flat on my ass. I blink up at her and hope I gave enough.

Did it work, Ani? Please, please tell me it worked.

It worked, Dragon Healer. And I am now forever in your debt.

A strangled cry comes from behind me, and I scramble to my feet just in time to come face-to-face with a vampire wielding a dagger. Anikêtos scorches him to ash.

"That was close." I suck in a breath, then drop to my knees as pain burns along my side. When I press my hand to my ribs, I find them sticky.

I know what I'll see when I move my hand, but I do it anyway. My fingers are stained red with my blood.

"Looks like he got a little closer than we thought, huh?" I force out a laugh as my head spins.

"Between us, we should have enough energy to at least stem the flow." Nazeel crawls up beside me, the deep wound in her thigh weeping with her own blood.

"Who did that?"

"One of the undead. It will be fine. My soldiers took care of him."

I glance behind her to see four heavily armored—and heavily armed—soldiers battling a group of warlocks. "When did they get here?"

"A few moments ago. Kameen sent them to bring me back, but they have too much honor to walk away from a battle." She takes my hand, places it over my wound, and rests hers on top. "Let us patch this up the best we can, shall we?"

I nod, grateful to her. Grateful she is alive and hopelessly anguished that Enora didn't make it.

CHAPTER
FIFTY-THREE

ALEXANDROS

40 MINUTES BEFORE THE LIGHT GOES OUT

"Alexandros!" Malachi snaps me out of the daze I was in, and I run to him. He is bound with silver chain, but there are no links and no obvious end point. No weak spot at which to break or snap or unlock. It appears to be forged from a single piece of silver, and the only way to break it is to snap the metal.

The silver burns my hands, but I ignore the pain and try to break him free. My efforts prove futile. I roar my frustration and glance at Axl, who is bound by the same magic.

Lucian lies bleeding out onto the unfinished cellar floor, his eyelids fluttering. "Wraith m-magic."

"I'm okay. Go help him," Malachi urges. I give the chains a final wrench that does nothing and run to Lucian.

Ophelia could break those chains, but that would mean leaving the protection of Anikêtos, crossing campus grounds, and potentially encountering the wraith. She is not doing that without me by her side. "As soon as Lucian is healed, I will fetch Ophelia and she will set you all free."

CHAPTER FIFTY-THREE

Axl nods. "We're okay. Help him."

I drop to the ground beside Lucian and cradle his head to my chest, squeezing the folds of his neck together whilst it heals.

Are you still protecting her? I ask Anikêtos.

Always, Dragon Whisperer, but we have a problem, he answers. *There are more coming. Hordes of shadows we cannot kill.*

What do you mean shadows you cannot kill? More wraiths?

No, Alexandros. They are the undead. Someone has opened a crack in the veil.

How do we stop them? How do we protect her from beings we cannot kill?

Elpis and I will set up a ring of Dragonfyre. None of the creatures will be able to cross it, not even the undead.

The veil has been cracked. How is this even possible?

CHAPTER
FIFTY-FOUR
OPHELIA

26 MINUTES BEFORE THE LIGHT GOES OUT

Nazeel grips my forearm while clutching her wounded thigh. She glances at the carnage surrounding us. "Ophelia. I was wrong."

I blink a drop of sweat from my eye and focus on the plea in her eyes. The chaos goes on unfolding around us. A battle cry from one of the undead pierces my ears, and I sense him drawing near, but between us, Nazeel and I form a protective force field around ourselves, and his shadowy sword strikes against it. "Wrong about what?"

"If we cannot send the wraith back to the netherworld and close the portal, then he must be killed."

"So how do we kill him? And what were you wrong about?"

Her vibrant green eyes shimmer with unshed tears, and she places a bloodied hand on my cheek. "I thought your destiny was to reign, Chosen One. I thought Lucian was the light who would swallow up the dark."

Realization hits me in a rolling wave, slowly settling into every cell of my being. I think I always knew this is how it

CHAPTER FIFTY-FOUR

would end. The kind of power I wield is unnatural. It is far too great for any one person to hold. "My destiny is to die, isn't it? I am the light that will swallow the darkness."

She doesn't answer, but she doesn't have to. Her eyes say everything.

"But how do I kill the wraith without a holy relic?"

A single tear cuts a path through the ash caked on her face. "My sweet, sweet Ophelia. You *are* the holy relic."

No. I can't be.

Except I know she's right. And somehow, I process a lifetime in a single moment.

Getting my degree. Traveling. Children. Grandchildren. All the things I won't have.

And all the things I already have: Love. Joy. My mates. Our bond. Losing them hurts the most, and if I allow it, the grief will overwhelm me. "What happens if we don't kill the wraith?"

"The veil will continue to splinter until the earth is overrun with darkness. When it falls, the light will be lost forever. And you will never be free. Never be safe. And neither will they."

"How do I kill him?"

"You must speak his name."

I frown, confused. "But nobody knows his name."

"You will learn his name at the end. Only at the end. Before the wraith takes your soul, Lucifer himself will give it to you."

No, that's way too easy. If that were true, anyone could kill him. "But how do I actually kill him?" With both of us depleted from the battle, our force field is cracking under the might of the hordes of vampires and warlocks who swarm us.

Nazeel glances over my head right as the force field splinters open and we are swarmed. "Trust your light, Ophelia" is the last thing I hear her say before she is swallowed up by at least six enemies.

Channeling my power, I throw off the undead that cling to

me. They are torn apart by the energy that rips through them, but they quickly reform, rolling into shadow and darkness before they return to the shape of men.

I glance back to where Nazeel was, ready to help, but she is fighting them off with spells as she runs for the safety provided by Anikêtos's Dragonfyre.

"Find the wraith, Ophelia," she calls. "He is at the ancient ruins where the darkness is strongest."

She must mean the ruins near the mouth of the river. Beside me, Ruby Dragon vampires battle a horde of the undead, beating them back again and again, tearing them limb from limb only for them to reform and return. They are exhausted. Everyone is exhausted.

I call out for Alexandros and my boys, but only he answers. *They are alive, little one. Stay with Anikêtos and Elpis within the ring of Dragonfyre. They will keep it alight as long as they need to. You must wait there for us. We will not be long.*

I love you.

Ophelia! Do as I say. This is not a request, agápi mou.

I know. I scrub the tears from my cheeks and wonder if my mind is strong enough to lie to him. *I heard you.*

Good girl. We will be with you soon.

"Ophelia!" Her voice is such a welcome sound.

Cadence! I spin around and see her running toward me, her auburn hair whipping around her face as she dodges a vampire. "Head for Anikêtos and Elpis," I call. "They'll protect you."

She glances in their direction. "Then let's go."

"I'll meet you soon. Go," I plead as she continues her path toward me.

Her eyes go wide, and I spin around to see the hooded figure of a warlock directly behind me, a silver axe held above his head as he prepares to bring it down. Lightning sparks from my fingertips, but before I can act, I'm shoved to the ground.

CHAPTER FIFTY-FOUR

When I sit up, Cadence's severed head rolls toward me, coming to a stop a few feet away from me. Her beautiful face forever frozen in terror. My wonderful, loyal friend.

Rage lights up my insides, and I direct it all at the warlock in front of me as he raises his axe once more. His body jerks, his limbs forking at unnatural angles. "She was my best fucking friend!" I bellow. "She was—" A sob steals the rest of my words, but he cannot hear me anyway. He cries out a counterspell, but there is no spell in the known universe that could stop me.

And when the shadowy forms of his undead comrades come to his aid, the lightning energy coming from my fingertips flows through them too. They fall to the ground, and so do I.

I cradle Cadence's headless body in my arms and let a river of silent tears drip onto her shirt. What is the point of all this power if I cannot use it to save the people I love?

"I'm so sorry, Cadence." I lower her body to the ground. I couldn't save her, but I will sure as hell save everyone else.

I call out for Sienna with my mind, and she answers me quickly. Last time I caught a glimpse of her, she was battling a swarm of enemy vampires with a group of allies who stayed behind to fight. *Get everyone to the dragons. None of these creatures can cross the ring of Dragonfyre. You'll all be safe there.*

And what about you?

I take off in the direction of the river. *I'm going to close the tear in the veil.*

Be safe, girl.

Always, I promise. And I wish I could mean it. Of course I'd be safe if I could, but all signs point to me being responsible for the tear in the veil by bringing the dragons back.

And now I am the only thing standing between the wraith and the end of the world as we know it.

CHAPTER
FIFTY-FIVE
ALEXANDROS

26 MINUTES BEFORE THE LIGHT GOES OUT

Giorgios's words return to haunt me. Anikêtos and Elpis returned through the veil, weakening it and allowing the wraith to crack it open. Had he bonded with Ophelia, then he and the Skotádi would have had the power they desired. The wraith would not have slipped back into the mortal realm, and we would not have armies of the undead storming the campus.

Now I see how we brought about our own downfall, but I am self-aware enough to admit that I would do it all again if it meant preventing him from taking her from me. I am no protector of man. I am *her* protector, and hers alone.

Alexandros! Her voice rings out in my head now. She calls for the boys too, but Malachi and Axl allow me to answer.

They are alive, Ophelia. Stay with Anikêtos and Elpis within the ring of Dragonfyre. They will keep it alight as long as they need to. You must stay there and wait for us. We will not be long.

I love you.

CHAPTER FIFTY-FIVE

That does not sound like an agreement. *Ophelia! Do as I say. This is not a request, agápi mou.*

I know. I heard you.

That is more like it. *Good girl. We will be with you soon.* As soon as Lucian is healed enough to walk, I will carry Axl, Xavier, and Malachi to her if I must.

"Why isn't Xavier waking up, Professor? If Giorgios is dead, shouldn't the magic die with him?" Malachi's concern saturates the dank cellar and snaps me back into action.

Xavier's heart beats a steady rhythm, and I feel our bond still firmly in place. He is very much alive but does not seem to be able to hear us calling to him.

"It's the wraith's magic," Lucian croaks. "Giorgios was merely the vessel. He never wanted the wraith to return to the mortal realm because he was able to channel sufficient dark magic through the veil. Now the wraith is the one in control, and the spell will remain in place until the wraith is either returned to the netherworld or until he's killed."

"The wraith has opened the veil. Do you have any idea how he might have done that?"

"M-my blood. Spilling my blood with the Sword of Skotos. The Skotádi forged the weapon from the shadows of the netherworld centuries ago. That's why they needed the one who first tasted her blood. That's why the wraith left. It went to the ancient ruins where the magic is strongest. Giorgios wanted him to tear the veil until it fell. Until there was no separation between the land of the living and that of the dead."

"Because if the entire world is in darkness, then she is dragged to the dark along with the rest of us?"

He nods.

"How do you know all of this?"

"I have been connected with Giorgios since I was a child.

His mind and mine ..." He squeezes his eyes closed. "It was a bond but ... forged with dark magic."

How could I have not known any of this? No, that is the wrong question to ask. How is it I let my son down so badly? He deserved better.

Like a rabid dog, he tries to shake his head from side to side, but I tighten my grip on him and continue holding the wound at his throat shut even as he struggles against me. It is as if he is trying to eject the bitter memories holding him hostage. And then he starts mumbling in ancient Greek.

"Lucian! Please help me understand. You can still help us stop this. How is it you tricked Giorgios into thinking you were dead?"

He sucks in a deep breath and mutters something unintelligible before his eyes return to mine. "I severed the bond with the help of the Skotádi warlocks. It was their last act of service to me before I killed them too. It was the only way to break the spell ..." He coughs, and blood trickles from his lips. "H-he ..." he sputters.

I stroke his face. *Save your strength. Speak to me in here*, I urge him.

I could force my way into his mind and comb his memories, but that would only earn me his unbridled—and deserved—anger. He would scurry away from me like a wounded animal. Besides, if we are to ever have any kind of relationship again, I cannot betray his trust in such a way. *The only way to break the spell Giorgios had you under?*

Yes. And because he believed me dead, I was able to enter his mind without him knowing. Observe his thoughts without detection.

Lucian's eyes close, and he sucks in a ragged breath. I lift my hand from his neck and blood runs from the wound like a river. Quickly, I clamp my hand over it once more. "Why is this not healing, Lucian?"

CHAPTER FIFTY-FIVE

The blade of Skotos. It was forged with unnatural magic. The blade continues to do damage after the cut is made. It will perhaps take a little longer than usual, but it will heal.

There is nothing to do but wait for it to heal, and although I bristle with impatience, I know I must focus on what else I need to know to stop the world from coming to an end.

CHAPTER
FIFTY-SIX
OPHELIA

15 MINUTES BEFORE THE LIGHT GOES OUT

Blood runs in a steady stream down my thigh from a gash on my hip, as the healing energy from the earth line that flows through me is far too depleted to close the wound. I run on, pain burning a trail through every ligament and every muscle. But I recall Cadence's lifeless face, Enora's silver hair as it was torn from her scalp. Sienna and Osiris, father and daughter fighting side by side, bloodied and bruised. My mates, all prepared to give up their lives in pursuit of the same goal—my survival.

But my survival is the one thing that cannot happen.

The words that have been spoken by so many echo through my thoughts: *Always trust your light, child. You are the holy relic, Ophelia. The Chosen One.*

Then lines from the prophecy, disjointed and out of order, ring louder:

And the light is tempted back from the darkness.

The child borne of fire and blood

shall be our ruin or our redemption.

CHAPTER FIFTY-SIX

To bring a balance that reigns through the ages.

A vampire barrels toward me, teeth bared, the scent of my blood thick in the air. I duck out of his way, dodging his heavy frame, and wince as sharp pain lances through my side.

I am right here with you, Chosen One. Anikêtos's deep voice fills my head, and the gust of wind at my back tells me he is right behind me.

What about the others, Ani? They need the Dragonfyre to stay safe.

Elpis is healed enough to sustain the circle.

Such a shame Dragonfyre can't kill a wraith.

It can kill everything else though.

Yes it fucking can. I raise my palms and flick my wrists, dousing my hands with Dragonfyre. The hordes of vampires and warlocks that come charging through the trees are no match for Anikêtos and me as we lay waste to the forest around us, along with every living being within it. Thankfully, the animals who call this their home all seem to have evacuated earlier. Screams of agony fill the night air, and the undead crumble from shadow to ash. But they slowly reform again, and there will be more. The wraith opened the crack in the veil, and only his death will close it. The burning forest warms my skin, flames licking at my feet as I plow on, channeling the air around us to quicken my pace.

I stumble over a rock and fall into the path of a grinning warlock. He raises his sword and is about to bring it down when I regain my footing and dive forward, sliding headfirst between his legs before flipping onto my back, where I place my hands on his calves and watch as the Dragonfyre engulfs his body.

Ani, you still with me? My breathing is harsh and ragged, my heart beating frantically in my chest.

Until the end, Dragon Healer. His words bring me comfort despite the inevitability of what's ahead.

OPHELIA

The wraith is waiting for us, his shadowy form ghosting through the ruins of the ancient stone church. My powers are limited here on sacred ground.

What do you need me to do, Ophelia? Anikêtos asks.

Just be here with me, Ani. Don't try to stop what's about to happen, okay? It's the only way.

As you wish, Dragon Healer. His usually gruff voice is gentle.

But its soothing quality is quickly forgotten as the wraith's unholy screeching pierces my ears. I can decipher its words now—perhaps because he wants me to. "I knew you would come, Chosen One."

I stand beside the crumbling altar that was once used for pagan sacrifices and lean on it for support as the pain in my side grows more intense. "Come to kill you and close the veil."

His laugh is a squall that threatens to burst my eardrums. "Such arrogance from such a pathetic little girl."

I roll back my shoulders and watch his shadowy tendrils slither over the stones around us. He grows closer. "We'll see just how pathetic I am when I take you down, asshole!"

"It astounds me how a creature of your apparent power has no sense of self-preservation. Giorgios would have allowed you to live at least. You could have reigned by his side. But I have no need of you now that the veil has cracked. I will find another power-hungry vampire to fulfill my earthly desires, and you, Ophelia Hart, will fade into obscurity. There will be no one to mourn your passing. You will leave this world as you have lived in it. As nobody."

CHAPTER
FIFTY-SEVEN
ALEXANDROS

15 MINUTES BEFORE THE LIGHT GOES OUT

I look at all four of my sons, incapacitated and in need of my help. Never in my long, long life have I felt so helpless. But there are more answers I need from Lucian. *When did you taste Ophelia?*

I used to watch over her. To make sure the Skotádi didn't find her. When she was five, she cut her finger on a broken bottle at the playground. Her foster dad was too busy flirting with any woman who looked his direction to pay her any mind. She was bleeding pretty badly, so I helped her. I must have gotten some blood on my finger. I wasn't careful enough. It was an accident.

And you felt her power then? From such a small taste?
I couldn't have not felt it.
And you protected her?

His body surges upward, and I have to fight to hold him down as a vicious snarl pours from his lips. *I watched her!*

Okay. I believe you. Please lie still so you can heal.

Our eyes lock, and I take his slow blink as acquiescence and loosen my grip. *So it was Giorgios who staged the attacks at the university. He tried to make me believe it was you.*

He closes his eyes and does not answer, and grief and guilt bond into a single blade that cuts me to the quick. *How did he become so powerful, Lucian? How did he gain such mastery over dark magic?*

He did not master it. He has never possessed dark magic; he merely borrowed it.

My scholarly big brother, with the kind blue eyes and sharp wit, the man who taught me how to curse in six languages before I was ten ... He borrowed dark magic? A mere four weeks ago, I could never have imagined the depth of his betrayal. *From whom?*

Lucian's eyes flutter open. They are hazel, just like his mother's, and I am filled with so much regret for what has passed between us that I struggle to catch my breath. *A warlock named Salem. When Giorgios was little more than a boy, Salem made him a deal. He promised to grant him the power of transportation and teach him the dark arts if Giorgios agreed to serve him.*

I have never heard of such a warlock.

He died almost two millennia ago. Giorgios somehow maintained the channel to his dark magic. It was how he formed the Skotádi.

Giorgios formed the Skotádi?

Lucian nods, then winces.

"Why is that still hurting you? Why are you not healing?"

I told you, it's the Skotos. It's still eating through my skin.

Despair fills me. *So you are not healing?*

I guess not. His rattling laugh is cut short by a coughing fit that has blood spraying from his lips. Droplets hit my cheeks, and I can only stare down at him.

He has been lying to me, allowing himself to bleed out in

my arms. For what? Punishment? Mine or his? *What if you take some of my blood?*

No. You can't. I can't. He thrashes against my hold, giving me another glimpse of the rabid beast that seems to live within him. *I won't!*

Why, Lucian? Why will you not let me try to save you? Perhaps he is trying to punish us both by dying in my arms.

His eyes are wild, glowing with delirium yet filled with an agony it guts me to witness. *Because I killed them! I did what you think I did, and for that, I don't deserve to live.* Tears and snot and blood drip from his face.

Of all the things I now despise my brother for, allowing my son to suffer in this way for centuries is chief among them. *But that was Giorgios, son. That was not you.*

I will never forget their faces. Their terror when they realized what I was about to do. I knew what he was, and still I joined him. I followed him blindly...

I glare at the remains of my brother and wish I could raise him from the dead only to kill him again. *You were a child, and he took advantage of you. I am sorry I was not a better father. Please let me be one now.*

Lucian coughs, and a bubble of blood forms on his lips.

I will bite my wrist so you can feed.

Taking your blood would cause us to share a bond once more. I cannot bear it. Not after all the pain I caused. That is not something I can withstand. Please, just let me go. He grabs at my sleeve, his fingers struggling to find their grip as he tries to cling to me even whilst begging me to let him go. His next word breaks me. *Dad!*

I rest my forehead against his. *I am here. I will not leave you, son. I promise.*

CHAPTER
FIFTY-EIGHT
OPHELIA

7 MINUTES UNTIL THE LIGHT GOES OUT

I wipe my sweaty palms on my pants, streaking more blood and dirt over the black leather. My knees tremble with the effort of standing while the wound in my side continues to ooze blood. And the wraith's last words, about how I have lived and will die as a nobody, seem to echo on the wind.

"I beg to differ." The sound of his voice makes my already shaky knees tremble, and I have to stop myself from bursting into tears. "You move an inch closer to her and I will end you, Salem."

Salem.

The wraith shrieks and shrinks back from us, retreating behind one of the stones.

Alexandros stares down at me, his dark eyes glistening with tears. "Did you think I would leave you to face the wraith without me, agápi mou? I would move all the heavens and every rock of the netherworld before I left you to face him alone."

CHAPTER FIFTY-EIGHT

I throw my arms around his neck but continue scanning the clearing and the sacred ruins for a sign of the wraith. He's still here. I feel the darkness and despair that seeps from him. "How did you know his name?"

"I was not sure it was his name until just now, but Lucian told me of a warlock named Salem that Giorgios took powers from. They were never stolen. Salem offered them in return for his lifelong service."

I step back from him, a spark of hope igniting inside me. "So now we can kill him."

He shakes his head. "Ophelia, without a holy relic we have no hope of killing him. We need to leave here. Now."

Oh, my dear Alexandros. I know how much this is going to hurt him, but perhaps one day we will meet again. Nothing is impossible, right? "We've had the ultimate holy relic all this time, my love."

He blinks, confused, but before I can explain what I mean, the wraith reappears, his shadowy tendrils curling through the air and heading straight for us. I use the last of my limited power to conjure a force field, but it's weak, and he's already bleeding through its cracks.

"Nazeel!" I shout her name, knowing that if she's alive, she'll be listening, even if she cannot be here. "Please tell him. Make him understand what needs to be done."

Ophelia is the relic, Alexandros. I hear her voice in his head as clearly as if it were in my own.

"No!" He grips my shoulders tightly. "You are not, Ophelia."

I hold out my hands to strengthen the force field, but it is weakening along with my body. I'm bleeding out from the wound on my side, and with every second, the wraith comes closer to reaching us through the failing barrier. Ignoring for a moment the fate that awaits me, I give Alexandros a smile full of love and gratitude. In only a few short months, he and his sireds showed me an eternity of love and happiness. I am ready.

The wraith can be killed with a holy relic, and any relic is holy if it is truly believed in. "You believe in me, don't you?"

His eyes bore into mine, and they're filled with pain and so much love, it makes my heart physically ache at the thought of leaving him. Of leaving them. "More than anything, Ophelia. But I would take the wraith to the netherworld myself before I allowed you to make this sacrifice."

"I am the relic," I repeat. "And I think you already know that. I think you know what being the Chosen One means, and that's why you've been so resistant to the prophecy."

He bares his teeth, although his eyes shine with unshed tears. "You think I would use you as a weapon? I would rather let this entire fucking world burn to nothing."

The wraith's shrieks get louder, and the air grows thick with despair and vitriol. "Know I am ready to leave this place truly understanding that I am loved beyond all measure. You do not have to use me as a weapon, my love." I lower my hands and place them on his face. The force field falls, and the wraith's icy fingers dust over the back of my neck. "I only need to be touching you."

Alexandros screams my name and tries to wrench my hands from his face, but it's too late.

I close my eyes and focus on my light. It grows brighter. Dazzling and sparking like the sun. It gets fiercer and hotter until I no longer feel the coldness of the wraith's embrace. Still, Alexandros's pained cries ring in my ears, and they are joined by Xavier's, Axl's, and Malachi's. Unable to bear the sounds of their heartbreak, I shut them out and channel everything into my light, willing it to burn brighter and more intensely than ever before.

The wraith grows closer still, sucking me into his shadows,

CHAPTER FIFTY-EIGHT

and when my soul is about to join his, right as it is slipping into his darkness, I say his name before Lucifer has to whisper it to me. *Salem.*

There is a dazzling burst of light, like what I imagine must happen when a star explodes. A blast of intense, bone-shattering energy that seems to vibrate through every living thing in the universe and then come back to me. Salem's long-lost soul returns to his body and is immediately dragged to the netherworld by Lucifer himself. I have never considered the notion that the devil is real, and perhaps it is merely my imagination, but his voice is much gentler than I expected it would be. *Your debt is paid, Ophelia Hart. The veil is closed.*

The veil is closed. Alexandros and the boys are safe. The world is safe.

The light goes out.

I can finally rest.

CHAPTER FIFTY-NINE

ALEXANDROS

"Ophelia, no!" I roar, but she cannot hear me. Even if she could, she would pay me no heed, for this is who she is. Who she was always going to be. The one who sacrificed herself to save the world—a world that will never even know her name.

She falls forward, and I drop to my knees with her, cradling her in my arms. Then I hear his voice in her head, and it sends a chill down my spine. Instinctively, I know who it is, although I have never heard him speak before—so very few have. The first fallen angel tells her that her debt is paid.

I will pay your debt. I will serve at your side for eternity! I implore him, but he is unreachable to me, locked away in the deepest recesses of his kingdom in the netherworld once more.

The wraith disappears, vanishing like a breath on the wind. And now she is gone too.

The depth of my pain is so intense it is impossible to feel it—for if I experience even a fraction, I will surely shatter into a million fragments of myself and scatter amongst the four winds. Although perhaps that would be a far less cruel fate than a world without her in it. I crush her to my chest and brush her

CHAPTER FIFTY-NINE

hair back from her forehead, waiting for her loss to eviscerate me. Waiting for the severing of our bond to slice my soul into shards of glass that tear through every fiber of my body. Waiting to become nothing.

The sound of bodies crashing noisily through the woods breaks the silence. A second later, Axl, Xavier, and Malachi burst into the clearing and are on the ground beside us, the magic securing the silver chains gone without Giorgios or the wraith to hold it in place. They silently implore me for an answer I do not have.

"Take me instead!" Axl screams toward the heavens. "Just bring her back." Then he turns his attention to me, his eyes wild. "Deals can be made with Death, right? I've heard you say it. So make him a fucking deal, Alexandros. Bring her back to us."

I drop my head, knowing I have let them all down. *I wish I could, only it was not Death who came for Ophelia, but Lucifer himself.*

"Lucifer?" Malachi says on a sob. "You're telling me the fucking devil has our girl?"

"No, for if he did, I would follow her to the netherworld and take her back from him. The devil does not take pure souls; he sets them free."

I look up to the dark sky, and the twinkling stars seem to mock me as my heart disintegrates into a billion particles of stardust. Perhaps that is the only way I can truly be with her. I will simply lie here with her in my arms until the end of time itself. Until everything turns to dust.

"Alexandros!" Xavier's pained cry rings in my ears now. "Do something!"

I rest my forehead against hers. Her skin is still warm. How I long to feel her soft breath on my face. What is the use in being the protector of man if I cannot protect the one human I was born to love? I place my hand over her heart, and it does not beat, but her blood still flows gently through her veins. My fangs protract. My heart rate spikes, jolting me back to life. What if I could ...?

"Do it," Axl says, not needing to read my mind.

CHAPTER SIXTY

AXL

I swear my heart feels like it's being physically torn from my chest. The moment the chains slipped from our wrists, we ran here faster than we've ever moved before in our lives, ignoring the searing pain in our limbs despite knowing it wasn't caused by the burns from the silver.

Ophelia is gone.

Yet still, we refuse to admit it. This is different from when we thought we lost the professor. More visceral in some ways, yet oddly less somehow.

I stare at her lifeless body cradled in his arms. How have I not turned to dust at her loss? This numbness must be some sort of defense mechanism. My body's way of protecting me. My brain won't let me feel all the pain at once because it would spell my destruction.

Malachi and Xavier are on either side of me, their shock bleeding into mine. She can't be gone. I won't let her go. I call out for her, and my heart cracks wide open when she doesn't reply.

"Take me instead!" I scream into the night sky. Surely someone will hear. Someone will take pity on her. She—of all creatures—doesn't deserve to die. "Just bring her back." I stare at Alexandros, memories of past conversations sending sparks of hope flickering to life. "Deals can be made with Death, right? I've heard you say it. So make him a fucking deal, Alexandros. Bring her back to us."

He drops his head, his shoulders slumped in defeat. *I wish I could, only it was not Death who came for Ophelia, but Lucifer himself.*

My blood is pounding so loudly in my ears that I'm sure I didn't hear him right. Because the devil doesn't fucking exist. Does he? If he does, he'd better give us our fucking girl back.

"Lucifer?" Malachi cries. "You're telling me the fucking devil has our girl?"

"No, for if he did, I would follow her to the netherworld and take her back from him. The devil does not take pure souls; he sets them free." The voice, so strained, doesn't sound like it belongs to Alexandros. He tilts his face to the sky.

What the fuck is this? Is he giving up? Letting her go?

"Alexandros!" Xavier yells, letting out a mere particle of the pain we're all feeling. "Do something!"

Alexandros returns from his trance and, gently lifting her, presses his face close to hers. My fangs ache. Maybe there's a chance. Maybe her soul still lingers close by, waiting to be tethered back to something. Back to us.

Alexandros can bring her back. He can save her if he'd just fucking try.

He places his hand over her heart. I cannot hear it beat, but I urge him anyway. "Do it."

CHAPTER
SIXTY-ONE
ALEXANDROS

Is this insanity? The final desperate act of a man who has not yet accepted that his world has ended? Perhaps. Probably.

But I would try anything to hear her say my name once more.

I dip my head and sink my fangs into her throat. The sweet nectar of her blood suffuses my mouth. *Please come back to us, agápi mou. I know you are still here somewhere. Please.*

Her blood trickles slowly into my mouth, filling me with everything she is. I slice a cut onto my tongue and let it flow into her vein. *Ophelia. Please! We cannot live without you.*

Her heart beats. Once. Twice. Or am I imagining it? Wanting it so desperately that I am hearing and feeling things that are not there?

Ophelia, I plead, allowing more of my lifeblood to slip into her vein.

"I'm here." Her voice is a mere whisper, but she may as well have roared the declaration. I pull my teeth from her throat in time to see her eyelids flutter open.

The cries of elation from Axl, Malachi, and Xavier surround

the two of us, and she blinks up at me, a small, sweet smile on her beautiful face. The relief I feel is so profound, it renders me speechless for a time. Never again, no matter how long I remain on this earth, will I take a single second of my time with her for granted.

The boys surround us, and the five of us become a single knot of unending gratitude.

I press my forehead to hers. "I thought we had lost you, little one."

"So did I," she rasps. "Did we do it?"

"You did it, Ophelia," I answer. "*You* killed the wraith and closed the veil."

Her smile grows, and I find myself grinning just as widely, and I know the boys are too. We refuse to let go of one another, remaining on the ground huddled in one mass of bodies. Whole again.

"You came back to us, baby," Malachi says.

Her blue eyes sparkle. "Yeah, I spoke to Lucifer."

"You had a chat with the devil, Cupcake?"

"I know. Crazy, right? He's actually kind of sweet. Even with his giant horns."

I cannot contain my laugh. Of course Ophelia did not find the devil even the slightest bit intimidating. She is fearless. But I am sure there are many who would disagree with her assessment.

Save your strength now, agápi mou, I tell her. Although I am desperate to learn more about how she returned to us, for I know I did not turn her. But for now, I am content to hold her in my arms.

I can still hear you in here, she says, surprised.

I rest my lips on her head. We have no idea how her powers have been affected, but she heard me calling for her, and I

CHAPTER SIXTY-ONE

hoped our bond would continue to allow us to communicate. *Yes, little one.*

"I felt you calling me back," she says with a contented sigh. "It was ..."

Axl takes her free hand in his and laces his fingers through hers. "We'll always bring you back to us, princess."

I squeeze Ophelia a little too tightly, and she winces. Some of her ribs are almost certainly broken, and she is bleeding heavily from a deep laceration on her side. "I will feed you some more of my blood, little one. It will heal you quickly."

Tears fill her striking blue eyes. "I can't heal myself anymore, can I? I can't feel my power."

I suspect if she has sacrificed her light, then she has sacrificed her power too, but now is not the time to discuss it. Now is the time to heal her, to take her home and rest before we count the cost of all we have lost. I stand with her in my arms, cradling her close to my chest, and she nuzzles against me. She is too cold for my liking. As we head back to the Ruby Dragon compound, she rests a hand on my chest. My mind drifts to the losses we have experienced today, and inevitably to *him*.

She blinks up at me, sensing my sadness. *I spoke to him, you know. He's going to be okay. He said it was what he wanted.*

Lucian. My firstborn son, who was willing to make the ultimate sacrifice just as she was. The light who turned back from the dark.

CHAPTER SIXTY-TWO

MALACHI

Alexandros gave Ophelia some of his blood back at the ruins, but all our energy is so depleted, it is taking longer than usual for us to recover. She still bleeds from the deep wound in her side, although it is healing. I step onto the path that leads to the Dragon Society houses with her cradled in my arms, having insisted I carry her at least half the way. We lost some vampires, but the ones who are left form a line on two sides, creating a path to our house, their heads bowed in deference as we pass. Not to me or Xavier or Axl, or even the professor, but in deference to her. My fucking warrior elementai who saved us all.

Her eyes are closed, her head resting on my chest, and I'm sure she's drifting in and out of sleep, but her heart beats steadily. She's alive. She has likely lost her powers, but we didn't lose her, and for that I am eternally grateful. When we realized what she was intending to do, I was filled with so much terror—awe and pride too—but mostly terror. And when we found her cradled in Alexandros's arms, when we thought she was gone ...

I have never experienced pain like that in my life. And

CHAPTER SIXTY-TWO

although it only lasted for a handful of minutes, that pain has etched itself into my soul and is a permanent reminder of what I almost lost. Now, my mind swims with the surreal notion that I get to spend the rest of my life at her side. Loving her and cherishing her. Protecting her.

A red-haired woman limps toward us, clutching a bleeding wound on her thigh, and Alexandros inclines his head in her direction. "Nazeel." It seems even the Grand Healer of the Order will need time to heal her wounds. Two women who look so similar that they can only be her sisters stay back as she approaches.

Nazeel gazes at my girl, a knowing smile on her face, and brushes a lock of hair from Ophelia's forehead. "I knew she would do it. I knew she was the one from the moment I first looked into her eyes."

I get it. I knew she was the one from the moment I met her too. My incredible girl who saved the entire goddamn world. Nazeel is looking at her with undisguised awe, and that's exactly how it should be. Every single being in this realm owes Ophelia a debt.

"She has sacrificed her light, Nazeel. I assume that means her powers too?" Alexandros asks.

Nazeel tilts her head, her vibrant green eyes shining with tears. "She has given up her power, but she is still an elementai, Alexandros. In every other way there is." She glances over her shoulder at four large men, all of them as bloodied and battle-scarred as we are.

"My guards give me no choice; I must return to Kameen," she says softly to Alexandros. "I fear this may be the last time we meet for a good while, old friend."

He nods. "Thank you, Nazeel."

She cups his cheek with her free hand. "No, thank you, Alexandros Drakos. Protector of man."

MALACHI

Protector of man, huh? Never in my wildest dreams would I have had our sire pegged as that, but I guess a lot's happened these past few months that I never could have predicted. His jaw tics, and I can tell the title doesn't sit comfortably with him, but he doesn't refute her. Nazeel limps across the lawn with her sisters at her side, followed by the guards of the Order, and we watch them until they disappear from sight.

Axl jogs up the steps and opens the door. "Let's get Ophelia inside."

∽

I LAY Ophelia on the bed, and her eyelids flutter open. "Are we home?" she whispers.

I sit beside her and take her hand in mine. "We sure are, sweet girl. You're safe now."

Her smile melts me to my fucking core. "We're all safe."

I nod. Yeah, we are.

Her mood turns on a dime, and the sudden sadness hurtling through her cuts me off at the knees. "Except for Cadence. And Enora. And how many others?"

Uncontrollable sobs rack her body, and I cradle her head to my chest and whisper soothing words in her ear, telling her that everyone who survived is safe thanks to her. Her pain at the loss of her friends slices into me like a blade, and I wish I could make it better. "You need to take blood from all of us, baby. It will help you heal faster."

Axl and Xavier voice their agreement. Alexandros stands at the foot of the bed, staring at her like he can't believe she's real.

Ophelia sniffs and nods. I slice open a cut on the pad of my thumb and slip it between her lips. Her eyes grow heavy as she suckles, causing warmth and pleasure to flow through my veins.

CHAPTER SIXTY-TWO

Am I taking too much? she asks, still able to communicate through our bond.

No, baby. You take as much as you need.

She suckles a little while longer before turning her head and sinking into the pillow. My cut heals over, and I trail my fingertips down her cheek. Alexandros kneels on the bed and starts removing her leather pants.

"Hey." She gives a short laugh, but it's listless. "Now? Really?"

"As much as I would like to, we need to check your wound, Ophelia," he says.

"Oh, right." She winces as he works the tight leather gently over her hips, revealing her previously white panties that are now soaked in blood. The scent of it has my fangs protracting, and I close my mouth so she won't see.

Axl groans with frustration as the scent hits him too.

"What's wrong?" she asks, her eyes wide with panic now.

I shake my head. "Nothing, baby."

"Oh, god." Her hand flies to her mouth. "If I lost my powers, does that mean I won't taste the same now? Do I smell different? Am I not vamp-nip to you guys anymore?"

Axl growls. "You still smell fucking incredible, princess. I'm desperate to taste you, but I'm not sure right now is the time to be feeding on your blood is all."

I nod, signaling I am in full agreement with his assessment.

Alexandros gently removes her blood-soaked panties and assesses the wound on her hip. It's healing well, but her sweet blood still oozes from the wound. "You taste just as delicious as you have always tasted, agápi mou. But let us take care of you before you tempt us all with your vamp-nip blood, okay?"

Her pale cheeks flush with a little color. "Okay."

As I lie down beside her, I hold her slender hand in mine, and I make her a vow that I will never let her hurt ever again.

CHAPTER
SIXTY-THREE
OPHELIA

Everything hurts. Every cell in every inch of my body. But I could deal with all of that if there weren't such a deep, gnawing ache in my heart. So many are gone. Crescent wolves and Dragon vampires whose names I don't even know. Vasilis. Enora. Cadence. And for what? Because Giorgios wanted more power? Did he not have enough already? And to what end?

I lie with my head nestled against Malachi's chest, aware of Axl and Xavier lying behind me and Alexandros sitting on the edge of the bed. Their concern for me is thick and cloying. I wish I could enjoy our victory, bask in their love and the comfort of their presence. But I'm too overwhelmed with guilt and grief, the weight of emotion crushing me.

Why did I get to come back when they didn't? Perhaps when I spoke with Lucifer, I should have bargained for their lives instead of selfishly asking for my own.

"You have nothing to feel guilty for, agápi mou," Alexandros says soothingly, his warm hand resting on my bare calf. "Those who made sacrifices did so willingly, and they did it because

CHAPTER SIXTY-THREE

they believed in you. They wanted you to live. Do not dishonor their memories by regretting that outcome."

I'm unable to agree with him, unable to stop a river of tears from pouring out of my eyes. The logical part of my brain knows he speaks the truth, but right now, it's still too much.

"How did you come back to us, Cupcake?" Xavier asks, his fingers trailing over my back.

Thankful for a change of subject, I shuffle into a sitting position and scrub the tears from my cheeks. "It was always supposed to be my light. That was the sacrifice that was needed. To kill a wraith, you have to return his soul, and to do that, you have to announce his name."

It was never supposed to be me. Those words resound in my head, and I know the boys and Alexandros hear them too. My eyes find his. "You gave me Salem's name, therefore Lucifer didn't need to take my soul in return for it. So, he gave me a choice." I can still recall the gentle tone of his voice. His obsidian eyes, full of both sorrow and compassion, when he asked me where I wanted to go next. "I wanted to come back, but then I was in the dark ..." I suck in a shaky breath, reliving the eerie feeling of being lost in the abyss. Of absolute nothingness. The fear when I realized I no longer had my light to guide me. And then they brought me back to them. "And then I heard you all calling for me ... and I followed the sound, and somehow, I found my way back."

Malachi presses a kiss on my temple. "We would have come and found you if we needed to, baby."

"M-maybe I should have—" I choke on a sob. "I should have asked him to save the others instead."

"When dealing with the devil, the only soul one can bargain with is one's own, Ophelia," Alexandros explains, his dark eyes boring into me. "It was not a choice you were able to make, so please grieve for your friends, but do not grieve for your return to us."

"And even if you had been able to, Cupcake," Xavier says, cupping my cheek and brushing away my tears with his thumb while his eyes shine with tears of his own. "You would have ended all four of us instead, because not one of us could live without you."

"The only person responsible for those we lost are the ones who took them," Axl says.

Xavier snarls. "And Giorgios."

"Why did he do it?" I ask. "Did you find out?"

Alexandros and the boys fill me in on everything that passed before Giorgios's death, and my heart breaks anew. For everything my mates endured. For Lucian.

It all hurts too much.

And I'm tired. So very tired.

Axl pulls me into his arms, and I curl into his body, my eyes closing despite how much I fight against it.

"Will she be okay?" he whispers.

"Yes," Alexandros answers. "But she has lost much, and it is in her nature to feel others' pain as acutely as her own. And she is exhausted. Let her sleep."

I want to stay awake, to bask in the comfort of their presence, but I can't. Too fatigued and too overwhelmed by guilt and despair, I let the heavy blanket of sleep take me under its weight.

CHAPTER
SIXTY-FOUR

XAVIER

Satisfied the tub is full and exactly the right temperature, I turn off the tap and head back into the bedroom, where Ophelia is suckling on Axl's wrist while Alexandros checks her over. She is battered and bruised, but fuck me, she is still the most beautiful thing I have ever seen.

When I think of what she gave up for us, of how much more she was willing to give ... When I allow myself to feel the pain of losing her, I can't fucking breathe. So I push the thoughts away and focus on the fact that she's here. She's safe. We all are. And now we get to spend the rest of our long lives loving and being loved by her.

I crawl onto the bed next to Alexandros and assess the damage. Her clothes have all been removed now, and only the cut on her hip remains, a cut so deep it still hasn't fully healed. Axl gently pulls his arm from her mouth, and she licks her lips. "Should I be enjoying blood this much?"

"When it makes you better, yes," Axl says.

"How are you feeling now, Cupcake?" She slept for four hours straight after she told us about what happened in the netherworld.

She offers me a faint smile, her eyes remaining closed. "Like I got run over by a horde of the undead."

I bite back a grin and skim my hand down the curve of her ribs. She doesn't wince, so her bones must have healed there. "A warm bath will help you feel better."

"Sounds like heaven." Her words float away on a whisper.

Alexandros dusts his fingertips over her hip. "The external wound should close soon, but the worst of the bleeding has stopped, so that is a good sign."

I dip my head. "Then let me help." I slice a cut on my tongue and flick it over the small open cut that still remains. The mix of my blood and saliva knits the skin back together fully, and her sweet taste coats my tongue. I heard her concern about her blood not tasting the same, which is ludicrous, but I'm happy to have the opportunity to reassure her now. *You still taste better than cupcakes.*

Thank you, Xavier.

When her cut has stopped bleeding, I pick her up and carry her to the bath, but she's still so exhausted that I can't risk putting her in the water alone. Any one of the others would happily jump in there right now and hold her, but this is my time to step up. Alexandros held her at the ruins, Malachi carried her back home, and Axl cradled her while she slept. Now it's my turn. I kick off my shoes and step into the tub fully clothed before sinking down into the water with her in my arms.

"Xavier, you're still dressed," she murmurs.

"Yep." I look at the soot and grime from my clothes darkening the water. We all stayed in bed with her while she was asleep, irrationally afraid to move in case she was taken away from us again. I really didn't think this through.

But she settles back against me and purrs like a kitten, so I wrap her in my embrace and rest my lips on the top of her head.

CHAPTER SIXTY-FOUR

She smells of fire and soot and blood, but she is still the sweetest thing in the entire world.

When Alexandros walks into the bathroom, he arches an eyebrow at the dirty water and shakes his head.

I hold her tighter. "I didn't want to let her go."

"I understand that." He reaches into the dirty water and pulls the plug, then grabs a fluffy towel from the rack. The pink one Ophelia brought with her when she moved everything from her dorm room. "Give her to me."

I stare at him.

"Whilst you remove your clothes and run some fresh water. I understand not wanting to let her go, but I will hand her back as soon as you are done."

I rest my lips on her temple. "We're gonna get out for a minute, okay?"

"I can hear you. I'm just keeping my eyes closed," she murmurs. "I'm so tired."

I look to him, concerned. *Is that normal?*

He nods. *She is healing, and she is grieving. Not to mention she destroyed a wraith. I would be concerned if she were not exhausted.*

Satisfied with his explanation, I hand him to her and jump out of the bath. While I strip and run some fresh water, he tells her that Axl and Malachi are taking a shower in the other room, and then they're going to make her some waffles and a milkshake because she needs food to help replenish her blood. And he tells her how much he loves her and how he'll never let her go again.

Although I'm aware he isn't speaking to me, the sound of his voice and his declarations of love soothe what remain of my rough edges.

"I love you too, Xavier." His tone is deep and sincere as he says the words I wanted to hear for so long. "All of you."

XAVIER

I keep my face turned away from him so he doesn't see the tears in my eyes. "I know."

When the bath is refilled, I sink back into the warm water, and he hands her to me. She leans against me again, and I gently wash the blood and grime from her skin. Again, she purrs, content and safe. And mine.

Alexandros turns on the shower and removes his own clothes. My eyes rake over him, from his taut muscles to his silvery scars. Every part of his body that I love.

He catches me watching him and smirks. *Later, pup.*

Fuck. Between Ophelia's soft body nestled against mine and him being, well, him …

Ophelia giggles, no doubt feeling my hard cock digging into her back. "Waffles and milkshake first."

"Whatever you want, Cupcake."

She yawns. "That's what I want."

She turns her body so she's sitting sideways on my lap, her cheek pressed against my chest, a relaxed smile on her beautiful face. Her breathing is steady and deep, her heartbeat a strong, rhythmic pulse.

She is incredible, is she not? Alexandros asks.

I hum my agreement. She's more than incredible. She is everything. She is mine. Ours. She is Ophelia Hart, still the most powerful being in the universe, with or without her light.

CHAPTER
SIXTY-FIVE
AXL

O phelia lies between Xavier and me, dressed only in a clean T-shirt of Malachi's, with her hands resting on her stomach. The final rays of the evening sun bathe the room in soft amber hues. A movie plays on the TV in the background, but none of us are watching it. Alexandros is reading quietly next to Xavier, and Malachi is lying next to me, his fingertips trailing up and down my spine.

It's an oddly ordinary scene given the extraordinary events of yesterday. Malachi scrapes his teeth over the nape of my neck now, his chest pressed up against my back. My dick stiffens. We've always been physical creatures, and this is how we reconnect. How we anchor ourselves back to each other after bad shit happens, and last night was the embodiment of bad shit. But I'm not sure if Ophelia is ready for that yet. We're all fully healed now, and although she slept most of the day away, she's still tired.

"You need anything, princess?"

She shakes her head. "Got everything I need right here."

Xavier's eyes lock on mine, and they're filled with longing. He wants what Malachi is teasing at too.

AXL

Alexandros gives me a sideways look, letting me know he can feel the growing sexual tension in this room as much as we can.

"I lost my powers, didn't I?" she asks, her voice small and quiet.

Alexandros closes his book and places it on the nightstand. "Do you still feel them?"

She shakes her head, biting down on her bottom lip.

"Like they are depleted or like they are gone?" he questions her further.

A tear rolls down her cheek, and it breaks my heart. She has lost so much in her short life. "Like they're gone, I think." I brush her cheek with the pad of my thumb. "I can still hear you all, but that's our bond, right? I don't feel the power anymore. The lightning in my veins. That simmering energy always right at my fingertips."

Xavier presses a tender kiss on her forehead. "I'm sorry, Cupcake."

Alexandros leans over Xavier and cups her jaw, turning her to face him. "You are still an elementai, Ophelia. You always will be. But yes, I believe you sacrificed your powers when you used your light to destroy the wraith."

"Is it bad that I'm glad they're gone?" Her voice is even quieter now. "Is it ungrateful? It's just ... I never wanted to be the Chosen One. I only want to be me."

The relief that consumes us all is palpable. I didn't want to admit that I haven't felt a moment's sadness for the loss of her powers. While I would be sad for her if she mourned them, it is so much safer for her—and for all of us—that she isn't some all-powerful being capable of saving or destroying the earth. That version of Ophelia would have always been a target. There would always be someone who wanted what she had and was

CHAPTER SIXTY-FIVE

willing to try to take it from her. She couldn't have had the normal life she's always dreamed of.

"It is not selfish, Ophelia," Alexandros assures her. "It is sensible, and it is a relief for all of us that you are no longer the target of every evil creature in existence."

A smile lights up her face. "So I can finish my degree? Become a social worker?"

Alexandros rolls his eyes, but I laugh out loud, and I'm joined by Malachi and Xavier. And then our girl's sweet laughter fills the room, and somehow Xavier's hand is on her thigh and my mouth is on hers. Soon, all of our hands and mouths are on her beautiful body—exploring, kissing, biting.

All five of us become a tangle of limbs, seeking the comfort and connection that only comes from this carnal union. I lose count of how many times I'm inside her, of how many times she falls apart with my name on her lips. But the sun is almost ready to rise once more by the time we finally fall asleep, our bodies wrapped together, our hearts beating as one.

CHAPTER
SIXTY-SIX
ALEXANDROS

The cold evening air feels good, almost cleansing as I take a deep breath and let it flood my lungs. There has been so much pain. So much loss and destruction. But there has been relief as well. And, dare I say it, joy. We spent yesterday and the better part of today counting our losses, and although they were great, the victory was greater.

Lucian?

Just because you force-fed me your blood and saved me doesn't mean you get to pop into my head whenever you want. The sarcasm eases my conscience a little. He did beg me to let him go, but there was more of him begging to stay. And I would rather him be alive and angry with me than dead. So I sliced my wrist and held it to his mouth, and he drank until his cut began to heal.

I believe force-fed is a tad hyperbolic. You suckled at my wrist like a newborn.

Fuck you, old man.

A smile spreads across my face. *Are you okay?* It is an incredibly complicated question, but he thankfully takes it at face value.

CHAPTER SIXTY-SIX

Yeah. I heard the elementai saved the whole world, and once I found out you were all okay, I figured I wasn't needed.

There is no malice or pity in his tone, but it still saddens me to know he feels that way.

I spoke to Ophelia. Told her I was okay, he goes on, no doubt sensing my sentimentality.

I long to tell him he is both wanted and needed, but I do not wish to scare him off, so instead, I simply ask, *Will I see you again, son?*

I am met with an onslaught of his pain, along with a bit of the madness that seems to sit so close to the surface. But he must find some peace amongst his chaos—at least enough to answer me with sarcasm and wit. *If I say no, you're just gonna keep talking to me in my head, aren't you?*

Yes, I will never stop talking to you again. Never again will I allow you to slip so far away from me. I do not tell him that either, though. *I am prepared to make you a deal. If you contact me once a month and you visit at least once a year, I will not invade your privacy. I will only reach out if there is something of grave import.*

He is quiet for a few moments. *I guess I can live with that.*

Sensing he is nearing his limit of our conversation, I tell him the words I am most desperate to say. *I love you, Lucian. You always have a home wherever I am.*

More silence follows before he speaks again. *See you around, old man.*

My heart is full of gratitude. The road in front of us is long, especially for him, but we have nothing but time to heal the wounds between us. I can only hope that one day he learns to forgive himself. That matters to me more than whether he is ever able to forgive me.

For now, my body is tired and my mind is weary. My shoes sink into the wet grass as soon as I stop walking and take a moment to look to the sky.

ALEXANDROS

Are you still here, old friend?

After Ophelia defeated the wraith, Anikêtos left to be with Elpis. Everything since has been fueled by such chaotic activity, and this feels like the first time I have had the opportunity to take a full breath. The first opportunity I have had to thank him.

His vast form blocks out the setting sun on the horizon. He comes in to land, and the swoop of his wings sends gusts of air furrowing through the trees.

He lands softly, unnaturally agile for a creature of his size. *I am here.*

I already sense the sorrow in the air. *But not for long?*

No.

You and Elpis are both leaving? She would never agree to be part of this conversation. Elpis abhors goodbyes. It is not in a dragon's nature to indulge such human traditions, for they view the passing of time so differently. But Elpis has always been an exception to that rule. She has always been the exception to so many rules.

We are.

A strange feeling of melancholy washes over me. It is not a sadness as such, but more of a mourning. A farewell to a past that has long since disappeared and which I have held onto for far too long.

How is the Dragon Healer?

Ah, my sweet Ophelia. A much more pleasant topic of conversation. *She is as good as can be expected. Fully healed with the help of blood from all her mates. She appears to have sacrificed her powers though—at least her elementai ones.*

Is she saddened by this?

I recall her lying in bed last night, surrounded by the four of us. *No. I believe it is something of a relief to her.*

And to me.

CHAPTER SIXTY-SIX

I glance out over the grounds of Montridge and the still-smoldering embers of the burned forest in the distance. But there is little more evidence of the battle that took place here less than forty-eight hours ago. *She saved the world from falling into darkness, and they will never even know her name.*

There are some who will always remember her name. I shall never forget the Dragon Healer.

That is true. All who know her will remember her always, for she is unforgettable in every way. And if I am being honest, I can say I would prefer that the world at large never learns who Ophelia Hart is.

And now we can look forward to a peace that will reign for the ages. His quote from the prophecy is not delivered with his typical disdain.

That is what they say.

Anikêtos stretches his neck and scans the horizon. *Already, I feel a shift in the cradle. Magic will rise again, and this time, without the shadows of the Skotádi.*

That reminder of Giorgios has me swaying on my feet as guilt and sadness barrel into me. *How did I not know, Anikêtos? All those years, he hid his true self from me.*

The darkness has always been adept at disguising itself within the light. And there is nothing darker than wraith magic.

My heart aches for the brother I lost—not the man he was, but the one I believed him to be. Despite his assertion that I was the cause of his evil, he sowed the seeds of his own destruction when he made a deal with Salem, long before he met Elena. Perhaps Elena's love would have turned him from the darkness, and that question will always give me pause, but it is one which can never be answered.

I feel Ophelia's presence before I see her, and she chases away the negative emotions slinking through my veins. *That* is her true power. She may have lost her light, but she is still able to spread it wherever she goes.

"I know you're not big on dinner, but Malachi and Osiris made a huge meal and everyone is sitting down to eat in a few. I thought it would be nice if we could all eat together."

Yes, let us sit down to a civilized meal after we almost burned the entire campus to the ground two days ago.

She jabs me in the ribs. "Hey, I heard that."

I wince. Although she has lost her other powers, the ones she inherited from me and the boys remain intact, and it is a struggle to keep her out of my head at all lately. Perhaps I simply do not try hard enough. "My apologies, little one, but it does seem a little ..." I pause, searching for the words.

Redundant? Indulgent? Ani offers.

"Ani!" Ophelia admonishes. But then her face breaks into a huge smile, and she blinks at me. "I can still hear him too."

Despite the circumstances, I cannot help but smile back. We both lost dear friends, and there is no avoiding the truth of that, but there is still happiness to be found if one only looks for it. "Yes you can. And he has a point, agápi mou."

I wrap an arm around her shoulders, and she snakes one of hers around my waist. "After everything that happened, isn't all of that even more reason to enjoy life, to bask in the company of friends while we have them?"

I draw in a breath and rest my chin on top of her head. She also has a point.

"I'm sorry you can't join us, Ani," she says.

Ani snorts. He considers such human pastimes as eating dinner together so far beneath him, I am surprised he does not take flight in a dramatic huff at the mere suggestion. But then I feel a sudden change in him. Not exactly sadness, but longing, perhaps. *Elpis and I will be leaving before twilight, Ophelia.*

Her lip trembles. *Returning to the netherworld?*

CHAPTER SIXTY-SIX

It would be too great a risk to breach the veil again when it is only so recently sealed. We will venture somewhere south. Somewhere less densely populated than here.

She stares up at him, her blue eyes shining with unshed tears. *I am sorry you can't return to your kind, Ani.*

It is what it is, Chosen One. He bends his head low and nudges her shoulder, and I am warmed by the affection he shows for her. *Elpis and I will have each other, and that is all we have ever needed.*

She wipes a tear from her eye, and I press a kiss on the top of her head. *I'm going to miss you, but we'll still see you, right?*

Perhaps is his only reply. Elusive as ever.

I am filled with nostalgia for times of old when he and Elpis would have remained by my side. But the world is a different one now. There is only one thing I can ask of him. *Do not stray too far, old friend.*

Of course not, Dragon Whisperer. He dips his head in my direction, then again, deeper, for Ophelia—the most profound sign of respect from a dragon. With a final shake of his scales, he takes flight, his vast wings stretching out and blocking what little remains of the sunlight, leaving Ophelia and me in his shadow.

"It still astounds me that people can't see him," she says.

"Can you imagine the ensuing chaos if they could?" I cup her chin and give her a gentle kiss before turning in the direction of our house. "So, tell me what culinary delights Malachi and Osiris have cooked up for supper this evening, then."

"Well, Osiris said to tell you he's reserved you his juiciest Kobe filet and that he will merely introduce it to the heat of a skillet before serving."

I growl my appreciation. A good, very rare steak is one of the few human foods I enjoy.

"He also said he won't bother with any of the trimmings

because they'd be wasted on your caveman palate." She holds her hand to her mouth and giggles, and the sound is music to my ears. My beautiful, gentle elementai. No longer the Chosen One or the world's redemption—simply my chosen one and the redeemer of my soul.

CHAPTER
SIXTY-SEVEN
MALACHI

CHRISTMAS EVE

"Just look at it though. It's all so shiny!" Ophelia squeals with delight, clapping her hands together. Her beautiful face is illuminated by the colored lights of the Christmas tree as they twinkle in the otherwise unlit room. We remodeled the house after the "incident," and the professor's quarters, with the exception of his study, have been combined with the main house to make one huge open-plan living area. All of which has been decorated with garlands and wreaths and colorful Christmas ornaments. I don't believe there's a square inch that has not been bedazzled by Christmas. Even Alexandros's old leather chair has been adorned with a Santa cushion. He's sitting on it now, reading his newspaper. At least he's pretending to, but his eyes keep drifting to the excitable bundle of elementai in the middle of the room.

There must be a hundred wrapped gifts stowed underneath the tree, adorned in a variety of shimmering red, gold, and green wrapping paper. I'd bet at least half of them are for her. We all decided to spoil our girl for the first Christmas we're celebrating together, especially given how we spent our last one. I can't wait to see her face when she opens her presents. There's nothing overly extravagant, but I can still imagine her face lighting up with each book, plushie, and unicorn-themed anything she opens.

Xavier wraps his arms around her waist and presses his lips against her neck. "You're shiny, Cupcake."

Dressed in sparkly green pajamas that make her look like an elf, she is fucking adorable, and I could eat her on the spot. A sentiment Axl, Xavier, and Alexandros all share in my head.

"You like my Christmas jammies?" she asks, giggling.

He snaps the waistband of her pants. "Yeah, I do. Gonna fuck my little elf soon."

"Am I to understand there are equally green and sparkly affairs upstairs that you'd like for us to wear?" I ask her.

"Nope." Xavier shakes his head. "Not being caught dead in no elf pajamas."

"Not dressing like an elf for anyone, princess. Not even you." Axl winks at her, while Alexandros remains conspicuously silent.

"Aw." She pouts. "But you would all look so cute."

If it makes her happy, I'll wear her Christmas pajamas, and so will they. But I can't resist having a little fun first. "I guess if the professor is down for wearing his Christmas *jammies*, then we'll all have to." Like the rest of us, he would do anything to make her smile.

She presses her lips together, her eyes shining with glee. Meanwhile, he studies his newspaper, continuing to pretend like he's not paying attention.

"I guess we wouldn't have much of a choice, then," Axl adds.

"You'd all look so adorable," Ophelia says sweetly.

"If the professor dresses in Christmas pajamas that look like

CHAPTER SIXTY-SEVEN

these ..." Xavier skims his fingers around Ophelia's waistband. "I'll nut in my fucking pants."

That gets his attention at least, but he simply looks up from his newspaper and amusedly raises one eyebrow.

Ophelia sighs, and I pull her back to my chest and rest my head on her shoulder. "Can we at least open a present?" she asks.

"No," Alexandros answers.

"Aw," Ophelia and Xavier whine in unison.

I vaguely remember celebrating Christmas as a small child, but it was nothing like this. Her joy is infectious, and it's making me giddy. I want to open presents too. "Not even one?" I ask.

"No," he says again. "You will all have to wait until tomorrow."

"Yeah, if we don't get to sleep soon, Santa won't come." Axl sniggers.

Xavier smirks, his blue eyes twinkling with mischief. "But if we go to sleep, Ophelia won't come."

"He's got a point," I agree. "Who needs to open presents when we have something so much more fun to unwrap instead?" I slide my hand under her pajama top in case there is any doubt as to what I'm referring to. She squirms, rubbing her juicy ass against me.

"But you already know what's under my wrapping," she breathlessly argues. "It won't be nearly as much fun as opening the gifts under the tree."

"Oh, Cupcake, I know you did not just say that," Xavier growls, and Axl voices his agreement.

I spin her around in my arms, and the sight of her flushed cheeks has me biting back a grin. "You're in so much trouble now, sweet girl."

She tilts her head to the side, and it makes her look even

more adorable. "Am I on the naughty list, sir?" Her purr goes straight to my cock.

Fuck, I love her so damn much. She has thrived this past year living here with us. Growing in confidence, acing her studies, and making new friends, she is finally starting to realize how incredible she is. She's embraced so many new things while still retaining her sweet, caring nature and everything else that makes her so uniquely Ophelia.

"Ophelia Hart, are you looking for a spanking?"

Alexandros's question makes her shiver, but she flutters her eyelashes at him over her shoulder. "Maybe."

I lift her and wrap her legs around my waist. "You are definitely on the naughty list, baby, and I'm gonna take you upstairs and unwrap you for your spanking."

Her breath catches in her throat, and her pupils blow so wide I can no longer see her vivid blue irises. I seal my lips over hers, grinding my hard cock against the heat of her center. Through our bond, I tell her all the filthy things we're about to do to her as I carry her to bed. Alexandros, Xavier, and Malachi follow close behind.

We remodeled upstairs too, and now there are only two bedrooms—one containing a specially made bed that comfortably sleeps five. Because life is way too fucking short for any of us not to spend every single night with her. Just like we're about to and like we do every single night—kissing and biting and fucking her until we all fall asleep, then waking up with her in our arms. I never thought I could feel anything remotely close to this level of happiness, and it's all down to this incredible girl right here.

She might not be able to summon all four elements anymore, but she is still the most powerful and incredible being in the whole goddamn universe if you ask me.

EPILOGUE

OPHELIA

THREE AND A HALF YEARS LATER

"That's it! My last class as an undergrad," I announce proudly as I burst through the door to Alexandros's office. He and Malachi look up from the book they were both poring over.

Malachi wraps me in his huge arms and spins me around. "I'm so proud of you, baby. You're going to be the best social worker ever."

"I have to get my master's first, Professor. And I don't even have my degree yet."

He grins at me, his green eyes twinkling. "You already know you aced every single test. And I'm not a professor yet, sweet girl."

"I'll still call you sir if you want me to," I purr, earning myself a sexy groan.

He's been teaching classes while he studies for his doctorate, and I'm so proud of him. He's a natural teacher, just like Xavier. But the latter is still resistant to the idea. One day, though, I'm sure …

Sealing his lips over mine, Malachi kisses me softly at first. When I part my lips, he wastes no time before sliding his tongue into my mouth and kissing me so deeply that I start grinding myself on him.

Damn hormones.

I'm pulled from Malachi's arms and into Alexandros's. He smiles at me, but his dark-brown eyes are full of fire and passion, and now I'm practically panting. I eye the desk behind him and lick my lips. It's been so long.

Alexandros arches a thick eyebrow. "It has been a matter of hours, Ophelia."

I wrinkle my nose. "It feels like forever, and I blame you entirely."

Humming, he splays his palm over my gently rounded abdomen. "How are my two favorite girls today?"

I blow a strand of hair from my eyes. "*I* am excited for whatever celebration you all have planned for our last day of school." I don't add that I hope it involves lots and lots of orgasms because I'm sure they already know that. Had anyone warned me that an elementai pregnancy would send my libido into hyperdrive ... Well, it wouldn't have changed my mind, but at least I would have been prepared. "And Cadence here is good too."

"So we have decided on Cadence, have we?" There is a hint of amusement in his tone, but he still has those authoritative professor vibes down pat—the ones that have me melting and ready to drop to my knees.

"Well, Cadence Enora, actually. The second elementai born in over five hundred years should be named after two of the bravest women who ever lived, don't you think?"

He tucks a strand of hair behind my ear. With his hands resting on my ass, he tugs me close so my body is flush against his. "If that is what you wish, agápi mou."

"It is. If that's okay with you?" I add. As the baby's father, he should get a say on the name. Although it would take a feat of epic persuasion to make me budge on my suggestion.

He trails kisses over my jawline before kissing me. *They are fine names for our daughter.*

I'm melting into his fiery kiss when Xavier and Axl burst into the room with the force of a tornado. They have taken over the Ruby Dragon operation entirely now that Alexandros is head of House Drakos, and they are both flourishing under the increased responsibility.

Alexandros groans before releasing me, and it takes less than a second for Xavier to take his place.

He flicks his long dark hair from his eyes and grins at me. "How are you doing, Cupcake?"

I bite down on my lip. "Good. You?"

He trails his teeth down my neck until I tip my head back and moan. "All the better for seeing you."

Oh god, it feels so hot in here. I'm burning up. My panties are damp, and the space between my thighs is throbbing with its own heartbeat. "Can we go home?" I whine. "Please?"

Axl presses his chest to my back and collects my dark-brown hair in his fist. He peppers kisses across the back of my neck. "We have the best surprise planned for you."

Does it involve cake and orgasms? This time I'm unable to stop the words from forming, even if only in my head. But they all hear me.

Xavier slides his tongue into my mouth while Axl grinds his hard cock against my lower back. *Lots of cake and lots and lots of orgasms, princess.*

Alexandros clears his throat pointedly. "Then let us leave before I am forced to begin the party here."

"I could go for starting the party right now," Malachi says.

Xavier hums into my mouth. *Me too.*

I'm about to agree, but the professor grabs my face and pulls my lips from Xavier's. He dips his head as though he's about to press his lips to mine, but instead, he takes Xavier's mouth in a bruising kiss. *We are not fucking our pregnant mate on my desk when we have a perfectly suitable bed at home.*

Oh heavens. Those words, watching these two kiss, and Axl's hard length nudging into my back ... Not to mention the pure heat in Malachi's eyes as he looks at me like he owns me—which I guess he kind of does. All of it combined has me about ready to implode.

Alexandros releases Xavier's mouth and immediately captures mine. It's as if he's trying to remind us all who's in control. Not that there's any doubt. He is always in charge, and we know it. It's how our happy family unit functions, and we are happy. More than happy, in fact. It took no time at all for all of us to adapt to our new normal—all five of us together and me not being the savior of the universe, just a regular ol' elementai.

"Can we at least run?" Xavier asks with a groan.

"Moving too fast makes Ophelia feel sick," Malachi reminds him.

Axl pulls me from Alexandros's lips and tips my head back so he can kiss me too. The professor growls his frustration, but he has become surprisingly good at sharing. However, he is not one to be outdone. He slips his hand underneath my skirt and tugs my panties aside before dragging a finger through my wet center.

"Always so soaked for us, little one." He dips the tip of his finger inside me, and my knees buckle so hard, he and Axl are the only things holding me up.

If we must go home, can we please leave now? I'm about to melt into a puddle here.

Axl releases me with a laugh. "Let's get you to bed, princess."

The five of us walk hand in hand over the quad toward home. We gave up caring what other people thought about our relationship a long time ago. And our ability to be open about our situation hasn't been hurt by the fact that the students at Montridge are a lot more diverse than they used to be. The university has been swamped with magical students the past three years: Witches whose powers lay dormant for their whole lives until recently and wolf packs who previously shunned other magical creatures. Even demons have returned to the university. Alexandros thinks it has something to do with the destruction of the Skotádi and all the dark magic they hoarded. Like the removal of so much negative energy has allowed other pockets of magic to flourish. He also says it's because of me, and that the rebirth of the elementai has restored a balance to the magical world that was absent for half a millennium. I don't know that for sure, but things definitely feel a hell of a lot calmer than they used to. And my life is a whole heck of a lot simpler now that I'm no longer the most powerful being who ever lived.

My life is unbelievable. I, Ophelia Ilyria Hart—orphan and lover of literature and unicorns, who didn't have her first friend until the age of nineteen—am adored by my four mates, about to get my degree, and pregnant with a baby girl of our own. So happy I sometimes feel like I might burst.

Of course there are times when I miss the friends I lost, but I focus on the friends I have. Sienna and Osiris; Melody and Shannon, the witch twins from my English class; Jenny, Sasha, and Aaron, the wolves Sienna introduced me to on my second Halloween here; and I can't forget my best human friend, Emma.

Then of course there's Lucian—he visits when he's not traveling the world, more frequently than I think any of us expected he would. Although his soul has found a measure of peace and he is much happier now, I don't think he'll ever lose his restless need to wander. He cried when we told him I was pregnant and expecting a daughter, but they were tears of joy, and I have never seen such happiness in him as in that moment. And the most unexpected friends of all, Elpis and Anikêtos, remain in the mortal realm. No matter how far they roam, I am still able to talk to them whenever I need to.

And, if you promise not to tell, I will let you in on a few little secrets, faithful reader.

It still rains when I'm sad.

I can still heal bites from my mates without the need of their saliva.

And sometimes, when I really concentrate and flick my wrists in exactly the right way, I can still summon Dragonfyre.

THE END

IF YOU ENJOYED this paranormal world and want more possessive, alpha vampires to swoon over, then be sure to dive into Sadie's upcoming series, co-written with the very talented LJ Morrow. Available to preorder now

A Curse of Blood and Fate

ALSO BY SADIE KINCAID

Books 1 and 2 of Sadie's latest series, Manhattan Ruthless are out now. Meet the James brothers in five stand-alone billionaire romances set in the heart of Manhattan, and you might just bump into a Ryan brother while you're there.

Broken

Promise Me Forever

Rebound

Played

Made

The complete, bestselling Chicago Ruthless is available now. Following the lives of the notoriously ruthless Moretti siblings - this series will take you on a rollercoaster of emotions. Packed with angst, action and plenty of steam.

Dante

Joey

Lorenzo

Keres

If you haven't read the full New York Ruthless series yet, you can find them on Amazon and Kindle Unlimited

Ryan Rule

Ryan Redemption

Ryan Retribution

Ryan Reign

Ryan Renewed

And the complete short stories and novellas attached to this series are available in one collection

A Ryan Recollection

If you'd prefer to head to LA to meet Alejandro and Alana, and Jackson and Lucia, you can find out all about them in Sadie's internationally bestselling LA Ruthless series. Available on Amazon and FREE in Kindle Unlimited.

Fierce King

Fierce Queen

Fierce Betrayal

Fierce Obsession

If you'd like to read about London's hottest couple. Gabriel and Samantha, then check out Sadie's London Ruthless series on Amazon. FREE in Kindle Unlimited.

Dark Angel

Fallen Angel

Dark/ Fallen Angel Duet

If you enjoy super spicy short stories, Sadie also writes the Bound series feat Mack and Jenna, Books 1, 2, 3 and 4 are available now.

Bound and Tamed

Bound and Shared

Bound and Dominated

Bound and Deceived

ABOUT THE AUTHOR

Sadie Kincaid is a spicy romance author who loves to read and write about hot alpha males and strong, feisty females.

Sadie loves to connect with readers so why not get in touch via social media?

Join Sadie's reader group for the latest news, book recommendations and plenty of fun. Sadie's ladies and Sizzling Alphas

Sign up to Sadie's mailing list for a free short story, and for exclusive news about future releases, giveaways and content here

Made in the USA
Las Vegas, NV
30 March 2025